THE SCOOP

ERIN VAN DER MEER

Copyright © Erin Van Der Meer 2026

The right of Erin Van Der Meer to be identified as the Author of the Work has been asserted by her in accordance with the Copyright, Designs and Patents Act 1988.

First published in Paperback in Great Britain in 2026 by Wildfire
An imprint of Headline Publishing Group Limited

Published in agreement with Grand Central Publishing

A division of Hachette Book Group, Inc.

Print book interior design by Taylor Navis

Jacket design and illustration by YY Liak. Jacket copyright © 2026 by Hachette Book Group, Inc.

1

Apart from any use permitted under UK copyright law, this publication may only be reproduced, stored, or transmitted, in any form, or by any means, with prior permission in writing of the publishers or, in the case of reprographic production, in accordance with the terms of licences issued by the Copyright Licensing Agency.

All characters in this publication are fictitious and any resemblance to real persons, living or dead, is purely coincidental.

Cataloguing in Publication Data is available from the British Library

Paperback ISBN 978 1 0354 3872 3

Offset in 10.56/14.08pt Dante MT Std by Six Red Marbles UK, Thetford, Norfolk

Printed and bound in Great Britain by Clays Ltd, Elcograf S.p.A.

Headline's policy is to use papers that are natural, renewable and recyclable products and made from wood grown in well-managed forests and other controlled sources. The logging and manufacturing processes are expected to conform to the environmental regulations of the country of origin.

Headline Publishing Group Limited
An Hachette UK Company
Carmelite House
50 Victoria Embankment
London EC4Y 0DZ

The authorised representative in the EEA is Hachette Ireland,
8 Castlecourt Centre, Dublin 15, D15 XTP3, Ireland (email: info@hbgi.ie)

www.headline.co.uk
www.hachette.co.uk

Praise for *The Scoop*

'A timely, commanding, blistering debut,
this one's sure to leave a lasting mark.'
Ashley Tate

'A darkly funny satirical peek into the world of late-night tabloid journalism and the chaos of our times. With explorations on grief, ambition, and privilege in the media industry, it quickly becomes tough to look away from.'
Natalie Sue

'I gorged on *The Scoop*. A devastating satire…smart, savage, and tinged with grief…required reading for anyone who has compromised themselves today for a better tomorrow.'
Ruth Madievsky

'This dark and propulsive tale sucked me in, left me feeling guilty about every time I've clicked on a story about a flailing actor and spat me out gasping. This is the book that everyone is going to be talking about.'
Chris Bridges

'An urgent, searing satire of the media. Through exceptional storytelling, it explores the cost of ambition, murky moral boundaries, and poses the question: in our perpetual pursuit of information, are we really any better than the news outlets whose articles we consume by the dozen? I loved it!'
Georgia McVeigh

'Snappy, fun, and set in the always-fascinating world of New York media. Loved it!'
Cat Marnell

'*Whiplash* meets tabloid journalism in this electric debut. *The Scoop*'s provocative, propulsive story and relentless protagonist kept me hooked and made me reflect on my own role in a culture of navel-gazing and the attention economy.'
Warona Jay

'Calls out the modern tabloid newsroom for the dark funhouse mirror it is – where outrage is currency, empathy is a liability, and even the most earnest idealists must learn to weaponize gossip and the private lives of others. Biting humour, sharp insight, and impeccable pacing.'
Andrew Boryga

'A thrilling page-turner about how far one ambitious journalist will go to land the story that could change her fortunes. I absolutely devoured it.'
Leigh Stein

Erin Van Der Meer is a writer and former journalist whose work has appeared in publications including the *New York Times*, *Daily Beast*, and *Elle*. She was a Spruceton Inn artist resident in 2024. Born in Sydney, Australia, she now lives in Brooklyn. *The Scoop* is her debut.

For my mother.

The public is unrepentant, for it is not they who own the dog—they only subscribe. They neither set the dog on anyone, nor whistle it off—directly. If asked they would say: the dog is not mine, it has no master. And if the dog had to be killed, they would say: it really was a good thing that bad-tempered dog was put down, everyone wanted it killed—even the subscribers.

—Søren Kierkegaard, *The Present Age*

Journalists justify their treachery in various ways according to their temperaments. The more pompous talk about freedom of speech and "the public's right to know"; the least talented talk about Art; the seemliest murmur about earning a living.

—Janet Malcolm, *The Journalist and the Murderer*

THE
SCOOP

PROLOGUE

SEVEN HUNDRED PEOPLE DROWNED WHEN a boat carrying migrants sank in the Mediterranean. The most popular story on our website was about a potato that looked like Elton John.

The Scoop occupied the seventeenth floor of an office building in Midtown. If there was a stomach-flipping view of New York City to behold from up there, I'm not sure I ever saw it. I worked at night, and at night there was no view. At night, the windows became a mirror, reflecting only the gray carpet, the endless rows of desks and chairs, our glowing computer screens, ourselves—a sight I found to be stinging and unwelcome, like bile in the throat.

A sense of urgency pervaded the newsroom at all times. Even in the middle of the night. Even though most of the stories we wrote were trivial, stupid. This was because we were judged not by the quality of our work, but by the length of the list of published articles I emailed to David at the end of each shift. Length as primary measure of worth—at Johnson News, the hypermasculine culture reached down to the most minute details.

We worked furiously, whether there was any real news to report or not. A love triangle among staff at a German zoo had resulted in the kidnapping of an endangered owl. The "armpit vagina" was the new muffin top. Sometimes a long-awaited pun opportunity would at last materialize, like if the actor Jon Hamm was photographed leaving a butcher shop. Fingers battering and clattering on our keyboards, we unconsciously adopted the performative flair of concert pianists, heads bobbing up and down, faces full of concentration. As though when we finally stopped, an audience might rise and give us a standing ovation.

To stay alert, we drank cup after cup of the bad office coffee and made ample use of Visine drops; the combination of the late hour, the air-conditioning, and the brightness of our screens meant that our eyes were always dry, sore, and in danger of closing. We joked that in order to stay awake until the end of the shift, we needed eye clamps, like that scene in *A Clockwork Orange*. The harsh fluorescent lighting in the newsroom was a drag, but it was even worse when, if none of us got up from our desks for a while, the smart lights, sensing nobody, switched off, shrouding us in darkness except for the glow of our screens.

Each month we were expected to produce more traffic than we had the month before. That was the only goal. Somehow, we had to elicit more clicks from people as they scrolled on their phones on the train, on the bus, on their cigarette break at work, on the toilet, during a commercial break, in bed in the middle of the night, staring, faces aglow. And so we had to be faster, more outrageous, faster, more shocking, faster, more terrifying, faster, faster, hurtling into the void. There was no endgame. There was no end.

It was not supposed to turn out this way. *I* was not supposed to turn out this way. I did all the things you're meant to do to avoid a life working through the night with the taxi drivers, supermarket shelf stockers, and sex workers (occupations that are all more noble than journalism). I went to college, moved to New York City, wore the right clothes, got a job at the right magazine, lived in the right neighborhoods (the East Village, and then a tasteful late-twenties move to Brooklyn), read the right books, went to the right bars, dated the right men. At the magazine company, I kissed the right asses. But then the social media age hit the industry as we knew it like an asteroid, turned everything upside down. The asses you were supposed to kiss changed, but nobody told me. No, that's not true. I *was* told, repeatedly. But I refused to listen, and then it was too late.

Some nights at my desk, a sensation came over me, strange and uneasy. It was like a portal to an abyss had opened up in the air in front of me. It paralyzed me for a moment, overtook me like a daydream, a roaring in the ears. Everything around me evaporated—my desk, my colleagues, the newsroom, New York City, the planet—and I was in the dark. I felt a dull, unnamable ache somewhere inside, in the rough location of my spleen, but deeper. Sometimes in this brief but all-consuming state—it would last no more than a few seconds—I'd have a vision of myself walking up to a stranger on a subway platform who was staring at their phone screen, transfixed. I'd take them by the shoulders, shake them, yelling, "We're all going to die one day!"

Sometimes it was a stranger. Sometimes it was my dead mother.

Everyone was always talking about leaving. We all had a plan, which we would share with one another in low voices as we watched Tupperware containers turn lazily in the kitchen microwaves. Or as we stood outside on Seventh Avenue, furtively indulging in the smoking habit we never needed until we started working there, stubbing the butts into the garden bed in defiance of the sign that implored us not to leave our toxic waste in the shrubbery. We were getting out of there, we insisted, always at a loosely defined time in the not-too-distant future, before summer, after the holidays, next year, in the spring.

Whether any of it would ever happen—the plan to train as a Pilates instructor, to become a florist, to go to wine school, to backpack through Southeast Asia should an ailing grandparent be generous enough in their will—was beside the point. We spoke with the air of the incarcerated, waxing hopefully about life on the outside, the fantasizing itself a coping mechanism necessary for day-to-day survival. Except ours was a prison with the door wide open, all of us free to leave at any time. Which made it all the more curious that so many of us did not.

1

THE RETIRED DETECTIVE BEING INTERVIEWED in the documentary about the murdered child beauty queen was describing how an undigested piece of pineapple was found in the girl's stomach. This fruit clue, he explained, helped investigators establish a timeline of her death. I shoved another sticky red handful of Swedish Fish into my mouth, considering as I chewed: If I were to die right then on the couch, what would the medical examiner think of what they'd find inside me?

Twenty-nine years old and eating cereal and candy for lunch, I imagined the doctor saying, tsk-tsking as their gloved hand fondled my small intestine, my secret shame exposed in the most undignified and unlikely of ways.

I swore to start eating healthier.

The intercom rang. Audrey—she was early. I peeled myself off the couch, the backs of my limbs sticking to the leather in the sweltering August-in-New-York-City heat, buzzed her in, clicked off the TV, closed the window, and turned on the window AC unit, even though Patti and I had agreed to use it only to sleep. ("The city's electric grid is more fragile than most people realize," my climate-activist roommate had said. "Also, I'm saving for Europe.") But Audrey grew up rich, and so wasn't hardy enough to handle such a hot afternoon with only the squeaking ceiling fan for comfort.

I opened the door to see Audrey clutching the banister, panting after climbing my walk-up's four steep flights of stairs, blowing strands of blond hair out of the pale oval of her face.

"I wasn't expecting you until—"

"You were so upset on the phone," Audrey said, still out of breath. "I was worried."

It made me cringe to remember how, two hours earlier, I'd called Audrey on the verge of hyperventilating, babbling garbled words through tears, unable to bear my moment of need and grief alone.

I stepped aside to let her in, feeling sheepish. Audrey was a Manhattan girl—she lived in the West Village and worked in Midtown—and often acted as though the part of Brooklyn where I lived was in another state. It touched me that she'd take the subway across boroughs for me.

"You took the 2/3?" I asked as I went to the sink and poured a glass of water, feeling bad it wasn't cold as I handed it to her. She dropped her bag to the floor and kicked off her shoes.

"God, no. I took a car—I'll expense it."

Oh, the casual excesses of the gainfully employed. Meanwhile, I'd spent the morning googling *How often can you donate blood plasma?* and *What happens if you donate too much blood plasma?* and *How much money for selling my eggs?* and *If I sell my eggs, could my genetic descendants find me in the future?*

I went to the fridge and took two of Patti's cans of Modelo, adding them to the running list in my head of her things I'd used and needed to replace (I saw it as "keeping the tab open"—not that Patti had agreed to, or knew anything about, this tab). I put one of the cold beers on the coffee table in front of Audrey, who had collapsed dramatically on the couch and was fanning herself with a copy of *The New Yorker*, and collapsed rather dramatically myself on the other end. Audrey didn't really like beer, but at least it was cold, and I wanted an excuse to drink. Audrey didn't ask if I had something else. She knew I wasn't well. That's why she was here.

"You didn't have to come," I said pathetically, a performance. We both knew she had to come.

"What happened?" Audrey asked, putting *The New Yorker* down, looking concerned.

I took a large swallow of beer, let out a deep breath, felt the tears threaten to start again.

"I thought this was the one."

Audrey reached across the couch and patted my arm.

"I thought I was done. Done looking, done with the apps, done with doing my hair and makeup, putting on my best outfit, and going to meet a stranger, hoping to feel a spark, and instead knowing after less than five minutes of stilted conversation that it's not going to work."

"I know you did," Audrey said, voice full of sympathy.

"Done with trying to prove my worth, prove I'm good enough. Done with trying to be enthusiastic and hopeful, while trying not to get too attached because of the risk of rejection. Done with waiting days, sometimes weeks, to hear from them again, only to receive some trite message saying that while they think I'm great, they've decided to go with another candidate."

Maybe I was overreacting to the news I'd missed out on the role of editor at *The SuperYacht Times*, a boutique magazine for boating enthusiasts. But it had been three months since the layoffs at *Marie Claire*, when I lost my job as features editor and Audrey lost her job as senior features writer, only the latest round of jobs to be slashed across the media industry, and I was starting to worry. Unlike most of the white people I'd met working in magazines, I wasn't rich. In fact, I was broke. The measly severance payment was almost gone, the state benefits I'd been receiving would soon run out, and I barely had enough in my bank account to cover a month of rent and bills. Then there was the matter of my several maxed-out credit cards, the total of which had recently blown out to five figures, on which I'd stopped making payments months ago (I'd had to block the numbers of Discover and American Express just to get some peace).

I couldn't ask my parents for money. My mother had been dead seven years, and I was estranged from my father, who left when I was twelve to move to Hawaii for a woman he met online (when she was still alive, my mom joked he had to go all the way to Hawaii to find someone who didn't know what an asshole he was). I got a one-line email from him every five years or so, presumably to check I was still alive—less often than a Pap smear, and more uncomfortable. I had no siblings; the only family I was in touch with were an aunt and uncle in San Francisco who sent a card every year on my birthday, which always included lots of warm sentiment, but never any cash. I didn't know what I would do if I didn't find a job soon. I'd heard people sold their dirty underwear, or pictures of their feet, and while the prospect of setting my own hours was appealing, I was the kind of person who worked best in a team. Also, I had a journalism degree and still believed that meant something.

Audrey nodded, pouted sympathetically, but she didn't get it. She was doing so well, couldn't have been doing better. Within weeks of the layoffs, she was announced as *The New York Times*' new media reporter, a position that was either her birthright or nepotism, depending on how you looked at it (growing up, I'd watched her dad anchor the nightly news and saw her mom's head atop a national newspaper column). The day Audrey called to tell me about her new job, I was glad she couldn't see my face as I did my best to hide my private torment, like I'd accidentally bitten into a chili at a wake, smiling politely through the burning pain. I wanted to be a good friend, wanted to embody a generous spirit, wanted to believe there was plenty to go around. But the success of someone so close to me as I smarted from the hot sting of rejection, after rejection, after rejection, felt like a spotlight shone cruelly on my own failures. I could hardly stand it. I'd swallowed down my envy, hung up the call, and screamed into a cushion.

"This is ridiculous," Audrey said now, indignant on my behalf. "What reason did they give? You're a *Marie Claire* journalist, for god's sake. *You* would've been doing *them* a favor."

It hurt to remember Susan, the recruiter from the small publishing company I'd been dealing with through weeks of calls, interviews, and writing tests. Forget any relative living or dead, ex-lover, or guy that ghosted me, lately my thoughts had revolved around one person and one person only: Susan. It was Susan I longed to hear from, Susan to whom I sent messages both electronic and telepathic at all hours of the day and night. I felt sick as I told Audrey about Susan's email. It had started off well, thanking me for my "patience and enthusiasm"—the praise, from Susan of all people, had made me beam—but that was the end of the good cheer. Susan regretted to inform me, but informed me nonetheless, that they had gone with another candidate, "someone with more boating-industry experience." She had signed off by wishing me luck in my future endeavors. Insultingly generic, I thought, given all we had been through.

"More boating-industry experience?" Audrey repeated, almost offended, as if Susan had talked shit about her mother. "Please, any chump can learn about boats. Starboard, port, nautical—"

"I think there's more to it than wearing striped T-shirts," I said.

"I hope the next time Susan goes boating someone pushes her overboard."

"Audrey," I scolded, though after the way she had betrayed me, it was hard not to take pleasure in the image of Susan flailing about helpless in the open seas.

"You're too good for them anyway. Moving on. What other jobs have you applied for?"

I led Audrey through the haunted house that was trying to get a job as a journalist in the summer of 2014 when you hadn't been born into media royalty. Aside from the one editing a magazine about superyachts, there was a gig at a weird lifestyle website writing oddly specific lists: *47 cheese puns for Instagram captions* or *72 sweet things to text her in the morning*. Cheat codes, I assumed, for people who outsourced their personality along with their laundry.

Then there was the writer role at *Surviving Cancer*, a small medical magazine.

"We need someone to write the short, snappy articles that keep things light in between the features about chemo," the editor had explained on the phone, weariness in his voice.

"Celebrities with cancer, bizarre misdiagnoses, that kind of thing. The editor in chief is a difficult man, so you do need a thick skin. But you'd have job stability. More than five thousand hospitals subscribe, and chemotherapy is a long, boring process, so we have a captive audience."

"Unless they find a cure for cancer," I'd said, my attempt at a joke. He didn't laugh.

"Grim," Audrey said when I was finished.

"Or is it hopeful?" I considered. "The magazine is about *surviving* cancer."

"It's still a magazine about cancer."

"True."

"What about *BuzzFeed*?" Audrey asked.

"Hiring freeze."

THE SCOOP

"*HuffPost?*"

"They just made a bunch of hires."

"Have you talked to Abigail at *New York Magazine*? She's great. Maybe she can help."

"I got her out-of-office reply. She's on some long summer sojourn. Does she think she's French?"

"Summer is the worst time to look for a job. Everyone is at the beach."

"I wish they would wash the sand out of their cracks and come back already."

I didn't want to admit it, but I was losing hope. I was coming to the realization I was part of a micro-generation in the media, those of us who graduated around 2008. We were too young to have a steady enough foothold to ride out an era of such tumultuous change, but also too molded in the old ways (and too expensive) for entry-level digital roles, the only kind opening up with any regularity. My magazine editor pedigree increasingly meant little in a digital world.

Because she was a good friend, Audrey pivoted the conversation to one of the few things that could cheer me up: people who were doing worse than I was. We spoke like octogenarians at a wake, somberly trading names of recently deceased acquaintances. Alex from *GQ* is writing SEO content from his parents' basement in rural Ohio. Such a loss. Jenna from *Elle* is telling everyone she's "freelancing," but everyone knows that's just something journalists say when they're out of work. Tragic. Celeste from *Harper's Bazaar* is illegally selling all the samples and gifts she's been sent from brands, spread out on a rug at McCarren Park on weekends. Just awful.

Audrey also regaled me with a story about a recent encounter with the well-known *Vogue* and *Atlantic* writer Elizabeth Waites. As the daughter of media royalty, Audrey often had juicy anecdotes from her rarefied plane of media existence, which I always lapped up greedily.

"She's involved in this thing, like Avon but more pyramid scheme-y," she said. "She's trying to rope half the Upper East Side into a multilevel-marketing network. Can you believe it? *Elizabeth Waites* tried to sell me an electric foot massager. The woman won a Pulitzer!"

I laughed, but it felt hollow, something about this gossipy offering leaving me not scandalized as intended, but sad. If Elizabeth Waites was forced to sacrifice her dignity to pay the bills, what hope was there for the rest of us? For me? I considered asking Audrey to put in a word for me at the *Times*, or with one of her parents' media power broker friends (I suspected this was how Audrey ended up at the *Times*, though she would never admit it) but I bit my tongue. Audrey had offered to help, once, a few weeks into my job search, but I'd blown off the suggestion, saying I had it handled. Audrey had helped me get my job at *Marie Claire*, putting in a good word for me with the editor when I was still a junior nobody at *Cosmo*, and my ego couldn't bear the implication I needed Audrey to survive in the industry. Months passed, and I'd realized how childish this had been, to refuse her offer to help me, like a toddler on their tippy-toes in an elevator, insistent on reaching up to press the button all by themselves to the chagrin of the waiting adults. Audrey didn't offer her assistance again, and I was much too proud to ask.

Outside the apartment door I heard the jangle of keys. Patti was home from work.

"Happy Friday, am I right?" she said too cheerfully as she stepped inside, her eyes wide as she took in the scene: her unemployed roommate drinking her beers with an unexpected visitor, the AC running full blast even though it was nowhere near bedtime. She struggled in, carrying under one arm a stack of large painted cardboard signs; I knew she had been at her girlfriend Sarah's place to paint ahead of the climate march happening in the city next month.

THE SCOOP

Patti, a lawyer at a nonprofit, had met Audrey only once before, at birthday drinks I'd had in the spring, even though I'd always hated birthday parties (mine, at least), and had organized only because I was newly single and in need of a photo of myself looking hot, happy, and surrounded by people to post on social media for Josh to see, should my ex look me up to try to find out how I was doing after he fell in love with another woman at work. I'd found out thanks to a balled-up note in the clean laundry, which had somehow survived the washing machine and the dryer, the paper disintegrating between my fingers as I unwrapped it but still intact enough for me to read: *me too, I am suffering here without you.* Found out, Josh had been sorry, begged for my forgiveness, offered to go to couples therapy, to quit his marketing job at the record company, but I wasn't about to stick around and wait for him to do it again, to "pull a Hawaii," metaphorically speaking. Two weeks later, I'd found the apartment with Patti and had spent the past year wondering if I'd done the right thing, denying my doubts to anyone who asked.

It would be an understatement to say that Patti and Audrey did not hit it off. Audrey represented everything Patti despised—rich people and their kids who got the sort of opportunities most others could only dream of, and who were largely insulated from the suffering of others. I'd told Patti that Audrey was different, that she understood her privilege, that she volunteered, that I'd spent four years sitting beside her at *Marie Claire* and could vouch for her good character. But Audrey could sense Patti didn't like her, and so of course Audrey acted cool toward Patti, which only confirmed Patti's assessment that Audrey was a snob.

"I came over to check on our girl," Audrey said by way of explaining her presence.

"What happened?" Patti said, dumping the signs beside the front door and staring at me.

"Nothing. I found out I didn't get that magazine editor job. That's all." I said this with an air of nonchalance, as though I hadn't been sobbing on the phone to Audrey a few hours ago.

"I didn't want to say it," Patti said, calling out as she went into the kitchen, "but I didn't think that job was right for you. You grew up in western North Carolina, four hours from the ocean. 'Fake it 'til you make it' doesn't work when it comes to maritime jargon and sea legs."

Audrey scowled, looking like she was about to start prattling on about hulls and jibs and ports again. It occurred to me only then that Audrey's parents had a summer home in Sag Harbor, that there was a boat tied to the private dock. I'd seen it the handful of times I'd visited.

Patti, probably figuring she ought to drink one of her own beers before they were all gone, not to mention get her money's worth of the excessive daytime AC use, returned from the kitchen holding a frosty Modelo can in her hand and settled herself cross-legged on the rug.

"Audrey, you're at *The New York Times* now, right?"

"Yes!" Audrey replied politely, nodding, though I could see she was already on guard.

"Tell me: what is going on with the climate change coverage at the *Times*?"

Audrey blinked back at her.

"What do you mean?"

"There's no sense of urgency in the reporting, despite how, well, urgent it is."

"The *Times* has a dedicated climate change reporter, who's done some great work—"

"But the stories are always buried! It should be on the front page! Every day!"

I watched as Audrey's smile gradually morphed into a grimace as Patti went on.

THE SCOOP

"Climate activists are only ever portrayed as loony outlier extremists, even though they're just everyday people concerned about their families and their communities. It's the trivializing of civil rights and anti–Vietnam War protesters all over again. Meanwhile, where is the scrutiny of the fossil fuel companies? If the *Times* doesn't ask them the hard questions, hold them to account, then who will? And can someone please shake the photo editors? A story on a heat wave will show images of people eating ice cream, when it would be more accurate to show people sick with heatstroke, or dead animals lying by a riverbed gone dry from drought..."

There was nothing I could do to save Audrey. Once Patti got started, there was no point trying to stop her—you just had to let her get it out. As I sipped my beer and watched Audrey squirm through Patti's polemic, my mind wandered to what Audrey had told me earlier, the story about Elizabeth Waites pestering media elites to join her MLM. The way Audrey said it, the mix of shock and pity, made it sound like Elizabeth was panhandling barefoot outside Penn Station. Audrey had been trying to make me feel better, but wasn't I just as pitiable? Just as pathetic? Weren't our industry friends probably talking about *me* like that? What was I going to do? Should I join an MLM? No, there were so many unemployed journalists around, everyone we knew had surely made enough pity purchases of Tupperware and essential oils to last a lifetime.

"Be right back," I said, slipping my phone into my pocket and going to the bathroom, ignoring the desperate plea in Audrey's eyes begging me not to leave her alone with Patti.

Perched on the edge of the tub, I stared at my phone, consulting it like an oracle, thumbs poised. I would figure this out the way I'd figured everything out, alone, for a long time now. I'd been on my own since Mom had died in my final year of college, a heart attack caused by her chronic lung condition killing her when she was only fifty-two, mere months before she would have seen me graduate. The summer after she died, I'd cleared out and cleaned her house and, when it was time to go, slipped the key for the real estate agent under the door. Then I'd sat in my car at the top of the hill, the back seat piled with boxes of her belongings I wanted to keep. The plan was to take the boxes to a storage facility, drive the car to the person who'd agreed to buy it, then take a taxi to the airport and fly to New York to start my new life. After a few minutes of tears, I turned the key in the ignition, ready to go. But the car wouldn't start. After a few tries, I realized that because the gas tank was almost empty, and I was parked with the nose of the car facing downhill, the engine wouldn't catch. I sat there, wondering what to do. I could have called AAA, but they wouldn't have come for at least an hour, if not longer, and if I'd waited that long I risked missing my flight. Nothing was going to make me miss that flight.

Before I could think about it, I released the handbrake. An action that would later frighten me, once I had a fully developed frontal lobe. I didn't think about the risk of driving head-on into the tree at the bottom of the hill where the road curved, the risk of my skin being cut open by shattered glass, the risk of bruises, broken bones, or worse. The car began to roll forward, slowly at first, then gaining speed. I kept one hand gripped on the wheel and with the other I turned the key in the ignition. As the car picked up speed, I turned, turned, turned it again. The steering wheel was locked. The bend at the bottom of the hill got closer. I was headed straight for the tree. I pressed my foot on the brake, but with the engine off it didn't work. I gained more speed still. And then, with only seconds to spare, the engine roared to life. I hooked the wheel to the right, pressed my foot hard on the gas, and sped toward the highway. Now, at twenty-nine years old, I was no longer so reckless. But I was no less determined, no less wired for survival.

THE SCOOP

There was one job I hadn't mentioned to Audrey, because I knew what she would say. I'd received an email from a recruiter at Johnson News, the conservative media company that owned dozens of newspapers and websites around the world, as well as the infamous cable channel, America Now. I'd ignored it, the words *Johnson News* conjuring images in my mind of the loudmouthed America Now hosts spouting lies, rumors of sexist executives insisting female hosts wear skirts and dresses, never pants, of Walter Johnson, the company's creepy elderly cartoon villain of a CEO. But had I been too quick to dismiss it? I reread the email. They were looking for a news editor at *The Scoop*, a website that had launched the year before. The recruiter wanted to know if I was available for an interview with the editor in chief, David Brown.

I opened a browser window and found *The Scoop*. I quickly discovered it was about as unserious as a news website could be, as though a group of bored and horny teenage boys suffering from brain injuries was in charge. The top story was about a woman in Australia who had broken the world record for drinking the most beer from a shoe; I reasoned it was important to celebrate women's achievements in male-dominated domains. Other stories on the home page included a priest in Italy going viral because his knee, from a certain angle, resembled the face of John Travolta, and feverish speculation on whether a certain reality show star's ass was looking bigger, again (the universe was expanding, and so was Kira Vincent's butt).

No. I couldn't, could I? Not Johnson News. I was a *Marie Claire* journalist. But then I remembered the box under my bed, the one that held the personal items I'd carried out the day I got laid off, still unpacked. Glaring proof that I wasn't a *Marie Claire* journalist, not anymore.

I hit reply and started typing. **Thank you for reaching out! It sounds like a great opportunity. I would love to learn more.**

Audrey knocked on the bathroom door.

"Frankie? You okay?"

I swallowed, my finger hovering over the send button. Was I really going to do this? It was the media-industry equivalent of the weirdest guy in the dive bar offering to buy you a drink. But if you have been lonely long enough, you will probably say yes. It feels good to be wanted.

Audrey knocked again.

I pressed send.

2

"So, tell me," David said, eyeing my résumé in his hand, "why do you want to work for us?"

The room was outrageously small, a windowless space closer in size to an airplane toilet than any meeting room I'd ever been in. Later, once I knew David, I suspected it was chosen on purpose. It was an optical illusion, a strategic move to make David—tall, broad-shouldered, though beginning to stoop and slacken with age—appear intimidating, an attempt to overcompensate for his diminishing importance in the world. It only sounds far-fetched if you didn't know David. That was him in a nutshell: a calculating mind protecting a fragile ego.

That late summer morning, high above Seventh Avenue, sitting opposite David at a too-small round table in what for all I knew was the janitor's closet with the cleaning supplies hastily removed, I wasn't sure I *did* want to work for him. For *The Scoop*. Still, I ignored the voice inside screaming at me to leave, now, and recited the monologue I'd practiced, the crux of which was: print is but one last resuscitation attempt away from dead, and I, Francesca Miller, Forbes 30 Under 30

List honoree (six years ago, but still) and trailblazing editor, who at *Marie Claire* oversaw a busy, award-winning features desk, contributing to a year-on-year rise in circulation in a challenging media landscape (this was a bald-faced lie; I prayed he wouldn't ask for proof), was ready to step out of the crumbling wreckage of the magazine industry and into the digital future.

"Did you ever have any fun?" David asked when I was done, staring down his nose.

"Excuse me?"

"You make it sound so serious. Aren't women's magazines all shoes and nail polish?"

It took all the restraint I could summon not to react. I'd barely been there five minutes and already David had said something sexist. I shouldn't have been surprised; this was Johnson News, after all. Still, it irritated me to hear him dismiss publications targeted at women as frivolous, nothing more than "shoes and nail polish," for him to trivialize my career by asking if I had "fun." He might as well have told me to smile. I almost laughed at the irony; it was exactly this kind of misogynistic attitude that made me want to be a journalist in the first place. As a teenager, it was in the pages of *Teen Vogue* and *Seventeen* that I first saw a life for women that was different from what I knew: watching my mom put dinner on the table every night for my ungrateful father like a 1950s housewife, hoping he wouldn't get drunk enough to scream at us or break anything that night, the men who slowed their cars to whistle at me as I waited for the bus. The magazines were a portal to another, better world, one where women had authority. A voice. Power.

Now I took in the sight of David: the receding hairline, the jowls that jiggled when he talked, the paunch that strained the buttons of his shirt, the dark, heavy brow that gave him the appearance of being permanently annoyed, the smug arrogance I considered unearned given the third-rate content on his website, and I knew it had been a mistake to come. On the subway on the way to the interview, someone was reading the *New York Post*, the cover story about twin three-year-old boys who died after being left by mistake in a hot car by their sleep-deprived mother, who was now on suicide watch. HOW COULD SHE? screamed the headline, and I wanted to be sick. Every time the doors had opened, I'd thought of getting off, taking the next train home. But something had kept me on the train, and that same something kept me there with David.

"Sure, there are shoes and nail polish," I said. "Alongside more serious features."

David sensed he'd caused offense.

"You'll have to forgive my ignorance," he said. "It's been a while since I picked up a magazine. I'd be surprised if anyone still reads them. You are right that the future is digital."

Then he changed direction.

"Tabloids are a special breed," he said. "Some people don't like what we do. Or at least they *pretend* not to like it. People who subscribe to *The New Yorker* will never admit to reading us, but we're the first website they check in the morning when they're on the toilet taking a shit."

I found David's needlessly vulgar description of reader loyalty repulsive, but he had a point. Most people shuddered at the word *tabloid*, seeing such publications—the *New York Post*, the *National Enquirer*, *TMZ*, and plenty more overseas—either as evil enterprises or as simply a joke. And yet, at *Marie Claire*, it was always the tabloid stories that made us run to each other's desks to discuss, from the juicy, like a celebrity's bad behavior at a fellow A-lister's Hamptons house, to the disturbing, like a murdered woman found frozen solid in a gas station icebox.

"Tabloids show the world as it is, not how we would like it to be,"

David continued. "All we do is hold up a mirror. But it's an ugly world. Some people can't bear to look. It's not easy, being the one who holds up the mirror, showing people what they'd rather not see. But someone's got to do it. At those magazines, you were in the business of creating a fantasy world. That's okay, people need fantasy. But human beings are flawed, and sordid. They lie, they cheat, they post things online that come back to bite them a decade later. That's *real*. That's *real life*. And I love it, all of it. I'd rather live an unglamorous truth than a polished lie, wouldn't you?"

To this I didn't know what to say, and thankfully, David didn't seem to want an answer. I was beginning to understand that for David Brown, the purpose of a job interview was not to assess the candidate's skill or suitability, but rather their capacity to endure his monologues.

"*The Scoop* isn't for everyone," David continued. "We don't run around on red carpets. We don't come in late or leave early. There are no slow news days. We work very hard here."

I thought I detected a question implicit in his words. *We work very hard here*. As if he was saying, *Will you work hard, Francesca?* A test, I was surprised to realize, I wanted to pass.

"Great," I replied, perhaps too quickly, too firmly. "I'm not afraid of hard work. I turned up in New York City from North Carolina, not knowing anyone, and worked my way up the ranks at the most prestigious magazine company in the world. Hard work? That's not a problem."

David stared at me for a beat, as if trying to decide if he believed me.

"I grew up in Reading, Francesca," he said when he spoke again. "I don't suppose you know where that is. It's about ninety minutes west of London. Manufacturing town. Working class. Very humble. I was the youngest of six. My father was a laborer. He broke his back carrying bricks for a living. My parents, God rest their souls, lived through

World War Two. They felt lucky to be alive, when so many had died. They were grateful just to have a roof over their heads. They thought I should be satisfied with the same lot in life. They didn't understand when I said I wanted to go to university, move to London, make something of myself. And while I did want it, I never once thought I *deserved* it. That the world *owed* me. All of these spoiled brats whose parents shell out for them to go to Yale, or Columbia"—he shook his head—"not only do they get doors held wide open for them, but they also have the nerve to think it's their God-given right, a place in this industry. That there is something *special* about *them*." He laughed.

Was David implying we were the same, me and him? The suggestion made me flinch. Though, I couldn't help thinking of Audrey. Her parents paid for her to go to Yale. While her mom had a column in a national newspaper, mine snipped the newsprint with scissors to cut out coupons. There it was, that twisting in my gut again, the feeling I kept telling myself wasn't jealousy as I thought of Audrey, only a few blocks downtown at the *Times*. It unsettled me, sitting there with David, to find myself agreeing with him, understanding him, as he talked.

"Our readers," David continued, leaning forward on the table, "get up at four in the morning to drop their still-sleeping children at their grandparents' house before they get on the train for a ninety-minute commute to work a twelve-hour shift at a hospital. They sleep in the cabs of the semitrailers they drive across the country for a measly wage. They don't give a flying fuck about why they should be eating sustainable sea scallops," he spat with a venom so specific that it made me wonder if David had somehow been wronged by a mollusk.

"If they were to read *The New York Times* for their news"—he laughed again, morphing from anger to amusement, as if he found the idea ridiculous—"they'd fall asleep in seconds and never read a damn thing. That's if they could afford a subscription, which most can't. The American media mostly ignores the working class—a fatal flaw, if you ask me, since it's the undereducated working class that is most desperate to be heard, and the easiest to influence."

David had my head spinning. One minute he was talking up his working-class background, ranting about out-of-touch elites; the next he was being elitist himself, saying anyone without a university degree was a backwards hick ripe to be fed lies. His sweeping stereotype of working-class people was maddening. My mom didn't go to college; she worked as a grocery store cashier and filled orders in an auto-parts warehouse, but she wasn't stupid. A voracious reader, she correctly guessed almost every answer on *Jeopardy!*, made people laugh with her wit. Sitting there with David, I remembered how my mother hated America Now.

"Half the people in this town have had their brains rotted by that damn channel," she would despair whenever we went to a restaurant and America Now was on the TV on the wall. I was betraying her, I knew, by being there in that building, while downstairs in the America Now studio, the maniacally grinning hosts performed like demented circus clowns, parroting made-up facts fed to them by producers scouring 4chan for the latest burgeoning conspiracy theories.

David sensed he'd rankled me, again. He lightened up all of a sudden, changed tack.

"*The Scoop* is the hot new thing at Johnson News. The eyes of the whole company are on us, all the way to the top. Shine here and you will have your pick of any job in the company: America Now, if television is something that interests you—boy, do they take home some fat paychecks there!—something cushy in corporate, a posting in London, *Business Day*..."

Business Day. It was the one Johnson News publication you could work at without bringing shame upon your family. The oldest, most respected financial newspaper in the country, *Business Day* occupied the same rarefied air as *The New York Times* and *The Washington Post*. Johnson News had acquired *Business Day* in a controversial sale a few years earlier; it was like new money buying a historic home on one of the most prized streets in Martha's Vineyard, painting it a retina-searing shade of hot pink, and turning it into a brothel. Since then, the once famously discriminating opinion section had been dirtied up by hokey writers pushing shady agendas. But for Ivy League graduates, it was hard to shake the emotional attachment. It was undoubtedly still impressive to work at *Business Day*, to walk into that storied newsroom in an I'm a Real Journalist Now, Daddy! starter kit of specs, cashmere sweater, and loafers.

There are still good people there, parents who had spent $100,000 sending their kids to journalism school reassured themselves, even though all the good people had long since left.

"Ah, now, that made your eyes light up," David said. "*Business Day*, the crown jewel of Johnson News. Tell me, what do you think of it?"

"What do I think of it? I mean, it's *Business Day*. It doesn't get much more prestigious."

Turns out I also was not immune to the fading luster of a legacy media brand.

"You'd want to work there?"

"Are you kidding? Of course."

"Great," David said, clapping his hands as if to say, *Case closed*. "So, you'll join us at *The Scoop* for a while. Help us get traffic up, make a name for ourselves. Then, in the new year, I'll organize your transfer to *Business Day*."

David must have been joking. Or I hadn't heard him correctly. I stared dumbly.

"*Business Day*? Really?"

"Sure. You'd be helping me out of a tight spot. If I can be frank, I'm in desperate need of a night editor at *The Scoop*. I can't sleep, wondering what dog turd of a front page I'll wake up to. These kids we hire, they're cheap, fast, and hungry as hell, but the messes they make..." David described a recent incident where a young reporter didn't know Tupac was dead. In the article, they referred to the rapper, assassinated in 1994, as though he were still alive. *Tupac is yet to comment*, the young reporter wrote in a story about a Broadway play based on his life. The mistake was caught, but not before some mischievous soul posted a screenshot on social media. *The Scoop* was mercilessly roasted for days.

But what had David said before that? Something about working at night?

"Sorry, did you say *night* editor?'"

"The shift is five p.m. until two a.m., Sunday to Thursday. Look, I won't pretend night shift hours aren't tough. But I think you'll be pleasantly surprised by the salary after your employment at those magazines. We pay our journalists properly, no unpaid internships and starvation wages. Plus, health insurance and all that. I know that's important to you poor bloody Americans. Financially ruined over a burst appendix. I don't know how you people live."

The salary was $10,000 more than what I'd earned at *Marie Claire*, the most I'd ever earned. In my mind I saw myself paying chunks off my credit cards, a steamy broke millennial fantasy, drooling as the balances drained down, down, down. I was almost aroused. Not to mention the health insurance, if I was the next *poor bloody American* with a medical emergency.

"You're offering me a job? Just like that?"

David shrugged. "I told you. We don't waste time here."

"I can see that."

Night editor? I felt like I'd been tricked. The recruiter hadn't mentioned *that*. But now it was so close: a new job, health insurance, being able to afford my rent and bills...and, unexpectedly, *Business Day*.

THE SCOOP

Had I found a loophole, a secret passageway to media greatness? A few months at *The Scoop*—it was August, and hadn't he said "in the new year"?—and I'd be at one of the most esteemed publications in the country. It was within reach again, the life I'd come to New York to pursue. The life I feared I'd lost forever after *Marie Claire*. The life I had begun building before I ever knew Josh. The one I'd closed my eyes and promised my mom, weeping that day in the car before I drove off from her empty house, I would never give up on. Maybe I wouldn't be the next Elizabeth Waites, the next tragic, washed-up joke of a journalist, after all.

David watched me, waiting for an answer. I felt the walls of that weirdly tiny meeting room closing in. I never could have imagined I would say yes. But how could I say no?

I had only one question.

"When do I start?"

3

THERE ARE THINGS YOU CAN get away with at night that you can't during the day. Graveyard shift at *The Scoop* was like a child's fantasy of being locked in somewhere you're not supposed to be after dark, like an amusement park once the gates were shut for the night: going on rides as many times as you can stand, gorging on cotton candy until you're sick, and, once spent, curling up to sleep in a bounce house—only if it was a sad, office-themed amusement park. I walked around barefoot, ate a greedy number of cookies from the jar in the kitchen, helped myself to a tube of expensive hand cream I found on someone else's desk. It was eerie, lonely, but oddly liberating.

Unlike a child trapped in a fun park after hours, there was no search party looking for me, no worried parent soon to arrive and take me home. No one was coming to save me, not from any of it: the watery, burnt-tasting Keurig coffee; the rows of empty desks and chairs that felt almost postapocalyptic, as if they'd been abandoned in a hurry; the stuffy air and strange silence after ten p.m. when the AC was shut off (because Johnson News refused to pay the overnight fee that would have kept it on); the row of clocks on the wall showing the time in capital cities around the world, reminding me of all the places I could have been instead; the jetlag feeling of being under the fluorescent lights after midnight when my body begged to be in bed asleep.

David wasn't there in the newsroom at night, his spot vacant at the head of the long desk where, in daylight, he'd shout orders at the tabloid's top editors sitting side by side, packed so tightly their elbows almost touched, David like a coach at the front of a rowing boat, screaming at his subjects to paddle faster, faster, faster. But I still had to deal with him. He called my desk phone often throughout the shift, the shrill, bleating ring a constant threat that kept me on edge.

There were also others.

Chris, the news reporter, was a quiet, peculiar man in his late forties. Tall, lanky, and pale, with prominent dark circles that suggested a serious vitamin D deficiency, Chris ate the same thing for dinner every night: a meatball sub from Subway. He would unwrap it at his desk, its spicy aroma filling the air, and proceed to tear hunks off his pungent sandwich, showering crumbs down into the cracks of his keyboard where, I assumed, they would remain for eternity.

Chris seemed to me like the kind of person who had unforgivingly bright fluorescent light bulbs throughout his home and washed his entire body, face to ass, with a bar of Irish Spring.

During my first week, I learned that years earlier Chris had won a Pulitzer. He'd been a young reporter at the *Chicago Tribune*, part of a team to receive the honor for a series about the mismanagement of city funds. It rattled me that a journalist could fall so far—from Pulitzer to "poop-etrator," as was the pun in his story about an unknown person in Arkansas who was shitting in people's mailboxes. Upon learning this, I found it hard to look at Chris, the way you might avert your gaze from an Oscar-winning actor whose face was tragically disfigured in a house fire.

Then there was Jocelyn, the photo editor, a loud, blunt, Italian American woman (she mentioned this often, giving it as an excuse for her loud-and-blunt-ness) about the same age as me, who chewed a lot of gum and was always running her fingers nervously through her brunette bangs. Her energy was like that of a hurricane brewing in the corner, the way she typed and clicked at manic speed, her fingers hammering away on her keyboard in a violent, thundering staccato. The frenzy only stopped when she took a cigarette break, at least once every couple of hours, sometimes more, bringing back with her the scent of smoke and perfume with notes of lilac, the latter I assumed to cover the cigarette smell. I preferred it to Chris's meatball subs.

On my first day, Jocelyn yanked open a desk drawer to show me the assortment of orange and white bottles, blister sheets of pills, and other pharmaceutical products crammed inside.

"Adderall, Xanax—you'll need those if you stress easy," she said, "eye drops, an herbal thing for UTIs... sometimes we get too busy to piss, and it causes problems, if you know what I mean," like this was totally normal, as if she were merely showing me how to work the printer.

But I liked Yenay, the entertainment writer, best. A twenty-two-year-old recent college graduate, she was at *The Scoop* in her first full-time job. Yenay wasn't jaded like Chris, or cranky like Jocelyn. She was bubbly, eager, and had shamelessly grand ambitions; Yenay dreamt of writing celebrity profiles for *Vogue*, *GQ*, or *Vanity Fair*. She would joke that as a Chinese American woman in the media, she felt a duty to break up the white male celebrity-profile-writer clique that overwhelmingly dominated the niche. On her "break" each night (supposedly we were allowed to take an hour, but leaving our posts for more than a few minutes was impractical), Yenay scarfed down her food while watching YouTube videos of Barbara Walters interviewing celebrities on *60*

Minutes. She reminded me of myself when I was her age, an ambitious, deeply determined young journalist in New York City, convinced there would be no limits to her success if she just worked harder than everyone else. That that was all it would take.

As I learned on my first day, in Yenay I had something of a fan. Washing our hands in the bathroom at the same time, she sheepishly admitted that when she was in college, she would cut out the column I wrote for *Cosmopolitan*—View from the Front Desk, an insider's look at the magazine from my perspective as editorial assistant—and stick it up on her dorm room wall.

"I wanted to *be* you," Yenay said, I think meaning to flatter, but only reminding me that I had once been someone important, admired, even envied—and that I no longer was.

Despite the occasional lull, or the odd excruciatingly slow shift (usually Sundays), the pace of the newsroom at night was mostly rapid-fire, chaotic, constant, a blasting firework display of pings, alerts, emails, and calls, all of which I had to respond to, often all at once. The only reprieve was when I stole a bathroom break (Jocelyn wasn't kidding about it being hard to find a moment to piss) or stood in the kitchen watching my dinner rotate in the microwave, the endless cups of black coffee and the pulse of the newsroom still humming in my veins. At the end of every shift, I was both caffeine-wired and brain-fried, my thoughts like a fistful of confetti thrust in the air, a scattered, swirling mess of fragments floating dumb and directionless. I felt strung out, dazed, comparable to what I imagined it would be like to be hung from the ceiling by my feet while being made to listen to the piercing strains of the Alvin and the Chipmunks cover of "Uptown Funk" on a loop for nine hours, as in some sick torture at the hands of a CIA agent. I wondered if this was what it would feel like to have a lobotomy. I decided it was strangely nice.

On Thursday night my first week, with less than an hour until the end of the shift, I was editing Chris's piece about a woman who claimed to earn $50,000 a month selling jars of her farts online. I was just glad it was Chris's byline at the top of the story and not mine. I was an editor, not a reporter, and so I comforted myself that I'd never have to suffer the indignity of seeing my name atop an article on *The Scoop*, on the atrocious content we pretended was journalism. When I left in a few months, I reassured myself, it would be like I was never there.

The shrill ring of my desk phone sliced through the silence, jolting me to attention. David called a lot, but 1:30 a.m. was late, even for him. It raised the question of whether the man ever slept, and there was every chance he didn't; Jocelyn said his family, a wife and two daughters, had not moved with him to New York City but stayed in London to not disrupt the girls' schooling. Living alone, as we understood it, with no pets, there was nothing to stop him from keeping strange hours, popping up throughout the night to send story ideas or order changes.

"Hi, David."

"Have you seen the *Daily News*?" he asked breathlessly.

"The *Daily News*?" I had heard him, but I feigned confusion to buy myself time.

"Yes, Francesca, the *Daily News*," he said, impatient. "The top story."

I typed *dailynews.com* in the address bar as fast as I could. What had I missed? A plane crash? A mass shooting? The death of a former president? The death of the *current* president? Once the page loaded, I scanned it, frantic. No photos from the scene of a plane crash. No headlines about a mass shooting. The top story was... Meryl Streep. At the beach.

I clicked on the story. The beloved Oscar winner was on vacation in the Bahamas, wearing a chaste aquamarine swimsuit, a white sarong wrapped modestly around her waist. She stood at the water's edge, a hand shielding her eyes. *This* was what had David all worked up?

"Where is our story on this?" David demanded, his voice rising an octave. "Hasn't the agency sent the pictures yet? They're not exclusive—*People* and *E! News* have them up."

What I didn't yet understand was that at *The Scoop*, paparazzi photos were often treated with the hysterical sense of urgency other news outlets reserved for the most serious of events; a celebrity nip-slip on the red carpet was our equivalent of war breaking out in Europe, in terms of the dramatic way the newsroom sprang into frenzied action. I could have understood the urgency, maybe, if the photos revealed that Meryl had a flaming skull tattoo on her lower back. But all I saw was a sixty-something-year-old woman in modest beachwear. Benign. A non-event.

Jocelyn snapped her fingers to get my attention. I covered the receiver with my hand.

"I sent you those!" she hissed.

"You did?"

"Yes! Two hours ago."

David was asking if I was still there, and what was going on. Phone still pressed between ear and shoulder, I went to my inbox and scanned it, panicked. Sure enough, there was the email from Jocelyn, sent earlier, unopened. How had I missed it? Or had I seen it but thought it was boring, because it was? Either way, I had to decide how to play it. If I told David I'd overlooked the email, it might plant a seed of doubt in his mind about whether I was capable of keeping up with the pace of the newsroom, as he had hinted at in the interview: The Scoop *isn't for everyone. We work very hard here.* No, better for it to be a difference of opinion, I decided.

I apologized for not prioritizing the photos, said I'd leave a note for the morning team.

"What?" David cried. "The morning? No, no, we need to get these photos up, now!"

But it was 1:30 a.m. Almost home time. Ludicrous, to keep the team back for this.

I explained that Chris and Yenay were finishing their last stories: Yenay an update on a celebrity divorce, Chris the news of a terrorist attack in Mogadishu, Somalia, in which hundreds of people were believed killed by a car bomb (world news was frowned upon at *The Scoop*, but permissible if especially violent or bloody, or with a death toll "high enough" to justify it).

"But aren't we here to report the news?" I'd tried when Jocelyn had explained this to me.

"I hope no one is getting their news from *The Scoop*," she'd said.

"I hope no one is getting their news from the media," came Chris's reply.

Now David had gone quiet long enough to make me wonder if he was still there.

"Do you think you know how to run this website better than me?"

I felt a shiver start at the crown of my head and spread down my body. There was a quiet venom in David's voice I had never heard before. I nearly laughed, wondering if he was joking.

"Well? Do you?"

"No, of course not," I managed to strangle out, realizing he was serious.

"Then forget fucking Mogadishu! Get the Meryl Streep photos live. Now!"

The pure rage in David's voice sent what felt like bolts of electricity shooting up my limbs to my chest, as if he were there in the office and not thirty blocks uptown in his Upper East Side penthouse. For a moment we were both silent. When he spoke again, he sounded calmer.

THE SCOOP

"We must never forget, Francesca," he said, "that the Man Upstairs is always watching."

"He's going to fire me," I said, holding one of Jocelyn's cigarettes up to my lips with trembling fingers as she lit it. She touched the flame of her Zippo to her own, then let it close with a snap.

We were outside the Johnson News building, huddled behind a concrete column to shelter our cigarettes from the breeze blowing down Seventh Avenue. I hugged myself to stay warm. It had been sunny and blue-skied when I'd left for work, one of those almost painfully perfect September days, so nice I had not brought a sweater. But during the evening a storm had rolled through; the ground shone with wet and there was a chill in the air. Jocelyn was better dressed for the weather in a leather jacket, opaque tights under her miniskirt to sheath her spindly legs, and black combat boots. With severe bangs, smudged makeup around her brown eyes, and deep berry lipstick that stained her cigarette, she seemed so suited to night shift I couldn't imagine her in sunlight.

"He won't fire you," Jocelyn insisted, as though I was being ridiculous. "That's just how it is here. One day two people can scream at each other in the newsroom, the next day it's like it never happened. Trust me, the next time you talk to David he will have forgotten all about it."

We were waiting for our cars, a service provided for night shift staff and the only discernible perk of working odd hours. Johnson News paid for us to be driven home in private vehicles not out of a sense of duty for our safety, I was sure, but to avoid the potential lawsuits that could result from the risk we would face riding the subway at that hour of the night.

I took a deep inhale of the cigarette, felt the smoke make my chest hot and tight, breaking the promise I'd made to my mom after she got sick with the lung disease that would kill her never to touch them. I imagined her clucking her tongue at what had become of me, puffing away steps from the America Now studios after being berated in the middle of the night by an old man with anger issues—and all over a photo of a woman at the beach. I wondered what she would have had to say about the turn my life had taken. *Glad to see that journalism degree being put to good use*, I imagined her teasing me. There was always a kernel of truth beneath her sarcastic quips.

"But what were you thinking?" Jocelyn said. *"Leave it for the morning?* Are you insane?"

I blew smoke into the night air, felt myself grow defensive. "How was I supposed to know a woman at the beach is more important than hundreds of people being bombed to death?"

Jocelyn rolled her eyes, fished her phone out of her jacket pocket, and brought up *The Scoop*. The Meryl Streep photos were in the "splash"—the top spot on the home page.

The devil wears (almost) nada! Meryl Streep, 65, showcases her bodacious beach body

"Does that woman not look good?" Jocelyn asked, turning her phone around and shoving the screen in my face. "Huh? Tell me she doesn't look incredible."

"I'm not saying she doesn't look good. All I'm saying is—"

"She's sixty-five years old, Francesca. The woman's got a flatter stomach than me, for Christ's sake. Don't tell me that's not a miracle worth stopping everything for."

I squinted at the photos again. I had to admit, Meryl *did* look good.

Jocelyn yawned loudly. "Yikes, I need to get to bed. You got someone waiting at home?"

It wasn't a subtle segue, as Jocelyn attempted to glean what details she could about my private life. But I was exhausted, shaken up, almost delirious, and wanted to stretch out this last moment of human interaction before the hours ahead, alone in my bed, lying awake, willing my brain to shut off and sleep before I saw the first hint of morning sun creep under the curtains.

I told Jocelyn I'd lived with a roommate in Prospect Heights for nearly a year now since the breakup with Josh. I said I'd been single since, which was true, though this tidy explanation of my love life failed to include that I'd spent my weird, unemployed, idle summer sleeping with strange men. All summer in the humid dark I'd prowled the streets of Clinton Hill and Fort Greene; this is where he resided, the particular breed of forty-something Brooklyn man recently separated from his wife I was self-destructively attracted to. I'd let the men with wives fuck me in their barely furnished studio apartments, let them pour me ice-cold glasses of Sancerre that stood on the dresser sweating beads of condensation as we acted like animals on dirty sheets, the sound of silverware clinking on plates from people dining alfresco on the street below floating up through the open window as, between moans, we tried not to whisper other people's names into each other's ears.

If I'd had the money to see a therapist, they probably would have said the unavailable-men thing was about the breakup with Josh opening up old wounds over my estrangement from my father, a longing to be "intimate" only with those who could offer no real intimacy, a subconscious avoidance. You know, some convenient, textbook, overintellectualized bullshit like that. Sometimes a woman just needs to get laid, and these men—sex starved as they were, just getting out of bad marriages—desired me intensely, which made me feel beautiful, despite my bloated face from all the daytime wine, despite the ugly scar of inadequacy I still bore from Josh's painful betrayal. When I took the job, the thought had crossed my mind that being forced to spend five nights a week in a newsroom could be good for me, healthy, since it would leave me only two nights a week to indulge in self-destructive debauchery, like a normal person.

"What about you?" I asked Jocelyn.

Jocelyn shook her head. "No. These hours are hard. In my experience, the only men who'll put up with it are chefs and musicians, aka the dirtbags. Chris and Yenay are single, too."

I found this depressing, but it didn't surprise me. I couldn't imagine Josh would have gladly gone to sleep alone in our bed while I was at the office, happily keeping himself entertained five nights a week without me. If the co-worker hadn't already broken us up, this job almost certainly would have. But if I hadn't left Josh, then I wouldn't have had to take the job at *The Scoop*; he would have supported me financially, at least for a while, so I could have held out longer until the right job came along. What would have been our fourth anniversary was coming up. Would he have proposed? Standing there on that Midtown corner in the middle of the night, I half expected to glimpse her through the window of a passing car, that old version of me. Or more accurately, the version of me I almost became but didn't. Strange, to have to grieve not just the things you once had and lost, but the things you thought your future held that would never be.

Our cars pulled up to the curb one after the other, indicators blinking neon in the night. We stubbed out our cigarettes in the garden bed beside us and headed across the forecourt.

"In the universe of *The Scoop*," Jocelyn said as we walked, "David Brown is God. Remember that and you'll make it here. Maybe."

THE SCOOP

The comparison of David to God reminded me of something he said on the phone earlier.

"*Is* David religious?" I asked.

"It's just a metaphor."

"No, I know. But tonight, on the phone, he said, 'The Man Upstairs is always watching.'"

Jocelyn began to laugh.

"No, silly. He means our evil overlord, Walter Johnson."

4

Was a brief choking scare too much to ask? A server performing the Heimlich maneuver on a diner whose lips were barely blue? Nothing too serious; I didn't want anyone to get hurt. All I wanted was for something so dramatic and astonishing to happen in the restaurant that we could speak of nothing else for the rest of the meal. So I wouldn't have to make my confession to Audrey. That I had done the unthinkable, and maybe unforgivable: I had become a tabloid hack.

When I'd made plans for brunch with Audrey and our fellow ex–*Marie Claire* colleagues Naomi and Jasmine weeks earlier, I'd been worried I would have to admit I was still looking for work, that I was still unable to convince anyone in the New York media I was worth hiring. Instead, I'd just had my first week at *The Scoop*. I felt tired and strange from going to sleep at sunrise and waking at lunch not at all refreshed, as if I were in a new time zone. I was still shaken after being on the receiving end of an explosion of rage from David so volcanic you'd think I'd set fire to a treasured letter from an old lover, his only copy—and all because I'd dared suggest readers could wait until the morning to see grainy photos of Meryl Streep at the beach.

But there I was, shoving down bites of mediocre eggs Benedict at a West Village brunch spot, the kind of place that charged double because Jake Gyllenhaal ate there once in 2004, my new life still a secret. I forced myself to chew and swallow, though I had no appetite, my stomach knotted with dread. I tried to listen as Jasmine, who had been the beauty editor at *Marie Claire*, filled us in on her new job as a copywriter at Aqueous, the luxury gym chain—or "premium well-being space," as she called it, clearly having drunk the Kool-Aid or whatever organic, sugar-free, fair-trade, shaman-blessed beverage they drank there. I could admit the perks *were* enviable. Sure, she had to keep a straight face while using words like *sacred* and *intoxicating* to describe a cardio class, but she also got a free Aqueous premium membership.

"Everyone is ridiculously fit and walks around wet-haired, smelling like the fancy bodywash in the showers," Jasmine said. "The place reeks of lemon verbena and geranium."

I'd thought when we hugged she'd smelled good, and now I noticed her pale cheeks were pink, and her brown hair was pulled up in a messy bun. She'd been at Aqueous on her day off.

This vision, of an office of impossibly fit and perfumed people, had Audrey swooning.

"The *Times* smells like stale bagels and dust. I can think of one colleague in particular who could do to shower more frequently. He's hot but lacks basic hygiene. It's so confusing."

Naomi looked to be enjoying the talk of our post–*Marie Claire* lives as much as I was, which was not at all. She'd been miserable since taking a job as a "social and community strategist" at an ad agency, an impressive-sounding title that obscured the mundane reality of her days: updating the social media accounts of her client, Hellmann's Mayonnaise. I'd followed Hellmann's on Instagram, trying to be supportive, and had been shocked to see they had 46,000 followers. Who knew so many people wanted updates from a condiment? Recently, Hellmann's and Hidden Valley Ranch had gotten into a (obviously contrived) feud. One of the posts got 14,000 likes. Naomi, former *Marie Claire* culture writer, was cosplaying online as a bottle of mayonnaise.

"I've never noticed how my office smells," Naomi said, glum. "Half the time I'm disassociating. The rest of the time I'm thinking, 'What would a bottle of mayo say?' "

"You said it's more diverse than *Marie Claire*," Audrey said, referencing some earlier conversation. We all remembered that Naomi had been the only Black woman on the team.

"Yeah," Naomi said, nodding, "but the bar is on the floor. *Marie Claire* was whiter than a Creed concert." She paused. "No shade to Creed. Those boys have some bangers."

I understood why Naomi found her job depressing, though when I thought about it, imagining what a bottle of mayonnaise would say if it were to become sentient and acquire a social media following was more compelling than anything I'd seen in *The New Yorker* lately.

Jasmine, seeing Naomi was spiraling, decided to change the subject.

"Audrey, I need to know more about the *Times*. How's it all going?"

Audrey smiled and nodded, said something vaguely positive about her boss and her colleagues, but I couldn't help noticing the way her shoulders reached to her ears as she talked.

"But are you enjoying it?" Naomi pressed her, frowning, as though she sensed trouble.

Audrey nodded vigorously as she swallowed her food. None of us bought it.

"All right, out with it," Jasmine said. "Tell us what's wrong."

"Nothing! It's *so* not a big deal. It's just that...I haven't figured out my beat. Media, obviously, but my beat within media. All my contacts are at Park Street, and the only exclusives I've been able to break so far have been about magazines shutting down, editor appointments, that kind of thing. Breaking stories about the magazine industry a few days before a press release would have gone out anyway? I don't know. I'm worried I'm not good enough for the *Times*."

It surprised me to hear Audrey express concern about her ability to keep up at the *Times*. She always seemed so confident, so sure of herself and her place in the industry, born into it as she was. She hadn't said anything to me about feeling insecure. Probably she didn't want to complain to me, of all people, because it would be insensitive—as far as Audrey knew, I was still unemployed, still in genuine emotional distress over being rejected by a magazine about boats.

"Give it time," Jasmine reassured her. "You're still new—everyone gets a grace period of a few months after starting a job. Before you know it, it'll be Thanksgiving, and everyone will mentally check out until next year. So, this year is basically a wash. I'd say you have until at least January to figure things out."

It was jarring, to realize how cushy all my jobs had been before *The Scoop*. Arriving at my desk at *Marie Claire* at ten a.m., or later. Generously long print deadlines. The over-the-top friendliness of magazine people (even if they gossiped savagely about you behind your back). Now, on a typical night, I edited at least ten stories, often even more, the ring of my desk phone triggering anxiety I was about to have my head bitten off by David again, all the while risking a UTI from holding in my piss because—breaking news!—a *Bachelor* contestant from three seasons ago had broken a toe and was posting a flurry of unhinged selfies from her hospital bed.

Jasmine turned to me. "What about you, Frank? How's the job hunt going?"

And just like that, it arrived. The moment I'd been dreading. I glanced around the restaurant but saw no indication anyone had a breakfast sausage lodged in their windpipe.

"Me?" I began, feeling like I'd been shoved over the edge of a waterslide and had no choice but to slip helplessly at breakneck speed to the bottom. "Actually, I... I got a job."

"What?" Audrey blurted, talking out of the corner of her mouth since she was mid-chew. I watched as her shock gave way to a wounded look, one of betrayal, and I felt a terrible pang of guilt. That week, I'd tried texting Audrey half a dozen times, even got as far as typing the words, I have some news, but deleted the message every time. I couldn't bring myself to hit send, wanted to delay just a little longer the moment I would be forever changed in the eyes of my best friend. I feared Audrey would view my tabloid-hack status like a zombie bite: an event that, while tragic, meant there was nothing to do but get away as fast as possible before I turned.

Jasmine and Naomi offered their enthusiastic congratulations, demanded more details.

Here goes nothing, I thought, the waterslide gaining speed as I hurtled to the bottom.

"Yes! It's, um..."

The three of them watched me, waiting. I couldn't seem to make myself say the words.

Naomi laid a reassuring hand on my forearm.

"Are you selling your body?" she said in a low voice, her face full of sympathy.

"What? No, nothing like that—"

"Is it PR?" Jasmine whispered, her eyes full of pity.

"God no," I said. I hadn't spent nearly a decade paying off my journalism degree with what was left of my pitiful magazine-industry salary to throw it in and spend my days sending emails that I knew, as a journalist who received plenty of them, were mostly dragged into the trash without ever being opened.

THE SCOOP

"I'm the night editor at *The Scoop*," I said at last. "It's a small news website."

From their nods and beaming expressions, I could tell Naomi and Jasmine hadn't heard of *The Scoop*. But Audrey had. I watched as her face changed from confused to concerned.

"*The Scoop*," Audrey repeated flatly. "You don't mean that Johnson News website?"

At the mention of Johnson News, Naomi and Jasmine's smiles evaporated. Their eyes flicked between me and Audrey and back again, as they sensed a wrinkle in the good cheer.

"That's the one," I said, taking a bite of soggy egg, determined to remain upbeat. I didn't look directly at Audrey, but I could sense the cogs turning in her mind as she absorbed the news.

"It's a Johnson News website?" Jasmine clarified, one eyebrow ever so slightly raised.

"Yeah," I said, my throat getting tight. I put down my fork. I had little confidence any of the servers in the restaurant could rise to the occasion and save a diner from choking to death.

"But it's not as bad as America Now. It is a tabloid, for sure, but it's not, like, evil, you know? Mostly lots of celebrity gossip, crime, oddball stories about UFOs, stuff like that."

Naomi nodded like she understood. "Right. Like the magazines at the checkout in small-town grocery stores? 'Whitney Houston reported alive and working at a ski resort in Switzerland!'" She giggled. I laughed, too. Yes, I liked this narrative. Harmless. A bit of silly fun.

"Exactly," I said. "Dumb stuff people click on because they're bored at work."

Audrey cleared her throat, stared at me with a puzzled expression. Like she was trying to make sense of it, that her best friend had gone over to the dark side of the media industry.

"From what *I've* heard," Audrey said, "I wouldn't say it's 'harmless.' One of my colleagues was talking about it the other day. The British tabloids are opening offices over here because they see the US as a gold mine, given our loose privacy laws compared to the UK. They send their own editors to run them, too, in the traditional Fleet Street way: aggressive, bloodthirsty, ruthless. My colleague told me about the big media-industry scandal over there a few years ago, where tabloid journalists were caught bribing doctors for medical records."

I looked down at my plate. Naomi and Jasmine had gone quiet. I knew vaguely what Audrey was talking about. Before the interview with David, I'd googled him. I hadn't found much except a few articles, mostly in British media-industry publications. David had been an editor at the now-defunct *National Herald*, the Johnson News newspaper that closed down abruptly following accusations of illegal activity by its reporters, including bribing, breaking and entering, and stealing. It had come to be known as the "spying scandal" and led to a government inquiry. But none of this worried me. David didn't seem to have done anything wrong—the journalists who were responsible served jail time—and the *National Herald* was no more.

"I'm not going to steal anyone's medical records," I said firmly. "It's only temporary, until I find something better." I considered telling them about the agreement I'd made with David, that he would soon transfer me to *Business Day*, to help them understand why I'd taken the job, but something held me back. A superstition it was unwise to share good news too early.

The others were quiet. They didn't seem convinced.

"I'm not exactly stoked about it either," I continued, trying desperately to squeeze a single drop of sympathy out of my friends. "But it's what I have to do. I ran out of options."

It was true. That morning, I'd gotten an email from my bank that said my credit score had gone down, again. I'd also searched for writer and editor jobs, David's screaming about Meryl and Mogadishu still reverberating in my head, driving me to see if it wasn't too late to find another job. But the situation was no less dire than it had been throughout my summer of unemployment. There was a copywriter job at a pharmaceutical company that required "rare-disease experience." (What was with these jobs requiring the most niche experience one could imagine?) My portfolio included nothing of the sort, but the thought had crossed my mind that they could not reject my application if I actually had a rare disease. I'd considered how I might go about this. "Rare" implied a certain exclusivity, but how hard could it be, in New York City, veritable bubbling cauldron of eight million people? Every rare disease in the world could surely be found in the Big Apple if one was willing to look hard enough, to venture to the farthest almond milk latte–deprived corners of the five boroughs. I'd post an ad on Craigslist soliciting anyone with a rare disease, ideally something curable (like a skin condition that could spread upon brief contact, given the time constraints) and then meet said rare-disease carrier in a darkened cinema and sit down beside them, where they would rub their bare arm and/or leg on mine for the duration of the film, or until I felt confident that their unique medical burden was now also mine to carry, in every sense. *If I can—bomp bomp—make it there*, I'd sing to myself as I left the cinema, *I'll make it—bomp bomp—anywhere. It's up to you, New York, New York.*

Or, I could just stay at *The Scoop*.

The mention of money, however brief, made Audrey frown and look down. I knew she hated being reminded that many of us didn't have a surplus of funds in our bank accounts, or a financially comfortable family to fall back on, because it made her feel guilty about her own good fortune. Often, she made throwaway comments about things "being so expensive lately" or needing to "rein in spending," to seem like one of us, when we all knew she never checked the balance on the screen when she bought groceries. I knew I'd won, that she would now back off.

The server came to clear our plates. Audrey asked him to bring the check.

"Maybe it's a good thing," she said, lightening, wanting to brush over the mention of money, as I knew she would. "They could do to have at least one ethical journalist in that building. Maybe you can stop *The Scoop* from becoming 4chan with a *Washington Post* budget."

The server brought the check. It was a dumb amount for very average-tasting eggs, especially when my account was close to zero since I'd just paid rent. I reminded myself I'd soon receive my first paycheck from *The Scoop*, and I could start digging myself out of my debt hole.

Audrey smiled at me across the table. Her joke was an olive branch, but it couldn't erase her obvious judgment of me for taking the job at *The Scoop*. What did I expect? She was a media reporter for *The New York Times*. Her father once went viral for an appearance on CNN where he called Johnson News "a cancer on democracy." How could she not be disappointed in me?

Naomi broke the awkward tension that hung over us. "Please, who's clean anymore?" She gestured at Jasmine. "Aqueous is owned by that Doctor Evil–looking motherfucker who raised millions for that awful homophobic Republican senator in Texas with the dead eyes."

Jasmine, not expecting to have the spotlight turned on her own ethical gray area, appeared taken aback. "Yes, that is something I've had to navigate. But I think that has to be balanced with the net-positive effect of Aqueous helping so many people to be healthier."

Naomi scoffed. "Correction: so many *rich* people."

Jasmine went red. Naomi put a hand on her shoulder. "Relax. I'm only kidding, Jaz."

"What about you, Hellmann's?" Jasmine shot back at Naomi, a mischievous smirk on her face. She was in on the joke now. "Saving the world one bottle of saturated fat at a time?"

Naomi laughed. "Okay, that's fair. Whatever it takes to make you feel better so you can sleep at night, since your paycheck is probably laundered global-pedophile-ring money."

Naomi was clearly still dating the NYU student who told her all the latest conspiracies. I hoped she wasn't about to start talking about chemtrails again. But it did make me feel better, knowing I wasn't the only one who had been forced to make an ethical compromise for work.

Jasmine asked me how the job was going. In my mind flashed a montage of my first week: the strange emptiness of the newsroom at night, the dumb stories about the mailbox shitter and Fart Jar Girl, the two a.m. drives home passing darkened storefronts and the eerily deserted but still brightly lit Times Square, Jocelyn's drawer of pharmaceuticals, David's wild outburst.

"Good," I said, pushing all this from my mind. "It's...different! The content is...refreshing. *Quirky*. And the people are...direct. Not afraid to say what's on their mind." I forced a laugh.

I could tell the level of detail was not to my friends' satisfaction. I had to give them more.

"The photo editor has this desk drawer full of pills: to wake you up, to help you sleep. She keeps it stocked with an herbal supplement to prevent UTIs because sometimes we get so busy we literally can't leave our desks to take a piss." I laughed again, too loud. "Crazy, right?"

The others didn't find this funny. Naomi pulled out her phone and looked up *The Scoop*. She turned her screen around to show the rest of us the home page—Kira Vincent's butt was looking even bigger. Jasmine and Naomi began to debate whether Kira had had surgery, perhaps implants, or whether her ever-plumper behind was the result of hard work in the gym alone. I heard David's words in my head: *People who subscribe to* The New Yorker *will never admit to reading us, but it's the first website they check in the morning when they're taking a shit.* Audrey looked bored, pretending not to be interested, but I suspected she'd look it up on the way home.

As we hugged each other outside the restaurant, saying our goodbyes until we would see each other at Audrey's birthday dinner in two weeks, Naomi whispered reassurance in my ear.

"You're in your Bad Sandy era," she said. "You're Olivia Newton-John, swapping the poofy skirt and blouse for leather pants and heels, smoking a cigarette. But you're still Sandy."

Still Sandy. A mantra I would repeat to myself in the weeks to come.

5

"WHAT'S GOING ON IN THERE TONIGHT?" David shouted down the line. "Have you all gone on strike? What the hell am I paying you for? Don't tell me you're voting to unionize."

The night it all began with Amanda Myles, David was in an especially bad mood. It had been a painfully slow shift, and David seemed to think calling incessantly to remind me of what a terrible job I was doing would somehow help. The shrill ringing of my desk phone made me jump every time. I was tense, on edge, anticipating his calls. Nothing we did was good enough.

"I want an angrier shark!" he cried in response to a stock image used to illustrate a story about a surfer mauled to death by a great white in South Africa. "It's not scary enough. I want to see sharp teeth, red gums, bursting out of the water, a crazed look in its eye. Think *Jaws*."

I'd begun to notice David's British accent, which during the day was almost tea-with-the-queen posh, at night slipped into something less refined, losing *t*s from the middle of words and *ing*s from the ends. The only explanation I could think of was that David was faking the upper-class affect, that at night he became too tired (or perhaps too drunk) to remember to maintain it.

I told myself I should be grateful he wasn't there to terrorize me in person, then considered the possibility he might be angry enough to come in. I imagined David on a street corner, hailing a taxi wearing a dressing gown and slippers, apoplectic, on the verge of blacking out from rage. This image disturbed me and so made me desperate to find something good.

Every so often I glanced up at the jumbo screen suspended above the newsroom that showed the front page of *The Scoop* in real time, overlaid with a constellation of numbers and symbols showing how each story was performing (a green, upward-facing arrow indicated it was popular and should be placed high up the page, while a red, downward-facing arrow meant it was bombing), and was seized by the crackling static of anxiety. Flashing red arrows everywhere.

The others felt it, too. We were like a small, floundering crew of a ship on stormy seas. Jocelyn disappeared to smoke even more than usual. Chris muttered and cursed under his breath. Yenay kept taking breaks to lie on the carpet to groan, complaining of a stomachache. I caught my hunched, harried reflection in the window and wondered how my life had come to this.

"We sure could use a celebrity death tonight," Jocelyn said. "I'm not saying I *want* someone to die," she was quick to clarify, "at least not anyone young. But a ninety-year-old *Cheers* star passing away peacefully in their bed? Something like that would be perfect."

I was appalled that Jocelyn would hope someone would *die* so we might hit our traffic targets—and even more appalled to find I secretly agreed. Anything to stop the increasingly irate calls from David. A bloody steak to throw to the beast gnashing its teeth at my ankles.

"There are no slow news days," said Chris, who had been listening to our conversation, in a strained, raspy voice in imitation of Yoda, "only unimaginative reporters."

"Confucius?" Yenay joked.

"David," he replied.

I trawled social media, looking for anything that could conceivably count as news—at least in David's sense of the word. A tweet from an account with twelve followers claiming unfounded gossip about someone famous would have been enough; in fact, this was common practice at *The Scoop*, and often proved fruitful, if not truthful. The protocol was to put in a request for comment to the celebrity's representative. But it didn't matter what the agent or publicist said, whether they confirmed, denied, or, as it often went, never replied. We got away with publishing the story, no matter how baseless or ridiculous it was, by littering the copy with lots of "allegedly" and "reportedly" and "claimed," and by including a line near the bottom that said the celebrity's representative had "been approached for comment." For example:

Actress Martha Kelly denies rumor she licked corncob at buffet, then put it back in fight with hotel staff after bacon runs out at breakfast

Unfortunately for Martha Kelly, dozens of other publications would cover the cob-licking denial, be it seriously or ironically, legitimizing it (*The Cut*: "The Martha Kelly Corncob Scandal We Didn't Know We Needed Because It's Only Tuesday and Everything Is Trash"). And so the non-story would take on a life of its own. "Martha Kelly corncob" would trend, leading many to assume Martha Kelly *did* do something untoward involving a vegetable. No matter the lack of evidence or her repeated, lifelong denials, it would probably still end up in Martha Kelly's *New York Times* obituary: "Kelly was a mostly uncontroversial figure. In 2014, she found herself at the center of a scandal when she was rumored to have licked a corncob at a hotel buffet and put it back, a claim Kelly repeatedly denied."

Yenay asked if she could write a piece about her favorite celebrity, the *Sports Illustrated* model–turned–cooking show host Annie Klein, who came from Yenay's hometown in Minnesota and for whom she felt a deep sense of pride and affinity. She brought up Annie almost daily.

"Why?" I asked Yenay. "Has Annie done something interesting?"

"Yes," she replied. "She cooked lasagna."

"That's not news, Yenay."

Yenay was polite enough not to point out that almost none of the stories we'd published that night—almost none of the stories we'd published ever—could reasonably count as news.

"There must be *something* from the photo agencies," I said, turning to Jocelyn.

"Zilch," she said. "Unless you count heavily staged photos of Tessa Abramson helping out at a soup kitchen—"

"I see her post-DUI reputation rehab is still underway," Yenay remarked drily.

"—and Amanda Myles shopping in the West Village."

Amanda Myles. The name echoed like something once familiar but long forgotten.

"Amanda Myles," Chris said. "The last time I heard the Valentines I still had hope."

"Chris, you've never had hope," Jocelyn snarked back.

Chris shrugged. "That's true."

"God, I *loved* the Valentines when I was a teenager," Jocelyn continued. "I bought all their albums, had their posters on my wall. What was that song? Their big hit? 'Almost There'?"

"Almost There." The words were a key that opened a hidden trove

of memories in my mind that had been locked shut for a long time. A moment from my childhood surfaced with no effort: in the car with my mother, both of us in puffer coats because it was often freezing in the mornings when she drove me to school, the windows fogged up, Mom turning the volume knob up as high as it would go, drumming her hands on the steering wheel, singing along to "Almost There" on the radio. A rare moment of lightness I always knew to savor before the clouds of her depression descended again. A happy memory, the kind that hurt to remember, because it made the loss of her sting all the more, and because it was always followed by the painful ones I wished I could forget. The call one morning from her neighbor as I crossed the courtyard at college, words delivered in regret and disbelief—*She was found on the floor in the living room, EMTs did what they could, I'm sorry, she didn't make it.* Horror at the realization that the reality I'd dreaded since her COPD diagnosis years earlier had come much sooner than I'd expected; she was only fifty-two. Speeding as I drove the two hours back to her house, our house, racing to get to her as fast as I could, unable to comprehend that there was no need to hurry because she was not there, not anywhere, at every traffic light looking at our last texts, certain if I wrote something she would reply, the alternative unfathomable. Once I did get there, going from room to room, her phone, keys, and wallet on the hall table, but no Mom. Dishes in the sink, no sound but the refrigerator hum. Her funeral, swigging from a bottle of Smirnoff in the passenger seat of my then-boyfriend's car, pulled over on a quiet dirt road near the cemetery, unable to bear the finality of her coffin being lowered into the ground, needing to make myself numb to endure it.

I snapped back to the room. Jocelyn was saying something.

"What?"

"I said, no one cares about Amanda Myles anymore. Right?"

"Who's Amanda Myles?" Yenay asked, popping up over her computer like a meerkat.

"You don't know Amanda Myles?" Jocelyn asked, incredulous. "What are you, twelve?"

"I'll be twenty-three in December," Yenay said, advancing her age as only the young do.

"But you must know the Valentines," I said. "Amanda was the lead singer with three guys. Their sound was like...like a modern, more poppy version of Fleetwood Mac."

Yenay's face was blank.

"Here," Jocelyn said, gesturing to Yenay to come to her desk. She opened YouTube and began to play a video, an acoustic MTV Unplugged version of "Almost There." I got up and stood beside Yenay to watch over Jocelyn's shoulder. Amanda was perched on a stool in front of a studio audience, in a long-sleeve black velvet dress and dark eye makeup. She looked like a witch. Eyes squeezed shut, achingly vulnerable, her voice cracked with emotion as she sang.

I blinked back the tears I felt beginning to form and clenched my jaw to steady myself.

"Guys, I've literally got chills," Yenay said when it was over. "I remember her now."

"What I remember," Jocelyn said, "is her acting like a crazy bitch at the MTV Awards one year. Do you remember?" she asked, turning to me. "She was wearing a dress that was basically a few squares of silk tied with string. When the actor she was presenting with looked her up and down, she gave him a death stare. It's like, girl, you do realize you're almost naked?"

I vaguely recalled the uproar. Some argued Amanda should have expected attention, given how shocking the dress was, especially for the time. Others said the guy was being sleazy.

"What did she say in that *Rolling Stone* interview..." Jocelyn muttered, trailing off as she searched to find an article about it online. "Here. She said, 'Men are secretly envious of women and their innate creative powers as the creators of life,' and that 'the lives of the majority of female artists throughout history have been destroyed by the men closest to them out of often-unconscious jealous rage.'"

"I'm sure her three male band members *loved* that," Chris said.

Yenay made a sound of approval. "Amanda sounds like a badass."

"Show me the paparazzi photos," I said. Amanda Myles was about as relevant and newsworthy as a Walkman, and yet the mere mention of her name had the four of us talking; maybe readers would be interested, too. Jocelyn opened the email from the agency and began to scroll through the images. Amanda was older, and now a brunette instead of the bleached blonde she was known for, but it was definitely her. In the first few pictures, Amanda, wearing a navy sweater over a long cream skirt and Converse sneakers, carried only a handbag. But in the following photos she was laden with grocery bags, on the way back from the store—and now, it was clear, aware of the paparazzo tailing her. In the photos taken on the way to the store, Amanda appeared relaxed, lost in thought. And then you could pinpoint it, the moment she noticed the photographer: a twist of her head, eyes wide over the top of her sunglasses, mouth in a tight line.

"Someone's not happy," Yenay said, noticing how Amanda's expression changed.

"Even better," Jocelyn replied. "We can say she was 'downcast.' Adds drama."

From across the desk, Chris laughed. "We'll leave out the bit about how Amanda looked 'downcast' because she was being followed by a strange man who was taking photos of her."

"You don't know that that's why, Chris," Jocelyn said. "Maybe she was constipated."

"Allegedly," Yenay quipped.

"What happened to the Valentines?" I asked. "Did they break up?"

I decided to answer the question myself and went back to my desk. A Google search revealed the Valentines went on "hiatus" in 2002 and never returned. Despite rumors for years after that Amanda would launch a solo career, it never happened. She disappeared from public life.

Yenay went back to her desk; then, after a few moments, she squawked with surprise.

"How is Amanda Myles not on social media? In 2014?"

"What, no Instagram, Twitter, nothing?" Jocelyn said. "That *is* weird. Plus, I just searched Getty Images. The last time she was photographed in public was over eight years ago."

Chris cleared his throat. "Maybe she wants to be left alone to bathe in tubs filled with hundred-dollar bills like any other obscenely wealthy ex–pop star who doesn't have to work for a living."

Jocelyn lifted her hands, framing a sign only she could see in theater marquee lights, and said, "Weirdo recluse Amanda Myles spotted looking older and fatter than you remember."

"Jocelyn," Yenay scolded, though I could tell she was trying not to laugh.

Jocelyn turned back to her screen for a few moments, leaned forward squinting at the image again, and then sat back and clapped her hands in front of her, making the rest of us jump.

"That's it, I've got it!" She beckoned me and Yenay to come over to her desk.

"Look, in the bags," she commanded us. "Do you see?"

Jocelyn typed and clicked until her screen was filled with a zoomed-in image of one of the grocery bags. I knew how ridiculous we must have looked, the three of us crowded around a computer like we were at the control panel launching a rocket into space, as if the lives of a dozen astronauts and whether they would see their families ever again were in our hands. But instead of a space shuttle on Jocelyn's screen, there was only the view of a woman's groceries. It was stupid, absurd, and something about it made me feel unclean. Yet I couldn't deny I was curious, to see what Amanda ate, what she kept in her fridge. It was both mundane and intimate.

Jocelyn began listing one by one the items she could make out.

"A wheel of cheese...I'm guessing Brie or Camembert...a bag of spinach, blueberries...spaghetti, mushrooms, sourdough, a pint of Ben & Jerry's..."

"Okay, so we know she's *not* lactose intolerant," Yenay deduced. She said this with a straight face, but I wondered if she wasn't subtly making fun of Jocelyn, of the situation. I sometimes felt sorry for Yenay, that *The Scoop* was her first and only newsroom experience. If I'd made it to the media party just in time for the last dance, Yenay had arrived at closing time.

"Do you see it? The story?" Jocelyn asked, impatient. "'Aging former Valentines singer Amanda Myles looks downcast as she is spotted sporting a fuller figure and buying comfort food in rare sighting of über-private star.' Yenay, you should be writing this down."

I couldn't help but laugh.

"You're not serious, Jocelyn," I said.

"What?"

"Come on, Amanda isn't fat."

"I didn't say *fat*. I said 'fuller figure.'"

I'd spent my career at *Cosmo* and *Marie Claire* working on articles about the dangers of body shaming, the toxicity of unrealistic beauty standards, the sexism inherent in the scrutiny of women's bodies especially. It was a reflex for me to call it out, almost as natural as breathing.

"We all know what 'fuller figure' means," I said.

"Okay, so she's not fat," Jocelyn relented, turning back to her screen.

She ran a finger over Amanda's chin, her stomach. "But definitely bigger, especially when you compare these photos to the version of Amanda Myles we remember. I think to *not* mention it would be weird."

She pulled up a photo of the Valentines from the early 2000s for comparison.

"That was ten years ago, Jocelyn," I said. "It's natural her body would look different."

"Look *fatter*."

I rolled my eyes. There was no way I'd allow the story to be published with the headline Jocelyn wanted. But the jumbo screen above the newsroom was still covered in flashing red arrows. We needed something. I decided we would publish the photos, but with a different angle.

"What about, 'Fans shocked as elusive pop idol Amanda Myles is spotted in NYC'?"

"Wait, are *we* the 'shocked fans'?" Yenay asked. I ignored her.

"Sure, that works," Jocelyn said, with a brief pause, "if you don't want anyone to click on it."

I knew she was right. I wouldn't click on that. But I could not allow the "fat" angle.

Besides, I was the night editor. David had put *me* in charge. It was my decision.

"Jocelyn, I appreciate the...advice," I said, watching her nostrils flare at *advice*, "but we're not going with that angle. Amanda Myles was one of the most famous people in the world; then she fell off the face of the earth. Now we have photos of her, and for the first time in a decade—that's the story." I looked to the others for confirmation, but Yenay and Chris stayed quiet, not wanting to be pulled into the disagreement between the new kid and the old guard.

"Fine," Jocelyn snapped, scowling as she turned to her screen. "I'll buy the photos now."

I was surprised she gave in, after being so adamant, but also satisfied to have won the battle. *That's right*, I thought, hoping I wasn't smirking with pleasure. *I'm the boss here.*

"Should I start writing, Frankie?" Yenay asked.

"Yes, please," I said, not needing to look at Jocelyn to know she was quietly seething.

As Yenay began writing, I went online to see if I could find a contact for Amanda. It was muscle memory for me; at *Marie Claire*, we always reached out to a celebrity's representative if we wrote about them, standard journalistic practice. Amanda had been out of the public eye for a long time, but there was still a contact email listed for someone at Triumph Music. In fact, I recognized the name, a music PR rep I'd dealt with a number of times at my magazine jobs.

> Hi Alice,
>
> Long time no speak! I'm at *The Scoop* now as night editor, and I'm writing to request comment from Amanda Myles on some new photos of her that have come across my desk. The images show Amanda shopping in the West Village on Tuesday. The sighting will be a welcome surprise to her fans, who have no doubt longed for an update from her since the Valentines' hiatus in 2002. Does Amanda have anything she would like to share with readers about her activities in New York today, or what she has been up to lately?
>
> We intend to publish tonight but we're happy to add a comment from Amanda as soon as we receive it.
>
> Thanks,
> Francesca

I hit send. Out of the corner of my eye, I caught sight of the jumbo screen, still covered in angrily flashing red arrows. I couldn't shake the thought from earlier, of an enraged and underdressed David turning up in the office to berate me in person, screaming at me until my face was covered in his spittle. I glanced at the door, the thought of it bursting open sending a chill through me. I would get ahead of it, just in case. I picked up the phone and dialed David.

"Yes? What is it?"

I sensed I'd interrupted him in the middle of something, though I couldn't imagine what. It was hard to imagine David having a life outside *The Scoop*. Anyone who knew David knew he didn't care about anything except the next story, the end-of-month traffic report, the next meeting with Walter Johnson, the next competitor we were going to destroy until there was nothing left of the media but Johnson News. Anything else, anything that got in the way of that, was an inconvenience, a banal fact of life to be endured, dealt with as quickly as possible, so he could get back to the real world—the news. Lucky for me, I was calling from the real world.

"David, it's Frankie. I've found something."

6

THE FOLLOWING DAY I WOKE with a start, a noise from the street below wrenching me from deep sleep. Disoriented, I fumbled with my eye mask. The clock on my nightstand read 2:15 p.m. Huh? I'd overslept, with no memory of snoozing my alarm. How could this have happened? Then I remembered the pill Jocelyn gave me as we packed up the night before, the tiny jade oval she pressed into the palm of my hand, *something to help you sleep.* A peace offering, I assumed, after our tense disagreement over Amanda Myles. Jocelyn knew I had trouble falling asleep after night shift, and then staying asleep once the sun was up and the noises of the city floated into my bedroom: the grinding rattle and clang of the metal roller door as the bodega downstairs opened for the day, honking horns from the traffic jam outside the school down the block, the whining and roaring of buses coming and going at the stop across the street. Then there were the noises inside the apartment: Patti's alarm beeping through the thin wall between our rooms, water in the pipes as she showered and got ready for work. The pill had blocked it all out, a blacked-out bliss.

I flopped back down on my pillow, watched as sunlight peeked through the curtain gaps, making strange shapes on the exposed brick, a hint of fall in the golden light. I'd overslept, but I still had two hours until I'd need to leave for work. *Work*. I groaned at the thought of another interminable night in the newsroom, forcing my eyelids open as midnight came and went, the jolt in my heart every time the phone rang, David aggravated over something trivial again. It made me want to drop my phone in the glass of water on my nightstand and pretend I was dead.

Lying there, I was surprised to find my mother on my mind. Had I dreamt of her? No, those were rare now, thank god, not like in the first year after she died when I couldn't even escape my grief in my sleep. It was Amanda Myles. Hearing that song "Almost There" for the first time in years, being slammed with the memory of my mom singing along to it in the car.

There were two versions of my mother that lived in my head now she was gone, and they were like two completely different people. There was the version of her that was smiling, animated, radiant, a real firecracker. Always the funniest person in the room, making people laugh with her own style of silly eccentricity, her auburn hair shiny and worn long, bringing out her big green eyes, chunky jewelry on her ears, neck, wrists, always the first to run to the dance floor when "Dancing Queen"—her song—came on the stereo at a party. It was that version of my mother who sang along to the Valentines in the car. I tried to remember her that way, but the truth was I had only ever seen glimpses of that woman and mostly knew her from photos taken before I was born, or in stories her friends told, back when she still had friends that visited. The other version of her I knew much better, the one I lived with most of my childhood: always dog-tired, weary, her humor on the bitter side of sarcastic, prone to moods she withdrew into, filling the house with dark clouds that wouldn't lift for days. Then there was the COPD diagnosis my senior year, the consequence of her smoking cigarettes since she was thirteen years old. An explanation, finally, for her worrying breathlessness and wheezing cough, though it brought no solution or relief. After that, a new level of darkness descended upon our house that never did lift. She stopped working, went on disability, and money got tighter. She started sleeping on a recliner in the living room instead of her bed, saying it eased the pressure in her chest. Dirty dishes piled in the sink for a day, then two, then three, loads of wet clothes sat forgotten in the machine until they stank and needed to be washed again. I cried when I researched the life expectancy of someone with moderate to severe COPD and it said an average of five years, cried more at the recommendation to quit smoking, get exercise, and eat healthier—she had done only the first, and even then, I once found a new pack of cigarettes and a lighter tucked at the back of a kitchen drawer. Evidence, it seemed to me, she didn't care to prolong her life expectancy, even for my sake. I didn't know what to do with that. So, I started doing more around the house, trying to take my mind off what would happen when I went away to college. I had the grades for Northwestern or NYU, was encouraged by a teacher to apply for a scholarship, but I couldn't bring myself to move that far from her. So I went to Elon, a two-hour drive away, so I could visit her on weekends, help her out. Told myself I wouldn't have gotten into a better school anyway.

I was right to worry about what would happen to her when I went to college. Often when I visited she smelled musty, like she hadn't showered or changed her clothes for days. Pizza boxes and wine bottles overflowed from a plastic recycling bin and onto the kitchen floor, and bags of groceries lined the hallway inside the front door—she would have them delivered but couldn't manage to carry the bags into the kitchen or put the items away. A thick layer of dust and dead bugs lined the windowsills, light bulbs always needed to be replaced; I'd walk into a room to find nothing would happen when I flicked the light switch. She was content to sit in the dark, the blue glow of the TV the only light. I came home more, pulling on rubber gloves to scrub the bathroom, carry out bags of trash, change the light bulbs. Mom would tell me to stop.

"Frankie, please sit down. Relax. You don't have to do all that."

"I can't *relax* in all this mess," I'd say. I probably could have said something kinder.

"I know, I know," she'd say, and I could hear in her voice the shame, which she would then try to cover. "Next week I'll give this place a good clean. I've been feeling better lately."

"Better" never came. She was never better, always worse, much worse. But somehow she convinced me to disregard what I saw with my own eyes. It was convenient for us both, this story. My mom didn't have to lose her pride, could keep playing the role of parent, and I was less burdened, didn't have to defer college to care for her, didn't have to delay starting my own life.

On those Sunday night drives back to school, I'd feel guilty for leaving, but also relieved to be out of there, desperate to get back to my dorm to shower, to wash off the unclean feeling on my skin, to not have to see the sad sight of my mom, an unmovable lump in her recliner. But I couldn't shake the frustrating paralysis of not knowing what to do. I wanted to ask for help, perhaps my aunt and uncle in California, whom I knew Mom spoke to on the phone sometimes but who were too far away to know what was going on. But then I imagined what would happen—my aunt calling her, asking certain questions, Mom catching on that I'd told her—and I felt scared. Scared Mom would be angry at me, say I'd betrayed her. My whole life I'd seen the way she told people she was fine when she wasn't, the way she vehemently resisted letting anyone pity her, or see her as weak. I couldn't bear the thought of her withdrawing from me, as she did during her dark moods, a punishment that left me feeling hopelessly alone. It felt safer to keep her secret.

The winter she died, I'd had a plan. After graduation, I would move home, live with her for the summer. Fill the fridge with fresh, healthy food, get her on a diet and exercise plan, stop her from sneaking cigarettes. Clear all the junk out of the house, give the place a new coat of paint, deal with the overgrown garden. See if I could get her back in touch with some friends. I was going to fix her, and then—my mother all fixed—I would go to New York City in the fall to begin my new life. It was the only way I could go to New York and not be racked with guilt.

I was too late. She died in February. I graduated in May.

But I tried not to think about that period of my life anymore, the gray, uneasy years from when she got sick until she died. It was a box under the bed I knew was there but never opened.

Head still on the pillow, I reached for my phone and saw a text from Audrey. She had sent a link to the Amanda Myles article on *The Scoop*, with the words, **this is really blowing up!**

What? I'd figured some people would be excited about the sighting of Amanda—that's why we purchased the photos—but it was hardly worthy of "blowing up." I clicked the link.

When I saw the headline, my stomach dropped.

> **EXCLUSIVE: Cheat day! Washed-up former Valentines singer Amanda Myles looks glum as she shows off fuller figure and stocks up on comfort food in rare sighting of private pop star**
>
> Nineties pop icon Amanda Myles has shocked fans by revealing her new fuller figure in a rare sighting, years

after the former singer of the Valentines disappeared from the limelight.

Myles, 42, was seen shopping in New York City's West Village neighborhood on Tuesday, the once-beloved singer behind such hits as "Almost There" going unnoticed by passersby as she headed to a grocery store to grab some essentials.

Dressed in a long, shapeless cream linen skirt, navy sweater and humble Converse sneakers, her brunette hair pulled back in a perky ponytail and hiding behind a pair of large dark sunglasses, Myles proudly showcased a significantly more curvaceous physique that will make her almost unrecognizable to fans.

Myles appeared downcast as she made her way through the West Village, hauling several bags of groceries. The very private star stocked up on comfort foods, including cheese and ice cream.

Mystery has long surrounded the circumstances that saw the Valentines, one of the most popular bands in the world in the early 2000s, with three Grammys under their belts, go on hiatus in 2002. Despite their millions of adoring fans globally, the band stopped recording.

Little is known about Myles' personal life. The California native has not given any interviews since the Valentines' hiatus began and is not publicly active on social media.

I sat up so fast the room tipped and spun, still agape at the image at the top of the article, which zoomed in on parts of Amanda's body—her chin, her stomach—and featured a close-up of her bulging grocery bags with angry red circles around the ice cream, cheese, and pasta, like she'd been caught breaking the law. Then I noticed Yenay's byline. It was the same story from the night before, only it had been completely rewritten. I squeezed my eyes shut in mortification as I remembered: I'd sent a link to the article to Alice, Amanda's rep, asking for a comment. Which version had Alice seen, last night's or this morning's? Panicked, I opened my work email and scanned my inbox. Nothing from Alice yet. I couldn't decide if this was a good or bad sign.

Then I remembered Audrey's comment—*blowing up online! No, no, no*, I whispered to myself as I opened Twitter, a pit forming in my stomach. Sure enough, I saw "Amanda Myles" was a trending topic. I clicked on her name and began to read the top results. I quickly gathered that a British reality star, known for calling out sexism and misogyny, had seen *The Scoop* article about Amanda. She had posted a screenshot of the headline, with Yenay's byline clearly visible.

> Disgraceful! This is not journalism—it's bullying, and it's disgusting. Shame on you @thescoop. Do better.

I scrolled through the comments, people slamming the article as sexist gutter journalism, toxic clickbait, many saying whoever wrote it shouldn't be allowed to call themselves a journalist. How had this grown so big, so fast? The UK was five hours ahead of the East Coast, so there had been time for it to snowball while I was asleep, oblivious to the brewing uproar.

I jumped out of bed, wanting to do something but not knowing what. I thought of Yenay, wondered if she had seen it yet. I went to text her, then stopped. If she was still blissfully unaware, I didn't want to panic her at home. Better to deal with it together, in the newsroom.

7

WHEN I GOT TO THE OFFICE, Yenay was slumped over her keyboard, face buried in her folded arms.

"I hope the worthless piece of tabloid scum that wrote this," Chris read from her screen, standing behind her, "dies covered in pigeon shit after a vigorous wedgie. That's... specific."

Yenay groaned under her arms, still face down on the desk.

"Chris, I don't think we need to keep reading out the tweets, okay?" I said, shooing him back to his desk. Kneeling on the floor beside Yenay, I gave her a gentle pat on the shoulder, an admittedly feeble attempt at comfort given the scale of what was rapidly unfolding that evening.

Anger over the article had spread quickly. *BuzzFeed*, *Cosmo*, *HuffPo*, *E! News*, and a dozen other sites covered the outrage. It was even discussed on an afternoon talk show. On my way to the office, I'd been glued to my phone, horrified at the rising tide of anger directed at us. Jocelyn had asked if anyone cared about Amanda Myles anymore; as it turned out, she was still rather beloved. Yenay received a deluge of messages telling her she was a vile excuse for a human being, some of them urging her to kill herself. I tried to reassure her they were probably just trolls, that people were angry but not *that* angry, but it was nonetheless unnerving.

Even some celebrities joined the growing chorus condemning *The Scoop*. In an especially brutal blow, among the famous names was none other than Yenay's beloved Annie Klein.

> The author of this article is female! Nothing sadder than a woman upholding the patriarchy instead of supporting the sisterhood.

It was this, more than anything, that had Yenay face down on her desk. I wished Annie, and the other celebrities, and the thousands of people piling on, knew who they were directing their fury at: a sensitive twenty-two-year-old from Minnesota trying to get her start in the media, who longed to write the kinds of in-depth, considered profiles celebrities loved. Not a maniacal villain who woke up each day rubbing her hands together with glee at the thought of who she was going to hurt. That although Yenay's name was on the article, those weren't even her words.

"We're going viral, baby!" Jocelyn cried with delight when she walked in with a hate-to-say-I-told-you-so swagger. A little too buoyantly, I thought, given the intensity of the vitriol.

"I'm glad you're happy," I said, standing up. "People are telling Yenay to kill herself."

"Congratulations," Jocelyn said, dropping her bag on her desk and then coming over and landing a solid slap on Yenay's back, "someone's got her first haters!" She sounded like a mother proud her baby's first tooth was coming through, while the child yowled in agony as an incisor emerged from its tender gum.

Yenay at last sat upright, appearing slightly dazed. Her eyes went to her screen and she read out one of the messages. "'Go jump off the George Washington Bridge, you dumb slut.'"

"But you live in Queens," Chris said. "More convenient to jump off the Queensboro."

"Oh god," Yenay said, spiraling further, "what if the trolls find out where I live?"

"You think this is bad?" He barked a bitter laugh. "David once changed the headline of an article I wrote about a woman in prison—for *murder*, mind you—to describe her as 'demented.' She wrote me to say when she gets out, she's going to come for me. I can only hope the parole board has enough sense to keep her locked up for the rest of her life or I am *toast*."

"See, Yenay?" Jocelyn said, pointing at Chris. "It's a rite of passage. You haven't made it as a journalist until somebody wants you dead."

None of this comforted Yenay in the slightest.

"Besides, what are you complaining about?" Jocelyn continued. "You should be happy! It's an exclusive, it's going viral, and your name is on it. It's a real story people are actually talking about, unlike the shit you churn out about ex-*Bachelor* contestants posting stupid selfies."

Yenay stood in a rush, nearly bumping into me, and ran down the hall to the bathroom.

"She'll be fine," Jocelyn said, waving a dismissive hand and returning to her desk. I considered going to check on Yenay but decided to give her some space. I sat down in my seat.

"I have to say," Jocelyn added in a loud whisper, "I think she's overreacting just a tad."

"Yes," Chris said, "she was only publicly insulted by a number of A-list celebrities and told to kill herself by hundreds of people on the internet. Not sure what she's so upset about."

THE SCOOP

As I logged in, I scanned the newsroom for David. I'd wondered if he might stay back until I arrived, to discuss how to respond to the backlash, since it was showing no signs of abating. I wanted to ask him how this happened, how Yenay's article could be so substantially rewritten without her having any say in it. But there was no David, only a few stragglers from the day shift packing their belongings, preparing to go home, watch TV, eat dinner, and go to bed before midnight, like normal people did. Then a thought occurred to me. I turned to Jocelyn.

"Did you go behind my back to David?"

Jocelyn turned slowly to face me.

"Excuse me?"

She had backed down too quickly the night before. It was all starting to make sense—Jocelyn must have decided that rather than argue with me, she would tattle on me to David.

"Did you email him and suggest the article be changed to the 'fat' angle? I don't see how else this could have happened—it was your idea."

Jocelyn cocked her head. "Do you really think I'd undermine you like that?"

I stared back at her. I didn't want to believe Jocelyn would do that, but I wasn't sure.

"If anything," Jocelyn said slowly, carefully, "I wanted to leave it, let it bomb, so that when it did, you would realize we should have done it my way. So you would learn your lesson."

We stared at each other. Chris chose this moment to start unwrapping his meatball sub.

"The answer to your question is *no*, Frankie, I didn't go behind your back to David. If I had to guess, I'd say David came in this morning, saw the photos of Amanda, had the idea himself, and ordered a reporter to rewrite it. I'm not sneaky. I don't pull shit like that. Okay?"

I decided I believed her. Jocelyn was too blunt and combative to do anything covertly.

Just then, David called.

"Have you seen the numbers on the Amanda Myles story?" he cried. "It's off the charts! Biggest story of the month so far—can you believe it? Fan-fucking-tastic."

I had never heard David sound so genuinely happy, hadn't known he was capable of experiencing such pure, boundless joy. I knew that meant I should be happy (the entire purpose of all of us at *The Scoop*, it was becoming clear, was to make David happy), and yet as he ranted on about page views and social shares, I felt the shock and confusion of the afternoon spill over.

"Yes, it's great news," I said, hearing the iciness in my voice, willing myself to snap out of my mood but unable to, "but I was surprised to see Yenay's article rewritten so drastically."

All the horrible, disgusting messages Yenay had received swirled in my mind.

"Yenay is getting messages from people telling her to kill herself. It's also put me in a very awkward position because I sent the piece to Amanda's rep, a contact of mine, so she—"

"And what would you have had me do?" David asked, a sardonic edge to his voice.

I should have known this question wasn't genuine, that of course my boss wasn't actually asking for my opinion on how he could do his job better. But I couldn't seem to help myself.

"Well, in the future I think my reporters and I should at least be consulted before—"

"Consulted?" David said, laughing. "At the crack of dawn? While you're all asleep?"

I was in dangerous territory, knew I should let it go. But my anxiety had been building for hours, and now that I'd found a release point for the pressure, there was no keeping it in.

"Couldn't it have waited a few hours? I think that reporters have a right to—"

"Thank you, David," he said, cutting me off.

"Sorry?"

"I said, *Thank you, David.* That's what I would have expected to hear from my night editor after she left an absolute turd on my home page that *I* had to spend *my* time polishing."

David was silent, waiting for my response. Would I argue back? I opened my mouth to speak but found I was speechless. Deep down, I knew arguing it was useless and naïve. As Jocelyn had warned me that night, David was God. I backed down, as he probably knew I would, told David he was right, and thanked him for fixing the story. I wished I could tell him what I really thought, or, even better, quit. Hang up, storm out. But I didn't, couldn't. I felt pathetic.

Satisfied by my groveling, David moved on.

"I want a new story on Amanda Myles, ASAP. Did you notice how furious she looked in the photos when she spotted the paps? I've got a sneaking suspicion she might be the next Britney Spears-shaving-her-head. Or the next Amy Winehouse-walking-barefoot-down-the-street—or Amy Winehouse pretty much any day of the week circa 2007. Those were the good old days. This is the kind of story that can make a tabloid, and that's what *The Scoop* needs. The Man Upstairs is eager for us to find a big story to help us make our mark. Amanda could be it."

I was alarmed by what David was saying. That we weren't backing off after the uproar—if anything, he wanted us to push harder. It made me uneasy. But before I could say so, he continued. "I've instructed Jocelyn to tell the photo agencies we'll take anything the paps can get of Amanda. I want the new pics up as soon as they drop. Let's ride the momentum." He hung up.

And just like that, David put a bounty on Amanda's head.

Eventually Yenay returned from the bathroom, and the night went on as normal, though she was quieter, more subdued than usual. At ten p.m. the AC shut off, making the newsroom so starkly silent I could hear every sniffle of Yenay's nose, every groan of Chris's stomach digesting his sandwich, every click of Jocelyn's jaw as she gnashed her gum. At some point, the cleaner who came through the newsroom every night appeared in the hall. As usual, she emerged from the kitchen and mopped the hallway, leaving in her wake the nostril-stinging scent of fake-lemony bleach, before moving through the rows of desks at speed, whipping each liner out of each little trash can and replacing it in one swift motion. I wondered how we looked to her, all of us with our heads down typing, frowning at our screens. Did she assume we were writing about important things, like politics, and the economy, and war? What could keep us there late into the night, away from our warm beds, but matters of utmost importance? Surely not the movements of a has-been pop star, or the latest update on a woman who makes a living by farting into jars.

Around midnight, my inbox pinged with a reply from Alice, Amanda's rep, a one-line email so devastating, that humbled me so viscerally, I nearly toppled off my chair and fell onto the floor.

> No comment. And don't contact me again unless it's a genuine attempt at journalism.

Later, as I took refuge for a few stolen moments in a bathroom stall, sitting on top of the closed toilet seat, Alice's words reverberated in my head. How could I have let this happen? How had I become involved in the kind of cruel, tasteless "journalism" I loathed? Shaming a woman for... the natural process of aging. For *buying cheese*. It went against everything I stood for. I had fought against the "fat" angle, tried to stop it, but I still felt culpable—Jocelyn had initially been dubious, and *I* had been the one to insist Amanda Myles was worth writing about.

I was no better than Chris, jaded, joking-to-hide-his-misery Chris, squandering an early-career Pulitzer, tumbling from the pinnacle of journalism to the pigpen. Now it seemed I, too, was doomed to shovel slop until the sweet release of retirement or death, whichever came first.

Then I remembered: *Audrey*. I hadn't replied to her text. I'd been in such a panic I forgot.

> Sorry I'm replying so late! Night shift has me all out of whack. I know, the story is disgusting. Ugh. One of my reporters wrote it but the editor made someone else rewrite it and add all the horrible stuff about her body. Audrey, how am I going to survive this place??

Three dots appeared. She wrote straight back.

> Really?? That's crazy! Yeah, people are pissed and rightly so. Eek, are you gonna stay?

Am I going to stay? What kind of a question was that? If I had an alternative, I wouldn't be at *The Scoop*. I felt the shift of the tectonic plates that sometimes rumbled between the surface of our friendship, the gap between our very different upbringings that could never be closed, which we both preferred not to acknowledge. Once, back at *Marie Claire*, the two of us were making lunch in the kitchen instead of buying takeout because we were on some money-saving or weight-losing jag (magazine people were always on at least one, if not both—for me it was undoubtedly the former, Audrey the latter), and Audrey had shamed me because my tin of tuna wasn't wild caught. That night we got drunk on free champagne at some media event and wound up at a nightclub. Ensconced in a toilet stall, Audrey pulled out a baggie of cocaine and tapped out lines on the closed toilet seat, without even a brief moment of silence for the underprivileged people with whom her drugs had hitched a ride to get to her WASP-y hands. Before I knew Audrey, I'd never even tried cocaine; I wasn't in the cool, flashy scene of kids who did that at college, and I spent so many weekends visiting my mom instead of going to parties. Besides some late nights with Audrey, the only other times I'd snorted straight white lines of powder with a rolled-up bill were with the separated Brooklyn dads. Separated Brooklyn dads *love* cocaine.

I took a deep breath, tried to release the bitterness I felt. I was being defensive, too sensitive. Audrey had only asked a question, and she had only asked because she cared about me.

> For now... but I need a strong drink at your birthday party on Saturday (so excited!!)

Still Sandy, I whispered. *Still Sandy*. I thought of *Business Day*. In just a few short months, all of this would seem preposterous, funny, a distant memory I'd never think about because I'd be busy writing about serious, important things, like politics, reproductive rights—

I heard the bathroom door open.

THE SCOOP

"Frankie?"

It was Jocelyn.

"Yes?"

"David's on the phone. Something about Fart Jar Girl having a rival now?"

I sighed. "Be right there."

8

I SHOULDN'T HAVE DONE IT. Don't know why I did. I hadn't checked Josh's Instagram profile for months; to look was the digital equivalent of lashing my back with a whip, self-inflicted torture. I was on the subway platform going to work when, impulsively, I typed his name. And there it was, a photo with *her*, the woman from work. She of the handwritten note, *I am suffering here without you.* Strings of exuberant fire and heart emojis filled the comments. They were official.

The train rushed in. The doors opened and I stepped on in a daze, let myself collapse into a seat by the window. I felt my face crumple, and then the tears came in a flood, a blindsiding sorrow that overflowed, threatened to drown me. It was my choice, wasn't it? I'd been the one to leave. So why, as the train screeched through the tunnels under Brooklyn, did it feel like this? Like my heart was straining and breaking apart with the pain of it? Hot tears blurred my vision as I stared at the photo, unable to look away from their faces even as it pierced my gut like a knife.

THE SCOOP

If I could have done anything, gone anywhere, at that moment, it would have been to lie in my mother's lap, to be wrapped in her arms. She could be moody, irritable, downright mean when she was tired, which was most of the time, and we fought, as mothers and daughters do. But when I was hurting, it was like whatever she was struggling with privately evaporated, and she never hesitated to drop everything and swoop in, to pull me in for a hug, to hold me as long as I wanted. Or, once I went to college, to stay on the phone with me, her voice a comfort like no other. In the years since she'd been gone, I'd cried on the shoulders of friends, been held by boyfriends, but nothing came close to my mother's embrace when I was truly in pain. I knew nothing ever would.

I could not reach for my mother now, but I wasn't so self-pitying to think I didn't have anyone, that I was completely alone. When the train at last emerged from the tunnel and trundled onto the Manhattan Bridge, filling the car with sunlight, I had cell service again. I texted Audrey.

> Josh and Miss America are Instagram official.

(The nickname came from mine and Audrey's admittedly weak summation of Josh's new girlfriend's personality based on our creeping of her profiles online—an unironically earnest photo of her in a long flowy skirt playing a guitar in a field of flowers; a status update in which she shared a humorless, self-righteously outraged opinion on a *Saturday Night Live* sketch about teachers doing drugs, which had the grating tone of a little girl making neat, safe declarations of right and wrong from her room in her parents' five-bedroom home, with four different musical instruments in her wardrobe and unexpired OJ in the fridge. Pat on the head, good girl!)

> Why am I crying over that Muppet-faced fuck
>
> Yes I broke a four-month streak of not checking his profile, don't be mad
>
> Yes I am aware of the role I am playing in my own suffering
>
> But please remind me of all the shit things about him again?

Three dots appeared. Audrey was replying.

> Remember the time you went axe throwing and he was really bad at it
>
> Remember how he made a face like a chicken being choked when he came
>
> Remember how when you met he called himself a "poet" but never showed you a single word of his writing
>
> Remember how he enjoyed comedy but wasn't actually funny
>
> Remember how he FELL FOR ANOTHER WOMAN AND THEN TRIED TO GASLIGHT YOU BY TELLING YOU THEY WERE JUST FRIENDS!!!

In spite of the streaming tears and runny nose, I started to laugh, a brief moment of levity before the weight would descend again.

THE SCOOP

Audrey had been my rock during the breakup with Josh, helping me move out, sitting with me countless nights as I cried over too many glasses of wine. And here she was, nearly a year later, still knowing exactly what to say to make it all okay, at least for a moment. I felt relief, too, that the tension I sensed between us the day before, when she asked if I would stay at *The Scoop*, seemed to have been washed away by this moment of connection over my stupid ex, who really did make the dumbest face when he ejaculated.

I savored Audrey's texts, reminding myself I broke up with Josh for a reason. She had burst the bubble of the romanticized fantasy that overtook me sometimes when I thought about Josh, wondered what could have been if I'd given him the second chance he'd wanted. When I discovered the balled-up note in the laundry and confronted him, at first he had dismissed it as nothing, gave me the *we're just friends* line. But I'd insisted it wasn't normal, pointed out that if they were such good "friends," why didn't he ever talk about her? I wore him down. He admitted he was attracted to her, that they'd worked together a lot and some "feelings of affection" had developed. When I asked Josh if he thought those feelings were mutual, he gave me a guilty look, said he knew they were. He swore he hadn't kissed her, let alone fucked her, that nothing physical had happened. But I'll never forget the look on his face when I asked if he wanted it to.

Since I was a child, since my father announced to my mom one Sunday afternoon while I was upstairs playing in my room that he had fallen in love with a woman he'd met online and was moving to Hawaii to be with her, after my mother had cried and begged him not to go, even though he was a drunk with a bad temper who treated her more like a maid than a wife—I'd always sworn that I would never allow myself to grovel so pathetically over a man. That at the first sign of any indiscretion or betrayal I would be out of there. Josh had been remorseful, said we had both played a role in the distance that had grown between us, that we had both let our sex life fade, but that he loved me, and was committed to me, to us, and was willing to do whatever it took to fix it: couples therapy, a new job to get away from Miss America. Maybe I was too young to be mature enough about it all, too impulsive to remain levelheaded, and sometimes I wondered if I overreacted that day, if I threw away our three years together too quickly. But as Josh and I stood in the living room of our Brooklyn apartment, the home we'd made together, all I could hear was the sound of my mother sobbing through my parents' closed bedroom door as my father retrieved the suitcase from the cupboard, unzipping it, packing his clothes. I saw the same scene playing out between me and Josh five, ten, twenty years down the line, this time with gray in our hair and our children playing upstairs in their own bedrooms, the cycle repeating.

No. I had to get out.

As the train descended from the bridge and slowed as it prepared to pull into Canal, I tried to focus on feeling grateful that Josh, along with his mommy issues, insecurities, moodiness, and irritating habits, like the way he'd sulk until I asked him what was wrong and never replace the coffee or laundry detergent when we ran out, was Miss America's problem now.

The Miss America nickname was a joke, a thin, easy way for me to try to feel superior to the woman my boyfriend just couldn't help but fall for even though he was supposed to be closed off to new romance. But, though I never would have admitted it to anyone, it was borne of the most painful part of the whole thing, perhaps even more painful than the betrayal and loss itself, which was the *kind* of woman Josh wanted instead of me. How different she was from me.

How did I know what kind of woman she was? I'm not proud of how deeply I stalked her, of the dark and dusty corners of the internet I found myself in, in my desperate search to make sense of what happened by gathering information (I *was* a journalist). It made me feel disgusting, the things I found, the things I knew, like eating week-old Thai takeout from the back of the fridge knowing you're risking food poisoning. It didn't help—or I should say it did help, helped very much indeed—that Josh's apparently irresistible co-worker had an uncommon name.

Oh, how I stalked this woman. I'm talking not just finding her Facebook, but her mom's Facebook, her dad's Facebook, her *grandmother's* Facebook. I clicked through every photo in an album of their 2007 family vacation to Cancun. I saw photos of her as a child in a gallery of images on her uncle's online obituary page, set to a poignant panpipe rendition of Bette Midler's "Wind Beneath My Wings." I found her Pinterest. The Pinterest was what made it all click for me. She had a board of recipes, she had a board of patterns for sweaters she wanted to knit, she had a board of jewelry, a board of cute hairstyles she wanted to try, of DIY projects, like turning old teacups into flowerpots, and clever under-sink storage hacks, all of which she updated regularly. She reeked of wholesome homemaker. She was in-your-face feminine, a real girly girl.

She was everything I was not.

I would have described myself as feminine, and yet I gave little thought to traditionally feminine things, like fashion or home décor. I had a handful of go-to, mostly head-to-toe black outfits I wore to work at *Marie Claire*, and simple jeans and seasonally appropriate tops for the weekend, and that was that. I'd worn the same two rings and neck chain since college. I hated to cook, found it boring. I didn't knit, or collect art, or take dance classes. It was foreign to me, this idea of having time and money to partake in things just for fun. I'd had to strive so hard, for so long, to fight my way from that gloomy house in the shade of the mountain, from the men who whistled at me at the bus stop, from America Now playing on the TV in my hometown's nicest restaurant, until anything soft in me had been snuffed out. There wasn't time for anything else when I'd been looking straight ahead, running, running, running, so my mother's darkness, the darkness that engulfed her and that house in her final years, would never catch up to me. I'd thought Josh loved me as I was, loved me *because* of how hard I'd strived, how far I'd come, thought he didn't care about superficial things like decorating a home with the right colors and trinkets, or flowing, floral skirts. But maybe some part of him longed for it, for warm banana bread just out of the oven and dangly earrings that caught the light, something pure and effortlessly graceful. Maybe he knew I couldn't give it to him, and so he couldn't resist it when it arrived right under his nose, a floating pretty pink cloud, a blooming and perfumed fever dream.

It was natural, I knew, given the circumstances, to feel anger, near-hatred for Miss America, even as I wished myself to be more evolved, wished I could resist falling into the tired old her-versus-me trap Josh had set. Still, why was it such an affront to me, this woman's overt femininity, her effortless grace? The softness and ease she embodied? Why did it cut so deep? What I saw when I saw Miss America was someone who had a mother who took her shopping at proper department stores, not just Goodwill, who didn't hold her breath when she got out her credit card at the counter, silently praying that it wouldn't be declined. A mother who took pleasure in taking care of her family by cooking, and sewing, and decorating, unlike mine, who more often than not white-knuckled through double shifts, barely had the energy to throw a TV dinner in the microwave for each of us. I'd never seen a woman genuinely enjoying womanhood like that, almost luxuriating in it, as Miss America seemed to do, only cursing its burdens.

Miss America represented all I'd been denied, except I hadn't known just how much I'd been denied—by my father's grinding down of my mom's spirit when he was there, and the life of exhaustion, stress, and worry when he was gone—until I saw *her*. Until I felt Josh's gravitational pull toward her. Grave evidence that seemed to confirm my worst fears: that my past had left damage that could not be repaired, left me permanently broken in some fundamental way, and no matter how far I ran, no matter where I went or what I did, others could see it, smell it. That it would follow me everywhere, seep into everything. That the life I'd convinced myself I could build was nothing more than a mirage. That my best days would always be spoiled by its shadow. That I'd never escape it. That softness, ease, would always be a language I didn't speak.

The train pulled into Bryant Park. The time for self-indulgent wallowing was up. On the street, as I crossed at the lights and hurried across the forecourt into the revolving doors of the Johnson News building, I steeled myself, tried to forget about Josh and Miss America and their grinning faces. At least with another night shift ahead, I'd be too busy to think about it. Too busy to think about anything except making the green arrows go up and giving David what he wanted.

9

"Anything new on Amanda?" I asked Jocelyn when I got to the newsroom. I had an email from David wanting an update and expected a call from him any minute to ask again. (He had also sent me a link to a study that found women who work night shift are at a higher risk for type 2 diabetes, cancer, stroke, and heart disease, which I had to assume was deliberate and personal.)

"Zilch," Jocelyn said. "Unless Amanda is coming and going in the dark using a rope of tied-together socks to rappel out of a back window, she hasn't left her house since yesterday."

Following the promise from David that *The Scoop* would pay top dollar for new photos of Amanda Myles, the paparazzi had held a nearly twenty-four-hour vigil outside her home. Motivated perhaps by the thrill of the chase, but more likely the chance to pay their children's school fees, they were assembled across the street, armed with cameras, ready to shoot. But despite the round-the-clock presence, they got nothing. Amanda was in hiding, refusing to give us what we wanted. At least that was how David saw it. A personal insult. I didn't see it that way, figured Amanda hated the photos we had published of her, loathed the attention after years of living so privately, and was waiting for it all to die down. But I cared less about the why and more about the how—how to get David something new on Amanda, to get him off my back.

"So, what do we do?" I said, speaking now to Chris and Yenay as well as Jocelyn. "Amanda won't come out of her house to be photographed. She isn't on social media. Her rep is...not exactly cooperative," I said, shuddering to remember the excruciating email from Alice that would probably still haunt me on my deathbed. "What do we do? Ideas? Anyone?"

Yenay pursed her lips in concentration, pushed them out like a duck's bill, thinking. Chris barely acknowledged me. That he was older than me, and had been at *The Scoop* longer, apparently trumped that I was night editor, that he was supposed to treat me with deference.

A deflating silence settled over us. What was with this team? I wondered. Where was the enthusiasm, the gusto? The problem was, none of us wanted to fuck each other. Sexual tension in the workplace is like a double shot of espresso, inspiring energy and motivation like nothing else can. They say America runs on Dunkin', but I'd argue that the real fuel of this corporate machine of a nation is the workplace crush, co-workers who are inappropriately horny for each other. Why else show up to another pointless meeting, or stay back late, unless there is somebody there whose performance in bed you've imagined at least once? But alas, it was hard to envision a more sexless foursome (the cast of *Seinfeld*?). Chris I could only picture using his hand in front of a computer, and Yenay was twenty-two—no one under twenty-five is having truly good sex and can therefore radiate a genuinely earned erotic swagger. As for Jocelyn, she was so controlling at work I assumed in bed she would long to be dominated. But I sensed she doubted any of us—Chris, Yenay, or me—would be up to the job. As for David, given his age and overall aura, when I considered him sexually, I imagined his face, beet-red, sweating and grunting. I'd have bet David Brown knew his way around a clitoris about as well as he did Mexico City.

Then I remembered Josh and Miss America. It was for the best, I was well aware, that I did not consider any of my colleagues fuckable enough to want to bang them in the supply closet.

"We could put Marcus on her," Jocelyn said eventually.

"Marcus?"

"The PI."

"Pee eye?" I repeated. I didn't understand.

"*Private investigator*," Jocelyn said, as if I should have already known this, *dummy*.

"Yes, we still do that," Jocelyn replied, a touch of defiance in the way she said this, with a hint of playful mischief. It was something I'd noticed among people at *The Scoop*, the way they acknowledged Johnson News as a sinister force while simultaneously getting a thrill from being a part of it. Like the faux remorse of a smoker who says they know they really should quit, waving away their putrid exhale while blatantly relishing every single suck. A perverse pleasure in being seen misbehaving, doing something bad, even dangerous, that bordered on the nihilistic.

I asked Jocelyn what we used private investigators for.

"What *don't* we use them for?" she said. "Addresses, car registrations, phone numbers, birth certificates, flight details. Locating people when the paparazzi can't track them down."

A private investigator? It sounded at once silly and sinister. The words conjured a mustached Tom Selleck in a convertible wearing aviator shades, but there was also something dark about it. Journalists could get away with almost anything in the name of public interest; you had to wonder what a PI might be tasked with. Surely nothing legal. Something felt off about it. Besides, we were journalists—wasn't that what *we* were for? To uncover info, stories, scoops?

"I think we can find something ourselves without calling up Sherlock Holmes," I said.

"As you wish," Jocelyn said with a shrug, though she might as well have said, *You'll see*.

But Amanda Myles, the question of how to find something new to write about her, would have to wait—there was other "news" to attend to. A man in Texas was suing a KFC because he found a roach in his chicken (KFC—KENTUCKY FRIED COCKROACH! screamed the headline). A woman in Romania had married a bridge. An A-list actress had walked a red carpet in a skimpy dress that showed a lot of tit. A heated discussion ensued in which the four of us gathered around Yenay's computer to debate whether the cleavage was most accurately categorized as side-boob or under-boob (initially Yenay and Jocelyn said side-boob, while Chris and I said under-boob, but after zooming in on the cleavage in question, Chris and I convinced Yenay it was under-boob, and the cleavage was officially declared as such). Between the four of us combined, we had more than sixteen years of higher education. Somewhere, my college journalism professor took another swig of bourbon and banged her head against a brick wall.

An email from David pinged my inbox. All it contained was some photos of a woman I didn't recognize. She was young and Black, and the photos were grainy. In one, she held a roll-your-own cigarette that looked like it might be weed; in the next, she was pecking a woman on the lips. In another, she was swimming in a lake, only her head and shoulders above the water.

The subject line of the email was **FW: calling you now**. In seconds my desk phone rang.

"David?"

"Have you got the photos?"

"The ones you sent just now?"

"Yes—figured I'd call and explain. Some photos have resurfaced of Ashley Thompson, that newish Democratic senator in California. Replaced what's-her-name, the old duck."

I squinted at my screen. The young woman in the photos looked to be in her late teens, early twenties at most. Senator Thompson, I guessed, was in her late thirties or early forties.

"That's Ashley Thompson?"

"Yes. In her young and wild days at UC Berkeley, I gather."

"Oh. Right."

"Let's get something up on these right away. Ask Chris to write it. For the headline, I'm thinking something like, 'Senator's wild partying past revealed! California Democrat Ashley Thompson caught smoking suspicious cigarette, kissing a GIRL'—put 'girl' in all caps—'and skinny-dipping as she prepares to lead Senate Committee inquiry into police use of force.'"

David had a way of turning something utterly mundane into the kind of story that made you stop everything and send it to everyone you knew, a skill that both awed and terrified me.

"Are we sure that's weed she's smoking?" I asked. "What if it's just a roll-your-own?"

"That's why we won't say 'weed,'" David replied slowly, condescendingly, like he was trying to explain the geopolitical history of the Middle East to a toddler. "We'll say, 'suspicious cigarette.'"

I wondered if David realized how he sounded, like an uptight, Goody Two-shoes tween, the one who would narc to his parents that some kids had snuck a beer to try at the Fourth of July barbecue, smiling a smarmy little satisfied grin as the others were grounded. *College student possibly smokes weed—shock of the century!* I looked down at my notepad, where I'd scribbled the headline he'd suggested. That's when I noticed.

"David," I began hesitantly, "I'm concerned that if we call out that Senator Thompson is kissing a woman in all caps, and mention it alongside the *alleged* weed smoking and skinny-dipping, it will seem like... well, like we're implying there's something wrong with that."

David scoffed. "We're just describing what's happening in the photos. Is she not?"

Now *I* felt like I was trying to explain something to a toddler. How to make David understand there was a decent chance the photo could out Thompson as gay without her consent? Not to mention the other person in the photo, while feminine in appearance, might not identify as a woman. David didn't exactly give me the impression he was open-minded about gender fluidity. Phone pressed between ear and shoulder, I googled *Senator Ashley Thompson gay*. Nothing. *Senator Ashley Thompson sexuality*. Still nothing. She kept her personal life private.

"What if Senator Thompson is in the closet, and with this photo, we out her?"

"Then she shouldn't bloody well pose for a photo carrying on with another woman."

Carrying on with another woman. The way David said it made my skin crawl.

"Where did these come from, David?"

"A trusted contact. The authenticity of the photos has been verified. Listen, I have to go. If Chris has questions, tell him to come to me. Now, let's get a move on. I want them up tonight."

"What was that about?" Yenay asked when I hung up.

"Chris's next story," I said. Chris peered above his computer monitor at me.

"David wants you to write an article on some photos that have"—what word did David use?—"'resurfaced' of California senator Ashley Thompson. From when she was in college."

"Ah, yes," Chris said, "the 'resurfaced' photos that only 'resurfaced' because we 'resurfaced' them. What's Thompson done to attract the wrath of one of Walter Johnson's pals?"

Was that what this was? David said they came from a "trusted contact."

"She's leading a Senate committee hearing into police use of force."

"Wow, what a *coincidence*," Chris said, like there was nothing coincidental about it.

A heavy feeling in my gut, a terrible twisting mix of guilt and steadily growing anxiety, told me this was even worse than the story calling Amanda Myles fat. How could this be anything but an attempt to discredit Senator Thompson? There was no way the timing, days before an important Senate hearing, was pure coincidence. Whose dirty work were we doing?

Jocelyn asked to see the photos, and she came over to my desk to inspect them. Out of the corner of my eye I saw Yenay shoot me a look. I knew what it meant: *Not again*. She'd barely recovered from the abuse she got over the Amanda Myles story. Not that Yenay would write this one, but still, the idea of *The Scoop* attracting negative attention again, so soon, unsettled her.

Me too.

Chris said he would approach Senator Thompson's people for a comment, and he started writing. Briefly, I considered if there was anything I could do to stop the story. But just as quickly, I let the idea go. I remembered all too well the night David screamed at me to run the Meryl Streep photos instead of the Mogadishu attack. How I'd pushed back on the angle of the Amanda Myles story, only for it to be rewritten. It was no use. Trying to fight it was futile.

Later, in the kitchen, my Trader Joe's Tikka Masala turning round and round in the microwave as I watched my precious two minutes and thirty seconds alone tick away second by second, Chris walked in, startling me.

"Sorry," I said, putting a hand on my chest to steady myself. "You scared me."

"You should be scared," he replied plainly. "I'm a youngish white man. We're the number one threat to public safety in this country, given the lethal combination of ready access to firearms and grievances we're supposed to believe are the fault of immigrants but are in fact due to decades of unchecked corporate greed that make us ripe for radicalization by extreme right-wing ideology."

I laughed, gathering this was Chris's attempt at humor. It made me think of a recent all-staff email from building management about active shooter preparedness training—held during the daytime, of course. On the night shift, it seemed, we were on our own. I said this to Chris.

"If a gunman came into the newsroom on night shift," Chris said, filling his mug at the coffee machine, "David wouldn't want us to 'avoid, barricade, confront.' He'd want a story. He'd want us to live stream it. He'd want us to track down the guy's neighbors for comment and find his Reddit handle to try to determine if he was an incel as he fired live rounds."

Chris began speaking in a terrible faux-British accent I took to be an impersonation of our boss. He puffed out his cheeks, furrowed his brow, and placed his hands on his hips.

"Use your shirt as a tourniquet to stop the bleeding and get to work! This is an exclusive! 'The Scoop journalists BLEED on NEWSROOM FLOOR as CRAZED GUNMAN opens fire.'"

I laughed to hide the bitterness I felt, like scalding hot coffee on my tongue. Chris was joking, but it was too close to something David would think, even if he wouldn't say it aloud.

Chris turned around and leaned back on the kitchen counter, watching me as I tried to peel the plastic layer off my microwave dinner without burning my fingers on the rising steam.

"You seem to be struggling—"

"I've almost got it."

"I was going to say, struggling with the obligations and contradictions of tabloid life."

I glanced up at him. It caught me off guard, that Chris had made an assessment of me. And an accurate one at that.

"Sure," I said. "A little. The story about Senator Thompson, digging up her past and twisting it to discredit her right before the Senate committee. That's... dark. I thought *The Scoop* was all just, like, celebrity gossip and paparazzi photos of Taylor Swift, or whoever."

"That's *why* we publish the celebrity gossip and paparazzi photos in the first place," Chris said, "to make the ad dollars to pay for the dark stuff, so Walter Johnson can buy himself political favors and fuel his dangerous right-wing, increasingly fascist worldview. *That's the whole point of the Taylor Swift pictures.* I call it the Kira Vincent to KKK pipeline."

Perhaps I'd been more naïve about what I was getting myself into than I'd realized.

"Wow, that's dark. Don't *you* struggle? Being a part of that?"

Chris gave a heavy sigh.

"'If the daily press were to hang out a sign like every other trade, it would have to read: Here men are demoralized in the shortest possible time, on the largest possible scale, for the lowest possible price.'"

"Huh?" I had no idea what he was talking about.

"Kierkegaard," he replied. "The Danish philosopher."

"I know who Kierkegaard is," I said, which was true, though I couldn't say with certainty I'd ever read his work.

"He predicted the current state of the media one hundred and fifty years ago. He said there is no limit to how far a newspaper can devolve, because it can always sink further to find new readers. He said the media 'will stir up all those dregs of humanity which no state or government can control.'"

"Right," I said, nodding like I understood where this was going. I wasn't in the mood for a lecture on media theory—not only was it after midnight, but also my dinner preparation was going disastrously, the tikka masala still almost frozen at the center. I flung it back in the microwave.

Chris laughed nervously, as if he felt silly for quoting a philosopher that died in the eighteen hundreds in the kitchen near midnight.

"Look, I have my gripes. But if I go somewhere else, it'll be the same shit, different stink. I'm older than you, I've been around the block a few times. It can be crazy here, but it's not so bad. Most people are decent, once you get to know them. In my experience, the ones at the so-called prestigious publications are worse. People here are more clear-eyed about the media—what it really is, or what it's become. Less given to illusions, delusions... about themselves most of all."

It sounded to me like Chris had Stockholm syndrome, had formed a deep emotional attachment to his toxic employer. Telling himself a story to hide the more uncomfortable truth: that his career had bottomed out and he was simply too lazy or cynical to do something about it.

"But don't you want to do better work?" I pressed, one eye on my dinner through the glass. "You have a journalism degree. Don't you find it demoralizing, having to write these stupid stories? 'Michael Jackson's ghost reportedly sighted at Home Depot'? 'Missouri woman arrested for failing to return a copy of *Weekend at Bernie's* to Blockbuster twenty years ago'?"

"Actually, I think the Blockbuster story is an entry point to explore the harm caused by overly broad and arbitrary laws. How our legal system exploits these laws to use poor, largely Black and brown people as pawns to maintain the prison industrial complex. Which is especially relevant as calls grow to expunge weed convictions as more states legalize cannabis."

The man could be insufferable sometimes. I tried not to roll my eyes.

"Well, someone should be locked up over *Weekend at Bernie's*," I said. "For crimes against good taste. Two guys parade their dead CEO's body around the Hamptons pretending he's still alive? And nobody notices he's dead? So stupid."

"I disagree," Chris said. "I think *Weekend at Bernie's* was a metaphor, an alarm sounded on what would happen to the human soul when the infinite growth required by the US capitalist system is favored at the expense of basic decency. A harbinger, a warning, that someday we'd all be propping up the dressed-up corpse of our ruthless economic model, in denial of its dehumanizing and destructive effects despite all the evidence, because it's easier than admitting its failure, easier than envisioning something new."

"Chris, how many of those have you had tonight?" I asked, gesturing at his coffee.

"I think four."

"Maybe switch to decaf?"

"Yeah."

For all Chris's insistence that at least some *Scoop* stories had more substance than it seemed at first glance, something still didn't add up. A Pulitzer winner, expounding on the prison industrial complex and the subliminal anti-capitalist message at the heart of an '80s slapstick comedy? I sensed there was something he wasn't telling me, a missing puzzle piece.

"So you really didn't feel conflicted? Writing the Senator Thompson story?"

Chris blew gently on his coffee, thought for a moment.

"Tabloids are as old as gossip, as old as palace intrigue. It's a natural human instinct to want to know about the lives of the people around us, especially people with wealth and power, like politicians and celebrities. In medieval times, maybe it would stop you having your head chopped off, if you knew not to flirt with Elizabeth, because she was having a secret affair with James, and James was known to order a beheading when he got jealous due to his unhealed attachment issues."

I considered this. "But doesn't it bother you that your name is on that article?"

Chris waved the question away, shook his head.

"I don't care about that. About my 'reputation' as a journalist or what anyone in this industry thinks of me. This job, this place... I'm just here for the money, to fuel my real work."

"Real work?"

Chris nodded.

"I write a climate change blog. Have for three years. I've got a pretty large following."

Chris smiled, looked quietly pleased with himself. His confession took me by surprise.

"A climate change blog? What prompted that? I mean, besides the fact that humanity is sleepwalking toward an extinction-level catastrophe and people should probably know about it."

Chris chuckled darkly.

"Once I realized *The New York Times* couldn't report with appropriate urgency one of the greatest threats the human race has ever faced because Exxon, Shell, Chevron, and the rest of the fossil fuel industry have them by the balls, certainly with ad dollars and probably also dark money–backed corporate thuggery, I knew the future of media wasn't going to be corporate."

I recalled Patti pressing Audrey about the *Times*' climate change coverage.

"You're so right," I said. "When are the *Times* and the rest of the corporate media going to stop portraying climate activists as unhinged lunatics when their response is actually sane? When will they grow some balls and start seriously holding fossil fuel executives to account?"

"Exactly," Chris said, nodding enthusiastically. "You get it." I could tell he was impressed. He didn't know I was merely parroting something my climate-activist roommate said.

I took in the sight of Chris, cupping his coffee mug, saw him anew. In an instant he looked different to me. I was taken aback. He had this whole other facet to him I'd never suspected. It was a mind-bending paradox: a journalist working for Johnson News, one of the world's greatest purveyors of climate change misinformation, writing a climate change blog.

"How can you stand to work for Johnson News?"

Chris gave a mischievous smile. "I like to think of myself as a kind of Robin Hood, taking money from the evil propaganda machine and using it to publish accurate information."

"Wow," I said, genuinely in awe. "That's amazing, Chris. I really admire that."

For the rest of the night, I couldn't stop thinking about Chris's revelation, his secret life as a climate change blogger. It explained why he seemed so detached about everything. He came into *The Scoop*, disassociated for nine hours, and then went back to his real life. The discovery made me feel betrayed. I'd felt superior to Chris, seeing him as this former Pulitzer winner who had fallen from grace, who had given up while I was still nobly reaching for journalistic greatness (brief detour aside). But that narrative had been flipped on its head. Now Chris was the noble one, accepting the fate of the corporate-owned media as increasingly useless, and instead seeking another avenue to make positive change in the world. I wondered now what *he* thought of *me*, if he saw me as the former *Marie Claire* editor who was now washed up and irrelevant.

I tried to reassure myself it was all okay. In a few short months I'd be at *Business Day*, doing important, valuable, essential work again. It was September. Next year felt so far away. I wanted to prove myself sooner. Maybe I could make it happen faster. I wondered how I could wow David, come up with a scoop so big he couldn't deny that I had held up my part of our deal.

"Can you send me Marcus's details?" I asked Jocelyn as we packed up that night.

"Sure," she said, raising an eyebrow at me, though she didn't ask any further questions.

Hi Marcus, I began the email. I'm the new night editor at *The Scoop*. I'd love your help with something. I need you to find me anything you can on Amanda Myles.

10

"'Park Street Publishing is now nothing more,'" Audrey said, reading aloud from her phone at the table, "'than an exceedingly glamorous hospice. Executives continue to claim print isn't dead, but we hear a number of magazine titles are under palliative care, the diagnosis terminal. The humane thing to do with these thin, lifeless versions of what they once were would be to euthanize them.'"

"Brutal," Jasmine said. The rest of us murmured agreement.

The chosen ones—those of us who made up the smallest ring of Audrey's inner circle—were gathered in the high-ceilinged dining room of her West Village apartment (it belonged to an aunt who had moved to Paris, or was it an uncle who had moved to London? I could never remember) to celebrate her thirty-first birthday. Aside from her cousin Dan, a lawyer, and her college best friend Ellen, who worked in finance, the rest of us were media people. We had all read the scathing *Page Six* gossip item that week, and now we needed to process it together.

"I can't believe that part about the hot desking policy," Jasmine said, shaking her head. "No one has their own desks anymore? People are getting written warnings for 'encroachment' for leaving a coat on the back of a chair overnight? What could possibly justify such brutality?"

I agreed it was outrageous, the report of the unnamed Park Street employee who found themselves in breach of company policy over a forgotten container of almonds, though *brutality* was probably too strong a word.

"It said they consolidated all the ever-shrinking magazine teams to a few floors, so they can rent out the other levels of the building," I said. "Fiscal conservatism in uncertain times."

"Come on," Naomi said, looking around at the rest of us conspiratorially, "isn't it obvious? They took away individual desks, one of the last remaining dignities of office life, based on some creepy study from McKinsey or whoever on how to psychologically control people in the workplace. They're subconsciously priming employees to have a scarcity complex, to see each other, rather than the executives, as the enemy, so there won't be enough camaraderie between them to unionize. To make them fight each other for the 'good' desks, which, if they thought about it for longer than a second, they would realize is absurd, and sad. Like spending fifty bucks on an arcade game to win a cheaply stitched stuffed animal with a wonky eye."

This disquieting imagery, a stingingly accurate portrayal of what a media career felt like lately, made us go quiet for a moment, a sad silence settling over the room. Then someone said how delicious the spiced carrots were, and we all *mmm*'d our agreement, and then someone complimented the branzino, and we *mmm*'d even more enthusiastically, and then we moved on.

I felt surprisingly cheerful, given the week I'd had—the photographic evidence of Josh beaming next to Miss America, getting berated by David countless times, the queasy feeling that stirred in my stomach over the things I did in the name of work. Senator Thompson had been forced to come out as gay after intense media speculation into her private life, sparked by *The Scoop* publishing her old photos. My good mood was mostly due to the wine, to which I helped myself regularly and generously. I just wanted to have fun, not talk or think about *The Scoop*.

And I was having fun, enjoying the company of all but one of Audrey's dinner guests: Patrick. Patrick was a British BBC correspondent temporarily based in New York, who was only at Audrey's birthday dinner because he was the date of Tessa, an *Elle* editor and a dear friend of Audrey's (they'd spent summers together for years because their families had homes on the same street in Sag Harbor). Patrick, it was obvious, at least to me, was exploiting his proximity to a *New York Times* journalist that evening by performing a shameless routine of flattery. It was clear from his prostrating, the way he laughed louder than anyone at Audrey's jokes, that his aim was to ingratiate himself so she might help him get inside the *Times*—a favor that even I, her best friend, hadn't asked of her. Add to that his overly formal way of speaking, reminiscent of a haughty *Downton Abbey* butler, and his mentions of attending Oxford and his parents' country estate outside London (a barely concealed attempt to let Audrey know he was one of her kind), and I'd disliked him immediately and intensely. All night I'd been unable to take my eyes off the jaunty scarf knotted around Patrick's skinny neck, which he kept on throughout dinner, despite the almost too-cozy warmth inside Audrey's apartment. Whenever he leaned down to take a bite from his fork, the tip dangled precariously close to his plate. I kept waiting for him to notice.

It was all I could do not to kick Patrick under the table, hard, and then pretend it was an accident. Whenever the urge gripped me, I drank more wine.

I was on my third, possibly fourth glass when someone mentioned Senator Thompson, and the media circus that exploded over her sexuality. I almost choked on a green bean.

"Forcing someone to come out..." Tessa said, shaking her head.

"Disgusting," Dan agreed. "There's no excuse."

Tessa nodded. "You know it's only because she's Black, and a Democrat. What about all the old Republican men who have been in the closet for years? Where are the stories on them?"

It shouldn't have surprised me that my friends had seen the news about Senator Thompson—it *had* been everywhere. I just hoped Audrey, Jasmine, and Naomi (the only ones at the table who knew I worked at *The Scoop*) hadn't caught the story's original source. Did they know? Out of the corner of my eye, I noticed Naomi, the sole Black woman at the dinner, wince. For her sake, I prayed the conversation wouldn't linger on the "whys" behind the story targeting Senator Thompson, knowing what would likely unfold: a table full of white guests clumsily trying to say the right things to prove they're "good" white people, real allies, all the while sneaking surreptitious glances at Naomi to see if they'd earned her approval and so could unburden themselves of their white guilt for the night, while trying to think of a way to casually drop a mention of something they remembered from *The New Jim Crow* for bonus points. Or was the wince about *me*—a sign that Naomi, who had initially supported my taking the job, felt differently now, given the proof that *The Scoop* published a lot more than just "harmless fun"?

"What's the name of that weird website that published the photos?" Patrick asked. *"The Scoop* or something like that? Never heard of it."

As he said this, the eyes of Naomi, Jasmine, and Audrey involuntarily wandered to meet mine. I stared back, willed them to receive the message I was sending: I did not want to talk about it.

Shut the fuck up, Patrick, I thought. I looked down at my plate, focused on cutting my chicken, but a noticeable silence fell over the table. Eventually I looked up and saw Audrey throwing nervous glances in my direction. Patrick picked up on our private communication.

"What?" he asked, as if waiting for someone to let him in on a joke. Audrey was still shooting looks at me, like I should say something. I pretended I hadn't heard Patrick's question.

"These green beans are delicious. They're garlicky but not *too* garlicky, you know?"

Hopeless. Everyone was staring at me now, somehow knowing. I drained my wineglass.

"*The Scoop* is a small news website," I said. "I work there. I'm the night editor."

Patrick's eyes went wide, and then he shot Audrey a look of concern, as if to ask if she knew that there was an intruder in our midst. A pleb from steerage had snuck into first class.

"Is it a tabloid?" he asked.

I shrugged, as if it were debatable. As if I didn't spend my nights disputing under-boob versus side-boob, or reporting a woman buying Ben & Jerry's and cheese as "breaking news."

"Who owns it?"

His question set me on edge. It was a normal thing for a journalist to inquire about, but Patrick asking me in front of the table, this threat of exposure, felt like an attack. I stiffened.

"Johnson News," I said, trying to sound nonchalant, almost bored by this fact. But now Patrick looked at me with barely veiled disgust, like I'd just finished describing in great detail a full-body rash I'd recently had. I saw Tessa's smile falter as she took in the news of where my post–*Marie Claire* life had taken me. My secret was out. I flushed hot with shame. More wine.

"Johnson News," Patrick repeated, as if speaking the name of an enemy of his family that went back generations. He eyed me warily, as if he believed himself to be in the presence of someone not to be trusted, even dangerous. I watched his scarf swing, skim the top of his plate.

THE SCOOP

"Frankie," Ellen said, either not aware of or choosing to ignore the tension that was growing between me and Patrick, "you have to spill. How did *The Scoop* get those photos?"

Thanks, Ellen, I thought bitterly while forcing a smile. But then I noticed everyone—everyone except Audrey and Patrick—nodding and leaning forward eagerly, excited to realize someone at the table might have juicy insider details on the story. I heard David's words again: *People who subscribe to* The New Yorker *will never admit to reading us*... Briefly, I considered telling them what I knew, to savor their attention and curious interest as long as I could, since it felt so much better than judgment. But feeling Patrick watch me like a lion ready to pounce, I refused to give him the satisfaction of proving I was the tabloid villain he assumed me to be.

"I don't know anything about that one," I lied. "I had nothing to do with it. Sorry."

Patrick stared at me with beady eyes. I wasn't sure if maybe I was just being paranoid, nervous under the spotlight of the table as I was, but I could have sworn he knew I'd lied.

"Who have they got running that?" he asked now.

"Excuse me?"

"Who's running it?" he repeated, unable to hide his irritation. "Who's the editor?"

I looked around at the others, longing for someone to find this inside baseball media-industry conversation boring and interrupt. But nobody did. Patrick waited for me to answer.

"I doubt you'd know him," I said. I cleared my throat. "His name is David Brown."

Patrick leaned back in his seat, a little breathless, apparently stunned to hear the name.

"David Brown? You've got to be joking."

"Do you know him, babe?" Tessa asked, sensing Patrick's agitation.

Jasmine, trying to break the tension, asked if anybody would like more of the spiced carrots.

"I know him all right," Patrick spat. He seemed to not know where to begin explaining how he knew David Brown, as if their history was so far-reaching and extensive it defied the limits of space and time, as if the two men had dueled over a beautiful woman in a past life.

"Put simply, David Brown is a disgrace," Patrick said, his face reddening. "He was a senior editor at the *National Herald* during the spying scandal." He looked around at his dining companions, expecting recognition before remembering which side of the Atlantic he was on. He went on to give a summary of the illegal activities and eventual downfall of the *National Herald*. He described David Brown and his type being at the "rotten heart" of the British tabloids, akin to the paparazzi who snapped photos of Princess Diana as she lay dying in the back of a crashed car in that Paris tunnel, negotiating deals for photos with newspapers as she took her last breaths.

"But it's all still rampant at the British tabloids, and no doubt at the ones over here, too. Now they just outsource the worst of it to private investigators so they can claim ignorance."

Patrick's mention of private investigators made me blanch. I put down my fork. It was only days ago that I had emailed Marcus, asking him to find what he could on Amanda Myles.

Patrick cleared his throat. "I don't know how you sleep at night, working for him."

I don't sleep at night, I thought. *I work.*

"Wait," Naomi said, turning to me. "This David Brown guy... that's your boss?"

It felt as though the others were seeing me differently now—the way Patrick saw me.

"Yes, David is my boss," I said. "I don't know what he was like years ago, but he's a fairly harmless old man these days." I pushed away the memory of *forget fucking Mogadishu*.

Patrick scoffed.

"Harmless? David Brown? He's a grown man with a reputation for bouts of explosive rage, kicking bins over and calling people cunts. He once famously screamed so hard at an editor that people noticed David's eye twitching for days afterwards. No, that man will be doing Walter Johnson's dirty work until the day he dies. You must have known when you took the job, Francesca. It's no secret—probably the first thing that comes up about him on a Google search."

I glared at Patrick, took another sip of wine. Why was I the villain here, when it was David Brown and Walter Johnson and those journalists at the *National Herald* who had done bad things? Sure, I'd been involved in the Senator Thompson story—David happened to send it to me—but if I'd refused to publish the photos, he would have just asked someone else to do it. And did none of them understand how hard it was to get a job as a journalist lately? Had they not all just heard the details in the *Page Six* gossip item about the dire circumstances at Park Street Publishing, about the hot desk policy, about the rumors of more titles soon to be closed down?

I wished one of my friends would jump in, defend me, tell Patrick to back off. Why weren't they? Audrey, Naomi, and Jasmine only exchanged awkward glances, looked at their plates, or helped themselves to more food. Then it hit me. How had I not seen it before? They'd seemed sympathetic, supportive, when I told them at brunch. But now I was seeing what they really thought. Or, maybe they had been genuinely understanding at first, but now the Senator Thompson story had changed things. I remembered Audrey's text: *Are you going to stay?*

"I did my research," I said coolly, increasingly aware there was little I could say to defend myself, to make the others understand why I'd taken the job. "But, to be honest, I didn't have much of a choice. I got laid off in May, and by the time the opportunity at *The Scoop* came along, I was about to run out of money. Out of options. Not that that's any of your business."

Humiliating, to have to admit to the entire table, most of whom moved in the same wealthy New York circles as Audrey, just how broke and desperate I'd been over the summer.

Audrey, I noticed, had gone quiet. The atmosphere at her birthday dinner had taken a sharp left turn. If she wanted to restore the good vibes, she could have said something to change the subject, steered the conversation away from Patrick's increasingly aggressive interrogation of me. But she didn't. She just sat there, prodding at something on her plate with her fork. I was angry at Audrey, I realized, not only for failing to step up to defend me from Patrick, but also, even though I knew this wasn't fair, at how well things had worked out for her since *Marie Claire*. At how dramatically our paths had diverged. For years, I'd faked my place in her world, with free clothing and bags from the fashion cupboard at *Marie Claire*, with invites to exclusive events to mingle with powerful people drinking expensive champagne, with a desk right beside hers. But now all that was gone, stripped away, revealing that I'd never really belonged at Audrey's table.

"Believe me," I said, hearing the bitterness in my voice, "if I could have retreated to my parents' estate to make calls to my Oxford alumni friends to help me out, I would have."

I knew Audrey was staring at me, but I refused to meet her gaze. I was talking to Patrick, but of course she knew the comment was meant for her, too. They were the transatlantic mirror images of each other. Audrey always made sure to talk about how hard she worked, a defense, I knew, against the assumptions she knew people made that she wouldn't be in the position she was in if it wasn't for her media-power-couple parents. I'd struck a blow where it hurt the most.

"Why not leave the industry?" Dan, Audrey's lawyer cousin, asked. "Like that article was saying, the media is going extinct, fast. You could probably double your salary doing PR or communications."

Jasmine and Naomi watched me carefully. This was, after all, what they had done.

"Ah, I see," I said, unable to keep the sarcasm out of my voice. "Instead of continuing the career I have spent the last almost decade building, I should give up on my purpose, my dreams, the life I know, and go do something else, right? Anything not to offend the moral sensibilities of who? You?" I said, turning to Patrick. "It's funny, I thought you would have better table manners than to let your scarf drag through your food all night, given the silver spoon it's obvious you were born with in your mouth."

"Frankie," Audrey snapped. She glowered at me, as if to say, *That's enough.*

"What?" I said. I knew I should stop but I was indignant at being painted as a villain. I found myself wishing Chris, Jocelyn, or Yenay were there to back me up, to support my argument no one else at the table seemed to understand. Then something occurred to me.

"None of my colleagues at *The Scoop* went to Ivy League colleges. They all have long commutes to work. Very different from *Marie Claire*, where it seemed like everyone lived walking distance or a few subway stops from the office. You can't tell me that's a coincidence."

Audrey cleared her throat. "But there are plenty of people at the *Times* who didn't go to Ivy League colleges, Frankie. What you're saying erases all those people and their hard work. What about yourself? You didn't go to an Ivy League, and you still worked at *Marie Claire*."

"Yes, Audrey," I said, knowing I should back down but unable to stop, "and just because there are still some polar bears wandering in the Arctic doesn't mean the ice isn't melting."

"Wait, you worked at *Marie Claire*?" Patrick asked, looking confused, like he couldn't compute it. I found this incredibly annoying, knowing he had *Marie Claire* and Co. up on a pedestal, as I admittedly once had, too. But it had occurred to me recently, as my time as a *Marie Claire* journalist moved further into the past, that the magazine was far from the bastion of journalism it purported to be. At *Marie Claire*, we wrote stories for the woman who had the time to flip through a magazine on the daybed by the pool at her Hamptons home, not the woman being paid very little to clean that rich woman's house. And which woman was more deserving of the resources and efforts of journalism? Which woman was in more urgent need of access to information? But that was not something someone like Patrick would have ever thought about.

I nodded. "*The Scoop* is only temporary," I said. "Until I can find something better."

Patrick raised an eyebrow. "But doesn't it concern you," he said, "that now you have been 'tainted,' so to speak? A reputable news organization would never hire a tabloid journalist."

A lump formed in my throat. Why would he say that? I stared into his face. I couldn't tell if he took pleasure in suggesting this or was apologetic; his expression seemed a mix of both.

"What are you saying? No one will hire me now because I work at *The Scoop*?"

Patrick turned to Audrey. "I mean, the *Times* would never hire a tabloid journalist, right, Audrey? How could they defend it? There would be a riot in the newsroom."

I looked at Audrey, beseeching her to deny what Patrick was saying.

"I suppose they might—"

"Oh, come on," Patrick said, as if this was outrageous. "It would never happen. Never."

"I don't know," Audrey said quietly, with a soft shrug, though it seemed to me she did know; she just didn't want to say.

At last, the truth. Hinted at in her message that night when I was at work—*are you going to stay?*—and now confirmed. Audrey saw my decision to work at *The Scoop* as a grave, fatal mistake, and I would never be the same in her eyes because of it. I was someone different to her now. We couldn't go back. The dining room all of a sudden felt unbearably warm, stuffy, too small. All those judgmental eyes. Patrick's food-stained scarf end. I couldn't stay any longer.

I stood. "I think I should go."

"Frankie, no," Jasmine said, along with some mild protestations from the others—not Patrick, of course. I hurried out of the dining room and went into Audrey's bedroom, where my jacket and bag were laid on the bed with everyone else's. I heard footsteps down the hall.

"Frankie."

I whirled around.

"So," I said, "you really took the side of some dude you just met instead of me?"

Audrey folded her arms across her chest as she stood in the doorway. "What? I didn't take sides!"

I couldn't help but roll my eyes.

"Yes, you did! Come on, Audrey. It's so obvious you agree with Patrick, that the *Times* would never hire someone who worked at a tabloid. Which means they would never hire *me*."

"I didn't say that," Audrey said, though I heard the falter in her voice. She looked down.

"That's bullshit, Audrey." I heard myself spit the words, unable to push down the angry hurt I felt bubbling up. "All my years as a magazine editor, all my years at *Marie Claire*, worthless now because of a few weeks at a tabloid? Seriously? How can you think that?"

"Because it's true!" Audrey exploded, meeting my gaze again.

"I knew it," I said under my breath.

"When you told us at brunch, I wanted to shake you and ask what the hell you were thinking! Any legitimate news organization is going to see Johnson News as a red flag. How could you be so reckless with your career?"

I was so stunned by Audrey's words I almost had to sit down on the bed.

"Reckless? Reckless with my career? How could you say that? You know better than anyone that nothing matters to me more. You know how hard I've had to work for what I've got, Audrey. Where I came from. I didn't have Mom and Dad to pull any strings for me at the *Times*."

I didn't know for sure if Audrey's parents had made calls on her behalf, or if she really had gotten the *Times* media reporter job on merit alone. But we weren't holding back now. We were out to hurt each other, and we both knew the precise location of each other's most tender spots.

I stared at Audrey, her face as red as mine probably was. We'd never had an argument that felt this serious before. It was only days ago she made me laugh with her texts, comforting me over Josh and Miss America. Now it might as well have been my worst enemy standing opposite me, staring me down. It felt like our friendship was slipping through the cracks of the fissures from the earthquake that had finally erupted between us, after years of faint tremors.

"David is getting me a job at *Business Day*."

Audrey snapped up to look at me.

"What?"

I nodded. I needed Audrey to know that I had a plan to get out of *The Scoop*, to get my old life back, or something like it. That this was just a season, one our friendship could weather.

"All I have to do is work at *The Scoop* for a few months and then he said—"

"Please. Frankie, you're not seriously that gullible? That is *never* going to happen."

"You don't know that."

"I do."

"How?"

"I just do."

"Cool counterargument. Very convincing."

Audrey sighed, rolled her eyes, then gave me a sad look. It felt like pity.

"It's so obviously a lie, to manipulate you, that it's not worth my breath to respond."

We stood there for a long moment, not saying anything. Hot tears pricked my eyes.

"You know, people have said to me that you can be cold. I couldn't see it. But I do now."

Audrey huffed with frustration. "When have I ever been cold to you, Frankie? When have I done anything but support you, help you? Even though you've always been jealous of me—"

"What? No, I haven't."

"You've tried to hide it, but it's so fucking obvious sometimes. I know you resent me because I grew up... comfortable. I've tried to be understanding, knowing that you don't have family, and then especially after everything that happened with Josh. And now you're nothing but ungrateful, and all because I dared to be the one to tell you the truth you don't want to hear."

I grabbed my coat and bag from the bed.

"Yes, good idea, leave." Audrey sounded angry, but I heard her voice waver, as if she was trying not to cry. I willed the sob in my chest not to force its way out until I was outside.

Audrey stepped out of the way. I didn't look back as I rushed toward the door.

11

"Bravo, night shift. Bravo!"

David towered over my desk, clapping his baseball-mitt hands in a standing ovation for Chris, Yenay, Jocelyn, and me. It was the last day of September, and according to website traffic, the Senator Ashley Thompson exposé was the most-read article on *The Scoop* for the entire month. The story about Amanda Myles grocery shopping was the third most read. It was the first time in a long time that night shift had a story in the top ten, let alone two. I wasn't sure how much of this effusive praise we deserved—it could be argued it was David himself who was owed most of the credit for both stories. But apparently our contribution was sufficient enough for David to stay back in the office until night shift arrived so he could congratulate us in person.

"I don't believe in this American culture of praising people for every little thing, throwing a parade for a child because they *made a doo-doo in the potty*," David said mockingly. "But I always give credit when it's due. The Man Upstairs is happy—let's keep it that way."

David's praise warmed me. On some level, I knew it was pathetic, to be so easily buoyed by his smile and applause. And I still felt uneasy, grubby, about both articles, and my involvement in bringing them into the world—it was only months ago, at *Marie Claire*, that I would have spoken of my disgust at such vile excuses for journalism, and the reporters who brought them forth. But it was nonetheless intoxicating to feel David's approval shining on me. Given he was so easily angered, often cruel, by contrast it made his praise feel all the more powerful, almost narcotic, soothing the ragged edges of my lonely days and long, long nights.

But nothing could dissolve the gnawing knot of dread in my stomach since Saturday night, after the humiliation I'd felt at dinner and the horrible argument with Audrey, which made angry tears prick my eyes if I thought about it too long. Moments from the evening haunted me in the shower, on the subway: Audrey's shrug, the way she equivocated when Patrick asked her if the *Times* would hire someone from a tabloid; her arms folded across her chest in the doorway, hiss-whispering at me; Patrick's scarf dangling in the red wine jus, almost sensual. Only Naomi had texted to see how I was; also to ask if I still had her copy of *Pedagogy of the Oppressed*.

"Now, tomorrow is October first," David said, fussing with a zip on his tan leather mailbag, the smile leaving his face, brow furrowed again. "You know what that means."

I knew what it meant to me. October first: only three months until January first—in other words, the new year, when, according to David's promise, I'd be headed upstairs to *Business Day*. But I doubted that was what he was referring to. I looked around at the others, hoping for an answer, but Chris and Jocelyn had their attention on their screens, only half listening to David. Yenay, who, like me, hadn't been at *The Scoop* long enough to get away with such obvious indifference when David was talking, looked how I felt: like a student desperately hoping the teacher doesn't call on them to answer the question in front of the rest of the class.

THE SCOOP

"It's politically incorrect celebrity Halloween costume season, of course!" David cried. "Tacky, tasteless, sexist, racist—the coming weeks will be a veritable feast of offensive impropriety in the name of festivity. At least a few famous idiots will make a misstep with their Halloween costume, and I want everyone on the lookout. It's been ten years since Prince Harry dressed up as a Nazi on Halloween. I don't know if you heard about that over here, but in Britain we sold more newspapers in one day than we had in a decade. Probably since his mother died."

David gazed out the window, lost in thought, as if recalling a cherished memory.

"Anyway," he continued, snapping back to the room, "in the coming weeks the paps will be lurking outside every A-list Halloween party both sides of the pond, on the lookout for celebrities in offensive Halloween costumes like hunters in deer season. You can bet they'll let us know within seconds of anyone somewhat well-known wearing an outfit that could be even vaguely construed as insensitive. This is a major opportunity for *The Scoop* as we work to increase our readership and visibility in the market. One white woman in a Pocahontas costume and we could hit our traffic targets for the entire month. But here's the thing: if the paps snap a celebrity in an offensive outfit, everyone else will have the story, too. But I want *The Scoop* to have an exclusive. That's why I've launched a project for the month of October for the entire team, but which I am asking night shift to lead: Project Black Lagoon. By October thirty-first, we're going to dig up at least one old photo of a celebrity in a controversial Halloween costume. It might be in the image archives, or a forgotten post on social media that hasn't aged well—Tom Brady must have worn a sombrero and a mustache at some point. That's why it's called Project Black Lagoon, because we're bringing something up from the dark depths to the surface. Get it?"

"What about Project Skeletons in the Closet?" Jocelyn suggested. "Because it—"

"No, no, it's Project Black Lagoon."

"But it works on two levels because—"

David made an impatient sound. "The name of the project is not the focus, okay? Just find me something. I'll send an update to the entire team tomorrow, but I wanted to brief night shift specifically, as I expect you to do most of the heavy lifting, since the day team needs to focus on the daily news cycle. It's going to be a lot of work, but it's also an opportunity. The Man Upstairs is *very* excited about this one. Let's not miss the chance to impress him, hmm?"

With that, David turned and headed toward the frosted glass doors of the newsroom.

As I watched him stride away, mailbag slapping his side, I was seized by a sudden panic. It was so rare for me to see David in person, and I didn't know when we would be face-to-face again. It could be weeks, even longer. Ego inflated by David's praise, and the urgency I'd felt to get out of *The Scoop* since learning of Chris's secret life only growing after the shame and judgment I'd felt at Audrey's dinner, before I knew what I was doing I stood and followed David through the newsroom doors. I found him waiting by the elevators, scrolling on his phone.

"David," I said, realizing as I spoke that I was out of breath.

He looked briefly surprised to see me headed for him, but quickly regained composure.

"Don't tell me you've found something already for Project Black Lagoon?" He lowered his voice. "I think Jocelyn's wrong, Project Black Lagoon is a much stronger name. Right?"

"Absolutely," I agreed, sensing that this was important to him. "And you can trust that we're on it, Captain," I added, inexplicably giving a military salute. David peered at me oddly.

THE SCOOP

"Sorry," I said, clearing my throat, trying to slow my breathing and pull myself together. "I thought since you're here tonight, it might be a good time for us to talk about *Business Day*."

"*Business Day*?" David repeated, frowning, as if he thought he'd misheard me.

"Yes."

"What about it?"

His expression was blank, as if he had no recollection of the promise he'd made.

"The job," I said, waiting for him to remember. "For me. We discussed it in my interview..."

David was still staring at me blankly. I realized then it had been a mistake to confront him. It was much too soon—I'd only been at *The Scoop* for a month. What had I been thinking? I saw then that what I'd intended as bold, chutzpah, must have come across as impatient, entitled.

But, to my relief, recognition at last registered for David. His expression brightened.

"Right, yes, of course. *Business Day*. How could I forget? You've been here how long?"

I flushed red, felt sheepish. It was so short a time I couldn't say it. "Sorry, I know I—"

The elevator doors opened with a ding. David stepped inside.

"No, not at all. You're... ambitious, Francesca. I like that," he said as he pushed the button for ground level. "Look, I doubt I'll get the green light for that until next year..."

The doors began to close. I leapt forward, thrust an arm in the way. They bounced open.

"...and everyone is so pleased with the progress on night shift. But tell you what: Peter Lowell, the managing editor at *Business Day*, is a mate of mine. Want to have coffee with him?"

Coffee with the managing editor of *Business Day*? Now we were getting somewhere.

"That would be amazing, David. It's just, I'm always thinking a few steps ahead and—"

"Wonderful. Now, I think you ought to take a few steps *back* or this elevator is going to take your arm clean off."

I jumped back, thanking David again before the elevator doors slammed shut.

"Yes!" I shouted to the empty hall. It was all I could do not to break out into dance right there by the elevators in some pathetically lame reenactment of the final scene in *Footloose*.

I took a deep breath and went back into the newsroom.

"Everything all right?" Jocelyn asked when I was back at my desk. I sensed Chris and Yenay were listening. I lied, said I had a few questions about Project Black Lagoon. I thought it might inspire jealousy in the others, if they knew I was only passing through at *The Scoop*.

"I still think it should be called Project Skeletons in the Closet," Jocelyn said.

"Welcome to October at a tabloid," Chris said, "the one month of the year where racism and misogyny go from being an invention of the liberal imagination to *real* and *important* issues."

I turned to Yenay.

"Yenay, can you get started on Project Black Lagoon tonight?"

"Sure, I'll see what I can find," she said, though I sensed immediately something was off with her. I thought she seemed quiet, a little subdued. I wondered if I was only imagining it, but then Jocelyn looked in my direction (not that Yenay could see) and raised an eyebrow; she'd noticed it, too. I wondered if Yenay was still smarting from the abuse over the Amanda grocery shopping article, and the brutal blow of criticism from her beloved Annie Klein; perhaps David bringing it up moments ago in celebration had reminded her of it. I considered sending Yenay a message, to ask if she was okay, but the idea floated out of my mind as quickly as it had come.

Instead, I privately thrilled at David's offer to schedule a coffee for me with Peter at *Business Day*. When would it happen? And what was Peter like? I made a mental note to do some research on him. *The Scoop* newsroom was still there, the jumbo screen with its flashing arrows, the scent of Chris's meatball sub wafting, a long night ahead of mind-numbingly inane headlines, the cold sting of eye drops, enough caffeine to risk cardiac arrest, the jolting bleats of my desk phone, my reflection in the bathroom mirror ghoulish under yellow lights. And while my body was still there, in my chair, clicking, typing, my mind had gone elsewhere. I saw myself in the hopeful near future, standing in the golden-white glow of pure, bright daylight once again.

12

I FIGURED IT WOULD TAKE MARCUS a week at least to find something on Amanda, maybe longer, if he found anything at all. But when I got to work the next evening, I had an email from him waiting.

You're welcome was all it said, two files attached. I held my breath as I clicked, watched them load, wondering what kind of ticking bomb Marcus had dropped in my lap. At first, when I saw the two documents filled with small text, scanned slightly askew, the anticipation I'd felt fell flat. No photo of Amanda snorting drugs in a hotel room? No surreptitiously snapped pics of her kissing a mystery man? But once I read the documents, I understood why Marcus had smugly assumed my gratitude. It was a marriage and divorce certificate, the latter dated barely a year after the former. Amanda, according to the documents, had a brief, secret marriage in her past.

"What's up?" Jocelyn asked, noticing as I leaned forward to squint at my screen.

"I heard back from Marcus."

"Ooh, what is it? Did he find something for Project Black Lagoon? Who's in trouble? It's Tom Brady, isn't it?"

"No," I said. "It's not for Project Black Lagoon. It's about Amanda Myles."

Hearing Amanda's name, Yenay's face popped up over her computer. She had seemed more like herself that night, chipper, softly singing a Taylor Swift song under her breath as she worked, but now her glow was gone. The words *Amanda Myles* still triggered something in her.

Jocelyn got up and came over to my desk, speed-reading the text over my shoulder.

"Amanda had a secret marriage," I said aloud for the benefit of Yenay and Chris, though Chris didn't even look up, apparently too engrossed in the article he was writing about Pierre, a "horny and lonely" dolphin seen rubbing himself on boats and kayaks and being a general menace to tourists in a French beach town. ("People love stories about randy animals," David had said when he emailed me the link to the dolphin story. I couldn't help wondering how he'd found it.)

"She married someone named Alexander Casteliani in 2001, then divorced him in 2002."

"Look," Jocelyn said, touching a finger to the screen. "It says they got married in Vegas."

I looked closer. It was true. Amanda had married some guy in Vegas, only to file to divorce him just over a year later. It gave the impression of a decision made spontaneously, only to be quickly regretted.

"Now, that's a headline," Jocelyn said. *"Amanda Myles's secret Vegas wedding.* Juicy!"

Yenay still looked uneasy, rattled, the mention of Amanda cuing her nervous system to press the panic button, but I could see the cogs turning in her mind as her journalistic curiosity got the better of her. She couldn't help herself.

"It's definitely not been reported before?" she asked. "What's the guy's name?"

"Alexander Casteliani," I said, spelling out his last name.

"There's nothing about it online, not that I can see," she said after a minute. "Amanda has had a few relationships, but there's nothing on a marriage or a wedding. She kept this quiet."

"What happens in Vegas," Jocelyn said with a cluck of her tongue. "A girl I know made out with her friend's *mom* at a bachelorette weekend in Vegas. It tore the whole group apart."

An awkward silence fell over us, none of us sure how to respond.

"The divorce happened in 2002, right?" Yenay asked. "Isn't that the year the Valentines went on the 'hiatus' they never returned from? That must have been a rough time for Amanda."

Jocelyn gasped. "Wait! What if the two things are connected, this lightning-fast marriage and divorce and the end of the band? It's too much of a coincidence for them not to be, right?"

"Look out, everyone, it's Woodward and Bernstein," Chris said drily.

"What?" Jocelyn shot back at Chris, arms crossed. "People have a right to know," she said, like we had received the tip about dangerously high lead levels found in the water supply in Flint, Michigan. I knew that to argue public interest in the instance of a washed-up pop star's marriage from more than a decade ago was a stretch. And yet I felt it—the jittery alertness, the slight uptick of the beat of my pulse, the feeling I always got when I knew something was a story. My excitement, I knew, was also at the prospect of finally bringing David a follow-up article on Amanda, who was still keeping a low profile, despite the best efforts of the paparazzi.

Jocelyn went back to her seat and began searching image libraries for photos of anyone named Alexander Casteliani, and for photos of Amanda from 2001 and 2002, especially any taken in Las Vegas. Yenay put Alexander's name into LexisNexis, the main database we used to find contact details, and began combing the results of anyone with the name. I trawled the archives of *The New York Times* and *Rolling Stone*, scanning old articles about Amanda and the Valentines for a mention of a husband, or a Vegas wedding, that would be too old to show up in a Google search. We carried on like that throughout the night, stopping only to publish a few other stories so that David, who monitored the website from home, wouldn't call up and, once again, accuse us of being on strike. (The biggest story of the night was the news that Nicole Kidman's emotional-support cockatoo, Maude, had pecked co-star Jeff Bridges in the eye on a film set in Atlanta, and producers were scrambling to write a believable reason for Jeff's character to wear an eye patch into the script. David claimed to have a hunch that Maude was in the country illegally, and had Yenay contact US Fish and Wildlife to get to the bottom of it.)

It was almost eleven o'clock when I found it. An article from July 1998 about an East Coast storm causing chaos for the summer music festival circuit.

The Valentines' manager, Alexander Casteliani, said the group would reschedule, read a line at the bottom of the article.

But I'd come across a mention of the Valentines' band manager, at some point, and it was someone with a different name. I clicked through my browser tabs to find the right article. *A.C. Williams*. It took a moment for me to notice. *A.C. Alexander Casteliani*. He'd used a different name for his manager work, which is why his name didn't show up in Google. But in the instance of this one *New York Times* article, his legal name *was* used. Found him. Jackpot.

"He was her manager," I said to the others, not believing my eyes. "Alexander was the Valentines' manager—at least he was in the late nineties."

"Wait, what?" Jocelyn said, slamming a hand on her desk. "He was her *manager*?"

"And," Yenay said, standing up and presenting a notepad with a list of names in messy handwriting, all of them crossed out except two, "I think I have his number. I've found two Alexander Castelianis who are the right age and living in the Los Angeles area, which would make sense for someone in the music business. One of them has got to be him, right?"

Jocelyn was almost feverish. "What are you waiting for?" she said. "Call him, now!"

A dryness in my throat, then. I hadn't expected to home in on Amanda's ex so quickly.

"It's almost eleven o'clock," I said. "Isn't it a bit late to call?"

"If he's in Los Angeles, it's only eight p.m. there," Jocelyn replied quickly.

But there was no point debating it—Yenay was already dialing a number. Someone answered. I heard her say she was calling from *The Scoop* and ask to speak to Alexander Casteliani. Then she asked if she had the right person: the Valentines' former manager.

"Hi, Alexander," she said, flashing a quick smile and a thumbs-up at us before returning her focus to her screen, the receiver squashed between her chin and her shoulder. "Thanks for taking my call. I'm hoping you can help me confirm some details for a story I'm writing…"

Jocelyn leaned across the desk, wiggled her brows at me. "This is big," she whispered, since Yenay was on the phone. "We might be able to give David an Amanda follow-up tonight."

I'd been caught up in the thrill of putting together the pieces of the story, excited at the prospect of finally uncovering something substantial to report on Amanda, just like David wanted. But now, with Yenay on the phone to Alexander, and Jocelyn saying we might be able to publish the scoop on Amanda's secret Vegas marriage *that night*, I started to get cold feet.

"Tonight? No, for something this big we should seek comment from Amanda first."

I cringed, recalling Amanda's rep's biting reply from last time: *Don't contact me again unless it's a genuine attempt at journalism.* The thought of contacting her again sickened me. I'd make Yenay do it.

"Why?" Jocelyn asked.

"Why? Because it's a big story about her personal life. She deserves a right of reply."

"But we won't be able to get ahold of her this late."

"Exactly, so we'll publish tomorrow. It's an exclusive. It's not like anyone can beat us to it."

"But, Frankie—"

Yenay hung up the phone and jumped to her feet.

"Alexander confirmed it. They married in Vegas after a Valentines gig—a spur-of-the-moment decision. He said the marriage was a last-ditch attempt to save their relationship."

"He told you that?" Jocelyn said. "Just now? What else did he say?"

Yenay beamed with the particular pride of a journalist that had just landed a scoop, her cheeks aglow with a post-orgasm flush, like any second she might light and smoke a cigarette.

"He said Amanda was"—she leaned down to read notes off her screen—"inappropriately close with a member of the band—he refused to say who—and even after they got married, it continued. He strongly suspects there was an affair going on. He used the word 'infidelity.' He said once their relationship ended, the Valentines was never going to survive."

"He really told you all this?" I couldn't help asking. It wasn't that I didn't believe Yenay—I didn't think she was making it up. But I was thrown by how fast it was all happening.

Yenay gave an awkward laugh. "Let's just say, if you hint to a man that people might think he's, um, 'not very big' or has 'problems' in the bedroom, he *will* give you the real story."

Chris had been joking when he compared Jocelyn and Yenay to Woodward and Bernstein, teasing them for acting like they were on the verge of uncovering the next Watergate (though such a "scandal" would barely raise an eyebrow in the freaky, twisted, utterly demented circus that was the twenty-four-hour social media–driven news cycle), but Yenay's read on Alexander, her ability to detect and leverage his insecurities to make him tell her what she wanted to know, was genius. I was surprised—and impressed. I hadn't known Yenay had it in her to be so sneaky and strategic in service of a scoop. It signaled a strong, natural journalistic instinct. I was sure she would make a great celebrity-profile writer someday, as she dreamed of being, a defiant rebuke of Patrick's doubt a tabloid reporter could get out of the game, get clean.

"Anyway," Yenay continued, "Alexander said we can use everything he shared with me as long as we don't use his real name. He asked to be called 'an insider close to the band.'"

"Yenay, this is incredible," Jocelyn said. "Let's publish the story tonight!"

At that moment, I thought of Amanda. I wondered what she was doing right then, perhaps watching TV, soaking in the tub, or in bed, believing that surely the glare of the public spotlight had moved on. Oblivious that at that moment, a group of scoop-thirsty tabloid journalists was uncovering her decade-old secret marriage and divorce, all thanks to a shady private investigator. As for me, I felt desperately torn. I wanted to make David happy, and for Yenay to receive the praise she deserved for scoring a scoop. But I was still the journalist I'd been at *Marie Claire*, even though I'd long since been kicked out of that office. It was wrong, I knew, unfair, to publish only one side of the story— Alexander's side—without giving Amanda the chance to give hers.

THE SCOOP

"Yenay, this is great work," I said. "But we can't allow someone's aggrieved ex-husband to use *The Scoop* as a mouthpiece to say whatever he wants without checking the veracity of his claims, especially an allegation as serious as infidelity. We have to seek comment from Amanda first and give her a reasonable amount of time to respond. You want to do this the right way, don't you?"

Yenay had been beaming, but now her face was creased with worry, no doubt recalling the people online who called for her death over the first Amanda story. I knew she understood, knew she didn't want to prove right the trolls who said she was nothing but a worthless hack.

Jocelyn started to laugh.

"Frankie, you know we can't do that. Sit on a scoop like *this*? If David finds out, he'll have a conniption. We publish tonight, request a comment, and add it once she gets back to us."

I tried to stand my ground. "An anonymous source—who we know is biased—has accused her of infidelity, leading not only to the end of her marriage but possibly the end of a beloved band. We can't publish one side of this story without at least *trying* to get the other."

"Call David," Jocelyn said, pointing at my phone. I could see she was upset, her apple cheeks reddening, her voice high and tight. It felt like the Amanda groceries article night all over again, when we'd argued about the right angle for the story, except this time she wasn't backing down. We were locked in a stalemate. "Call him, now. I'm telling you that's what he'll say."

Before I could argue back, Jocelyn jumped up, came over to my desk, picked up the receiver of my phone, and pressed the speed-dial to call David. She put him on speakerphone.

"Mmmpphhh?" was all we heard when it picked up. It sounded like David was eating.

Jocelyn stabbed a finger at the phone, urging me to start talking. I'd been cornered.

"Um, David? It's Frankie," I began, stumbling over my words. "You're on speaker."

"Hmmph? Yes, I'm here, what is it?" He sounded irritated. I thought I heard chewing.

Begrudgingly, shooting daggers at Jocelyn the whole time, I told David what the private investigator had found, the marriage certificate and divorce papers. I told him about the anonymous quotes from Amanda's ex. When I was finished, David erupted with pure glee.

"Brilliant!" he cried. "Absolutely brilliant. I knew that sneaky woman was hiding something. There's got to be some photos of her trashy secret wedding out there somewhere. Tell Marcus to keep digging."

Jocelyn jumped in. "We'll look into it. Also, David, Frankie's asking if we should wait to publish," she said, "to give Amanda a chance to respond first. She said it's not 'fair' to her."

I felt my face burn hot with embarrassment. I could have slapped Jocelyn. What she said was, technically, correct, but the way she phrased it... I knew she was trying to make me look bad in front of David.

David scoffed and spluttered down the line.

"Wait? Why on God's green earth would we *wait*? We can't be beholden to a washed-up pop star getting back to us whenever she damn well feels like it. Give her rep a heads-up tonight, but it's on *them* to keep up with *us*. I want something live as soon as possible. Within the hour."

Within the hour? Amanda would be totally blindsided. I knew how that felt; the most painful moments of my own life—my mother's death, the balled-up note in the clean laundry—were precisely so painful because they seemed to come out of nowhere, with no warning. The shock, the having not seen it coming, seemed to amplify the pain tenfold. I knew it was important for us to publish exclusives, and to move fast, but this just felt so... cowardly. Unethical. I looked around at the others, to see if anyone else was going to speak up. But Yenay was too junior, Chris was too cynical, and Jocelyn was too stubborn. I racked my brain, wondering what I could say to slow, if not stop, this. The only thing I could think of was to voice concern for Yenay, who had suffered torrents of online abuse over the first story about Amanda.

"David," I said, venturing cautiously, "my main concern here is for Yenay. The online abuse she received after the first story was disgusting, and I'm just wondering if we should—"

"So why don't you write it, Frankie?" Jocelyn said. I looked up at her. She flashed a saccharine smile, too sickly sweet to be genuine.

"Yes, brilliant idea," David chimed in. "I think it's good for editors to write every now and then, so they don't lose touch with what they expect from their reporters." I thought I heard something slyly teasing in his voice. "As long as you don't have a problem with that, Yenay?"

I looked at Yenay, willing her to claim her exclusive, to insist she wanted to write the story, but she shook her head. For a moment, I was surprised—she'd been so excited about it—but I realized she was smart enough not to pointlessly incur David's wrath. Plus, if *The Scoop* received criticism over our new Amanda Myles story, this time she wouldn't be the prime target.

"Fine with me," Yenay said quietly.

"That's settled, then," David said. "Now, since we've wasted all this time dithering, I want it live in half an hour."

"Half an hour?" I said, unable to hide my growing panic.

"Yes, Francesca," David said, warning in his voice. "If it's not in the splash in thirty minutes, I'll assume you are no longer interested in doing your job, and I'll have security come and escort you from the building."

Before I could reply, he hung up.

I stared at the phone in shock, the dial tone bleating until Jocelyn placed the receiver back in the cradle. I couldn't look at her, or at Chris or Yenay. I knew I had lost.

"Hello?" Jocelyn said, waving a hand in front of my face. "Did you not hear him? He said if it's not live in half an hour you're getting fired. And possibly manhandled by security."

"David wasn't being serious, though," I said. "About calling security. Like you said, sometimes people here say things in the heat of the moment, but they don't really mean it."

"Are you willing to take the risk? You now have"—she checked her wrist—"twenty-nine minutes."

The grim realization rose like a blood moon: my byline was about to appear on *The Scoop*. Either that, or I walked out. Quit on the spot. But I'd given too much by then to give up.

"Send me Alexander's quotes, Yenay," I said, accepting my fate. "As quickly as you can."

I started writing.

13

EXCLUSIVE: Amanda Myles' secret Vegas wedding! Marriage to the Valentines' band manager revealed as insider says side fling with fellow band member destroyed short-lived nuptials

By Francesca Miller

They were one of the most beloved pop-rock bands of the '90s, breaking the hearts of millions after going on indefinite "hiatus" only to never record another song again.

Now *The Scoop* can exclusively reveal the real reason behind the end of the Valentines: a secret marriage and a love triangle — with none other than the band's lead singer, Amanda Myles, at the center.

According to documents obtained exclusively by *The Scoop*, Amanda, now 42, married the Valentines' band manager, Alexander Casteliani, in 2001 (less than a year before the band's announcement of an indefinite hiatus in early 2002) in a secret Las Vegas wedding ceremony.

But the pair's honeymoon period was short-lived, with the couple filing for divorce just six months after tying the knot. And according to an insider who spoke to *The Scoop* on condition of anonymity, the main reason for the split was Amanda's "inappropriately close" relationship with an unnamed Valentines band member. The pair's flirting was "relentless," with some questioning why Amanda started dating Alexander in the first place, given the intense chemistry with her bandmate.

"There was always sexual tension and lots of flirting between Amanda and this other band member — even more than what you'd expect from two people who wrote and performed music together," the insider said. "Everyone thought it would stop once Amanda and Alexander got together, but it didn't, and it drove him crazy. The marriage was a Band-Aid. It didn't work."

It's understood Amanda and Alexander — who was 14 years her senior — made the decision to marry spontaneously after a Valentines show in Las Vegas, a last-ditch attempt to cement their status as an exclusive couple and put an end to the feelings between Amanda and the "other man."

But it didn't work. Amanda kept up her "relentless flirting" and close "friendship" after the wedding, and for Alexander, seeing Amanda behave like a lovestruck teen, whether backstage or in front of a crowd of thousands, became too much, and they called it quits.

The love triangle was "absolutely a factor" in the band's decision to go on hiatus.

THE SCOOP

"After Amanda and Alexander's split, things got really messy. Alexander stayed on as manager, but Amanda refused to be in the same room with him. How can a group survive when the lead singer can't even hold a conversation with the manager? It drove a wedge in the band, communication broke down and they never recovered. Instead of making music, all they did was fight."

Despite persistent rumors that Amanda Myles would release a solo album, the singer disappeared from public life and has not recorded since. After over a decade of obscurity, the very private Myles was recently seen shopping near her home in New York City's West Village neighborhood, the star showcasing a fuller figure.

The Scoop has contacted a representative for comment.

14

Alone in the bathroom after publishing the article, I stood and stared at myself in the mirror.

In movies when people splash their face with water, the pink leaves their cheeks, and they look soothed, refreshed. But after I turned on the faucet, bent over the sink, and scooped the cool stream onto my face, I inspected my reflection to see I had mascara, black and mucky, clumped beneath my eyes, dark streaks down my cheeks. The cheap paper towel I used to try to wipe it off disintegrated, leaving a faint dusty white residue. I looked eerily like the mug shot of a woman in a recent crime story, a kid's party clown charged with child endangerment after showing up drunk to a fifth birthday party and dangling one of the kids over a balcony railing. I was not drunk, nor had I endangered the lives of any children, but I did feel like a clown.

When I took the job at *The Scoop*, I'd believed that as an editor, I would not have to write articles, that my byline would never appear on anything. This would mean that hardly anyone, save for a few close friends, would ever know I'd worked there, and I'd avoid sullying the Google search results of my name with the stains of a tacky tabloid.

I wouldn't leave a trace. I understood now how foolish I had been to think I'd get in and out unscathed. My name, the one my mother gave me, was on a story revealing Amanda Myles's secret marriage, alleging without basis it was the reason for the breakup of the Valentines, and littered with anonymous accusations by her bitter ex-husband, without giving her a chance to respond before publication.

Dishonest. Dirty.

I'd asked if I could use a generic byline—"by a *Scoop* reporter," or something like that—but Jocelyn informed me (with unconcealed pleasure) that David didn't allow generic bylines. *A reporter should stand by their work*, was his view. It appeared not to matter that I'd written the article under duress, had been threatened with being fired and carried out by security if I refused.

How had I fallen so far?

Publishing Amanda's ex-husband's claims without checking if they were true made me feel disgusted with myself. I could imagine what Josh would say about me if he was given the chance to tell his side of our breakup unchecked by a tabloid reporter. I shuddered to think what my father would say about my mother if given the same opportunity. A man will cling insistently to a convenient narrative when he has caused a woman harm but also hopes to sleep at night.

Strange, for my father to be on my mind in that dimly lit office bathroom after midnight. But then it was just the sort of place the ghost of him would find me. I thought of how he made my mom feel powerless, first with his cruel words and explosive rages, and then by leaving her to raise me alone. The particular sting of marrying her, only to rob her of what a husband was supposed to be—supportive, caring, loving—and then leaving the first chance he got, treating her like a used scrap to be discarded, headed somewhere warmer to start over, begin anew. Was I still angry about it? Or was it really about Josh and Miss America? I didn't know anymore.

A flash of memory: my college graduation ceremony, striding across the stage to accept my diploma, looking into the crowd expecting to see, on instinct, the face of my mother. But there was only my aunt and uncle from California, who had insisted on coming to stand in her place. I was struck at that moment by a profound ache in my chest, like a bolt of lightning from above straight to my heart, cracking it open, oozing a kind of cosmic love into my veins. I promised my mother then, just in case she was listening, that I was going to do the only thing that could make this right. I was going to build the kind of life no one could take from me. I would not end up powerless and alone in the shade of the mountain. I would do it for both of us.

I couldn't turn back now. My dirty secret was out, my name right there on the home page of *The Scoop* for all to see. I couldn't undo my decision to take the job, to walk into that building, to do the things I'd done. Audrey called it reckless, joining Johnson News, but she didn't get it, never would. I decided I no longer cared what Audrey, or strangers on the internet, or anyone else thought of me. I'd do whatever it took to survive, like I always had. I was the girl who put the handbrake down and rolled. I would get a job at *Business Day*. And to do that, I knew, I'd have to do whatever David wanted. I'd have to think like him, be as ruthless as him. *Be* him. Besides, what did I have to lose anyway? Now that my name was attached to a sleazy tabloid article, all other doors back to honorable publications had closed—at least according to Patrick and Audrey. All except for one: *Business Day*, through the secret back passageway I had discovered, via David's influence at Johnson News. It was all I had left. The only way out.

And then, once I proved myself at *Business Day*, my reputation restored, who knew? *The New York Times* or maybe even *The Washington Post*? Journalists at *Business Day* made that leap all the time. Or maybe I could worm my way into CNN or MSNBC, become a foreign correspondent, report live from a war zone. Far enough away from gunfire so as not to be in any real physical danger, of course, not close enough for a bullet to whiz right by my head, but still required to wear one of those serious PRESS flak jackets and a helmet so I could pose for some photos, which I would then post online for my college peers to see, especially the ones who chose to go into PR or communications, smug in the proof I was one of the ones who made it.

Or maybe that wasn't what I wanted anymore, especially if it meant spending my days surrounded by the Patricks of the world. For as much as Johnson News deserved all the criticism and scorn it received, it was undeniable that at Johnson News you could come from nowhere and make something of yourself. You didn't have to use the word *summer* as a verb, didn't have to know your way around the Hamptons or Nantucket, didn't have to play tennis or ski in the right places with the right people, didn't have to play tennis or ski at all. All you had to do was work hard, and hard work was a language I understood. Despite how much the industry at large loathed Johnson News, there was undeniably serious power in the halls of that building. *Business Day*, America Now, a posting in London, big money and influence in corporate. I imagined myself boarding a helicopter at a pad on the East River, flying to the Johnson family mansion upstate for a meeting of top editors, a member of Walter Johnson's inner circle, just like David.

Then I had a thought that made me laugh, grin wide in the mirror: I could work my way up at *Business Day* until I was even more senior and respected at Johnson News than *David* was. I imagined myself calling him, complaining about something on *The Scoop*, telling him to sort it out, hanging up without a word. Another fantasy: Patrick accosting me outside the Johnson News building one day as I come out of the revolving doors and head to my chauffeured car, a huge black SUV that was to take me to a private airport, headed somewhere important for something important. Patrick asking if I remembered him, if we could have coffee, the weasel wanting something from me now that I called big shots at Johnson News and half the media outlets we'd once known had been killed off. I imagined telling him to call me, brushing him off as he says, *But I don't have your number*, the car door slamming in his face, Patrick with his hands pressed against the window, unable to see through the tint before the car drives off, that dumb skinny food-stained scarf probably still hanging from his stupid skinny neck. Yet another scene: I imagine my father learning of my success and emailing me to ask for money. I never reply.

I smiled bigger and wider still in the mirror, as unnatural as it looked and felt. I worked harder than everyone else, and I wanted it more than anyone else. This, I believed, was enough.

15

THE NEXT AFTERNOON, WALKING TO the subway, fall had arrived; there was enough of a chill in the air for me to wrestle my coat from the back of my closet and brush off the mothballs. The change of season came as a welcome relief. All through the summer, the sting of losing my job at *Marie Claire*, the pain and grief from the breakup with Josh still fresh, tender, had made me feel like I'd had a protective layer peeled off my skin: raw, sensitive, exposed. Out of sync with the joy I saw around me; the tinkling music of ice cream trucks on street corners, children running under the spray of open fire hydrants, couples kissing on picnic blankets in Prospect Park. I'd convinced myself strangers could sense my gloom amid the revelry; I was the Grim Reaper, ambling down the Coney Island boardwalk, black robes flapping in the salty ocean breeze.

But now, as I passed the Halloween decorations beginning to appear out front of the buildings of Prospect Heights, clusters of jack-o'-lanterns with wide grins on stoops, huge black spiders and their webs covering the fronts of brownstones, fake plastic skeleton hands reaching out of the soil in garden beds, I had the feeling that, finally, things were getting better. I'd been carried by a new surge of energy in recent days, and it wasn't just the humidity leaving the air.

The article about Amanda Myles's secret Las Vegas wedding, and the claim it led to the end of the Valentines, had gone viral, having been picked up by the *New York Post* and *People*, as well as a few music news websites: *Rolling Stone*, *Pitchfork*, *Spin*, and *Billboard*. The lack of solid reporting underpinning the story—the whole thing based on the claims of one "insider" who refused to go on the record—was overlooked by the reporters who wrote these articles, frantic workers on the churnalism assembly line who needed to sling their own content as fast as possible to get their clicks, hit their targets, and move on to the next, trying not to break under the feverish, relentless pace journalists a decade earlier couldn't have imagined, surely would have rioted over. And so, the claims, dubious as they were, repeated enough times, reported by enough different publications, morphed from rumor to truth. The legitimizing of the story helped me forget about the journalistic ethics I'd compromised to publish it. It felt good, the forgetting.

That wasn't all. I had a meeting scheduled with Peter Lowell, managing editor at *Business Day*. Just as I'd hoped, David had emailed Peter, cc'ing me, asking if he was available to meet "one of the brightest stars at *The Scoop*" for coffee, to give me the "inside word" on *Business Day*. We were to meet the following Monday at eight a.m. at the Le Pain Quotidien across the street from Johnson News. I balked at the early hour—I'd be lucky if I got three hours' sleep that night—but a *Scoop* editor, even "one of the brightest stars," wasn't in a position to negotiate with the managing editor of *Business Day*. It was a miracle it was happening at all.

I'll be there! I look forward to meeting you, Peter, I replied, standing on the subway platform, debating the exclamation mark for a neurotic amount of time. *Would it make me seem unserious?* I wondered, before deciding that I worked at *The Scoop*, so there was no point trying to pretend to be anything *but* unserious. Besides, people tend to respect you more for owning what you are rather than trying to be something you're not. This briefly seemed to me an enlightened thought, something I should perhaps write down, until it occurred to me it was not; I was just sleep deprived and had been spending nine-plus hours a day consuming the dumbest content on the internet, waterboarding my brain nightly with digital sludge in a slot-machine fugue. I made a mental note to buy a brain-health supplement, something with B vitamins, omega-3 fatty acids, and ginkgo biloba, and to start playing one of those games that are supposed to strengthen your memory, like sudoku, or whatever. A mental note I immediately forgot.

When I got to the office, a few minutes late, the others were already there. I could tell right away something was up. Jocelyn was on the phone, saying, "Yes, okay, wow, I'm so sorry."

I mouthed, *What happened?* at Chris and Yenay, but they just shook their heads and shrugged, in the dark as much as I was. The wait felt interminable until Jocelyn at last hung up.

"Amanda punched a pap."

"What?" I nearly shouted. I swiveled my chair to face Jocelyn, who appeared grave.

"No way," Yenay said slowly, taking in the news. Chris let out a long, low whistle.

"Just now? Where?" I asked, just as Yenay blurted, "Has she been arrested?"

Jocelyn took a deep breath, held her hands up to quiet us, and started from the beginning. That morning, David had asked the photo agencies to send any paparazzi they could spare to Amanda's place, promising *The Scoop* would pay any price for exclusive photos of her in the wake of last night's article. Amanda hid inside most of the day, the only sign she was home the occasional rustling of an upstairs curtain. And then, a little before five o'clock, the paps showing no signs of leaving, she emerged. Dressed in a plain white T-shirt, sweatpants, and sunglasses, barefoot, she came out into the courtyard just beyond her front door and began asking the paparazzi to leave. It was clear she was upset. But the paparazzi weren't about to leave; they were finally seeing some action after an excruciatingly dull day of waiting. And so, the paps burst into action, snapping pictures madly, jostling to get closer to Amanda, shutters clicking, the bright white of their flashing bulbs blinding. Each member of the pack so determined to beat the others to the best shot, to secure a higher pay day, that soon the group was pushing forward as one wild, erratic organism, a terrifying hydra, moving from the sidewalk into the courtyard of Amanda's property, surrounding her. Amanda pointed and screamed at them to leave, threatened to call the cops—they were trespassing—but it did nothing to deter the paps, now in a frenzy, the value of the pictures only growing higher the more visibly distressed and enraged she became.

What happened next unfolded in a matter of seconds. Camera bulbs still flashing, one of the paps called out to Amanda, asking if it was true she was an unfaithful cheater. She snapped. It didn't matter who said it; she grabbed the pap closest to her and tried to take his camera, and a struggle ensued. That was when Amanda hit him. In seconds, some of the other paps, looking out for one of their own, were dragging him back to the sidewalk as Amanda disappeared inside.

As Jocelyn told the story, I felt lightly nauseous, as at the very top of a roller coaster before the plunge. Amanda had been provoked to violence by a question about the allegations in our story the night before, about her secret Vegas wedding and her ex's cheating claims, by a paparazzo staking out her house, motivated by the money we'd pay for new photos of her. On some level I noticed this, the crashing domino effect of Marcus's discovery to this troubling development, but there were so many questions firing rapidly in my mind, I couldn't dwell on it.

"How do you know all this?" I asked when Jocelyn was done. "Who was that on the phone?"

"The paparazzo she punched," Jocelyn replied. "He's sending the shots over as we speak. He said he's got a close-up of Amanda looking like a wild beast going in for the kill. He's going to make us pay through the nose for these, but who can blame him? He did take a hit to get them. He deserves to buy himself a strong drink—and possibly a visit to urgent care," she quipped.

"Is he hurt?" I asked.

"Nah. He's just a bit shaken up."

I was aware that we were, yet again, only getting one side of the story. *Of course* the paparazzo would say Amanda "punched" him. But what if he was exaggerating, even just a bit?

"She definitely punched him?" I asked. "Socked him one right in the jaw, or the nose?"

Jocelyn exhaled sharply. "Amanda hit his face with her hand," she said, irritated by the question; I wasn't sure why. "Was her fist technically open or closed? I don't know. Does it matter? She physically attacked a dude just doing his job. It was violent—and uncalled for."

Yenay cleared her throat. "There's got to be dozens, if not hundreds, of photos of the moment, right? We'll be able to tell from the pictures if she full-on punched him or not."

"Is he pressing charges?" Chris asked.

"I doubt he will," Jocelyn said. "The cops don't have a whole lot of sympathy for the paparazzi. I think Amanda would have to shoot him before he considered involving the police."

When the photos came in, Yenay and I huddled around Jocelyn's computer, analyzing them like a touchdown replay. In the clearest shot of the incident, Amanda's hand was half open, half closed as it connected with the pap's cheek. It was difficult to tell if she was intentionally trying to hurt him or only trying to push him away, since they were locked in a scuffle after she'd latched on to his camera. What *was* clear was that Amanda was out of control. She looked almost deranged, her face red and contorted with rage. No one in their right mind would behave like that, and for the first time I considered her mental state, wondered if perhaps she wasn't well. But the thought was quickly overshadowed. The photos were gold. Traffic gold.

"Amanda Myles punches pap—this is going to *explode*," I said as I went back to my desk to get to work, my mind already churning with possible headlines, considering which pics would look best in the splash. I asked Jocelyn to cut a custom image that showed the three most shocking shots, with a cropped-in close-up of Amanda's hand connecting with the pap's face.

"Maybe we can find some witnesses to confirm what actually happened," Yenay suggested, still standing beside Jocelyn's desk but now turned to face me. "The other paparazzi will side with their own, of course. But maybe a neighbor, or a nearby business owner, saw."

"There's no time," I said. "A dozen paps were there, who are on the phone right now selling their pics. We have half an hour, tops, before the story breaks. We need to publish now."

"But shouldn't we call it a 'physical incident' or a 'scuffle' until we can gather all the details? You can see as well as I can that she might be pushing him away because she's scared."

"If you think David isn't going to call up and bite my head off when he sees a weak headline like that, while our competitors, I guarantee you, will call it a punch, then I have to wonder if you've been paying attention, Yenay. If we're wrong, we'll correct it later, okay?"

I didn't mean to sound as harsh as I knew I did, but we didn't have time to equivocate, and Yenay was slowing us down. I didn't look up from my screen to see what she thought of my blunt response to her concerns. Out of the corner of my eye, I saw Jocelyn glance in my direction, her eyes lingering on me for a moment before turning back to her screen. I knew what she was thinking. It wasn't long ago that I would have agreed with Yenay. I would have been insisting that we exercise caution, refrain from claiming Amanda punched anyone until we had all the facts. But after a few weeks at *The Scoop*, I was starting to understand that we couldn't lose. All we had to do was put the word *punched* in quotation marks in the headline and say Amanda *allegedly* punched him—because the pap had alleged it—and our asses were covered. Like always, we would seek comment from my biggest fan, Amanda's rep, Alice. And if it turned out Amanda had not punched the pap, that perhaps it was an accidental knock as they tussled, we'd report that, too. But for now, there was nothing to stop us from reporting it and bringing in hundreds of thousands, even millions, of clicks, from making the green arrows soar.

"I'll get started, then," Yenay said stoically, stuffing down her dissent as she returned to her desk, fingers poised at her keyboard, ready to write the copy. But that wouldn't be necessary.

"You know what?" I said. "I'm going to handle this one."

Yenay snapped up to look at me, waiting for me to explain why she would not be writing it. But I didn't have to explain. I was the boss. I refused to look at her even as I felt her staring.

It was unorthodox, to write it myself instead of assigning it to Yenay. But I wanted the story done right. Plus, why should Yenay get the recognition from David and the Man Upstairs? Before, I'd been afraid to have my name on *The Scoop*, but then it happened, and the sky hadn't fallen. Besides, where had doing things the "right" way gotten me? Sure, in the magazine world I'd worked my way up slowly, patiently, with integrity, and I'd become someone reasonably important. But as I'd so brutally learned, the magazine world was a bubble—a bubble soon to burst into nothing. I'd been wrong, thinking *patience* or *integrity* would get me anywhere. It was better to be seen, at any cost, than to be unknown, irrelevant. Fart Jar Girl had taught me that.

I hoped Audrey was seeing my bylines on *The Scoop*, and that smarmy human toothbrush Patrick, too. Forget "still Sandy." I'd crossed over to the dark side, and I was beginning to like it.

16

AMANDA MYLES 'PUNCHES' PAP! Troubled Valentines frontwoman allegedly assaults photographer outside her West Village home in chaotic scene following bombshell reports of a secret marriage and explosive cheating claims

By Francesca Miller

Shocking images have captured the moment Amanda Myles allegedly punched a photographer outside her New York City home Wednesday evening, as the singer's personal life continues to spiral.

Paparazzo Anthony Lopez, 32, was on the job snapping shots of the Valentines frontwoman when the beloved '90s star emerged from her home and reportedly asked the paps to leave.

A witness said Myles, 42, was infuriated by the presence of the paps and began a heated verbal exchange with Lopez. As pictures of the dramatic scene show, a scuffle ensued, in which Myles appeared to grab Lopez by the collar in an attempt to take his camera. Moments later, Myles appeared to hit Lopez on the left side of his face. Other members of the paparazzi dragged Lopez to safety.

"I think he would have ended up in the hospital if he hadn't been pulled away from her," an eyewitness, who asked not to be named, told *The Scoop*. "That lady was out for blood."

Lopez, a married father of two from Queens who has worked as a professional photographer for 10 years, said he does not intend to press charges against Myles. It's unclear if police are investigating the incident. *The Scoop* has reached out to the NYPD and Myles for comment.

Myles, the voice behind the '90s hits "American Bitch" and "Almost There," has been back in the spotlight recently following troubles in her personal life. Fans expressed shock after she was seen looking unrecognizable, showcasing a fuller figure, with some saying she looked "weary" and "haggard" compared to her days as a hitmaker. She has also been the subject of cheating rumors, after an insider close to the band claimed Myles married her manager, Alexander Casteliani, in Vegas in 2001 and that Myles' infidelity led to their divorce — and the eventual demise of the band.

Myles has not commented on the reports; her rep has not responded to multiple media requests.

17

I WOKE UP WITH THE TASTE of Ring Dings on my lips, chocolate crumbs and vanilla frosting smeared on my face. My bedsheets felt gritty. Through bleary eyes, I counted the signs of disorder: the empty wine bottle and purple-stained glass on my nightstand, the closet door ajar, a chaotic tangle of clothes, shoes, spilling out like a landslide. A disaster, all of my own making.

It was past noon. I lay there, eyeing a smooshed Ring Ding on my pillow, until the memories came. The green pill Jocelyn had pressed into my hand as we left the newsroom, the one I'd asked for because I was so wired I feared I wouldn't be able to sleep at all. The deserted city out the window on the ride home, neon lights shining orange and green against shuttered metal roller doors. A spontaneous decision, spacey from the pill, to ask the driver to pull over and let me out three blocks early at the twenty-four-hour bodega, where I'd roamed the crammed aisles under yellow lights before taking an armful of snacks to the counter, paying for my goods under the watchful eye of a cat perched atop the newspaper stacks. I didn't need to read the headlines.

In bed, uncorking some wine I'd found in the cupboard (Patti's—I added it to my secret tab), tearing open the Ring Dings and salt-and-vinegar chips, stuffing fistfuls into my mouth, gulping merlot, I'd read my story about Amanda's paparazzi fight over and over, refreshing Google to see the results as news outlets around the world covered the story, *my* story, drunk on the power (also, just drunk). I'd been nominated for awards, written magazine cover stories, but it all paled in comparison to the high of my story exploding across the world, urgent, infinite.

I reached for my phone and turned off Do Not Disturb. Notifications poured in.

Jocelyn: "Not a punch"—LOL whatever you say, bitch!!

Yenay: This is getting out of hand—you okay?

Twitter: You have 37 new mentions!

My booze-broken brain struggled to make sense of the scattered jigsaw puzzle pieces. What had I missed? I googled Amanda's name. The first result was a link to an article on *People*.

> **EXCLUSIVE: Amanda Myles paparazzi 'punch': Star blasts 'tabloid lies,' says incident was 'misreported'**

I sat upright, ignoring the steadily worsening pain in my head, a seasick feeling swirling through me, the hangover or anxiety or both, I wasn't sure. A pit of dread in my stomach, I clicked the headline. A few paragraphs led into a statement from Amanda. I saw that it was long.

> I don't usually comment on articles written about me, but I want to correct false accounts of an incident that took place between myself and a photographer outside my home on Thursday.

THE SCOOP

The claim made by *The Scoop* website (which has since been covered by many others) that I "punched" a photographer is blatantly false. I would like to clarify what really happened.

At the time of the incident, at least 10 members of the paparazzi were loitering on the sidewalk outside my home, blocking foot traffic and causing such a disruptive, intimidating presence it made entering or exiting impossible. After 10 hours of nonstop surveillance by the paparazzi, I came out of my front door and asked politely for them to leave. Instead of respecting my wishes, they began to not only take photos with blinding flashbulbs but also trespass onto my small courtyard, shoving each other and crowding around me. I became afraid for my safety.

As the group shoved closer, still taking photos, one of them repeated recently reported false accusations about a matter in my past that remains painful for me. I became emotionally activated and reached for the camera of one of the men. In hindsight it was not the right thing to do, but I was alone, overwhelmed, and afraid for my safety. The man, whose name I now know is Anthony Lopez, placed his hand on me roughly, causing me to fear I would lose my balance. As a matter of self-defense, I pushed him away from me, at which time my hand grazed his face. It was not a "punch" as widely reported, nor an act of violence, but merely a woman protecting herself.

It has been many years since I released any music or toured with my former band, the Valentines, and so I have found the sudden, intense attention on me lately,

> following a number of senselessly cruel articles published by tabloid website *The Scoop* — one commenting on my physical appearance, another spreading lies about my personal life — overwhelming.
>
> I'd also like to note my disappointment over the misogynistic tone of the articles *The Scoop* in particular has published about me in recent weeks, whether commenting on my "fuller figure" (tabloid-speak for when a woman's body changes in a way some people deem unacceptable) or perpetuating a tired trope of the "scarlet woman" in an unresearched article about my past marriage, which was based entirely on the claims of one anonymous person, who is lying.
>
> (It's worth noting all the articles were authored by women.)
>
> Tabloids have long profited from the demoralization and debasement of women — I am not the first target and I will not be the last. They are a tool of oppression, used to shame any woman who dares to go against patriarchal expectations, and to frighten every other woman enough to make sure she never steps out of line. Still, I am disturbed by the resources and attention being dedicated to my personal life when there are far more important and urgent things happening in the world. I will be making no further comment and ask that the media respects my privacy.

I couldn't take it in. Or refused to. It was too much to absorb, alone in my room in the curtained dark. Numb, I opened my work email—anything to avoid processing what I'd read, to not have to think about that line: *It's worth noting all the articles were authored by women.*

I watched dozens of messages pour in. One in particular caught my eye, sent at 7:03 a.m.:

Sender: Amanda Myles
Subject: Why?

Francesca,

Because of you, I have been up all night, unable to sleep, crying my eyes out.

Words have power. You, of all people, should know that.

I want you to know that the words you have written about me hurt me. I am a real person. A human being.

You want a comment? Here you go: You should be ashamed of yourself.

I stared at the words on the screen, struggling to believe what I was seeing. How did Amanda Myles get my email address? It took a minute, but then it clicked: Alice must have forwarded one of my requests for comment to her. I sat in quiet, dazed shock for a few moments. Then I started to laugh. Not that I thought it was funny, Amanda's obvious pain—and it was obvious, more palpable and raw in her email than in the statement. I just didn't know how to process it, the outrageous fact of the email, not from her rep but Amanda herself. For a celebrity to contact a reporter directly, rather than via an agent or publicist, was to take the rule book of the celebrity-journalist relationship and set it aflame. Why would she do it? I read her words over and over, the email making less sense every time. The vulnerable confession, that she had been "up all night crying"—why would she expose herself? Why would she willingly show her soft underbelly to the person who'd caused the pain? Around my own wounds, I'd built stone tombs.

Then came the bizarre, unsettling awareness, jarring and surreal, like time itself had glitched, like something fundamental had shifted: Amanda Myles knew who I was. Knew of the existence of little old Francesca Miller, who as a kid had Amanda Myles's posters on her bedroom walls, who'd watched her music videos on MTV in the mornings getting ready for school, who'd heard Amanda's unmistakable voice over grocery store speakers while choosing between ice cream flavors. Not only did she know me, but she also *hated* me, or at least it felt as though she hated me. Our worlds had merged, a seemingly untraversable distance between Amanda and me now shrunk down to nothing. Adding to the strangeness was the relative closeness of our physical proximity; she was in the West Village, barely a twenty-minute cab ride away. I braced for a knock on the door, imagined opening it to see Amanda there, livid.

Guilt washed over me. Until that moment, I think I'd convinced myself Amanda would never read the articles, that her agent didn't pass them on, that she was too mercurial and offline. Or maybe until that moment, to me Amanda hadn't seemed like a real person but a character, existing on a different plane, one where a news article wouldn't reach her. But here was the proof it had, and judging by her email she was angry, deeply wounded by the words. *My* words.

Shaken, feeling slightly queasy, I got up and went to the kitchen, where I stood at the sink and chugged a glass of water, then another. For a moment I was lost in thought, about *The Scoop*, and Amanda, and the enormous mess that seemed to be spiraling out of control, until I looked down and saw a roach poking out from under the stove, belligerently flicking its spindly little antennae. I squealed, almost dropped the glass, and lurched to the other side of the kitchen island, horrified and disgusted. Patti and I had mostly given up fighting our building's indefatigable roach population, for nothing worked on them; these were Brooklyn roaches, battle-hardened and deeply proud, the kind that did not scurry away into the shadows if disturbed but instead stood their ground preparing to fight, and I had always hated confrontation.

Something about the roach sighting, this egregious crossing of the unspoken agreement we had with the roaches that the kitchen was ours during daylight and theirs after dark, made the shame that had been stirring in me since Amanda's email morph into frustration. Resentment.

What was Amanda doing at that moment? Oh, you know, she was probably getting an "emergency" massage from a house-call masseuse to melt away her stress while her assistant booked her a private jet to a yoga retreat in Ibiza until the drama blew over. I knew she did not live in a roach-y old Brooklyn apartment that meant a daily forty-minute commute to work on the filthy, sometimes feral subway, where I'd seen a pile of literal human shit more than once.

Sure, I could see how the articles were hurtful, how having a group of men lurking outside your house would be uncomfortable. How everyone thinking that you punched someone, when maybe you actually didn't, would be infuriating. Fine. But didn't Amanda understand that media attention was part of the deal? The media-celebrity relationship, after all, was a mutually beneficial one, often leveraged by celebrities themselves, who planted stories that they were rumored to be under consideration for an Oscar-worthy role when they weren't, or posed for a wholesome at-home-with-the-family photo shoot after a DUI to make the stink go away. Not to mention media coverage had helped the Valentines sell concert tickets and albums, helped Amanda secure huge endorsement deals, all of which had become the wealth that now afforded her a seven-million-dollar West Village brownstone in which to cry over the mean articles.

Besides, it wasn't like I wrote the articles for my own enjoyment, nor were they borne of some vendetta. It wasn't personal. I was only doing my job, a job that, forgive me, I'd deemed preferable to spending my days writing about fucking *cancer*. Those, it seemed, were the only options left for those of us clueless enough to have chosen journalism as a career without knowing the editor of *The New York Times* or the head of a TV network, or unlucky enough to have been born into a family that couldn't spring for Yale. Amanda, meanwhile, hadn't had to work in a decade. She was so wealthy she would probably never have to work ever again.

I grabbed my phone, opened Amanda's email, and hit reply. I began drafting a response.

> I'm sorry to hear you're upset, but

No. This was like a car accident—never admit fault. I deleted the line and tried again.

> I'm shocked and, frankly, disappointed to receive such an unprofessional note from you. We at *The Scoop* are only doing our jobs and approached you for comment countless times.

But I wasn't in a position to send a message on behalf of *The Scoop*. I deleted that, too. Probably I shouldn't reply at all. But what *should*

THE SCOOP

I do? Tell someone? Who? In the past, I would have gone straight to Audrey, but we still weren't speaking, and even if we were, Audrey would have just told me to quit, which I couldn't do. Not with a job at *Business Day* so close now.

I texted Jocelyn: **What are you doing tonight?**

18

"Boo-hoo, let's all shed a tear for the rich lady, crying into her champagne and wiping her eyes with wads of hundred-dollar bills in her multimillion-dollar brownstone while people starve."

It was weird, seeing Jocelyn outside of work. Disorienting, uncomfortably intimate somehow, like bumping into your dentist at the grocery store, witnessing their frustrated squeezes of a series of rock-hard avocados, all that power they had over you when you were laid out in the chair, as they pressured you into making a promise to floss, revealed to be nothing more than a performance of authority. Perched on a stool at a high-top in the back of an East Village dive bar (her suggestion), Jocelyn was at least less intimidating than she was in the newsroom, a softer, less spiky version of the woman who all but growled at anyone who dared to disagree with her.

"Besides, any publicity is good publicity for these spoiled brats," Jocelyn was saying, still holding my phone to read the email from Amanda, which she had begged me to show her. "No one has cared about Amanda Myles in years, and now everyone is talking about her—all thanks to us! Just you wait, next week Amanda will announce the launch of her designer shoe line, or her organic candle company, or whatever. That's the thing with these people. They can't lose."

Jocelyn handed back my phone and sipped her vodka soda with lime. I chugged some of my second (third?) beer. Yes, I liked this take. That what we had done was in Amanda's best interest, that we were helping her, even. That she should be *grateful*. All day I'd flip-flopped between guilty regret and defiant refusal I'd done anything wrong. But the more I listened to Jocelyn, the more I let go of the former and dug deeper into the latter, told myself she was right.

"You know, she's probably not even really upset," Jocelyn continued. "She's just trying to make you feel sorry for her, to manipulate you, to stop the stories. Like those Nigerian email scams that swindle lonely old women out of their life savings—a dirty trick. Don't fall for it."

"You're right, you're so right," I agreed, nodding vigorously, pushing away intrusive thoughts of Amanda appearing in the bar trailed by a pack of hired goons, my nemesis pointing at me and shouting, "There she is!" as I scrambled over the bar top to the back exit, where I would trip over a rancid pile of trash bags and fall face down in a puddle of fresh urine, the depositor of said urine still zipping up his fly, the karma Amanda would no doubt say I deserved.

There was just one thing that made me doubt my innocence, one thought I couldn't seem to push away, and as the booze flooded my bloodstream, I couldn't stop myself from voicing it.

"Do you think Amanda might be...unwell?"

"Unwell? In what way?"

"Don't you think it's odd? To email me like that? Irrational. And why *is* she so reclusive? She could be making a fortune as a judge on *The Voice* or whatever. David seems to think so."

"Really?" Jocelyn asked. That it was David's opinion apparently validated the argument.

"Yeah. He said he thinks Amanda could be the next big celebrity train wreck, headed for a Britney Spears 2007–style meltdown. Sounds like he hopes for a head-shaving any day now."

"He's probably right. The look on her face as she lunged for the pap? I can't unsee it."

"Does it worry you?" I asked.

Jocelyn cocked her head. "What do you mean?"

"I don't know," I said, though I did know, I just didn't want to come off as alarmist, or paranoid. "Like, what if she does do something Britney Spears 2007–esque?"

"Shave her head?"

"Worse than that. An overdose, a car crash, you know... hurt herself, or someone else."

Jocelyn shrugged. "So, she'll check in to a rehab that's more like a five-star resort, lie low for a few months, come out restored, pay for the best PR to fix her reputation, and move on like nothing happened. All fixed. Do an interview with Oprah and land some million-dollar endorsement deal. Thank you, next, cha-ching. That's how it always goes. Nice life, huh?"

I told myself Jocelyn was right. Amanda was wealthy. She could only fall so far. Us and the paps, meanwhile? Without our paychecks, we'd be out on our asses. Amanda would be fine.

I glanced around the bar, which was steadily filling up with the Friday night crowd. It was dark inside, with no windows to let in any light. When I'd gone to the bathroom, there was an empty space above the sink where a mirror would usually be, because no one wanted to see themselves in a place like that. We seemed like the oldest people there, apart from the bartender, by at least five years. Jocelyn read my mind.

"I used to come here all the time, when I lived around the corner.

I was dating a drummer, and this was where the band came after shows. God, it feels like a lifetime ago."

It was rare for Jocelyn to share something about her private life. The chaos of the busy nights in the newsroom meant it rarely felt natural to make personal disclosures. It occurred to me then that despite spending five nights a week with the woman, I knew so little about her.

"When did you move to Jersey?" I asked.

"About two years ago. I grew up there, so it was a move back. I live with my parents."

I nodded, not judging. If I could have lived with my parents and worked in New York to save money, I would have. But Jocelyn looked somewhat tortured about this admission.

"My mom got sick," she said, staring down into her drink, "is still sick. ALS—it's early to middle stage, progressing fast. I moved into the granny flat out back of their place, to help my dad. That's why I took this job, so I can stay with Mom during the day while Dad is at work."

It was like a final puzzle piece had been clicked into place that allowed me to see clearly the mystery that was Jocelyn. It all made sense now; why she was always so quick to snap, the endless cigarette breaks. She carried an invisible weight, having to bear the daily paper cuts of witnessing her mother's slow, inevitable decline. The cranky woman from Jersey who spent her nights at *The Scoop* transformed in front of me into the photo editor who lived in the city, dated a drummer, stayed out too late in bars, until her carefree youth was cruelly ripped away from her.

Was I only now meeting the real Jocelyn? I was beginning to suspect she wore a mask at work, an armor, as a form of self-preservation, her own brand of swagger and bravado to shield herself from the hypermasculine, ruthlessly competitive, darkly toxic culture. A mask she dropped as soon as she walked out the door every night—something it had never occurred to me to do. I could see how it would help, to perform a character at *The Scoop* as a kind of survival strategy, to avoid having inconvenient human responses to the things we did, like feeling conflicted or guilty over, say, a celebrity emailing to say a story you wrote made them cry.

"I'm so sorry," I said. "That must be really difficult, being a caregiver for your mom."

Jocelyn nodded, gave a tight-lipped smile. I sensed her bracing for me to ask a question that was naïve, or insensitive, to say something that revealed my lack of understanding of what she was going through, thereby making her feel even more alone in the experience than before. I wanted her to know I got it—sort of. That I had my own scars born of the pain of mother loss.

"My mom got sick when I was in high school," I said. "She started getting fatigued and out of breath. Senior year she was diagnosed with COPD. She died my final year of college."

Jocelyn drained her glass. "Jesus, that's horrible. I'm sorry. Did you look after her?"

An innocent question, and yet it felt like a slap. Within it I heard an assumption, that I must have stayed home to care for my mother when she was sick. And this implied a judgment, at least that's how it felt, of the fact that I didn't.

There was a simplicity available in hindsight that obscured the confusing haze of my mother's final years—how believable she sounded when she said, *I'm feeling better lately.* Or, at least, believable enough for a young woman who thrashed desperately inside, felt like she was drowning every time she stepped into that dark, dirty, unraveling chaos of a house. Every time she found the messes she'd cleaned on the previous visit had returned, worse than before. Every time she saw the vegetables in the fridge spoiled, untouched, more cases of wine purchased against doctor's orders. Staggering, the fantasies we build to deny what's in front of our eyes.

A memory struck: the day before I left for college. We'd had a fight. I couldn't remember what started it—an item I'd packed she didn't want me to take? My mom snapped at me, viciously, out of nowhere it seemed, and then we were both yelling, and then we were both crying.

"Are you mad at me for leaving?" I asked through tears. "Do you not want me to go?"

"Why wouldn't I want you to go to college?" she replied, exasperated. "That is *exactly* what I want for you, Francesca. What I've always wanted for you. How could you think that?"

"I'm worried about you," I admitted, hearing my voice crack and quaver. "You're sick."

My mother stepped forward and hugged me, holding me as I cried into her shoulder.

"Please don't worry about me," she said after a minute. "The *parent* is meant to worry about the *child*, not the other way around. Listen to me: You are bright, and full of potential, and because you are so much smarter than me, you are not going to throw away your future by staying in this town. There's nothing here for you! You asked if I was mad at you for going—I'm not. But I *will* be mad at you if you stay. And I'll be even more mad at myself for being the reason you stay. Your future cannot wait. You have to grab it with both hands, right now. Understand?"

I pushed the memory away. "No, I went to college," I told Jocelyn. "But I visited a lot. It's what she wanted."

"*Of course* that's what she wanted," Jocelyn agreed warmly, perhaps detecting my defensiveness. "And look at you, a journalist in New York! Your mom would be so proud."

I tried to smile. It was a generous thing to say. I used to think that, when I was at *Marie Claire*. Whenever I had some success, like a cover story, or a promotion, or a nomination for an award, a bittersweet feeling always crept up on me that made my eyes wet and my throat tight, knowing I was living the life my mother wanted for me. But since taking the job at *The Scoop*, I was no longer sure of that. I thought of this most evenings when I walked past the America Now studios. Sad, but oddly freeing, the awareness it was no longer possible for me to disappoint her.

Jocelyn asked if I wanted another drink. I did. In a few minutes, she was back with our next round, somehow getting the bartender to serve her before a dozen others already waiting.

"So, what are you going to do with it?" she asked.

"With what?" It was loud in the bar now, and I almost had to yell.

She looked at me like I was stupid. "With Amanda Myles's personal email, dummy. Don't you see the gift that's fallen right in your lap? You've got a direct line to her, no agent, no middleman. And if David's right? If she's *this* close to shaving her head in public? Jackpot."

"What are you suggesting?" I asked, wary but curious.

"Ask her for an interview," Jocelyn said, sucking down vodka through her straw. "Tell her some bullshit about giving her 'the chance to set the record straight.' They always fall for it."

I laughed. "Did you read the email? Amanda hates me. There's no way she'd do it."

"You would think that, wouldn't you?" Jocelyn said. "But they're narcissists, these celebrities. Bottomless pits for attention. They just can't help themselves."

"Maybe some of them. But Amanda's been living like a hermit for years. She seems genuinely upset over the recent attention. I really don't think she wants to be in the spotlight."

"So that's why she put out a statement? That's why she emailed a journalist?" She shook her head. "Nonsense. She's pretending to be upset, but she wants it. Fame is a powerful drug—once people get a taste, they're forever chasing the high. I'm telling you: request an interview, give her the old *tell your side of the story, control the narrative* bullshit. Amanda will say yes."

"Maybe," I said, hating the idea more with every passing second. But I figured I should at least humor Jocelyn. "But there's no way *I'm* sending that email. She might actually try to kill me." I glanced up at the door of the bar again, half expecting to see Amanda's furious face.

"Even better. What a story! Just the kind of scoop the Man Upstairs wants us to get."

Jocelyn hunched forward on the tabletop, like a skilled salesman homing in on a target.

"Frankie, if David finds out you have a direct line to Amanda and you didn't use it," Jocelyn continued, "he'll flip. And, honestly? I don't think you have many strikes left."

I didn't want to admit it, but I could see Jocelyn was right. Plus, what Jocelyn *didn't* know was how close I was to *Business Day*, the reason I'd taken this cursed job to begin with. The meeting with Peter Lowell was days away. It would have been foolish of me to risk pissing off David at such a critical juncture. There was also the fact that now Jocelyn knew about the email. Would she tell David? She swore she didn't go behind my back with the first Amanda Myles article, that David came up with the "fat angle" on his own. But I didn't know for sure.

"Okay, okay," I said, "I'll do it. Next week at work."

"Nuh-uh. Do it now." Jocelyn tapped the table with her finger. "Before you chicken out."

"It's the weekend."

"So?

"And it's late."

"You're the *night* editor."

I was too tipsy to be emailing anyone, especially in a professional capacity. But I could see Jocelyn wasn't going to give in. I decided I'd write the message, get her input, make her feel involved, and save it to drafts. Mull it over in the days to come without three (four?) beers in me.

I opened my work email and started typing out the message. When I was done, I handed my phone to Jocelyn for her to see. I watched her eyes flick back and forth as she read it.

"Love it," she said. Then she tapped a finger hard on the screen. "Sent!"

"What?" I wrenched my phone from her and checked the screen. The message was gone.

"Jocelyn!" I went to my sent items. Sure enough, there it was. It felt as though I'd been summoning the courage to jump into the water from a high rock, only to be shoved over the edge from behind with no warning, and now I was in free fall.

"I can't believe you," I said. I wanted to push Jocelyn off her stool. She just laughed.

19

CHIC MAGAZINE CLOSED DOWN. BUZZFEED ANNOUNCED another round of layoffs. *USA Today* was rumored to be mulling major budget cuts. But me? I was fine—better than fine. I was earning more than I ever had, I was now on a first-name basis with Peter Lowell, and I knew it wouldn't be long before I pulled off the career revival no one expected: tabloid journalist to *Business Day*.

In my private life, things were not going so well. I was looking at the photo of Josh and Miss America every day, sometimes multiple times a day, even though it made me feel sick, unable to resist even as I willed myself to block him, forget him. I couldn't help myself creeping on her Pinterest either, in an admittedly tragic and misguided attempt to know her, understand what she had that I didn't, why Josh had been willing to risk our relationship for her. I knew I'd have to quit this dirty habit, this compulsion, before, among the dresses and shoes and vegetarian recipe ideas, I'd begin to see engagement rings, and then wedding dresses, and then baby cribs. Maybe I wouldn't be able to stop, and I'd still be silently watching, decades in the future, as she pinned arthritis remedies and gift ideas for the grandkids. I'd be there, lurking, as she made a Pinterest board for "chic funeral and wake ideas." I hoped I could stop before then.

I still hadn't spoken to Audrey, both of us stubbornly waiting for the other to be the first to reach out, and I'd been wounded to see photos on social media of her, Naomi, and Jasmine hanging out without me. Naomi and I were still in touch, occasionally texting each other, though never mentioning *The Scoop*. Jasmine, however, was less subtly shunning me, taking days to reply to texts, and when she did reply, it was with the bare minimum of words. (I think it would have hurt less if she had stopped replying altogether.) But I tried not to think about that. Mostly my thoughts circled around work: constantly checking to see if Amanda had responded to the interview request, bracing for David's next angry outburst, hunting for stories that would please him, make people click, make the arrows on the jumbo screen turn green and shoot up to the sky.

Like the missing Georgia woman.

I was excited about the missing Georgia woman. Not excited that she was missing, obviously; how horrible for her loved ones. But I thought it had the potential to be a big story, one of those true crime tales that captures national attention, the next Laci Peterson. It was well known at *The Scoop* that nothing reliably rated better than a missing or dead woman, with a caveat: she should be young, pretty, rich, a wife and/or mother, and white, or at least check four out of the five. "Men should want to fuck her, and women should want to be her," was how Jocelyn once put it to me, which she said was how David put it to her, which was probably how Walter Johnson put it to him. If there were any indications she might be a drug addict, or a sex worker, don't bother—the clicking public liked their victims wholesome. The Georgia woman was single, no kids, so she did have a couple of marks against her in terms of eliciting enough sympathy to break traffic records, but she was at least young, pretty, and white, and came from a family that owned horses—a cute detail. Back at *Marie Claire*, I'd once assigned a story on "missing white woman syndrome," about the disproportionate amount of news coverage white women and girls received compared to women of color. In other words, I knew better. But there was something about the Georgia woman I knew David would love—I think it was the horses. I asked Chris to write it as Jocelyn searched social media for photos of her (ideally with horses).

"I tell everyone," Jocelyn said as she right-clicked and saved photos of the woman from her Facebook profile, "in the event you go missing or die a newsworthy death, make sure you have a public album of nice photos of yourself. No sunglasses, and nothing taken by a professional, because of copyright. Make the job easy for the stressed-out, overworked photo editor who has to illustrate the story in between cropping pics to zoom in on famous women's tits and having their head bitten off by their unhinged asshole boss. Otherwise, millions of screens will be plastered with some hideous photo taken of you from an unflattering angle at a wedding nine years ago that your aunt Margaret tagged you in. If you're not dead, you'll wish you were."

I laughed at the dark inner workings of Jocelyn's tabloid-twisted mind, even though I was still mad at her for hitting send on the email to Amanda. Chris laughed, too. Yenay said nothing. She was still acting strange, quiet. I couldn't stand it any longer. I decided to send her a message.

> Got a sec to chat in the kitchen?

I stood, grabbed my water bottle, and walked quickly across the newsroom and down the hall. I was in the kitchen filling up my water bottle at the sink when I heard Yenay walk in.

"Is everything okay?" she asked. I turned to face her. She was leaning back against the counter, arms crossed.

"That's what I was going to ask you," I said. "You haven't seemed like yourself lately. I've been wondering if something's wrong."

She frowned, shook her head.

"Come on, Yenay. Something's up. Tell me what it is, so I can help."

For a beat we held each other's gaze, a stalemate, neither of us backing down, until eventually Yenay gave a heavy sigh and relented, dropping the *nothing's wrong* performance.

"It's not any one thing," she began hesitantly, searching for the words. "It's...it's everything. It's being told to kill myself by strangers on the internet. It's being accused of 'upholding the patriarchy' by Annie Klein," she said, looking queasy at the memory. "It's being called a slimy hack—and a traitor to my gender—in Amanda Myles's statement. It's the nights spent scrounging through internet cesspools, trying to dig up someone's shameful Halloween—"

"Anything yet?"

"No. I thought I found Tom Hanks in Ku Klux Klan robes, but it was a ghost costume."

"Tom Hanks? No, the media has been trying to find something on him for years. But the guy's got a cleaner record than Mother Teresa. I doubt he's ever had an overdue library book."

"I know, I guess I was feeling desperate. Anyway...it's just not what I imagined, when I moved to New York to be a journalist."

"What? You didn't go into a hundred thousand dollars of student debt to report on the daily inflating or shrinking of the size of one woman's ass?" A joke, to try to cheer her up. It didn't work.

"I know I should be grateful," she continued. "There are people I went to college with still making coffees and driving Uber, who can't get a full-time job. I know I'm one of the lucky ones. But..." She trailed off. "It feels like everyone hates us—"

"That's because they do."

THE SCOOP

"—and I understand why. Look at the stories we publish! I didn't think I would ever be *that* kind of journalist, you know?"

"What kind?"

"Sleazy. And kind of evil?"

I understood Yenay's frustration. Of course I did. I was right there with her, being punished with a time-out in the naughty corner of journalism, enduring indefinite exile from my media elite tribe, my days feeling more like some kind of humiliating hazing ritual than regular employment. But moping wasn't going to get her—us—anywhere. It was time to snap out of it.

"I get it, Yenay. I do. You want to be one of the journalists the celebrities like. The ones who get invited to a hotel suite to sit on a plush white couch to interview them about their new skincare line, scribbling down a detail to include in the piece describing how they had their bare feet curled beneath them on the couch, leave carrying a bag of goodies, and receive a bouquet of flowers at their desk with a handwritten note on publication day. I know, because I used to be one. And I won't lie, it felt good—to feel special, the proximity to such immense glamour and fame. But you know what? They don't really like you. They don't respect you. They're just using you. It's like patting a dog on the head. *Good boy. Sit. Stay.* No matter what you write, to them you're still a dog."

As the words left my mouth, I was amazed at my own insight, half expecting poignant orchestral piano and violin to start playing from somewhere. And the realization kept unfurling.

"Isn't this—what we're doing at *The Scoop*—the *real* journalism? Kira Vincent's ass aside. Writing the stories celebrities don't want published? What was it Orwell said? *Journalism is printing something that someone does not want printed. Everything else is public relations.*"

If I'd thought about it more, I would have considered that *The Scoop* and the state of the media in general were themselves an Orwellian nightmare, the investment of enormous amounts of resources into mostly shallow content while the world's truly powerful were rarely held to account. But I was on a roll, and I was grateful that Yenay, if she thought this, too, didn't say so.

"Sure, sometimes they aren't *one hundred percent* true," I continued. "Sometimes the details are slightly off, but the subject is always given a chance to correct us, to tell the truth—we seek comment! They know how to reach us! Those fluffy, ass-kissing cover stories at *Marie Claire* and every other magazine, written only when a star has a movie to promote, are for the celebrities themselves, not the readers. Readers don't care about that stuff—a celebrity's thoughts or opinions or hopes for world peace, not really. What readers want to know is their secrets, their haunted past, who they are rumored to have fucked or are fucking or want to fuck, what they have in their fridge, how much they weigh, the horrible, unhinged thing they said to a co-star on a movie set after a seventeen-hour day. Readers want to know the things the celebrities don't want them to know—*that's* what's interesting to them. That's what we're for."

I remembered then what David had said in my interview: *I'd rather live in an unglamorous truth than a polished lie, wouldn't you?* I hadn't understood it then, but it was starting to make sense to me.

I had convinced myself with my little speech, but apparently not Yenay. She nodded politely but still looked glum. A troubling thought occurred to me then: *Was Yenay going to quit?* Was that why she'd been so quiet? Yenay couldn't quit! She'd come so far from her hometown in Minnesota, clearly had such a natural aptitude for journalism... and what about the white male celebrity-profile mafia? They still dominated the pages of *GQ*, *Vogue*, and *Esquire* every month... and what would that mean for me if she left? I'd be down a reporter until we replaced her, and what if that delayed my transfer to *Business Day*? No, Yenay could *not* quit.

"Yenay, if I tell you something, do you promise not to tell anyone?"

Yenay nodded, though she looked slightly terrified, as though she feared I was about to make a confession she would never be able to unhear, perhaps something involving bodily fluids, or a loud noise during a late-night drive followed by the discovery of a large dent in the fender.

I told her about my agreement with David when I took the job, the promise of a transfer to *Business Day*, that I was having coffee with the managing editor the very next morning.

"Once I get there," I said, speaking in a low voice in case Jocelyn or Chris came down the hall, "I'll take you with me. I'll put in a good word for you, insist they have to hire you."

I thought Yenay would brighten at the possibility of not just a way out of *The Scoop*, but a straight shot to *Business Day*, which had the prestige and credibility I knew she desired. While she did smile and nod, listening as I talked, her response wasn't as enthusiastic as I'd expected.

"So, it's a job interview?" Yenay asked, frowning slightly. "For what position?"

"It's not *technically* an interview," I explained, irritated that Yenay couldn't see how exciting this was, not just for me, but for her, too. "It's coffee. But the fact that David organized it, and that Peter said yes so quickly...it bodes well, that it won't be long until I'm there. Until *you're* there, Yenay. This is an opportunity for you, too. I mean...*Business Day*!"

Yenay smiled, though I thought it seemed forced. "It's so nice of you to think of me, Frankie," she said. "But don't worry about me—at least not until you're actually there."

Something in Yenay's eyes told me she was dubious that I would go to *Business Day*. I was aware, on some level, that I was promising something not mine to promise. Like inviting someone to my Lake Como villa, the villa I was going to purchase with my winning lottery ticket, the ticket I was yet to buy, then getting upset when they wouldn't commit to making a date to visit. It was hard to make Yenay see it was real, and it was happening. But I kept trying.

"David will let me go to *Business Day* once I give him what he wants," I continued. "A big scoop for Project Black Lagoon. Or something new on Amanda Myles. Just think," I said as I grabbed my water bottle, and we began walking back to the newsroom, "you and me at *Business Day*. *Business Day*! Imagine how jealous Jocelyn will be."

The possibility of inspiring envy in Jocelyn made Yenay's eyes light up. Jocelyn had been unsympathetic to Yenay when she got trolled, and I could tell she still hadn't forgiven her.

"Okay," she said, her voice low as we neared our desks. "I'm in. I'll see what I can do."

I knew she'd come around. Spite is an incredibly potent source of motivation. I could've found the strength to lift a small car in the air with the spite I felt for Josh and Miss America, could probably solve world hunger in a day if it meant making Audrey and Patrick look stupid.

Back in my seat, Chris popped up over his computer.

"Yes, Chris?"

He cleared his throat. "The Georgia woman has been found."

I perked up. *She'd been found? She'd been found! Jackpot!* I asked Chris where the body was located—a shallow grave in the woods?—and if the police had a suspect, or any leads. Was it an ex-boyfriend or ex-husband? It was almost always an ex-boyfriend or ex-husband. I wondered how quickly we could track down all her exes on social media, maybe even take the list to the cops, see if they'd be willing to confirm any were suspects. Now, that'd be a scoop.

"No, no, she's not dead," Chris said. "She's alive. Sounds like a miscommunication between her and her family. I don't think she was ever really missing. She's completely fine."

Wait—the Georgia woman was *alive*? There was no story?

"Damn it," I snapped, thumping my fist on the desk. "What a fucking waste of time."

The others stared. I could still feel the spot where my hand hit the hard edge of the desk. A shock wave of dark energy reverberated through my body; it frightened me. I hadn't meant to react like that. I didn't know where it came from.

"I mean, I'm glad she's okay," I added, turning back to my screen, pretending to be reading something important, in the hope the others would forget what just happened.

"We'll find something else!" I said with a laugh, but it sounded unnatural, high-pitched.

"Are you okay?" Jocelyn asked after a beat. "I thought you were about to lose it, Steve style."

"Steve?"

"The old night editor."

No one had ever said anything to me about a previous night editor.

"Where did he go?" I asked.

Behind his computer, Chris let out a sharp sigh. In response, Jocelyn's mouth fell open, and she thrust out her palms, instantly on the defensive like an innocent woman unjustly accused.

"What?" she said, giving Chris an aggressive look I'd only seen in dive bar parking lots.

"Why would you bring that up?"

"It's not a secret."

"No, but..." Chris huffed again.

I looked between Jocelyn and Chris, waiting not at all patiently for someone to explain.

Jocelyn began to speak again, but she stopped herself when Chris stood abruptly.

"I *really* don't need to relive this," he said, turning and heading for the kitchen.

Now Yenay was peering over the top of her computer. I gathered it was the first time she had heard about Steve, too.

"What happened to Steve?" I asked again.

"Psych ward," Jocelyn said finally. "Somewhere upstate."

"Are you serious?"

"Oh, yeah. Guy went crazy."

"What do you mean, 'crazy'?" Yenay asked. "Did he have a breakdown or something?"

"Almost every night, toward the end," Jocelyn said, sounding oddly nonchalant given what she was describing. "He would disappear down to the Irish pub on Forty-Fifth Street for hours, then come back and either pass out drunk in a meeting room for the rest of the night or otherwise remain conscious and terrorize us. Stumble around. Curse. Scream. Throw things."

"Throw things?" I said. "You're joking."

"I wish I was."

"Like what?"

"Mugs. Books. Chris started keeping his copy of *Infinite Jest* in his bag after that."

Yenay and I locked eyes. I wondered if the images running through her mind were as disturbing as the ones in mine.

"His computer once, cords and all," Jocelyn continued. "Then there was the time he threw a stapler at Angela—the entertainment reporter before Yenay. It only grazed her face, but I hear the payout was decent. I wish it was me he hurled it at. I would've taken the money and caught the next plane to Rio de Janeiro."

What a nut, I thought. Tragic, really. Some people just aren't cut out for journalism.

"I'll never forget Christmas Eve," Jocelyn said, a kind of awestruck wonder coming over her as she reminisced.

"Toward the end of the night, I go into the kitchen," she began, lowering her voice like a camp counselor trying to scare children around a fire. "You know how the lights in there turn off if they don't detect movement for ten minutes? Well, I see the lights are off and assume nobody is in there. But when I step in and the lights come on, what do I see but Steve, on the floor against the wall, barefoot, an open bottle of champagne in one hand, a fistful of roast chicken in the other."

"What?" Yenay whispered, almost wincing at Jocelyn's description, clearly creeped out.

Jocelyn nodded solemnly. "The chicken and wine were supposed to be for the people working on Christmas Day."

The disturbing image of a man, gut bulging over his midsection, drunk, greasy, and ravenously mauling an entire roast chicken with his bare hands lingered in my mind until the ping of a new email pulled me back to the present. I checked my inbox to see it was Marcus.

> Need anything? Amanda's marriage and divorce certificates, that was nothing. I can always go "code red"—just say the word.

Code red. What did that mean? I was curious. Tempted. After all, Yenay hadn't found anything for Project Black Lagoon yet, and surprise, surprise, Amanda Myles had not responded to a hastily drafted email from the woman she probably suspected was the Antichrist requesting an interview. Maybe it was time to use Marcus again. But something in me hesitated. If I was totally honest with myself, it was what Yenay had said in the kitchen earlier, about us being "sleazy, and kind of evil." As confidently as I'd argued with her, that what we were doing at *The Scoop* wasn't so bad, that it was justified, Yenay's words had stirred up the uneasy feelings, the guilt I'd felt upon receiving Amanda's email: *You should be ashamed of yourself.* And I knew using a private investigator was worse than us finding scoops on our own, through old-fashioned journalism. So, I didn't reply to Marcus, not right then. We'd do it on our own. We'd do it right.

The breaking news app pinged. There was a chance an asteroid the size of Yankee Stadium could crash into Earth next Thursday. I imagined the asteroid hurtling across the sky, flaming orange and red, saw myself at the moment of impact, staring at my screen, oblivious.

20

I WAS HALF A BLOCK down from the Le Pain Quotidien opposite Johnson News, watching coffee-cup-clutching people file into the same building I'd exited in the dark only a few hours earlier. I checked the time on my phone: 7:58. Two minutes until my meeting with Peter. Almost time.

The chaos of Seventh Avenue in morning peak hour, with its incessant honking of horns and people rushing past on the sidewalk, was a brutal assault on my senses; I felt nervy, on edge—not surprising, given I'd shut my eyes barely an hour before my alarm went off, and now had four shots of caffeine running through my veins. But I ignored the exhaustion I felt, forced my eyes open wider, plastered on a grin. This meeting with Peter could change everything, change my life forever. Journalists, at least in New York, rarely got jobs because of a superior level of knowledge, skill, or experience; there was always a pool of equally suitable candidates. No, journalists in New York got jobs by being well-liked by the right person—everyone knew that. Make a good impression on Peter, and I could be saying goodbye to *The Scoop*, to night shift, to David, to the judgment of everyone from friends to celebrities. I slapped my cheeks a few times, trying to look awake, checked my reflection in a store window, and headed inside.

I spotted Peter sitting at a table by the window and strode over.

"Peter, hi," I said, jutting out a hand with an energy and confidence I hoped he couldn't tell was fake, praying he couldn't feel my nervous jitters. He shook it firmly as we subtly looked each other up and down. Peter was roughly late forties, with dark, slicked-back hair sprinkled with gray. He looked older and portlier than in his headshot I'd found on the company website, not that I was one to talk—since working night shift, my face had surely aged a decade.

"Francesca, wonderful to meet you," he said as he pumped my hand. I detected a British accent. So, he was someone David knew from London, I guessed. Peter was warm and genial enough, but, I sensed as he sized me up, slightly suspicious. I wondered if I looked strange, sickly, my makeup failing to hide my dark circles and pasty complexion. Or if Peter was always wary of ambitious young women who wanted something from him. Peter already had a coffee, so I took off my coat, hung it on the seat back, and then spent the next five minutes trying not to make eye contact with him as I ordered, and then waited awkwardly for, my large cappuccino.

"It's just occurred to me that this is early for you," Peter said when I sat down, looking at his watch with concern. "You're on the night desk, right? You should have said something."

A fascinating peek into the male psyche, the suggestion someone would simply ask for what they needed, without fear of consequences or retribution—conscious or not—from the other party. I waved away his concern.

"It's fine," I said, searching for a convincing reason why it was, indeed, fine that I'd finished work at two a.m. and gotten into bed at three, my racing mind preventing me from drifting off until after five, before my alarm jolted me awake again at six, eyelids feeling like sandpaper.

"Sleep when we're dead, right?" was all I came up with, followed by a too-loud laugh.

"Yes," Peter replied. Impressed, concerned, or threatened by my apparent lack of need for sleep, I wasn't sure. He continued on. "David says you're doing a great job at *The Scoop*."

Had David really said that? There was no way to know, though the praise felt like a drug flooding into my veins all the same. Out the window, people were still streaming past the America Now studios and into the revolving doors of the Johnson News building. It felt closer than ever that I might soon be one of them, moving in daylight again. I plunged ahead.

"Well, David is a great boss," I said, nauseated by my own insufferable ass-kissing. "He's taught me a lot. This is my first job at a tabloid. Before this I was at *Marie Claire*—"

"How do you like working for David?" Peter asked, cutting me off, then continuing to talk before I could answer. "He can be a loose cannon," he said, laughing and shaking his head. "I worked for him briefly, before I came over here. Once, he had me call up a police station to confirm a story about this bloke fucking a chicken. The story was real—he really did fuck a chicken—but it wasn't a genuine follow, just a prank. As I asked the cop at this tiny village police station for details about the chicken fucking, the whole newsroom was listening, laughing behind their hands. And he's got a hell of a temper. I'm sure you've seen him blow his top."

I didn't know what to say. I was stuck on the casual mention of bestiality before nine a.m.

"David's like that TV chef—what's his name?" Peter said. "The one who goes to shitty restaurants..."

"Gordon Ramsay."

"Yes, Gordon Ramsay. David can get really fired up, but it's only because he loves it so much—the news. He really cares. He might be the only person in the industry who still does."

Care. An interesting way to put it. I tried to think of it as *care* when David screamed at me to *forget fucking Mogadishu*, *care* when he threatened to have me removed by security.

"How long have you known David?" I asked, not bothering to try to steer the conversation back to my experience or accomplishments. I knew all that really mattered was that Peter left the meeting feeling he liked me, even if he recalled little of what we'd talked about.

"We go way back. We first met when I was a cadet on *The Times* of London almost thirty years ago. David did not fit in there, to say the least," he said with a chuckle. "David was smart and hungry, but a bit rough around the edges. He rubbed people the wrong way. He might have fit in better if he'd played the game a little, but, well, that's not his style. *The Times* was the kind of place where you got promoted because you played tennis with the right people after work—at least it was back then. David hated that. He thought the hardest worker who brought in the best stories should win, that it shouldn't matter where you grew up, who your mates were, how expensive your suit was. Once he got to the tabloids, he thrived. They don't care who you are, where you come from, as long as you bring them a killer story. But you know that, you're at *The Scoop*."

Peter smiled, quiet for a moment as he sipped his coffee, eyeing me again with curiosity.

"So, David said you're interested in coming over to *Business Day*. I've got to ask—why?"

A predictable question, and one I'd prepared for. But there was something about the way Peter asked it that struck me. Not as though he was trying to see if my intentions were pure and true, or if I'd be a good fit, but like he genuinely couldn't fathom why I'd want to work there.

"My background is in magazines," I said. "Long-form, more serious content. Don't get me wrong, *The Scoop* is...fun. I've learned a lot. But...I don't know how to say this without sounding snobbish...I didn't study journalism to edit stories about reality stars, and animal videos, and fake outrage. To be pressured to publish so fast there's no time to fact-check."

Peter nodded like he understood. "I don't think any of us saw it coming—the dumbification of news—at least not as fast and extreme as it's been. You know less than ten percent of people read all the way to the bottom of an article? Most are barely more than a thousand words. But who can blame them, when the article has been sloppily thrown together by a college grad who hasn't been given the proper training because nobody has the time nor resources to..."

Peter stopped and squeezed his eyes shut for a moment, like he knew he was spiraling.

"But I digress. What I mean to say is, are you sure you want to go back to long-form, more serious work? It's satisfying to write, sure, but the audience doesn't want it anymore. All of that is going the way of the dinosaurs. It's like saying you want to be a steamboat captain."

Exhausted as I was, functioning on so little sleep, it didn't take much to deflate me. My face must have fallen, because Peter began trying to reassure me.

"Hey, you're one of the lucky ones," he said. "You've got a full-time job at a website that's making money and is low-cost to run. That people *actually read*. *Business Day* is the opposite: old-school and expensive to keep afloat. Dusty old fossils like me running things, mired in bureaucracy. It's going to kill us, if I'm honest with you. There's a guy blogging from a trailer in Tuscaloosa with more clout than some entire newsrooms. In my opinion, Francesca—and this is just my opinion—you're better off staying where you are. Once tech is done hollowing out the media in a decade or so, I think the only ones left standing will be *The New York Times* and *The Scoop*, and not much in between. You'll probably be in charge of half the industry. Meanwhile, I'll be in a hut in rural Connecticut catching rabbits to feed my family."

In my mind I tried to picture a future media industry where the only publications left were *The New York Times* and *The Scoop*. I saw Audrey, in smart black reading glasses and a blazer, sitting at a desk overlooking her esteemed newsroom full of journalists working studiously—and then down the street, me, in David's seat at *The Scoop*, wearing a clown costume and honking my big red nose every time a story got over a hundred thousand views.

"Especially if you follow in David's footsteps," Peter continued. "You know, don't be afraid to get some blood under your nails or lose a tooth for a story—metaphorically speaking."

Metaphorically, sure, I thought, still plagued by thoughts of Amanda coming after me.

"That's why Walter Johnson brought David over to the States to run *The Scoop*," Peter said. "He's not precious or pretentious, like a lot of American editors are. He gets the job done."

I tried to listen, but I was stuck on Peter's bleak prediction for the future of the media.

"You really think the outlook is that grim?"

Peter sighed sadly. "I don't know. The fat *will* continue to be trimmed, and trimmed, and trimmed some more, until it's nothing but skin and bones. Impotent. Pointless." He paused for a second, as if wavering over whether he should say something. "You know, part of me won't be all that sad to see it go. Not when you look at what it's become. Will something better sprout from the ashes? I don't know. But if I were you, Francesca, I would stay right where you are."

I nodded as if seriously considering what Peter was saying. But privately, I thought Peter was a sad, pessimistic defeatist. Yes, the industry was changing, rapidly, and would look a lot different in the future. But people still read physical books, and people—or at least *enough* people—would always read longer, well-written, well-researched features that made them feel informed, that helped them better understand the world. And I was going to be one of the journalists who wrote those features. I was *not* going to spend the rest of my career at *The Scoop*.

It would not be wise to disagree with Peter (men hated that, especially when it was a woman disagreeing—and a young woman at that). I was trying to get him on my side, make him like me, as important as that was for getting anywhere in the media. But I couldn't let my chance of a job at *Business Day* slip away. Not when I was this close. It was my only real hope.

"You might be right, Peter. And look, I'm certainly not in any rush to leave *The Scoop*," I lied, "not at all. It's just that I'm still relatively young, and I have a lot to learn. David has been... *incredible*, but I know at some point I'm going to want to keep growing. I think working at *Business Day*, for brilliant, learned editors like yourself? I would gain a great deal from that."

Flattery worked, as it usually does. Peter began to nod, as though this was simply a fact, how *brilliant* and *learned* he was, how much wisdom I could absorb by osmosis just by being in his presence. Despite his grim warning about the coming media apocalypse, and his doubt that there was still any good reason to work for *Business Day*, all of a sudden Peter perked up.

"I hear you, Francesca," he said. "It's easy to stagnate. It's important to keep growing as a professional. Well, listen, I wouldn't want to steal you away from David..."

Please steal me away, I thought. *Kidnap me. Right now. I won't struggle.*

"... but you should reach out when you're ready for a change. Not tomorrow—David might actually kill me if you jump ship too soon. But when the time is right. Let's stay in touch."

I almost floated down the block after saying goodbye to Peter, watching him hurry across the street and into the Johnson News building. *You should reach out. Let's stay in touch.* I cackled to myself, ignoring the glances of passersby, remembering how I massaged his ego. Incredible, how easy it was to manipulate someone desperately clinging onto what little power they had left as the world they knew disappeared minute by minute, their total irrelevance looming.

I stopped at the end of the block, wondering what to do for the next eight and a half hours. I checked my work email. When I saw it, my stomach dropped. A reply from Amanda.

> Meet me at 3:30 at San Mateo's. Off the record, no photos, no recording, no one else.

21

I'D ARRIVED TEN MINUTES EARLY to the restaurant, one of those small but subtly moneyed West Village spots with crisp white tablecloths and servers who move with the careful poise of ballet dancers. Seated at a table in the dimly lit back corner, my hand trembled as I lifted the glass of tap water the waiter kept stopping by to top up, my stomach gnawing itself with sharp teeth.

Nervousness I'd felt meeting celebrities at *Marie Claire* now seemed quaint compared to the rolling thunder and lightning cracks of anxiety that crashed over me as I watched the door, waiting for Amanda to walk in, though a small part of me doubted she'd show. Could I really do this? *Irrelevant*, I told the anxious knot in my stomach, my shaking hands, my dry mouth, my racing heart. *You must.* If I could get Amanda to give me something I could publish (she'd said "off the record," but that could be negotiated), I wouldn't have to ask Marcus to go "code red," whatever that meant. I could give David something new on Amanda, his appetite for anything on the woman he'd deemed the next big celebrity train wreck still insatiable. Then, David satisfied, and given I was basically best buds with Peter Lowell, *Business*

Day would be mine. I imagined Audrey hearing about my job at *Business Day*, pictured the scowl on her face as she was forced to swallow the bitter pill that I had been right and she had been wrong. That it hadn't been a mistake to take a job at *The Scoop*—it had been genius. I was, undeniably, very spite-motivated.

The tinkle of a bell and a cool gust of air snapped my attention to the door. And there she was, Amanda Myles. She had really come. A few of the restaurant staff rushed to her in the entryway, saying how wonderful it was to see her again, offering to take her coat. So that was why she had chosen this place—she was a regular. She wanted the upper hand of home turf.

For a brief moment, I forgot all about the sickening nerves and general sense of terror that consumed me as I was struck by the sight of Amanda in the flesh. She was beautiful. Shorter than I'd expected, with her polished chestnut hair—this is how she would have been described in an article on *The Scoop*—tied back in a sleek ponytail. Her jutting cheekbones instantly made the infamous description of her "fuller figure" absurd; I was probably larger in size than Amanda. I was no better than an oafish football fan watching the game on TV, mocking a kicker who missed the goal from the comfort of the sunken dent made by my ass in the couch cushions.

As Amanda threw her head back with generous laughter at something one of the waiters said and shrugged out of her coat—a fur, real or fake, I couldn't tell—I took in her outfit, a long, ankle-length deep-blue silk dress that glimmered sapphire. Tottering in strappy black heels as she whispered conspiratorially to one of the servers, charming the staff with ease, she radiated glamour, but also something harder to define, an aura that marks someone as different. Special. Some other diners turned to look, and a few seemed to recognize her, whispering, eyes wide in surprise, while others only frowned and returned to their conversations, either not knowing who she was, or having been in New York too long to be impressed by seeing a celebrity. Then, as incongruous to me as it surely was to everyone else, Amanda glided an elegant path between tables toward the back and headed straight for me—the awkward, seasick-looking woman.

"So," she said, lowering herself into her seat and placing a black leather purse on the table before looking me squarely in the eyes. "You're the one who's been making my life hell."

It felt like the restaurant floor dropped away and I was hovering in midair, about to plummet. It was exhilarating and terrifying to be face-to-face with Amanda, without a screen or locked newsroom doors to hide behind. I steeled myself for an attack, verbal or even physical.

"Funny," she continued, openly scrutinizing me, "I'd half expected you to have horns."

A wry smile, a flash of mischief in her big hazel eyes. Amanda had... made a joke?

"Horns? Yes, I had those surgically removed," I said, unsure how I mustered the boldness to banter with her, given how close I was to puking from nerves. Amanda barked a laugh. Through the haze of anxiety that made everything seem slow, echoey, and far away, I began to see that Amanda was amused. Entertained. She flashed another playful grin. I had expected Amanda to be cold, wary, or even aggressive, and this gulf between what I'd prepared for and what was actually happening threw me, forcing me to plot a new course of action in real time.

Amanda leaned back in her chair, crossed her legs, staring, taking me in. I saw no sign that she was, like me, in a hurry to fill the silence. I stared back, noting the delicate gold chain that gilded her slender neck, an immaculate manicure, details that conveyed a sense of order.

But there were things that hinted at something messy beneath the glossy surface, some private struggle; the whites of her eyes marked with red lines, as if she'd recently been crying, or hadn't been sleeping (that would make two of us); dark circles that betrayed a weariness. I watched as, in seconds, she seemed to shift back and forth between two selves; a big smile and defiant eyebrow raise one minute, a hollow stare, nails scratching her arm, her neck, the next.

A server came to take our order. Amanda reached up and put a gentle hand on his arm.

"No food today, Stefano," she said calmly, smiling up at him. "Just two martinis, dry."

The man apparently named Stefano nodded, swiftly removing the unneeded wineglasses and cutlery from the table and disappearing without acknowledging me. Was Amanda serious? I was astounded by her entitlement, her arrogant assumption I'd be happy to drink whatever she was drinking. Amanda clocked my reaction, lifting her chin in my direction like a challenge.

"What? You don't like martinis?"

"Sure," I said, almost laughing at the brazen nerve of it but forcing myself to bite my tongue instead. "A martini sounds great." I made a mental note to sip it slowly. If you didn't count that one measly hour, I hadn't slept. I needed to stay sharp, alert, get what I came for.

Amanda began to glance around the restaurant almost comically, swiveling in her seat.

"So, which direction should I face?" she said, her voice dripping with sarcasm, twisting in one direction, then the other. "I want to make sure the hidden camera captures my best angle."

"I promise you, Amanda, there is no camera."

"And I'm supposed to believe the word of a tabloid journalist?" She seemed edgy all of a sudden, her playful energy dissipating. "You must have a recording device in your bag, then."

I reached down to the floor for my handbag, picked it up and opened it in Amanda's direction. "I'm not recording. You can search my bag and check if you don't believe me."

She waved the bag away. "Jesus Christ, I'm only kidding. I'm not the TSA."

Stefano returned with the martinis. Amanda lifted hers and sipped without pause—clearly, this was not a cheers-ing situation. I did the same, trying not to grimace as the liquor burned my throat. I hadn't eaten all day, had barely slept, and as the booze hit my stomach, I felt instantly dizzy, off-kilter. But it gave me the courage I needed to take control of the conversation.

"Thank you for agreeing to meet with me," I said, still in shock that *the* Amanda Myles was sitting on the other side of the table. "I wasn't sure you would say yes, after everything."

Amanda shot me a tight smile as she gently placed her martini back down on the table.

"Well," she said, thoughtful as she leaned back in her seat, folded her hands in her lap, "when I got your email, I was skeptical. I found it hard to believe your offer was genuine, and not just some sneaky trick. But I thought about it, and it occurred to me that maybe, just maybe, if we met face-to-face, if you saw I was a real, flesh-and-bone human being, you might pause before you hit publish on a story filled with horrible lies about me. Then I got curious: Who *is* this person, so indifferent to my suffering? Why is she doing this? I wanted to understand."

Of all the reasons Amanda Myles could have had for agreeing to meet, I never would have guessed it was because *she* was curious about *me*—even if her curiosity was self-motivated.

"So," she continued, "you used to work at *Marie Claire*, is that right?"

The city might as well have ground to a halt around us. I tried to compute what Amanda had just said. She knew where I used to work? She'd looked into my background? My briefly stabilized heart rate began to race again. What was happening? I was the journalist. I was supposed to be asking *her* the questions. Yet somehow Amanda had wrestled control of the conversation, had her hands firmly on the steering wheel. I didn't know where she was taking us.

"What?" she said, noticing my surprise. "You think I wouldn't do my research before agreeing to meet a tabloid journalist?"

Trying to hide my panic as the direction of the conversation spun further and further out of my control, I eventually found my words and confirmed that I used to work at *Marie Claire*.

"And now *The Scoop*? That's a long way to fall. Who did you refuse to fuck?"

"Excuse me?"

I stared at her, sure I mustn't have heard her correctly. Amanda only raised an eyebrow.

I squirmed under the spotlight Amanda had turned on me, eyeing the exit. But maybe it was only fair, if I expected Amanda to open up to me, that I should have to open up to her, too.

"It wasn't like that," I said. "It was more like, refused to see the writing on the wall, that print journalism was dying, or was already dead. Refused to pretend to be genuinely enthusiastic about search engine optimization. I guess I did neglect to kiss the asses of the right people."

"I know all about what happens when you refuse to kiss the asses of the right people," Amanda said. "You know my ex-husband, Alex. Seems like you two are best buddies now."

So, Amanda *had* guessed that the "insider close to the band" in the article was Alexander. She wasn't an idiot. I kept my mouth shut, said nothing, though my eyes probably confirmed it.

"Please, those comments were classic Alexander. I'm not the least bit surprised that when you came calling, my ex-husband jumped at the chance to trash me. I'm just amazed he was able to form coherent sentences. I hear he spends most of his time in the desert doing ayahuasca."

Still, I said nothing. I wasn't about to let her pressure me into revealing the source.

"So *now* you're going to play the ethical journalist?" she said, rolling her eyes. "You know, that story brought up a lot for me. It was an incredibly painful time in my life, the breakdown of my relationship with Alexander and the end of the Valentines. It took me years to get over it—not even 'get over it,' but be able to function normally on a day-to-day-basis. So, to have all of that dragged back into the public arena out of nowhere..." She trailed off, looking down into her martini for a moment before meeting my gaze again. "It fucked me up."

A sadness crept into her eyes as they locked on mine. I could see she was telling the truth. Still, Jocelyn's words from the night at the bar rang in my mind: *She's just trying to make you feel sorry for her, to stop the stories. Don't fall for it.* I couldn't rule it out, that Amanda might have a hidden agenda, perhaps to try to elicit an admission of guilt from me as part of planned legal action. Maybe she was secretly recording us, as she'd jokingly accused me of doing. I ignored the pang of sympathy I felt for her. I had to do my job. I wouldn't let her derail me.

"But you know what hurt even more?" she went on. "The first article. The photos of me walking with my groceries. Can you imagine what it's like, to have your flaws pointed out for thousands of people to see? To have cruel comments made about your body for an audience?"

Her confession surprised me. I'd assumed Amanda would be the most upset about the article blaming her for the end of the Valentines, claiming she had cheated on her husband. Or the paparazzi "punch" (which, at least according to her, was not a punch, but self-defense).

"The close-ups on different parts of my body," she continued, shaking her head, looking miserably into her drink. "It was so invasive, so personal. It made me feel so...ugly. Exposed."

Amanda looked like she might cry. Only a monster would refuse to show remorse upon hearing how their actions had hurt someone so deeply, but that's what I had to do. I glanced at the clock on the wall. We'd already been talking for fifteen minutes. I could feel it slipping away, my chance to coax some useful piece of information out of her. I had to wrest back control.

"I'm curious to know why you disappeared from the spotlight for so long, after the Valentines went on hiatus. There were rumors you would have a solo career. But instead you disappeared. Surely you understand the interest, in someone so popular vanishing like that?"

Amanda was about to respond when Stefano returned and asked if we wanted another round. Amanda said yes. I noticed her glass was empty; mine was half full. I said yes anyway. I didn't want Amanda to become self-conscious about drinking more than me, which might make her more careful about the words coming out of her mouth. She was just starting to open up.

"There were a few reasons," she said once Stefano was gone. "For a while, I had a stalker. This was many years ago, and it's over now, but while that threat was active—he was a very unwell young man—I had no choice but to lie low or otherwise risk attracting him. I decided nothing was worth the daily fear of being followed, or even attacked, by a man who believed he needed to impregnate me to bring the next Jesus Christ to earth and save humanity."

She said this matter-of-factly, but I was rocked. My face must have betrayed my horror.

"Oh yeah," she said, eyes wide, nodding, "you wouldn't believe the freaks that come out of the woodwork when you're a woman in the public eye. Especially at that level of fame."

The sympathy for Amanda I was trying to suppress bubbled again, along with some guilt, that part of Amanda's reason for going underground was for her personal safety. With that first article, *The Scoop* had forced her back into the spotlight. I took a numbing swallow of my drink.

THE SCOOP

"But I don't like to dwell," Amanda said. "And that wasn't the only reason. The truth is, I reached a point where I could no longer handle the attention. After the split from Alexander and the hiatus, I was in a bad place for years. Things got really dark. But I went to therapy, even got sober for a while—not anymore, obviously," she said, raising her glass and taking a big sip, something about this sending a chill through me. I wondered how recently she'd started drinking again. I hoped the *Scoop* articles, the media attention, the stress of it all, hadn't made her relapse.

"And then my mother died," she continued. "Not two years later. Just as I was picking myself up from what I thought was the worst time of my life, an even bigger wrecking ball hit."

I knew from Wikipedia that Amanda's mother was dead, but it was only then that it clicked, that we shared the experience of losing our mothers. "Wrecking ball" was about right. That was what it felt like for me, too, that first year or so. Before my mother died, I'd expected to feel profound grief and sadness when the day came. What I wasn't prepared for was how much my sense of self, how it felt to be a person in the world, had fractured and broken apart with the loss. A sudden, brutal forced death and rebirth, cleaving me into two selves: the version of me who existed when she was alive, and the version of me who'd experienced the loss of her, and was now forced to go on without her. *Call me when you get there*, my mom had always insisted when I traveled, and dutifully I always did, as if it were some safety law I was obligated to abide by or otherwise risk some unspecified but serious consequence. The first trip I took after she died, it felt like a rope had been cut, or an anchor untied, the reality sinking in that I no longer needed to call her when I got there, never had needed to. No alarms were set off, nothing fell from the sky. Just a quiet, invisible, permanent shift as I rolled my suitcase to the taxi rank.

Amanda began to look different to me all of a sudden, as if the light in the restaurant had changed. The golden fall afternoon rays still streaked through the windows onto the white tablecloths and glassware, but I felt it distinctly, that something in the atmosphere had shifted.

"I read the article you wrote for *Marie Claire* about the loss of your mom. The one about grief and anniversaries."

My breath caught in my throat. Amanda had read one of the articles I was most proud of in my career, a reflection on the pain and beauty of death anniversaries, which I'd published on the *Marie Claire* website on the fifth anniversary of her passing. I couldn't believe she'd read it.

"What you wrote, about the anniversary being like a bend in the river, passing the place where you almost drowned but didn't, a reminder of your strength—I was very moved by that."

Amanda's words seemed genuine, despite my awareness that she might have come there that day to trick or manipulate me—into what, I still couldn't say. Maybe she was only playing to my ego. Still, I felt the wall between us coming down, fast. For a brief moment, I forgot the circumstances that brought us to that West Village restaurant. We felt like old friends, reunited.

"It's so unfair, isn't it?" Amanda said. "Losing your mom young. You're still at the age when she's the worst—suffocating, and yet at the same time doesn't understand you, somehow both too much and not enough. Then you grow older, and you start to get it: why she was like that, so racked with worry at what the world might do to her daughter. But by the time you're mature enough to actually want her advice, you can't ask her, because she's gone. It's cruel."

"Yes" was all I could manage to stammer out as I tried to maintain my composure.

"I've never been able to lose this feeling that we were on the precipice of a new era, one where she didn't have to wear the mask of 'mother' with me. Like we were about to really know each other."

I sipped my water to try to stop myself from crying. Amanda had verbalized something I'd been feeling toward in the dark for years but had not yet touched, though I'd come closer to it lately. Not that it was unfair that my mom died when I was young—I knew what had been stolen from me; the years, the birthdays, the Thanksgivings, the Christmases, decades and decades of them. The possibility of her meeting my theoretical future children, and decades and decades of time with them; my mother, eighty-something, me, sixty-something, both of us watching my adult daughter blow out the candles on her thirtieth birthday cake. It was too much, too big, to truly fathom, the full reaches of the loss into time and space. I already knew, too, that I blamed myself, regretted not sending up a white flag to someone for help before it was too late. And no matter how many friends, therapists, self-help books, lifestyle gurus, and weirdly intense yoga instructors said it wasn't my fault, that I should release the burden of the guilt I carried over it (which, according to said weirdly intense yoga instructors, I carried in my stomach, the true root of my occasional digestive issues, definitely not a sensitivity to dairy), I knew I never would.

What I hadn't been able to articulate, perhaps because it would have taken me until I was closer to Amanda's age to do so, was that with more maturity on my part, and some added years of wisdom for my mom, too, we might have been able to take off those masks required of a mother raising her daughter. When she died, I was still keeping her at arm's length as I fought to become my own person, form my own separate identity. I know she kept a lot from me because she thought I was still too young and immature to know, or because she wasn't quite ready to cede her parental authority. I got the first clues of this at her funeral, based on the stories my aunt and her close friends had recounted from my mom's wild, younger days—the time as a teenager when she took mushrooms and spent the night in a hall cupboard "talking to the man who was giving her jellybeans"; the satirical poems she wrote about the nuns at her small-town Massachusetts Catholic school that got her caned across her hands as punishment; the man she was in love with before she met my father who broke it off suddenly, which took her years to get over, if she ever really did. But there, at the restaurant, it hit me with full, shattering force: the loss of not just birthdays, Thanksgivings, and Christmases, but of who she was yet to become, and who I was yet to become, and what might have bloomed between those two strong-headed women, so alike, when given the chance to put down the weapons they held up toward each other.

The words tumbled out fast and uncontained.

"There's a Valentines song that was special to me and my mom. 'Almost There.' One of my favorite memories of her was this one time she drove me to school. She was happy, silly—which was rare, because she was always so tired. She had depression. But on this morning, she turned the volume up and was singing along, drumming her hands on the steering wheel. Free."

Amanda gave a small, sad smile. She looked briefly lost in thought.

"Did she get to see you graduate from college?" she asked.

"No—she died a few months before. But she knew my plans, to move to New York City and become a journalist, and she was excited. She wanted me to have a better life than she did."

"And you've been trying to make a dead person proud ever since."

She said this not like an accusation, but with a knowing. I nodded.

"That's why I was surprised, when I read your essay. How could the same woman who wrote it work somewhere that twists the truth, publishes lies, spreads hate?"

THE SCOOP

Her words came down like a hammer, smashing the illusion we'd briefly inhabited that we were just two women connecting over grief, pain, and loss—not a journalist trying to fish for a scoop, and a fed-up celebrity possibly gathering information on her enemy. I felt angry at her for breaking the spell. Had all that dead-mom talk been a strategy, to get me to drop my guard?

"Are you married?" she asked suddenly, glancing at my finger. I told her no. There had been a long-term relationship, I explained, but it ended a year ago. Nothing serious since then.

"You're better off," she said. "Better to be single than with the wrong person, and I believe that with my whole heart." She shook her head. "Alexander pursued me for years, made it known he was attracted to me, wanted to be together. I resisted and resisted...something in my gut just knew. I'd glimpsed things that gave me pause—his sensitivity to the slightest criticism, his impatience that blew up into rage, moping for days over minor disappointments..."

I could tell by now Amanda was tipsy. I was, too; I had to work harder to focus on what she was saying, stay sharp. I tried not to pick up my drink. Something was unfurling in her, and the way she spoke now seemed more confessional, almost careless. I didn't want to miss a word.

"But he was our manager, and, for all his flaws, he had this way of making me feel safe. Over time I convinced myself that he only had these strong emotions and reactions to things—sometimes to me—because he cared for me so deeply. I convinced myself that was love.

"So, I gave in, and for a while it was great. It felt good, to have arms embracing me when I walked offstage, to see his eyes shine with admiration on a new level as I sang. But I soon learned a hard lesson about men: they see something shiny, decide they want it, and do anything it takes to get it. But once they get it, they realize that admiring a shiny thing from afar is very different from having that shiny thing right up in your face all day, every day. Before you know it, something flips. Then the shiny thing they longed to claim is too bright—much brighter than them—and it shines on all their insecurities. They start to resent you, blame you, and it becomes so uncomfortable for them, so unbearable, that subconsciously they start trying to extinguish it."

I tried not to let my surprise show, that Amanda was sharing all of this with me. We'd agreed the conversation was off the record, but even so, there was no need for her to open up in this way. And not just to any journalist, but me, the one "trying to ruin" her life. Amanda *was* tipsy, but not enough to not know what she was saying, and to whom she was saying it. Then I remembered what Jocelyn said, about famous people yearning for attention, the fame a drug that, once tasted, the body never forgets, never stops craving. Amanda did seem lonely. It would be hard to resist for anyone, the intense gaze of another person interested in you. But especially for the lonely, for whom the gaze of another can feel like the most intoxicating thing in the world.

"Things started falling apart with Alex, and, at least according to him, it was all my fault. He convinced himself there was something going on between me and Toby, our drummer. There wasn't—we were band members, friends, that's all. If there had been anything there, it would've happened years earlier. Before I know it, I'm agreeing to 'prove' my love to Alex by marrying him in Las Vegas one night after a show when we were on tour. Dumbest decision of my life.

"When we officially broke it off a few months later, Alexander and I couldn't be in the same room together; he'd end up screaming, and I'd end up crying. Horrible. I spoke to the rest of the band, suggested we get a new manager—but Alexander was one step ahead. He'd already bad-mouthed me to every exec in the music industry, saying I was crazy and that I'd cheated on him with Toby in the next room on tour, which was a flat-out lie. But this was the early 2000s. The industry was even more of a boys' club than it is now. No one wanted to work with us—sorry, with *me*. We could have continued searching until we found a new manager, but the drama created a negative energy around the Valentines—not just in the industry, but inside the band itself. A bad smell we could never get rid of. We went on hiatus, hoping with time things would resolve themselves, but something had shifted, permanently. It was the end. I blame myself."

"You shouldn't blame yourself, Amanda," I said. "It's not your fault that your own band manager and husband, someone you trusted, treated you so badly and bad-mouthed you—"

"But I do. I cared so much about the Valentines, more than anything. Being in that band was a privilege, and it was my responsibility to make the right decisions, to protect it. I failed."

"But you were so young, Amanda."

She shook her head, and I could see she was almost in tears, her eyes glassy. She took a big swig of her martini, placed it down on the table less carefully than before, the liquid sloshing.

"Anyway, it was a long time ago. I've made peace with it. At least, I thought I had, until the article," she said, the still-burning embers of the anger she felt for me visible in her eyes.

"There were people in my life I'd never told that Alex and I got married, you know."

There it was, that churning guilt twisting in my guts again. Briefly, I wondered if I should stop with the questions. But Amanda had agreed to come, hadn't she? And I was beginning to feel it, the buzzing, staticky sensation, an electric pulse, the machinery of my mind whirring faster, the unmistakable intuition that I was closing in on... *something*. I was starting to pick up on what was at the root of Amanda's pain: the particular loneliness of feeling misunderstood. By Alexander, who claimed she was "unfaithful"; by the music executives who wrote her off as "crazy." No one could go back and change the past. But what did Amanda want now? Revenge?

"There was no chance of a solo career?" I asked. Then, figuring a little flattery wouldn't hurt, "No offense to the others, but you were what made the Valentines special, Amanda."

She smiled sadly, shook her head. "Alexander made sure that was never a possibility."

"Why not?"

"Are you kidding? Like I said, no one wanted to work with me after that. 'Crazy Amanda Myles' who 'cheated' on her poor husband with a band member? I had meetings, but I could always see in their eyes nothing was going to come of it. It's a leap of faith, to invest the money and time into launching a solo career. And the record companies had their pick of young, hot new things to choose from instead. There were a couple of influential men who were considering working with me, but..." She trailed off. "Let's just say I would have had to compromise myself too much. I was done appeasing men with dollar signs in their eyes and a bulge in their pants."

She raised an eyebrow at me as if to say, *You're a woman, you know what I mean.*

"Anyway, a few years went by and then it was the YouTube discovery era. All of a sudden, you didn't even have to be in LA to get signed by a major record label. There was a moment when that could have happened, and it passed. But I've accepted it all now. Mostly."

Mostly. Amanda clearly still had a deep well of rage inside over what had been taken from her by these men—by Alexander, by the music industry suits. Possibly even her Valentines band members, for not doing more to support her. Her reputation had never been repaired. *Mostly.* She still longed for it, for justice, for the record to be corrected, maybe even the solo career she never got. If she let me tell this story,

Amanda could repair her public image, finally get to tell her side. And this was exactly the kind of story I'd been searching for—something exclusive, big enough to impress David, but that would at the same time return my lost journalistic integrity. Genuine news. We could both reinvent ourselves. Help each other do it.

"How come you've never spoken publicly about any of this before?" I asked.

"Journalists would contact me from time to time, but I knew how it would go: I'd talk to them, then they'd go to others to corroborate the story, including Alex, and the master manipulator would twist everything until it was his version of events that got told. The only person I'd have trusted was Oprah, but she never called." She shrugged. "The moment passed."

"So why not let the world know the truth now?" I said. "What's stopping you?"

Amanda shook her head, her mouth in a tight line.

"I know you're afraid to trust me, Amanda. But...this isn't the real me. Working at a tabloid, I mean. It was never in the plan to end up at *The Scoop*, editing stories about celebrity nose jobs, or a 'psychic' panda that predicted 9/11—"

"Wait, what?"

"It was most likely a coincidence—it doesn't matter. Look, I know we got off to a rocky start. But you read the essay I wrote for *Marie Claire*. *That's* the real me. Let me tell your story."

Amanda frowned. I could tell she didn't believe me. But I needed her to.

"I don't know..."

"It's just like you said," I tried, saying whatever I could to convince her. "These powerful men—in Hollywood, the music industry, or the business world—see women as something to use and throw away once there's nothing left to squeeze from them. I think it's noble, that you walked away and took the consequences that came with that instead of compromising yourself."

I'd offered this purely to stroke her ego, but as I heard myself say it, I realized it was true. Amanda had given up on her dream, the future she'd wanted for herself, but at least she was no longer allowing herself to be demeaned, no longer allowing herself to be exploited for her desires. I could not say the same.

Amanda watched me warily. I could see she still wasn't satisfied. Earlier in the conversation, when I'd opened up to her about my career, how I'd gone from *Marie Claire* to *The Scoop*, I'd felt how I'd pulled her toward me. She'd said it at the very beginning of the meeting, that that was why she had come—to understand who I was and why I was writing the articles about her. This was the key, I realized, to give her another taste of what she came here to get. I needed to be vulnerable with her again. I decided to tell her about David and *Business Day*.

"Hearing you talk about what happened with Alexander, and the music industry executives, about how they abused their power over you... I can relate. That's sort of what I'm going through right now at *The Scoop*, with my boss, David Brown."

"I knew it," Amanda said, slamming a hand on the table. "I knew there was more to it."

I told Amanda how after losing my job at *Marie Claire*, I'd grown more desperate as the months passed and accepted the offer for an interview with David. I told her how he offered me a role on the spot, the highest salary I'd ever earned, how he had also promised to get me a transfer to the more prestigious *Business Day*. That I was now beholden to the whims of this man, who could technically withhold the offer as long as he wanted to. Dread sat heavy in my stomach as I acknowledged this aloud for the first time. Amanda nodded as I talked, and I could see it in her eyes, the way her view of me slowly shifted. It was her story, with only a few details changed.

I felt tears prick my eyes. I didn't try to hide them. "My life has gone off course. But I'm doing everything I can to get it back on track. Let me do this. Let me help you get your revenge."

Amanda shook her head firmly. "No, I'm not interested in getting revenge. Revenge is driven by anger, and I'm not angry anymore. Revenge only continues the cycle of hurt. If I were to ever talk about that time in my life, what happened to me, it wouldn't be to get revenge."

I nodded, even though I found this difficult to understand. Didn't she want to show the world how she had been wronged? Own the narrative? Didn't she want to rub it in the faces of those who had hurt her? I must have been a childish person, because the thought of getting revenge gave me great pleasure.

"It's been years since I've given an interview; after being burned a few times, I promised myself I never would again." Then, with a small smile, she added, "But I will think about it."

I believed she meant it.

22

With *The Scoop*, Johnson News revives toxic tabloid culture for the digital age

By Audrey Holt-Crawford, media reporter

Johnson News, the global media empire that locally owns conservative cable channel America Now, and ruffled feathers several years ago when it acquired *Business Day*, is again stirring controversy, this time with its tabloid website, *The Scoop*, where journalists emulate the aggressive tactics of Fleet Street hacks.

Since they launched *The Scoop* a year ago, Johnson News has invested millions in the digital-only website, which the *Times* understands employs around 25 full-time staff (eight editors, five photo editors, and at least a dozen full-time reporters) working out of Johnson News HQ on Seventh Avenue. The team has been producing upwards of 100 articles a day, a surprisingly high number, given the head count, until you examine the quality — or lack thereof. The vast majority of articles are rewrites of other publications' stories with no additional reporting, not to mention riddled with typos and errors. (Troublingly, the *Times* hears staff are under such intense pressure to crank out stories that regular bathroom breaks are often impractical, and that in order to keep up with demand, journalists are encouraged to take herbal supplements to prevent UTIs.)

But it's *The Scoop*'s reckless "publish now, ask questions later" style that has raised the most concern, after Democratic senator Ashley Thompson from California recently made the difficult decision to come out publicly as gay after *The Scoop* published old photographs of her from college, including one that depicted her kissing a woman. In a statement, Senator Thompson, 47, said she had not yet come out, as she was still "privately grappling with" her sexuality. The timing of *The Scoop*'s "exposé" is also raising eyebrows, given the story broke just days before Thompson was due to participate in a Senate committee on police use of force. (Johnson News did not respond to a request for comment.)

Thompson isn't the only high-profile figure who has felt the wrath of this bullish new tabloid. Amanda Myles, who many will recall as the lead singer of '90s pop-rock band the Valentines, who in recent years has deliberately chosen a life out of the spotlight, was subject to a story that dissected paparazzi photos taken of her on the street near her West Village home. The article, written by *Scoop* reporter Yenay Tan, described Myles as "washed-up" and cast judgment on specific items in the grocery bags

Myles was carrying. It also commented repeatedly on her appearance, describing her as "showcasing a fuller figure."

"I wasn't 'showcasing' anything," Myles told the *Times* when contacted for a comment, her first media interview in more than a decade. "I was literally just walking."

A second article, published by editor Francesca Miller, a once-respected magazine editor, again took aim at Myles; the journalists, apparently looking to repeat the "success" of the first article, dug into Myles' private life and turned up documents revealing the star briefly married her band manager in 2001.

The articles have seen Myles become a prime target of the paparazzi. Tensions flared last week, leading to a physical altercation between Myles and one paparazzo. *The Scoop* published the photos with a headline claiming Myles "punched" him, but Myles insists she was only using her arms to keep the man away from her; she'd felt unsafe as the group swarmed her to take photographs. Myles says *The Scoop* did not contact her to confirm the details of the incident until several hours after publishing the headline alleging the violent attack.

Myles voiced her concern for younger, more vulnerable people entering the entertainment industry, and the mental health toll such relentless and unforgiving attention could take.

"I don't think the tabloids will be happy until they have ruined my life, and everyone else's, for the sake of a few clicks."

23

I GRIPPED THE BASEBALL BAT, felt its cool metal in my hands, the heft of it, swung, and slammed it down onto the desk with a crack. The items resting on its cheap wooden surface—a computer monitor, a keyboard, a picture frame with a portrait of a lobotomized-looking blond family, a mug bearing the words *Today's good mood is sponsored by coffee!*—jumped into the air with the force of the strike and crashed back down again. With one swift movement, I kicked a black leather office chair out of my way; it skidded across the room and toppled over on its side.

There wasn't much time left. When the desk at last split in half, sending the items on it down onto the floor, shattering the picture frame, I turned my attention to a Xerox machine in the corner. Panting, my arms growing weak and shaky, I couldn't help letting out a guttural groan with every whack, like a tennis star slogging it out in a Grand Slam match. *Match*! If only I had matches. I'd take some paper from the Xerox machine, set it alight, and watch the place burn.

An alarm startled me. *Whoop-whoop-whoop.* I let the baseball bat drop with a clatter.

In the foyer, I removed my hard hat and safety glasses, peeled off the plastic coveralls I'd worn over my clothes, and shoved them down a chute as instructed. Nearby, a dozen New Yorkers were zipping up their own coveralls and selecting tools of destruction, waiting to unleash their pent-up fury over four-across sidewalk blockers, horn-honkers, and elusive G trains.

"Better?" Patti asked as we clinked our drinks at the bar attached to Precious Things, "a safe space for women to express the rage accumulated in their daily lives as the result of interactions with men who have not done the work to unlearn toxic patriarchy." Fed up after I'd spent the weekend moping around the apartment, unshowered, drinking all her booze, she'd forced me to dress and dragged me to the rage room, where I could "express anger in a healthy way." Windowless, no sunlight inside at all, it was the only place I could bear to be, aside from my bed.

I nodded, sipped my beer, tried to smile, but in truth I did not feel any better. Destroying a fake office, while cathartic in theory, had done nothing to alleviate the alternating panic and dread that had consumed me for the last twenty-four hours, ever since the publication of Audrey's article. She had humiliated me, for our entire industry to see—any peers who'd missed my bylines on *The Scoop* were surely well-informed of my tragic fall into tabloid purgatory now.

Once-respected magazine editor. She really wrote that. *Once-respected.* I couldn't think of two words Audrey could say to me that would be more cutting, not even "fuck you." It *was* a fuck-you.

When Audrey had shared at brunch that she needed to start bringing in some stories that weren't just Park Street Publishing gossip, for fear of being seen to be underperforming at the *Times*, I hadn't realized that one of her scoops would be...me. I couldn't have imagined it, and still didn't want to believe it. The chance of us reconciling now seemed all but impossible.

THE SCOOP

What made Audrey's betrayal sting even more was that she had gotten an interview with Amanda. Did Audrey talk to Amanda *before* or *after* my conversation with her at the restaurant? No way to know. But I couldn't stop stewing over it, the possibility that Amanda sat opposite me, making me work for it, swearing she didn't give media interviews anymore; meanwhile, she'd just been blabbing to the *Times*. Whether Amanda gave that interview to Audrey before San Mateo's or went running to the *Times* right after, either way, I felt like I'd been duped by both of them.

"Frankie?"

Patti was staring at me, waiting for me to answer a question I hadn't heard.

"Huh?"

"I said," Patti repeated, summoning her patience, "have you spoken to Audrey again?"

I had not. Not since Thursday, when I woke at lunchtime and checked my inbox to find an email from her, sent at 9:03 a.m. I held my breath as I opened it, wondering if the apology I'd been waiting for, ever since the dinner party, had finally come. Instead, she'd sent me a few paragraphs from an article about *The Scoop*, an article that mentioned me, and asked if I had any comment to make before it went live in an hour. Clinical, cold. No explanation, no apology, no suggestion we talk about what happened between us, nothing like that. By the time I saw it, it was after midday, and instinctively I went straight to *The New York Times* media section, where I saw the piece was already live. In horror and disbelief, I read Audrey's words, words thousands of people, including people we knew, had no doubt already read—including the detail about the herbal UTI supplement in Jocelyn's drawer. Something I'd told her in private, as a friend.

Soon a text had come from Yenay. She was crushed, as shocked and mortified as I was.

Isn't Audrey your friend? she'd asked. I couldn't bring myself to reply to that.

I called Audrey. She answered. I demanded to know how she could do this to me.

"Really? You couldn't have at least given me some more warning this was coming?"

"Once my article was ready to publish, my boss didn't want to wait. You of all people should understand that, Frankie. From what I hear, *The Scoop* often gives no warning at all."

A taste of my own medicine, is that what this was? How unbelievably petty. Then I remembered the pettiest part of all.

"'Once-respected,' huh? So not anymore, right? At least now I know what you really think."

"You're the one who took a job at the McDonald's of journalism, but this is somehow my fault?"

"What's wrong with McDonald's? I've seen you inhale a Big Mac more than once. And if you want to play 'who's the more ethical journalist?' how dare you publish the thing about the UTI supplements? I told you that in private, Audrey. As a friend. I thought I could trust you."

I didn't know what else to say; I was so angry I couldn't think clearly enough to form another sentence. I hung up and wept like a baby. Five years of friendship, gone. I wondered how I didn't see it coming; that at some point, the different worlds we came from would come to claim us back. The natural way of things brought back into balance. As I sat there with Patti, nursing my drink, it seemed impossible that I might never speak to Audrey again, and yet just as impossible to see how our friendship could come back from this. How I could ever forgive her.

"No," I said, still smarting from Audrey's betrayal. "What else is there to say?"

"You two are such good friends," Patti said. "You'll work it out. Let things cool off."

"I thought you were going to say, 'I told you so.' You've always hated Audrey."

"'Hate' is a strong word. I never said I *hated* her. The girl's got a stick up her ass, for sure, but she's not the devil. Also, don't shoot me for saying this, but... I don't blame her."

What? Was Patti about to turn on me, too? She was the only person I had left. I knew I shouldn't have been so brazen with how much of her food and drink I'd put on my secret tab.

"How could you possibly be on her side?" I asked, gripping my beer bottle tighter.

"Would you relax? I'm not on her side *or* your side. Don't you see? Audrey is as stuck as you are, working her ass off for clicks, to make her boss happy, to keep her job. Just like you."

"We're *both* stuck? Come on, you know about her parents, her wealth. We are *not* the same."

I saw in Patti's eyes a flame of irritation. A loud eruption of laughter from a nearby table not enough to pull her intense gaze away from me.

"You're not understanding me. I'm trying to get you to see it's not personal. That this is so much bigger than you and Audrey as individuals. The competition between workers in a late-capitalist system denies them the possibility of authentic connection, because their fundamental disempowerment, and their false belief in the need to hoard supposedly 'scarce' resources, means they see each other as—"

"Spare me the lecture, Pat. No offense. I'm not in the mood for a teachable moment."

Not personal? I had been blindsided, betrayed, by one of the few people I trusted. Or at least *thought* I could trust. I didn't know how to be the bigger person. I couldn't see beyond it.

Patti cast her gaze downward into her drink, looking like a parent feeling tempted to give up on her disappointing child. I felt bad for shutting her down the way I did, but when attempting to enlighten your roommate about class consciousness, you have to choose the right moment, and that day was not it. It was hard not to feel like a shitty person next to Patti sometimes, with her climate activism and pro bono work helping people who couldn't afford a lawyer, and that feeling of moral inferiority was only getting worse every week at *The Scoop*. But I was turning things around. I just had to get through this difficult chapter; then, once I got to *Business Day*, I'd overhaul my life. I'd start donating to Planned Parenthood and the ACLU, finally buy some groceries to put in the community fridge on my block I walked past every day. Once I got the *Business Day* job, I decided, that was the kind of person I was going to be. I just had to get there first.

"So, what now?" Patti asked. "What are you going to do?"

"What do you mean? What can I do? Everybody's read it by now. Even if Audrey could take my name out of the piece, I know she wouldn't. She's always been so goddamn stubborn—"

"I don't mean Audrey's article, Frank. I mean, are you going to stay at *The Scoop*?"

Not this again. First Audrey, now Patti. If I couldn't leave before, I really couldn't now.

"What other choice do I have? The entire industry thinks I'm bottom-feeding scum."

"So, leave the industry. If someone like you is forced to churn out pointless clickbait, to degrade yourself like this just to stay in it, it's the canary in the coal mine."

Patti threw back what was left of her negroni and looked at me with a serious expression.

"There's something I've been meaning to talk to you about. I wanted to wait to bring it up until I saw you in person, but I've hardly seen you with these crazy night shift hours..."

I stiffened, felt my pulse beat faster, wondering what could be so serious that Patti couldn't just text me about it. That she felt the need to wait until we were face-to-face to discuss.

"The article about Senator Ashley Thompson. The one with the old photos of her, that forced her to come out. Did you have anything to do with that?"

It surprised me that Patti had seen the story, though I didn't know why. Maybe I'd assumed she didn't read mainstream media outlets, thought she got her information from alternative sources. But then, the story did go viral. I felt a pit like a river stone in my stomach.

"No, why?" The lie came even easier the second time, after first denying it at Audrey's.

"Okay," Patti said, and I panicked once I realized what was coming. "It's just that, when I saw that *The Scoop* was the original source of the photos, I recognized the name as the place you work. And when I clicked on the link to see the original story on *The Scoop*, I didn't recognize the journalist's name—just some dude—but I saw the time stamp. It was published at night."

Shit. I took a pull of my beer as I decided whether to double down on the lie or come clean.

"Frankie, you can tell me the truth. Believe it or not, I won't judge you. Like I said before, about you and Audrey—this is about more than just you on an individual level."

Patti looked me dead in the eye. I couldn't lie to her, not when she was looking at me like that.

"I tried to push back, Pat, I swear I did. When David sent the photos, dictated the headline to me, I warned him it was—"

"Please don't get defensive," she said, raising a palm to silence me.

"It's not helpful. I need to tell you how I feel, so I can let it go. Can you please try to hear me, instead of explaining?"

I sealed my lips and sat in silence as Patti described how upsetting it was for her, that the person she lived with, shared her home with, had played a part in publishing that article. The way the headline referred to two women kissing, making a joke out of it, making it seem disgusting.

"Frank, I know how badly you needed a job. When you got it I was happy for you, even knowing what I do about Johnson News..."

It was true. When I told Patti I'd signed the contract with *The Scoop*, she'd been overjoyed, her happiness only increasing when I explained I would be working night shift (which meant she would have the couch and TV to herself in the evenings). I probably could have told her I'd made a career pivot to become an arms dealer and she still would have suggested we break out the champagne. New York City's obscenely expensive and nearly-impossible-to-navigate rental market will push even the most upstanding and principled people to their limits.

"...because we all have to make compromises in this unjust system we're forced to participate in, or otherwise starve. As an activist, I sit with it all the time: by blocking off this street for a protest, what if it makes someone late for their job and they get fired and can't support their family? Or someone can't get to a person they're a caregiver for? It's not easy. But when there's something bigger and more important at stake, trade-offs must be made. So, if you think you can salvage your career in order to do valuable work in the future, and that this is the way to do it...well, you're the only one who can make that call. Only you can decide. No one else can tell you what is right for you. No one else has to live with your choices. It's up to you."

24

I'M NOT SURE WHAT I THOUGHT would happen once I'd done it. Once I emailed Marcus and told him to go "code red," to do whatever he had to do. Maybe that the horns Amanda joked about would spontaneously sprout from my forehead? Or I'd be attacked by a swarm of locusts? That the universe would send me some kind of instant, undeniable sign that I had strayed too far from the path of what was good and just? But there was nothing; no spooky, synchronistic slap on the wrist to frighten me back into more honorable territory. It felt like getting away with shoplifting, like I'd slipped a bracelet into my coat pocket and walked straight out, face posed in bored innocence. I kept waiting for the alarm to sound, to get caught in the act, but there was only silence. I never imagined it would feel so easy, so normal. That it would feel like nothing at all.

When there's something bigger and more important at stake, compromises must be made, Patti had said. *Only you can decide.* And so, I had. I'd decided that I wasn't going to let *Business Day* slip through my fingers—it was so close now. One big scoop to please David, to impress Peter, maybe even big enough for Walter Johnson to know my name, was all that stood between me and the version of myself I just *knew* I was destined to be. The kind of journalist who people at parties hovered nearby wanting to talk to, who had tens of thousands of followers, who won awards, who got to stand onstage holding a hefty trophy made of 24-karat gold, who would tearily thank their late mother for the sacrifices she made for her, but ultimately dedicate the award to the tireless journalists at that moment fearlessly reporting from a warzone somewhere, the true heroes of the industry, as one solitary tear is slowly wiped from her cheek. I'd been on my way at *Marie Claire*, until the path had abruptly disappeared. But I was clawing my way back. And the only route back to media respectability for me now was *Business Day*.

Marcus didn't make me wait long.

I'd almost forgotten about the email I'd sent him when, a few days later, his name appeared in my inbox. I was on the subway platform on my way to work, stuffed into my puffer coat, the unmistakable acrid scent of fresh piss from a puddle nearby filling my nostrils.

Dredged this up from the black lagoon, the note said, with an unsettling winking emoji.

I began to sweat as I clicked on the attached file. Once it loaded, it took me a moment to understand what I was looking at, who I was looking at: Amanda. She was young in the photo, couldn't have been older than twenty, which made the image at least two decades old. In it, she wore a gold minidress covered in fringed beads, matching glittery gold heels, and what was obviously a wig—a shock of shaggy, brassy hair with blond highlights. I immediately recognized that Amanda, clutching an oversize fake microphone, was dressed up as the rock-and-roll icon Tina Turner. The reason it took me a few moments to realize it was Amanda was because she was wearing a conspicuous amount of bronzer, heavy, all over her face, chest, arms, and even her legs, making the whites of her eyes appear whiter, her skin several shades darker.

Amanda, I realized with horror, was in blackface.

Paranoid, I moved away from the other people on the platform to keep my screen safe from prying eyes. I felt hot, my heart thudding faster in my chest as I stared at the image, dumbfounded. Questions swirled in my mind. When and where was the photo taken? Was Amanda aware of its existence? Had she understood the costume amounted to blackface, or was she too young, dumb, and white-privileged to realize it? It was unclear how old she was, but she looked past the age when one should know better. How did Marcus get the photo? Did I want to know? When the train whooshed in and the doors sprang open, I stumbled on in a daze and flopped down in an empty window seat, as usual. A woman in a hairnet dozed nearby, mouth open. I would have to decide what I was going to do about the photo by the time I got to work.

Atlantic Ave—Barclays Center.

I should have been thrilled. Marcus had found more than any desperate tabloid editor in need of a scoop could hope for: Amanda Myles in a racist Halloween costume. It was like both of David's white whales had fucked and spawned a grotesque white whale love child. Project Black Lagoon would be a success—that I had cheated, sort of, by using a private investigator felt beside the point. David would be pleased, unable to deny that I'd fulfilled my end of our deal.

Dekalb Avenue.

And yet, my first instinct was to guard it. It was a life-destroyer, no two ways about it. Blackface was indefensible; Amanda's reputation would be ruined, probably forever—and deservedly so. So why did I wish I could simply delete the email? Pretend I'd never seen it?

As the train rushed out of the underground and trundled onto the Manhattan Bridge, the sunset streaking the East River pink, purple, and orange, I watched the boats and ferries stream across the water below, leaving delicate ripples across the surface. The Johnson News building stood somewhere in the cluster of skyscrapers beyond, shooting defiantly up to the sky. I felt the weight of it, the power I now possessed. I realized then that this was where my hesitation came from; not from some misplaced sympathy for, or desire to protect Amanda—what she had done deserved to be condemned—but from my own responsibility. If it weren't for me, if I hadn't ordered Marcus to dig, dig, dig, the photo of Amanda would likely have stayed buried forever. I could not be extricated from it, from what would come of publishing it—for Amanda or for anyone else. The consequences of *my* choice, expected or unforeseen, intended or never imagined, would be irrevocable. I was a necromancer, raising the corpse of her shameful secret from the dead. Once out, it could not be put back where it came from. What would I unleash?

The reason Amanda agreed to meet—so I would feel viscerally her humanity the next time I went to publish a story about her—had been a move of near genius. And it had worked.

Almost.

Grand Street.

Publishing the blackface photo would, without question, explode any remaining chance, however minuscule, of me interviewing Amanda for *The Scoop*. I'd already convinced myself that it wasn't going to happen, was probably never going to happen in the first place. But what if? What if that moment at the restaurant, when it felt like Amanda and I understood each other beyond celebrity and journalist, was real? What if her gut told her to trust me? What if she saw me as more than a tabloid hack? Saw me as I really was, or at least as I saw myself: tangled up in something I was trying to fight my way out of. Stuck, like everyone.

Broadway-Lafayette Street.

But now I didn't need an interview with Amanda. Revealing that a once-beloved pop star had worn blackface was serious, the kind of story that would get so much attention that even Walter Johnson would hear about it. Maybe I wouldn't need David to get me a transfer to *Business Day*. Maybe I could get to Walter myself—track down his email or phone number, even ambush him on the executive floor—and make him see I was being wasted at *The Scoop*. Then David would no longer have something to hold over me, to control me.

West 4th Street—Washington Square Park.

I thought of Amanda, wondered what she was doing at that very moment. Curled up cozy on the couch in her brownstone, maybe? Laughing to herself, pleased with her plan to dangle an interview in front of that gullible tabloid hack to bring any further *Scoop* stories on her to a halt?

No, I decided. Amanda probably wasn't thinking about me at all.

When the doors opened at Bryant Park, I shoved my way through the wall of commuters forcing their way onto the train and hurried up the steps to the street. By the time the Johnson News building came into view, I knew what I would do. I'd do what Audrey did when she called me *once-respected* in *The New York Times*, published something I'd told her in private. I would do what Josh did when he thought, *Hey, I wouldn't mind getting to know that pretty colleague of mine by the printer a little better*. I would do what David did when he called to shout at me in the middle of the night. I would do what Amanda did when she told me to my face she didn't give media interviews, only for her comments to the *Times* to be published days later. I would do what was right—*right for me*. Everybody else was.

25

"It's her, right? I mean, it's *her*."

Amanda Myles's egregiously darkened face filled my computer screen as the others crowded around to see—this was serious enough to get even Chris off his ass. I paced back and forth by the window, munching a cupcake; a PR rep had sent a box to promote *No Scrubs*, a reality show about a woman who cleaned crime scenes for a living looking for love, the show's subject matter weirdly not enough to make them unappetizing. I'd kicked off my shoes; the first wear of my boots for the season had left welts on my heels. In the kitchen earlier, I'd sucked down a few mouthfuls of a bottle of white wine I'd found in the fridge; as I swallowed bites of cupcake, I realized I was kind of buzzed. A woman, a straggler from day shift, looked at me funny as she passed on the way to the elevators. I didn't care. I was too busy preparing to ruin Amanda Myles's life. Her accusation, the first thing she said to me when we met at the restaurant, was about to come true.

"It's Amanda, all right," Jocelyn said, clucking her disapproval. "Unless she has an identical twin the public has somehow never heard about, which is possible, but unlikely."

"The private investigator found this?" Yenay asked. "Where? How? Did he say—"

"Nuh-uh-uh," Jocelyn interrupted. "No, ma'am. That is none of our business."

"But it is, isn't it?" Yenay continued, undeterred. "What if he did something illegal to get it? Like hacked into her email? Or bribed her housekeeper to steal it from her mantelpiece?"

"I doubt she would display *this* on her mantel," Jocelyn said, making an awkward face.

"You know what I mean," Yenay pressed on, frustrated. "The source matters, right?"

"The less we know the better," Chris said, going back to his desk. "Assume everyone is operating within the bounds of the law despite the pressure, unrealistic expectations, and ferocious competition, wink, wink. Then, when a reporter does something illegal, say you didn't know, because you didn't. Get rid of the 'bad apples' to keep your reputation untarnished and the business operating as normal—that's how things have been done at this company for decades."

Chris was being derisive of the unscrupulous ways of Johnson News, but he was right. That's just how it was. The machine was too big and powerful for any of us to change it, even from within. The only thing to do was use the machine for our own purposes, and then get out.

I sat down in my chair. There was much to do, and no time to waste. Yenay and Jocelyn, lingering by my desk, got the hint and went back to their own. Out of the corner of my eye I could see Yenay, saw she had her arms crossed and that she was biting her lip, lost in thought.

"So, should I email Alice?" she said after a beat. "Request a comment from Amanda?"

"No," I said quickly, through another mouthful of cupcake. Yenay just blinked at me.

"I'm not giving her a chance to spoil our scoop," I said. "She could get ahead of us, put out a statement, go to her *friends* at the *Times* or *People*. Then it won't be a scoop anymore."

Besides, all the other times we sought her comment, she never gave one. What was the point?

I looked at Jocelyn for confirmation, that this was the right course of action. She nodded. I could see on her screen she was already cropping the blackface photo, preparing to publish.

"But..." Yenay began, then stopped herself.

"What?" I said, frustrated. I needed Yenay writing copy, but she was slowing us down.

"Amanda got into a *physical fight* with the paparazzi. She gave comments to *The New York Times* about the mental health toll the recent media attention has taken on her. I'm not saying she doesn't deserve the criticism, the repercussions—people deserve to know when someone who's made a lot of money off of the public has done something like this. But shouldn't we at least give her the chance to include a response in the article?"

What was Yenay thinking? This was the Project Black Lagoon scoop we—*she*—had been searching for, for weeks. Now Marcus had delivered it, just in time, with a week to go until Halloween. The green arrows on the jumbo screen would soar, she would have her name on a big exclusive story sure to go global—a genuine scoop, outing a major celebrity for the sin of having worn blackface—and night shift would be the darling of *The Scoop*, maybe even the whole company. She knew this would all but guarantee me the transfer to *Business Day*, and I'd told her I was going to take her with me. Now it felt like she was trying to sabotage it—sabotage me.

"Ask for forgiveness, not permission," I said, unsure for a moment where it came from. Then I remembered: It was something Josh used to say. One of those stock phrases recited by the worst corporate bro you know, who thinks he's so clever, before weaponizing his incompetence all over everyone's faces. I used to think it was stupid. I also used to be incredibly naïve about the way the world works.

Ask for forgiveness. Except I knew Amanda would never forgive this.

"Are you forgetting what Amanda said about us in her comments to the *Times*?" I asked Yenay. "Don't you want to get back at her for slandering our names in the paper of record?"

"*Get back at her*?" Yenay repeated. "This isn't the fifth grade; she didn't yank my ponytail in class. It's beside the point. What happened to 'doing things the right way'?"

I'd never seen Yenay like this. She'd certainly never spoken to me, or the others, this way before. Jocelyn glanced over at me with a tense look that said, *Get your reporter under control.*

Doing things the right way? After a moment I realized she meant the Vegas wedding story, when I'd insisted we seek comment from Amanda before publishing. It felt like a long time ago, months, even years, but it was only a few weeks. I barely felt like the same person.

Then I remembered how Jocelyn made me call David that night. *David.* I perked up at the thought of what he'd say, how happy he'd be, to hear we'd found something big on Amanda, another development confirming his celebrity-train-wreck narrative. If I called him, I could double-check my decision not to alert Amanda to our scoop until we had published the piece.

I picked up the phone and dialed David. It was the moment I'd been waiting for—finally, I'd reeled in a big one. I almost salivated at the anticipation of David's praise, hearing him erupt with raucous, unbridled delight that we had finally caught Amanda Myles behaving badly.

He answered on the first ring. I explained everything as quickly as I could: Marcus found an old photo for Project Black Lagoon. It was Amanda Myles, her skin conspicuously dark with makeup. Finished,

I waited for his response, for him to explode with glee. But he was unmoved.

"Great," he said curtly. "Why are you calling me instead of publishing the damn thing?"

David must not understand what this means, I thought. So, I again described the image, taking pains to make clear, for the benefit of the old guy, what bronzer was, that Amanda had used enough of it to darken her skin in impersonation of a woman of color to be in blackface.

"Yes, yes, I understand," David replied impatiently. "What I *don't* understand is why you're wasting time yapping away about it."

"I...I thought you would want to know," I strangled out. "I found an old photo of a celebrity in an offensive Halloween costume for Project Black Lagoon, like you wanted."

"You mean Marcus found it."

"But only because I asked him—"

"Congratulations, Francesca. What do you want, a medal? For doing your fucking job?"

David's words stung. I'd expected him to shower me in praise, but instead he was cold.

"No. I thought you'd want to know. That's all." I couldn't hide the hurt in my voice.

"What I *want* is to not have to babysit my night editor. Just publish the story. Now."

David hung up. I sat there dumbfounded, the phone still up to my ear, the dial tone bleating. The others watched me, perhaps picking up on my woundedness. He'd hung up before I could ask if we should seek comment from Amanda before publishing or not.

"David says full steam ahead," I lied, hoping they hadn't heard that I didn't get the chance to ask him.

Yenay stared at me for a moment, her mouth in a tight line.

"Okay, well I—"

"I'm writing it," I said, cutting her off. "So you don't need to worry about that, Yenay."

I watched as she opened and closed her mouth a few times, not knowing what to say.

"You can email Alice with a comment," I said. "But don't hit send until I say so."

An hour later, I'd written the copy. The photo of Amanda in blackface was at the top of the story in the content-management system. All I had to do was hit the publish button in the top right corner and Amanda's secret would be a secret no longer. The world would know. The others gathered behind me, for a few moments all of us silent in shared reverence for the fact that Amanda Myles's life as she knew it was about to change, forever. She just didn't know it yet.

EXCLUSIVE: Photo surfaces of the Valentines singer Amanda Myles in blackface Halloween costume, as woes pile up for troubled star after violent scuffle with paparazzi and infidelity claims

Beneath the headline was the incriminating photo of Amanda, grinning dumbly.

"This is going to ruin her," Yenay said, matter-of-fact. "Not that she has much of a career to ruin anymore, but still. There's a big difference between a has-been and a *racist* has-been."

Jocelyn scoffed. "She'll be fine. Look at Mel Gibson. He was caught making antisemitic comments and using the N-word. I saw him on a movie poster last week."

"But what you're forgetting, Jocelyn," Chris said, "is that Amanda Myles is a woman."

I clicked the button. **Are you sure you want to publish?** an automatic prompt asked. For a moment I hesitated. I knew as my finger hovered over the mouse that two different futures for Amanda stretched out, and I had more power and control than I'd ever imagined to influence which future she would live. But I'd come too far, given too much, to turn back now. *Click.*

And then, it was done. In seconds, the story autopublished to *The Scoop*'s social accounts, the photo of Amanda's goofily grinning face flooding the feeds of thousands, soon to be millions of people around the world. Two minutes later it was the top story on the home page, her face filling the space above the fold. It took less than ten minutes for *TMZ* to cover our story, and a dozen others weren't far behind—*BuzzFeed*, *E! News*, and more. Across New York City, the country, and all over the world, overworked journalists just like us churned out their own versions of the story, all so they could hit their traffic targets, keep their jobs, afford their rent, pay off their student loans—loans from the journalism degree they'd earned but could hardly afford, believing they would make a name for themselves, become A Serious Journalist.

Believing it would be more than this.

Yenay hit send on the email to Alice. Amanda would soon know. *Such a shame*, I thought, unable to stop the smile that crept across my face. *It didn't have to be this way.*

David would call to congratulate me soon, I knew he would. I'd caught him at a bad moment on the phone earlier, that was all. I got him what he wanted, just in time. Now it was his turn to give *me* what *I* wanted. And if he didn't, I'd find a way to go over his head to Walter Johnson. Whatever it took, I would get out of *The Scoop* and get to *Business Day*, once again the kind of journalist, kind of person, I was supposed to be, used to be, before it all went wrong.

The buzz of my cell phone vibrating on my desk startled me. An unknown number.

THE SCOOP

"Hello?"

"What the fuck, Francesca?"

A woman's voice, familiar. Was it Alice? No, I'd never spoken to her on the phone.

"How could you do this to me?"

Amanda. It was Amanda.

"Where did you get it?" she demanded, her voice hoarse and cracking like she was about to cry. "I've never even seen that photo. I barely remember that night. Who gave it to you?"

I heard my pulse in my ears. Lightheaded, I put a hand on the desk to try to steady myself. How did she get my number? Then I realized that it was in my email signature.

"Amanda, I'm—" I caught myself. Car crash rules. "I wish I could tell you that."

When they heard me say Amanda's name, the others looked up and stared.

"This is...I can't...How did..." she sputtered, and I wondered if she was going to hyperventilate. "How long have you had it? Did you already know you were going to do this when I met you at the restaurant? Opened up to you? Empathized with you, after everything?"

Had you already slammed me to The New York Times? I thought, but didn't say.

"To think I was going to trust *you* with my story. You're nothing but tabloid scum."

I wasn't surprised Amanda was upset. But "tabloid scum"? That was harsh. I thought we could at least try to keep things professional. I grabbed a half-eaten cupcake and took a bite.

"I'm only doing my job, Amanda," I said between swallows of cupcake. "God knows I need it, because I'll never get another one after that *Times* media section hit job of yours! But that's just life, right? Anyway, let me guess: you're calling to finally give me that interview?"

Amanda made a sound—a curdled combination of a groan and a shriek so piercing I had to lift the phone away from my ear. Yenay and Jocelyn watched me, eyes wide with shock.

"Do you know what you are, Francesca? You're a pathetic excuse for a journalist, and a pathetic excuse for a woman. A pathetic excuse for a human being. I'm glad for your mother, that she can't see you now—how ashamed she would be to have to call you her daughter."

Classy, I thought, so stunned Amanda would go that low I almost started to laugh.

Amanda hung up. Calmly, I placed my cell phone back down on my desk.

"Was that...?" Chris asked, not needing to say her name.

I nodded, still not quite able to believe myself what had just happened. The others waited for me to explain. Despite myself, no matter how hard I tried to keep my face straight, I started to laugh. Laughter that shook my shoulders, made tears spring to the corners of my eyes. Jocelyn, Yenay, and Chris all looked at me like I'd gone mad. I guess in a way you could say I had.

Hand on my chest, I forced some deep breaths in and out until the laughing fit subsided and I could speak. I didn't tell them Amanda called me a pathetic excuse for a human being, or said my mom would be ashamed if she were still alive. But I shared the most important thing.

"Amanda said: *I barely remember that night*. Do you know what that means?"

"She confirmed it's her in the photo," Jocelyn said.

"Exactly. Now we can take out the *allegedly*s and *apparently*s. Even better, she never said 'off the record.' You know what that means?" I laughed again. "She provided a comment!"

I opened the article and added a new line a few pars from the top.

THE SCOOP

Myles has confirmed to *The Scoop* that it is her in the photo, admitting, "I barely remember that night."

Later, in the kitchen, I again stood in front of the open fridge door. After spooning someone else's expensive organic coconut yogurt into my mouth, indifferent to the sign on the wall begging, PLEASE DO NOT TAKE THINGS THAT DON'T BELONG TO YOU, washing it down with a few more swallows of the cold white wine, I decided to finish off the cupcakes, biting into the crime scene cleaner's smiling gelatin face. This woman, who spent her days confronting the ugliest parts of life, of people, somehow still hadn't given up on love. Still had hope. One by one, I plucked the sickly sweet treats from the box, tearing them apart with my fingers, ramming hunks into my mouth, licking icing off my fingers. Did I still have hope? After what I'd seen, what I'd done? What *did* I hope for? I had trouble remembering, right then, what it was all for.

26

Bright morning rays streamed gold and white through the newsroom windows. I'd never seen the office drenched in sunlight before. I'd come to work on Friday, a day off, after having barely slept once again, instead staying up to watch the blackface story catch fire, set the world's media ablaze, watching it grow and grow, now beyond my control. All the major news and celebrity gossip websites had covered the photo of Amanda in blackface. Her name was trending on Twitter with thousands of mentions every hour. It had even been discussed on the *Today* show.

"Incredibly disappointing to see anyone in blackface, but especially someone you've idolized," said Natalie Adams, the show's Black co-host, shuffling her papers.

Rachel Leigh, the show's white co-host, nodded in agreement. "Yet another white woman who really needs to go to therapy."

Why had I come to work? Hard to say. Nobody asked me to. But I couldn't stay away. It would have been like lighting the fuse of a firework and not watching the sky to see it explode.

Now I stood in a snaking semicircle in the middle of the office, alongside faces I mostly didn't recognize, some sipping from coffee cups, others fiddling with notepads and pens or sneaking looks at phones, all of us with our bodies turned to face the person at the center: David. Tall and serious in a navy suit and polished black dress shoes, he commanded attention as if onstage at a theater in the round. I gathered this was the daily morning news meeting. The atmosphere felt tense, like on *Survivor* before tribal council, only without the flickering tiki torches—a good thing, given the damage David could already do without access to an open flame.

David opened his mouth, about to speak, but as he did so his eyes fell on me, and his expression bloomed into one of surprise. Others followed his gaze, to see what had stunned him into silence, until almost every person in the room was staring at me. All I could do was smile, squirming under the sudden attention, feeling the ache in my bleary eyes, wondering if I looked insane; I hadn't showered or brushed my hair before leaving my apartment. I was also wearing yesterday's clothes, though at least there was no way for anyone from day shift to know that.

"Francesca," David said, regaining focus, "I'm surprised the sunlight isn't making your skin smolder. Everyone, if you haven't met her, this is Francesca, our nocturnal night editor."

Mumbled greetings and hearty laughs rippled around the semicircle—the kind of laughs employees must force in response to the jokes of the person who controls their paycheck. Not knowing what to say, since David had already introduced me, I just kept grinning.

"I'd have thought you'd be sleeping it off, Francesca," David said, peering at me, a question not asked but implied: *What are you doing here?*

David seemed to be waiting for me to explain my presence there in the newsroom on my day off, and during the daytime, no less—a fair inquiry. Except it felt excruciating, to be in the spotlight of David and these strangers; I was used to moving in the shadows, backstage, after-hours, mostly unseen. On the spot I had to think of a rational explanation to give, even though I'd not so much made a decision to come to work on my day off but rather obeyed an impulse.

"I thought I should come in," I managed, "in case I can help. With the Amanda story."

I looked David in the eye, defiantly held his gaze. This was it, the moment I had been waiting for. I'd caught him in a bad mood the night before, that was all. But now he would acknowledge, in front of everyone, my achievement: that I was the one who had completed the task he had set us with Project Black Lagoon. On the jumbo screen hanging above the newsroom behind David, Amanda was still on the home page, in third spot—proof. I watched David, waiting, almost giving him a nod to encourage him, to urge him on. *Say it*. But he glanced down.

"Help?" David repeated, before looking up at me again.

"Yes," I insisted, not giving up. "It's such a big story, an exclusive—I'm sure you saw it was covered on *Today* this morning. I figured I should be here, since it's my story, so—"

"But that's yesterday's news. Or, I should say, *last night's* news."

David held his penetrating stare, as if he wanted to make sure there was no way I could miss, or misinterpret, his insult, veiled as a joke. A few people coughed and cleared their throats, shifted from side to side restlessly, finding the palpable tension between us awkward, or otherwise wanting to get on with the meeting. I saw myself through their eyes, the weird night editor lady, looking a mess with bags under her eyes and rumpled clothes. I wished I could show them who I used to be, someone who stepped fresh-faced into the *Marie Claire* office every morning, someone they would have respected. Instead, I was enduring David's condescending, belittling attitude, at a loss to explain it. Odd, to share him with dozens of others. I was conscious then of a bizarre, certainly not healthy kind of intimacy that had formed between us, during our late-night phone calls. In the daytime, with all these people, David wore a mask. But at night on the phone with me, he took it off. I felt I knew him better than the others. But now he was treating me like all the rest, just one of his many minions. Like I wasn't different, or special. And I was—special. I would have bet he didn't offer a job at *Business Day* to just anyone.

"We've got it handled. But by all means, do stick around. We're happy to have you."

David couldn't have sounded more insincere if he'd tried. I wondered if the others could smell my desperation for his approval, wondered if David could. It was humiliating, to crave it, need it, and yet I couldn't stop myself from trying to get it. That he was withholding it from me didn't make any sense. Why was David being so cold toward me? Had I said something at the meeting with Peter Lowell that I shouldn't have, and Peter had relayed it back to David? Did Peter tell David that I hated *The Scoop* and was desperate to get out, desperate to get away from him? This was, technically, true, but I thought I had been careful to hide my eagerness. Besides, David put me in touch with Peter precisely because we had an understanding that I was going to move on to *Business Day* after a short while. I didn't see what I could have done wrong. There had to be a way to fix it, to get us back on track. All I had to do was figure out what that was.

"Now," David said with a single loud clap of his hands to regain the full and undivided attention of the newsroom, "let's get on with it. What have we got coming today? Callie?"

A short blond woman stepped forward from where she had been standing behind David and began reading off her phone a list of celebrity stories the team was prioritizing that day. So, this was Callie King, head of entertainment, whose name I'd seen around. David stayed quiet while she rattled off headlines until one about Amy Matthews, the Grammy-winning country singer who had posed for *Rolling Stone* naked but for a python positioned strategically to cover her breasts and vagina. The story was already on the home page, and doing well, judging by the green arrow that hovered over it on the jumbo screen. David turned and squinted at the screen.

"Why is naked Amy in sixth spot? Why is naked Amy *below* the Mozambique flood?"

A short, stout, ruddy-faced man, who I gathered was from the news desk, began to speak.

"The photos of the flood are dramatic, David—there are images of the shoes of the dead lying along the river's edge. Haunting stuff. They're saying the death toll will hit a thousand."

David barely paused for a breath.

"Unless the river is the Hudson, the Thames, or the Seine," he said, "I don't care. Amy up, flood down. Next."

Callie kept talking. "Emily Brent has been photographed not wearing her wedding ring."

"Ooh," David said, rubbing his hands together like he had just been presented with a tray of delectable pastries. "Trouble in paradise, huh? What do we think, is she headed for divorce?"

"Oh, no," Callie said, looking sheepish. "Sorry, I should clarify: she was photographed in character on a film set. That's why she isn't wearing her ring. But it's a great headline, right?"

"Absolutely," David crowed. "Nice work."

What was happening? Why was David praising Callie for a story that was totally made up, but couldn't bring himself to congratulate me for the Amanda blackface exclusive? A lump formed in my throat. It seemed undeniable that David was deliberately trying to punish me.

"Okay, Dennis," David said, "you're up."

The stout man from before began, like Callie, reading out a list of upcoming stories from his phone. David stopped him at a story about a personal trainer in Arizona that died of the flu.

"This was a woman, you said? Twenty-five years old? How'd you find that?"

"GoFundMe.com," Dennis said. "It's a treasure trove of tragic tales and general misery."

Gross. Still, I made a mental note to start trawling GoFundMe.com to look for stories. Maybe I'd find something there David would really want. Had he become bored of Amanda?

"Can I get a look at her?"

A photo editor who remained seated at their desk near David clicked a few times until some images of the woman were on the screen: smiling on vacation, holding a soft fluffy cat up to her face.

"Why is she wearing a sweater in all of them? She's a personal trainer. Haven't we got anything a bit sexier? Wearing a sports bra, perhaps? Is a bit of cleavage too much to ask?"

"I'll keep looking, David," the photo editor said.

David looked around at the gathered editors and reporters as if wanting confirmation he was right. "Nobody wants to see a personal trainer in a sweater, alive or dead. Am I wrong?"

Cautious laughter rippled through the semicircle, along with a few disapproving *tsk-tsks* and head shakes. I looked around at the faces of my colleagues. Some clearly feared David, eyes wide, expressions tense with worry he might call upon them—and if he did, that they'd disappoint or irritate him enough to receive one of his famous beratings; nobody wanted to be called a cunt, at least not before breakfast. Others seemed in quiet awe of him, enraptured by this man and his strange, unorthodox ways, like something from a bygone era—because he was.

David relished the attention, that much was obvious. The easy wins of performing for a captive audience. I wondered if he understood that if they weren't all being paid, they wouldn't bother to remove an earphone if he asked them a question on the street. I wondered, feeling my resentment toward him bubble, if he knew that it was only his mediocrity, lack of integrity, and deep craving for approval from men who were actually powerful that had gotten him to where he was. The exact combination of traits that made him the perfect tool for Walter Johnson to exploit. And, of course, the most crucial trait of all to be successful at Johnson News: obedience.

After the meeting, I was walking back to my desk when Callie appeared beside me.

"Will you be around later? Some of us are going for drinks at five. You should come."

I wasn't sure how I would stay awake until then, but I thanked Callie for the invite and told her I'd be there. Callie spent her days sitting beside David. I wondered if I could glean some information about him from her. I needed to figure out how to get him back on my side.

At three o'clock, my desk phone rang. On the screen were the words FRONT DESK.

"Hello?"

"This is Dale from front desk security. I have someone here for you. Amanda Myles."

That name, a bolt of electricity straight to my core. I'd nearly dozed off at my desk, but now I was wide awake, like someone had zapped me with a cattle prod. Or was I asleep, dreaming?

"Ma'am?"

Surely this couldn't be real. I felt a heady rush of adrenaline, blood pumping faster in my limbs. Why would Amanda come here, to

THE SCOOP

Johnson News? What did she want? In my mind I saw Amanda forcing her way into the office, picking up stacks of papers and throwing them up in the air, pulling off a shoe and pelting it at someone's head, splashing red paint everywhere like a PETA activist, screaming, *Tabloids are murder!* I saw myself running across the newsroom to get away from her, Amanda chasing me, catching me, tackling my legs, pinning me to the ground as I lay there, helpless, Amanda's face close to mine, her teeth bared, almost growling.

I looked around for someone to help me, but everyone was preoccupied—heads down working at their desks, coming and going from meeting rooms, huddling in the hall to gossip.

"Amanda Myles?" I repeated back to Dale, trying to buy myself a few more moments.

"Yes, ma'am."

Why couldn't I have stayed home on my day off like a normal person? When Amanda showed up, I would have been on the other side of the Brooklyn Bridge, at home, in my apartment, safe, and someone else would have had to deal with her. This was my punishment, for never having learned how to master work-life balance. For not having a hobby. Cycling, indoor rock-climbing, knitting, a pet parrakeet, even an adult coloring book might have prevented this.

That's when it clicked: I didn't have *work-life balance*. I didn't have a *hobby*. Only losers without a purpose, who were totally unserious about their careers, had *work-life balance* and *hobbies*. No, I was a journalist—from the moment I opened my eyes each day and checked the news apps to when I laid my head on the pillow and drifted off to sleep fantasizing about winning a Pulitzer. I got my thrills from finding exclusives, hitting deadlines, breaking traffic records. Yes, I was a journalist, and this—Amanda being downstairs—was a story. I wasn't going to waste it.

"Should I send her up?" Dale asked, beginning to sound impatient.

"No," I told him. "I'm coming down."

I hung up the phone, stood, and hurried over to the other side of the newsroom to Callie, who was sitting at the head of the long row of desks that belonged to the entertainment team. As quietly and quickly as I could, I explained that Amanda Myles was downstairs in the lobby, and that she was asking to see me. Now. Callie's eyes flew wide.

"Wait, are you serious?" she whispered. "Amanda Myles is downstairs? Now?"

I nodded.

"I want you to follow me down there," I said, looking around to make sure no one could hear us. "I'm going to talk to her. I want you to hide nearby and film it. Record what happens."

Callie stared at me in terror and admiration, like she couldn't decide if I was of unsound mind or a fearless genius. I was a journalist; I was both. Her face broke out in an enormous grin.

"Let's go."

When the elevator doors dinged open and we stepped out into the lobby, the row of turnstiles was all that now stood between Amanda and me. Scenes of her tackling me to the ground played in my mind again.

"If it turns physical," I told Callie, "don't stop filming to help me. Keep recording."

Callie didn't argue. She hurried over to a spot against the wall we had discussed on the ride down that would give her a clear view of the lobby but keep her protected behind the turnstiles. She did look nervous, a little shaky, but determined, like she'd been asked on a whim to interview the president. Like the moment she'd been preparing for her whole life had arrived.

Me? I felt strangely calm. I didn't know what would happen. But I gave it over to fate, decided to accept whatever unfolded, to surrender to the moment.

I was also sleep-deprived.

I pushed through the turnstiles and scanned the lobby. It was late afternoon on a Friday, and so it was chaos, swarms of people darting past laden with bags as they ran to catch buses and trains. My eyes roamed the scene until I spotted Amanda. She was standing in the corner beside a large potted plant, arms crossed, chewing on her lip, wearing a T-shirt, no jacket, even though it was chilly out, almost November. I noted her loose, faded jeans and grubby white sneakers, her hair high and messy on her head, a bird's nest. She looked gaunt, like she hadn't been eating. I almost couldn't believe this was the same person from the restaurant days ago. Without the expensive clothes and makeup, she didn't look glamorous, or famous. She looked... ordinary.

I took a deep breath and walked over to her, fiddling with my security pass to hide the fact that my hands were shaking. Amanda sensed me, her head snapping up as I approached.

"Where did you get it?" she demanded.

No niceties, then.

"Tell me how you got the photo. I've never seen it before. Who gave it to you? Was it Alexander?"

There was that *s*-word again, trying to come out of my mouth. But I couldn't say sorry, wouldn't. "I understand you want to know," I said, "but I'm not at liberty to reveal that."

I'm not at liberty to reveal that was good. It sounded official, like something a lawyer would say; perhaps I'd overheard Patti say it to someone on the phone before. I stood taller.

My phone buzzed in my hand. I checked and saw a text that appeared to be from Callie.

> Can you go outside? Light is weird in here. Street
> backdrop will look better. I'll follow.

I glanced at front desk security. I was reluctant to move farther away; they knew me from my two a.m. exits every night. They'd step in if things did turn physical with Amanda. The way she was looking at me, it wasn't out of the realm of possibility. But I needed usable footage.

"Amanda, why don't we step outside?"

Her nostrils flared.

"Did you just ask me to *step outside*?"

"I don't mean it like *that*," I said with a nervous laugh. "But it'll be easier to talk out there." I headed toward the revolving doors, knowing Amanda had no choice but to follow me outside if she wanted to say, or do, whatever she had come to say, or do, to me.

Outside, I stopped in the center of the forecourt, trying to ensure Callie would have a clear shot. When Amanda caught up to me, I saw that her eyes were brimming with tears.

"My boyfriend," she choked out, "he left me. He had a 'family emergency' and flew to Italy to his parents' place. Doesn't know when he'll be back. But I know the truth—he thinks he'll be 'canceled,' lose his endorsements, if he's associated with me. I'll never see that man again. Who can blame him? Who would want to date the 'secret racist' Amanda Myles?"

Amanda had a boyfriend? Who, it appeared, had dumped her over the photo? No wonder it wasn't enough for her to stay under her bedcovers at home and cry until the news cycle moved on. No wonder she had taken the extreme step of coming to the Johnson News building and demanding a scalp. Amanda's pain and anger were palpable, threatening to erupt. She needed to put it somewhere, the fury over her life being blasted open and ripped apart in an instant. And what better place to put it but with the person who had pushed the button to detonate?

She took a step closer, and then another, causing me to flinch. She cocked her head.

"I don't know where or how you got that photo, but I'm going to find out. If you did something illegal, Francesca, you or someone else at *The Scoop*, then I'm going to get the best lawyer in the city, and I'm going to sue Johnson News, and you, too. I'm going to ruin you."

Amanda had her finger pointed at my chest. One or two people passing by glanced at us, but it was New York City—they had probably already seen at least three stranger things that day.

I stared back. I knew what Amanda was trying to do. She was trying to get me to break. To make me cry, admit fault, say I was sorry, beg her to forgive me, not to hurt me, sue me, or ruin me. I knew there was a chance that to get the photo, Marcus had done something shady at the least, illegal at worst. But I didn't care. The chances of Amanda being able to successfully prove that, let alone bother with a court case against a company with pockets as deep as Johnson News, were slim to none. I had nothing to lose. In fact, I had something to *gain* by infuriating her further. Amanda might even lay a hand on me. Now, *that* would be a story.

"Amanda," I began, standing up taller, not stepping back even though she was towering over me, uncomfortably close, "don't blame me for what *you* did. You have to live with the choices you make," I said, remembering what Patti said to me, liking the way it sounded. "What would you have me do, when a photo of a celebrity in *blackface* comes across my desk? Make it disappear? Bury it to protect you? I'm a journalist, Amanda, not your personal publicist."

"Isn't that convenient?" Amanda spat, leaning closer. "Because that day at the restaurant, you were selling me on the powers of positive spin, what great PR it would be to tell my story about Alexander's abuse and the sleazy music industry executives. Was all that just bullshit?"

She laughed.

"You're nothing but a two-faced liar."

"*I'm* two-faced?" Now it was my turn to laugh. "You told me you were considering doing an interview with me, with *The Scoop*, even though you 'never' do interviews. Then I see you give comments to the *Times*! You lied to my face. You were never going to give me an interview. You just wanted me to think you would so that there'd be no more stories about you on *The Scoop* because I wouldn't want to piss you off. Well, you were wrong. I'm not that easy to manipulate."

"But I *was* considering doing an interview with you. I believed you, in the restaurant, when you said that all this stuff at *The Scoop* wasn't the real you. I'd already agreed to provide comments to the *Times* when we met."

She gave a frustrated sigh. "The *Times* reporter reached out to me a few days before we met. That's *why* I decided to respond to your request, from weeks ago, asked you to meet me at San Mateo's. The *Times* journalist, the story they were writing about me and Senator Thompson and the tabloids, was what prompted me to wonder: Who is this person, and why are they trying to ruin my life? And then I met you, and we talked, and I believed you, could see your heart was in the right place—or so I thought. I was reluctant to have such an important story published by *The Scoop*, of all places. But I saw it as a kind of correction, to balance the other articles with the truth, finally. I believed you when you said you would tell it right. I decided, after hearing your story, about your boss, that you deserved a second chance. But I was a fool to trust you."

I swallowed, struggled to take in what Amanda was saying. So she hadn't, as I'd believed, gone running to the *Times* after our meeting as some kind of revenge? A deliberate slight to spoil my big opportunity, what would have been her first interview in a decade? She was going to give me an interview after all, if I'd followed up with her? No, she must be lying.

"Thank god you never followed up," she said, shaking her head. "I would have said yes."

Out of the corner of my eye, I could see Callie, behind Amanda, out of her view, near the America Now studios. I was so stunned by what Amanda said I'd briefly forgotten Callie was filming. Amanda had pushed on something deep within me, and I felt the rage threatening to boil over. I couldn't stop myself. And why should I? I might as well push her over the edge.

"Why did you come here, Amanda? Was it just to abuse me? Or did you come to get some answers? The truth? Because if it's the truth you want, I'll give it you. Are you ready?"

I didn't wait for a response.

"You're a washed-up has-been. You're here right now because as much as you like to pretend otherwise, your ego craves attention. You're a self-obsessed narcissist with a black hole inside that can never be filled. But you're trying anyway, because it's better than looking directly at the truth, which is that it's not the fault of your ex-husband, or some music industry executive, that you went nowhere after the Valentines. The band was propping you up, and once it was gone, you realized the truth, which is that you were simply never that good. You were mediocre. Still, you could have pushed on, could have kept trying, but you were deeply afraid of everyone seeing the truth. So, you hid away and started blaming everyone else. That's what you're doing now—blaming someone else. It's not *your* fault that *you* wore a stupid racist Halloween costume, but *mine*? Unbelievable."

Amanda and I stared at each other. Now it was time to make this a story worth telling. It was a gamble, what I was about to do. But if it paid off, it would be worth it. Maybe it was what Peter Lowell had said that day at coffee: *Don't be afraid to get some blood under your nails or lose a tooth for a story.* "Metaphorically speaking," Peter had joked. Metaphorical, until it wasn't.

"Amanda, I've wasted enough of my time," I said. "You do know some of us have to work for a living? I'm going back upstairs now."

I turned and began walking back toward the building entrance. After a few steps, I felt Amanda's hand roughly grab my arm. The gamble had paid off.

"Don't touch me!" I shouted, spinning around and yanking my arm back from her, rubbing it dramatically for effect—it didn't actually hurt.

"Put a hand on me again and I'll get security."

It took all my restraint not to look over in the direction of Callie to see if she got the shot.

Amanda looked down at her hand, seemingly bewildered at what she had just done. I took one last look at her, then turned and walked as fast as I could back to the revolving doors, breathing hard, convinced with every step that I was going to feel her hand on me again. But soon I was inside the foyer, and then behind the turnstiles, and then in the elevator. I was safe.

And I had a story to write.

27

I CAME TO FACE DOWN on the floor, the light pouring in the windows stirring me awake. I sat up with a start, unsure of where I was, until I registered the familiar gray carpet, the rows of desks and chairs, the jumbo screen. For reasons then unclear to me, I'd spent the night in a meeting room at work. A sharp pain pulsed in my head, the kind that lets you know you drank too much the night before. I looked down at myself to see I was, inexplicably, wearing a banana costume.

"Unnngggghhhhhheeerrrrr," I said to no one.

Someone had left a bottle of water beside me, and at the sight of it I yearned to slake my parched throat, which felt cracked and tasted ashy, like I might have spent the previous evening as a volunteer fire fighter, putting out a blaze, though was more likely the result of the much less heroic act of smoking cigarettes. Next to the bottle of water was my phone. I reached for it, slid it across the carpet toward me, checked the time: 7:15 a.m. I saw I had some texts from Callie.

> Couldn't get you downstairs to put you in a cab so left you in the meeting room to sleep it off

ERIN VAN DER MEER

> Text me when you wake up to let me know you're okay
>
> And great work last night!!

Unsteadily, I got to my feet. To my relief, the newsroom was empty. On weekends the team started at eight a.m. I had to get out of there before I risked being seen in my hungover, still-unexplained banana-costumed state. I staggered over to my desk to collect my things, head pounding harder now, and saw it was littered with red cups and empty wine bottles, the sight of them making my stomach lurch. Sweeping the evidence of debauchery into a trash can, memories from the previous night returned: Callie and me, skipping the team drinks to stay back and publish the video of my dramatic encounter with Amanda, followed by another story revealing she'd been abruptly dumped by her boyfriend over the blackface photo (Amanda never said our conversation was off the record), and yet another, once Amanda released a statement, in which she apologized "unreservedly" to all those she had "offended" with her "ignorance."

Callie, appearing with a bottle of wine she'd procured from somewhere, both of us kicking our feet up on my desk, watching the green arrows on the jumbo screen soar as the stories went viral. Then, once the wine was gone, deciding to go to a bar; me rummaging in Jocelyn's drawer for an Adderall, to help me stay awake despite the exhaustion of having not slept the night before. Out on the street, passing a Party City, going inside, leaving a few minutes later wearing the banana costume, Callie doubled over laughing. The bar was a dark blur; I had no memory of leaving, or how I ended up sleeping on the office floor instead of at home in bed.

I chugged some water, gathered my coat, bag, and security pass, my drunk-dulled brain forming a step-by-step plan: *Go to bathroom. Pee. Take off banana costume. Call car. Go home.*

That's when I looked up at the jumbo screen above and saw it, really *saw* it, the story in the top spot on the home page, a grainy still of Amanda and me on the street outside the building.

EXCLUSIVE: Out-of-control Amanda Myles attacks journalist in shocking new video

You couldn't see my face; my hair mostly covered it since I'd turned away from Amanda to walk inside. Her hand was on my upper arm, and I was beginning to lurch away from her. But anyone who knew me would recognize me: Audrey, Naomi, Jasmine, Patti, Josh. I imagined them all, their shock if they saw it, and almost couldn't bear the shame. I pictured Josh specifically, leaning over to show Miss America his phone: *See, I told you Frankie was nuts.* Amanda looked worse—she was the one reaching for me—but it didn't take a genius to guess she had probably been goaded into it, that it was no coincidence the moment was captured on video. Standing there, neck craned to look up at the screen, the stupidity of what I had done, the recklessness, began to sink in. *Reckless.* Wasn't that what Audrey called me, the night we argued? *How could you be so reckless?* The truth of it swamped me: I'd proved her right.

In the back seat of an Uber, headed home, focused on trying not to be sick each time we rounded a corner, I was beginning to doze lightly against the window when my phone buzzed.

> Fantastic work, Francesca. Keep it up. People are noticing.

David. No question asking if I was okay—I had been "attacked" after all—or if I'd been hurt, or if I needed help. *People are noticing.* Okay. But were they the right people? And what exactly were they noticing? That I seemed like the type of person who would get in a bar fight because someone skipped my song on the jukebox? And why was David being warm toward me all of a sudden? Why did I deserve praise over this, but not the blackface story? How had I gotten to this point, where it felt like my fate had become dependent on the mercurial moods of an erratic old man? A man who seemed to feel contempt for me one moment, adoration the next?

At home, Patti wasn't there. I showered, forced down a piece of plain buttered toast despite the protests of my roiling stomach, and lay down in bed. I had texts and missed calls from Jocelyn and Yenay, both no doubt shocked by the video of me and Amanda and wanting details. I ignored them. My room was a mess, one side of my bed piled with clothes clean and dirty, my nightstand covered with dirty glasses and empty snack packets—sure to lure the intrepid roaches from the kitchen. I thought of my mom, the way she rarely got off the couch on those last few visits home from college, thought of the stacks of old magazines, the overflowing recycling can, the rows of empty wine bottles, the baskets of laundry everywhere. How when the phone rang, she never answered, saying she'd call back whoever it was later, though something made me doubt it. I'd been running from it for so long, the darkness in her that I knew was in me, too, my inheritance. Convinced myself if I kept moving forward and didn't look back, didn't stop for a second, I could outrun it. But despite my insistence I would never let that darkness catch me, I couldn't ignore the evidence to the contrary—the roaring hangover, laundry everywhere, the scrunched packets, the unanswered texts, my curtains blocking out the sunlight.

That night I had a dream my mother was trying to call me. I heard my phone ringing from inside my backpack, on the seat next to me at an airport terminal. Somehow I knew it was her. I groped through the bag, reaching and reaching, the phone ringing and ringing, until

THE SCOOP

at last I yanked it from beneath the jumble of objects in the bag, my joy like finding someone alive in the rubble after an earthquake. Face up in my palm, on the screen it said: **Mom**. But I couldn't answer. I couldn't work the phone, or maybe it was frozen. I tapped desperately on the screen, but nothing I did helped. She was right there. *Please, please, please.* But the ringing stopped.

I could not answer the call.

28

A FEW DAYS LATER, a little after six p.m., Jocelyn's desk phone rang. It was a pap who often trailed Amanda. I knew something was wrong when I heard her say, "Is an ambulance on the way?"

I locked eyes with Yenay above our screens. Chris stopped typing. Jocelyn nodded, said, "Uh-huh, yes, I see," for what felt like an unbearably long time. She hung up and turned to me.

"There's been an incident at Amanda Myles's house. That was one of the paps—he heard it over police radio. Someone called nine-one-one for a woman found unconscious."

"Jesus Christ," I heard Chris mutter. Yenay put a hand to her mouth.

"Is he sure?" I asked. "The pap definitely has the right address?" I didn't want to believe what I was hearing, so it was easier to try to prove it wasn't real, that there had been a mistake.

"It's definitely Amanda's address," Jocelyn said, her expression grim. "The pap is on the way there now. He's on a motorbike and not far away; he'll probably beat the ambulance."

Chris got up and went to the window, hands clasped behind his back, quiet, contemplative. He looked downtown, as if he might be able to glimpse Amanda's house.

"Frankie, you should call David," Jocelyn said. "This could be big. And...bad."

Everything felt slow, strange, dulled as I picked up the phone and hit the speed-dial button to call David. When he answered, I relayed it all quickly, hearing my voice wobble as I said *Amanda* and *unconscious* and *ambulance*. When I was finished, David didn't miss a beat.

"So, what are you waiting for? Send somebody down there!"

"You're saying we should go? To Amanda's house?"

"For Christ's sake, of course! We could have a celebrity suicide ten minutes from the office. We need to find out what's happened—this is too big to rely on the paps. Call me back when you've sorted it."

He hung up. I looked around at the others, who were waiting for me to tell them what David said.

"He wants someone to go down there."

I had to decide in an instant who would go. I looked between Yenay and Chris, considering the options. Chris was the more experienced reporter, but he'd been so checked out for so long, had gotten rusty; I knew he wouldn't be able to muster the urgency the situation required. Yenay was too green for this; straight from college to a newsroom where she'd been chained to the desk. There were so many things she didn't know about reporting in the field, had never been given the chance to learn. I didn't have faith in either of them to handle it. Or maybe it was really that as the situation spiraled further out of my grasp, I thought that by going to the scene, it would give me some control. That maybe I could figure out how to fix it.

"I'll go," I said, standing up, pulling on my coat, and gathering up my things. Chris and Yenay didn't argue. Jocelyn tried to say something, but I barely heard her as I ran for the door.

In the back of a cab as it flew down the West Side Highway, I gripped the handle above the window as we weaved in and out of traffic. Like something from a movie, I'd thrust a fifty-dollar bill at the driver and told him to do whatever he had to, to get me to Amanda's address as fast as possible. It was dusk, the sun almost gone, and as I watched the blurry streams of light from cars and buildings rush by, I swallowed the saliva pooling under my tongue, tried to breathe. I was having trouble holding on to a single clear thought. I tried to reassure myself the panic was probably for nothing. Maybe Amanda had merely fainted or tripped down some stairs. Frightening, but not life-threatening. An accident, not deliberate. Or maybe it wasn't even her; she was rich, she probably had staff. Our assumption could be totally wrong. The ambulance was on the way, probably there now, and all would be fine. David's voice rang in my head: *We could have a celebrity suicide*... But my mind wouldn't allow me to look at it head-on. It was too much.

I felt an urge, nonsensical as it was, to text Amanda, ask if she was okay. And then I was in the past, remembering the neighbor calling about my mom. The words, *I'm sorry, she didn't make it*. Hanging up the call, refusing the images that rushed in to fill the gap of all I did not know. The way I had gone to our last messages and stared, sure that if I texted her and asked what happened, she would reply. The alternative—that we had exchanged our last words, would never speak again—unfathomable. Impossible, unthinkable, that she had slipped soundlessly from my grasp, like the string of a balloon from the hand of a child. Gone. But this wasn't like that, I told myself. Not the same. David was overreacting. Amanda would be alive.

"I can't go any farther," the driver said, pulling me back to the present. We were at the top of Amanda's street. A few feet away the scene of chaos began. Two ambulances blocked the road; an enormous gaggle of paps huddled across from Amanda's building, cameras poised.

I opened the door and hurled myself out of the cab, running down the block until I reached the commotion outside Amanda's brownstone. All around me were paps on the phone, yelling, negotiating prices and deals, shouting and gesturing wildly, promising exclusives.

"What's happening?" I asked one, trying to catch my breath. "Has anyone come out yet?"

"Not yet," he said, without turning to look at me or lowering his camera. "The EMTs went inside about five minutes ago. A young woman let them in—she looked distressed."

"No way, bro," I heard another paparazzo yell into his phone. "If Amanda Myles's dead body is brought out on a stretcher, that's six figures, easy. Don't try to stiff me on this."

Just then, all the paps perked up, began to jostle for position, cameras clicking. A curtain rustled inside Amanda's place and then the front door was open and the EMTs were coming out, carrying a stretcher. Camera bulbs flashed. In a few seconds Amanda came into view. She was tucked under a white sheet and had an oxygen mask strapped over her face, her eyes closed. My stomach plunged at the sight of her, vulnerable, weak, seemingly unconscious. At the same time, my heart leapt to see the oxygen mask. Amanda was, at least for now, still alive.

"Get out of the way!" one of the EMTs yelled at a half dozen of the paparazzi, who'd left the main scrum across the street and begun swarming Amanda on the stretcher, cameras pointed at her face.

They were blocking access to the ambulance. The EMTs shoved their way through the pack, loaded Amanda into the back, slammed the doors closed, and sped off, siren wailing.

Moments later, two women emerged from the house. One, a young woman, red in the face as though she'd been crying, held a hand up to shield her eyes from the flash of the cameras as she hurried down the sidewalk toward Sixth Avenue. The other, an older woman, set off across the street. I was gripped, then, by a panic: David would call any minute, wanting exclusive details for our story. I'd be caught empty-handed, nothing to show for being at the scene. The first woman had already disappeared. On instinct, I ran down the street after the older woman.

"Excuse me," I called out, stopping her as she reached the top of the stairs of a brownstone, about to go inside. She whipped around and faced me, looking for the source of the sound. She saw me and frowned.

"Hi," I said, trying to catch my breath. "I'm...a friend of Amanda's. What happened?"

"You're her friend?" she asked sharply. I could tell she was suspicious.

"Yes," I lied, allowing the emotion that had been sitting on my chest since that first call from the pap to bubble up and catch in my voice. I fought back tears, and I wasn't faking it.

"We were meant to meet this afternoon at San Mateo's—we all know how much she loves the place—but I couldn't get ahold of her," I continued, stunned at the story I was weaving on the spot. "It's not like Amanda, so I decided to come around. I can show you our texts," I said, gesturing at her with my phone.

I was bluffing, but the woman bought it. I watched as her face slackened and she came back down the stairs. When she reached me, I saw her eyes were filled with tears. She wrapped her arms around herself.

"I saw the ambulance lights flashing out the window," she said. "I haven't seen Amanda in a while, but I used to talk to her sometimes, and I got worried."

She wrapped her arms around herself tighter.

"That was Amanda's sister. It looks like it was an overdose. Prescription pills."

"Not deliberate?" I blurted. I longed for the woman to say it was an accident, a mix-up of sleeping pills and other meds. To tell me Amanda hadn't intentionally wanted to harm herself.

"Hard to say." She looked at me sadly, then added softly, "It seems that it was."

No, no, no, don't say that.

"But she's okay, though, right?" I pressed. "She's going to make it?"

For a moment, the woman looked reluctant to say. "They gave her a shot of something, and it roused her. But if she was there like that for a long time..." She trailed off. "The EMTs wouldn't answer any of my questions. I don't know. It made me think...it doesn't look good."

In the newsroom, in the elevator, in the cab, waiting with the paps, I'd refused to consider the possibility that Amanda might not survive. But something about the look on the neighbor's face, a look like she was surrendering to something terrible, inevitable, forced me to consider it as a real possibility, a probable one, even, for the first time. I realized I was about to be sick.

"Sorry...I just need to..." was all I could manage to say before I turned and walked off down the block, hand on my mouth as the saliva pooled under my tongue again, like in the cab, but worse. I made it to the corner before I had to stop and heave over the spikes of a low iron fence into a garden bed, and then I was helpless, emptying the contents of my stomach again and again and again.

Dazed, shocked tears stinging, blurring my vision, I stumbled around the corner to a bus stop, where I collapsed on the bench, tried to breathe, sobs rising heavy from my chest. I stayed there like that, oblivious to passing people and cars, until I heard my phone vibrating in my bag.

I fished it out and saw Jocelyn's name on the screen. I knew I should answer, but I could only stare as her name flashed and flashed. It was as though I were watching myself from above, like my brain had lost contact with the rest of my body. I couldn't make myself press the button to answer. I missed the call. Jocelyn called three more times before I forced myself to pick up.

"Frankie?" Jocelyn said when I finally answered. She sounded panicked. "The stretcher pics have just come in—Jesus Christ. Are you still down there? Do you know what happened?"

Across the street, I could see a woman walking a few feet behind two children, probably her children, who were riding on scooters. The woman had the kids' backpacks slung over each of her shoulders, carrying the weight so they could ride free. Oblivious to the events that had unfolded nearby just moments ago. It was dark out now, the streetlights had come on, and the night covered me. I felt cold, even in my coat, and my mouth still held the sour tang of vomit. I tried to focus on Jocelyn's voice, what she was saying. She was asking for details. What I'd found out was on the tip of my tongue. I knew it was wrong, that I'd lied to obtain the information, and I felt wretched, knowing the neighbor only told me because she believed I was Amanda's friend. But imagining what David would say or do to me, upon hearing I had been at the scene but didn't have an exclusive story, sent a chill through me. I told myself that at least the information I'd been given was true, and that was better than speculation or rumors. I told Jocelyn what the woman shared with me, said it was a neighbor who didn't give me her name.

"Do they think she's going to make it?"

I couldn't bring myself to tell her what the neighbor said.

"No one knows yet."

THE SCOOP

Jocelyn was quiet for a beat. In the background I heard muffled voices.

"Can you get back here?" she asked then, almost pleading. "David's here and—"

"David's there? In the newsroom?"

"Yes," she said. "He's going nuts. Yenay walked out—"

"She *walked out*? Where did she go?"

"I don't know. But I don't think she's coming back." Jocelyn lowered her voice. "Can you please come back? David's furious. With you and Yenay gone, it was left to Chris to get a story live, but he was too slow. *TMZ* broke the news that Amanda was found unconscious and taken to the hospital. Now David is ranting about how this is our story and we're blowing it. I don't understand half of what he's asking me to do. He keeps asking for you. Please come back."

29

BY THREE O'CLOCK IN THE MORNING, the newsroom was deserted except for David and me. Quiet, at last, after the chaos of the night that had just unfolded. A riotous scene of phones ringing nonstop, orders being shouted, footsteps running. No one could reach Yenay, who did not respond to calls or texts, and so David had sent out an urgent request for any willing *Scoop* reporters to come in and work the story. This meant hounding anyone who knew Amanda—family, friends, former band members—for comment, harassing staff at the hospital for an update on her condition, and preparing an "in memoriam" piece, a hastily slapped together tribute to Amanda detailing the highlights of her life, for publication in the event that she died.

David commanded the newsroom from his spot at the top of the editor's desk, stiff and silent as an obelisk except for when he broke concentration to bark an order or answer the phone. From across the room at the night shift desk, I stole looks at him when I could, each time expecting to see a grave expression indicating we were in deep shit, or feverish, unbridled lust as the traffic soared. But he was largely unreadable, giving no clues about what might be to come.

THE SCOOP

With David in command for the night, my role was to follow his orders, and I didn't put up a fight. I was delirious, numb, detached. None of it felt real: the sight of Amanda being carried out of her house on a stretcher, the replay of the scene on the televisions on the wall. The possibility that at any moment we could hear she was dead. Jocelyn, Chris, and I hardly spoke, aware David was monitoring us, expecting the same focus and attention of brain surgeons mid-operation. Not that any of us had the words to articulate how horrible things had been, still were.

When the last bleary-eyed reporter went home, David pulled up a seat at my desk and began directing me through a task that required, as he put it, "discretion": to make edits to a number of *The Scoop* articles about Amanda, and to delete one entirely, like it never existed.

"Legal are worried her family could file a lawsuit—if she dies," he clarified. A recent case of a celebrity suing a news website over the publication of a sex tape, and the enormous potential costs of the settlement, had "everyone running scared," David spat. "So much for the First Amendment. Spineless. But the bloke from legal was chucking a fit, and Walter always listens to those weasels—giving away money is his worst nightmare. If there's one thing I've learned in all my years at this company, it's that you never say no to the Man Upstairs."

And so, David beside me, so close I could smell his stale breath, we got to work. We deleted specific words from the headlines of various stories about Amanda, words like *crazy* and *washed-up* and *unhinged*. A side-by-side image in the grocery shopping article, comparing Amanda's body during the peak of her Valentines fame with a recent photo, the latter marked with red circles around her chin and stomach to indicate weight gain, was also removed. The article to be deleted entirely concerned a meme that had spread online after Amanda's altercation with the pap. Someone had photoshopped Amanda's face next to a shirtless, cigarette-smoking Brad Pitt in a scene from *Fight Club*, and our article included dozens of screenshots of tweets mocking Amanda's "deranged outburst," as the author of the story, someone from day shift, put it. The other articles could be justified, legal said, but the *Fight Club* meme piece was harder to defend, as it amounted to little more than a celebration of bullying, and included nothing that could legitimately be considered in the public interest. *Gratuitous* was the word the lawyer used.

It shocked me to see at least a dozen articles about Amanda published in recent weeks I hadn't known about, written as they were by reporters on day shift. Only then did I realize just how relentless *The Scoop*'s coverage of Amanda had been. How overwhelming the onslaught.

I don't know how long we were there, David and me, on a quest to locate and destroy the most damning evidence of *The Scoop*'s campaign against Amanda, but it was long enough for the overhead sensor lights to go out, leaving us in darkness but for the blue glow of the screen.

By the time we finished, it was after four o'clock and David said it was time we both went home. We rode the elevator down in silence. I kept waiting for him to say something as we passed through the lobby with a nod to front desk security, as we pushed through the side door and stepped out onto the forecourt, awash in the bright white lights of the America Now studios.

A quickly mumbled "good night" was all he offered by way of parting words, turning on his heel and walking away from me. After everything that had happened. That still might happen.

"What if she dies?" I called out. David stopped, slowly turned around to face me, and then walked back to where he'd left me.

"What if she dies?" I repeated, barely croaking the words out this time.

David sighed. "It's four o'clock in the morning, Francesca. It's been a big day. I can see you are very tired. Let's see what tomorrow brings, hmm? For now, go home. Get some sleep."

"*Sleep*? How am I supposed to sleep when, for all we know, Amanda could be dead?"

David shook his head, like he wanted to dismiss the suggestion as melodramatic.

"If Amanda dies," David said plainly, as if it pained him to have to explain something so obvious, "the fault will lie with no one but herself. She swallowed those pills on her own."

"But the changes we made just now, to the old articles. Why would we do that unless—"

"Because our scared-shitless legal department has no bloody backbone, that's why," he said, his voice shaking with anger. "And it seems to me right now that you're no better. Listen, whatever happens to that woman," he said, unable, I noticed, to say her name, "in the coming weeks, there will doubtless be a hysterical media frenzy—especially from the holier-than-thou, bleeding-heart liberal elites, fingers pointed everywhere, looking for someone to blame. And they will almost certainly be pointed at us. Even though most all of them will have gotten plenty of traffic and made plenty of ad dollars reporting on her downward spiral. Even worse will be the readers, the biggest hypocrites of all, calling to boycott us when they clicked on every article, couldn't get enough. They will point fingers everywhere but at themselves. That's just how it is."

But wasn't David doing the exact same thing? Pointing a finger of blame everywhere but at himself, at us? I stared up at his towering figure, not knowing what to say but not wanting to let him walk away, into the night, knowing he would probably have no trouble sleeping at all.

"You know, I had my doubts when I hired you, with your magazine background and portfolio of fluff pieces. You knew nothing about real news, the speed, the grit. But I recognized a hunger in you, a hunger that sets a journalist apart from the rest, a hunger you can't buy with an Ivy League degree or Daddy on the board. I thought you could handle it. Don't prove me wrong."

After everything I had done, David was calling me weak. Weak, when I'd risked a punch in the face to get the video of Amanda grabbing me outside the office, steps from where we stood right then. Weak, when I'd returned to work after throwing my guts up in a garden bed after being at the scene of her attempted suicide. Weak, after I'd stayed back until almost sunrise to help him cover the tracks of all we had done to Amanda these last weeks, under his orders. What else could he possibly expect me to "handle," expect me to do, to prove myself to him?

"Now go home, get some rest, get a hold of yourself, and come back tomorrow. There will be plenty more tragedy and ugliness to cover. And if you won't do it, someone else will."

With that, David turned and walked off again, leaving me alone in the predawn gloom.

I made it through the car ride home, the climb up the four flights of stairs, and into the shower before I broke. Beneath a stream of near-scalding hot water, the weight of it all—the exhaustion, the chaos of the newsroom that night, the confusion of the scene outside Amanda's house, the way the paparazzi swarmed her limp, barely conscious body on the stretcher, the unbearable not-knowing of whether she was still alive—came down on me all at once, and then I was down on my knees on the floor of the tub, folded over myself. Sorrow, raw and uncontained, rushed through me like a geyser pushing through the cracks of the earth and bursting open, the sound of the water disguising the small cries that escaped my open mouth as I wept. It was a familiar pain, an old pain, one I knew I had been carrying since long before that moment.

How I wished for someone to come, lift my wet, naked body, gently wrap me in a towel, dry me off, help me dress, and tuck me into bed. Lay a loving palm on my forehead, tell me everything was going to be all right, that I hadn't done anything wrong. That things had simply gotten a little out of hand, out of control, beyond my grasp, but there would be a way to fix it.

But nobody came.

There was only me.

30

THE YEAR I MOVED TO New York City, I saw a shark at the Met. It was a conceptual work by the British artist Damien Hirst, a thirteen-foot tiger shark embalmed and suspended in a formaldehyde solution and encased in glass: *The Physical Impossibility of Death in the Mind of Someone Living*. A mighty thing of nature, controlled, conquered. I stood before it, both awestruck and disturbed, gazing into its frightening open mouth, its rows of enormous, jagged teeth, my mind playing tricks on me, that the shark might jerk to life, rush at me, strike, leave me bleeding out on the museum's polished concrete floor. I remember the way my skin prickled with primal fear. The longer I stared at this apex predator overpowered, I became aware of the clusters of people inspecting it with mild interest before continuing on with gossip, or tedious discussion of which nearby restaurant might be open for a late lunch. I remember feeling frustrated, angry, there in that antiseptic room humming with dull talk. Pointless, for a wild, powerful thing to be destroyed and presented, all so humans could remark upon it dumbly.

That's what I dreaded more than anything, then, at twenty-two:

waking up one day, at forty, fifty, or sixty, to realize I'd been caged. Like my mom, then dead less than a year, hidden away in a dark, drafty house where no one ever visited and nothing much of anything ever happened, kept there so long by lack of money, a toxic marriage, and the obligations of motherhood that she forgot she was a wild thing and never bothered trying to leave even once she could have. I'd believed, in the way a person can believe something without ever consciously articulating it to themselves, that becoming a journalist would inoculate me against the same fate. It would be a guarantee of power, control, freedom. A guarantee that I would really live.

But now, on the verge of turning thirty, spending my nights in a newsroom that produced little in the way of any actual news, at the whims of one cranky old man's moods, going to increasingly more outrageous and dangerous lengths to earn those precious clicks *The Scoop*—and the entire industry—needed to survive, I could come to no other conclusion than that I'd spent the last seven years doing the opposite of living. Rather, I had been observing life at a remove, peering at its frightening force through the glass in a sterile room. By reporting on the world, I'd been taking raw, wild, unpredictable, adrenaline-in-your-veins-air-in-your-lungs-jump-in-the-ocean-agony-and-ecstasy life, and turning it into something ordered, contained, controlled. Kept it at a distance, because it felt safer than truly living. I'd called it a life, my days at the office, staring at a screen, writing, editing, thinking. But I'd started to suspect it had only been a proxy. That it had been naïve to think that *reporting* on life was equivalent to *living* it.

After my mom died, after I packed up her house at lightning speed and prepared to leave for New York, I locked her belongings in a storage unit, and, in a way, I also locked away my confusion, guilt, rage, and grief. And it worked, boxing up and hiding away my pain, at least for a while. And when something works, when we find a way to maneuver around pain, chances are we will do that same thing again the next time life becomes too much. I wasn't obligated to stay with Josh after his betrayal, but instead of bearing the vulnerability of exploring what it would look like to forgive him, or at least try to, instead of being willing to see what might have been on the other side of that, I shut him out, pushed him away, acted like it never happened, like *we* never happened. Audrey and I shared the blame for the way our friendship unraveled, but instead of calling her, demanding we fix the rupture between us, instead of facing the discomfort of what she might have said, of her rejecting me, I stayed silent. And the more I stayed back, looking from behind the glass instead of living, not only did I grow lonely, but I also became numb to my pain. Which was a relief for a while, since the loss of my mother had almost engulfed me. But then I also became numb to the pain of others, blind to the hurt I caused them. Caused Amanda.

Was Amanda the tiger shark? Tamed and displayed as a specimen to be observed, analyzed, judged? A place for the public to project its fears, regrets, shame, desires, resentments, and unlived lives, because that feels easier than to acknowledge all that's inside us—the messy, the complicated, the contradictory, the ugly, the embarrassing, the inconvenient, the frightening?

Yes, that was Amanda. A wild thing of beauty and power, neutralized, captured, and presented for our amusement. All so the rest of us could keep looking outward, never inward.

I'd been on the outside, looking through the glass, for long enough. It was time to live.

31

David drummed his fingers on the gleaming mahogany between us. The meeting room was much bigger than the tiny space from the day of my job interview. It had a conference table that could seat ten, and windows, through which I could see a slab of orange and indigo sky, sunset. Did the choice of meeting room mean I'd at last earned his respect? Surely I'd earned something, after everything I'd done. But probably it meant nothing at all. I was exhausted from trying to read the signs, trying to interpret his every nonsensical, contradictory word and action, of trying to make things make sense. It seemed like a long, long time since anything in my life had made sense.

"So, Amanda is home and resting up," David said with a small smile. "But the photos of her arriving home from hospital didn't rate well at all." He shrugged. "Readers have moved on."

The paparazzi had been there to capture it, the moment Amanda climbed out of a black SUV wearing large dark sunglasses, her sister holding her arm to steady her, and beelined to her front door, keeping her head down as she pushed through the mob. We'd known for a few days she was in a stable condition, but it was still a relief to see it with my own eyes—Amanda awake, walking. Alive. But *The Scoop* article reporting it got barely a tenth of the clicks the other articles about her did. Amanda, as a subject of public interest, had reached saturation point and was beginning to wane, eclipsed by the news that an A-list couple had filed for divorce, and that Fart Jar Girl, after being hospitalized for severe abdominal pain caused by eating an excessive amount of beans in an attempt to stay ahead of the competition from her rival, Gassy Gal, had been forced into retirement on the advice of her doctor. She was said to be pivoting to feet pics.

"Anyway," David said, moving the conversation along with a clap of his hands, "I spoke to the Man Upstairs, and we're both *very* impressed with the way night shift handled the situation—the exclusive you got from the neighbor," and it made me queasy to be reminded of this, "the way Jocelyn and Chris stepped up in your absence when the news broke…"

At the mention of Jocelyn and Chris, David paused almost imperceptibly, and I could tell he was remembering how Yenay had quit that night, walking out of the newsroom in protest shortly after I left for the scene, refusing to write the article about Amanda found unconscious in her home (at that stage unconfirmed), refusing to ever write another word for *The Scoop*.

"I'd rather go back to Minnesota and be a Pilates instructor," she said on the phone when she finally returned my call, days later. "If that's what I have to do? To make it as a journalist? It's not anything like I thought it would be, when I was in college, when I was obsessed with magazines. Back when I would have killed to be the next Francesca Miller."

Killed. We fell into an uneasy silence at that word. That day on the phone, Amanda was still in the hospital, her condition unknown. I spent the weekend in bed, barely able to force myself to get up to go to the bathroom, nauseated, paralyzed with dread at what might happen. That Amanda could die. That the evidence was right there on *The Scoop* website, article, after article, after article, targeting her. That my own name was atop several of them, not least the blackface story and the video of her "attacking" me, the obvious tipping point of it all.

"I know I let you down," I'd told Yenay, meaning it. She'd contemplated quitting *The Scoop* weeks ago, all but said it that night in the kitchen, but I'd encouraged her to stay, insisting I'd take her with me to *Business Day* if she helped me find a scoop for David. I'd dismissed her concerns, was so focused on getting to *Business Day* that I ignored anything that got in my way.

"I really am sorry. For convincing you to stay, when I could tell you wanted to leave. For not doing enough when you got trolled over the first article about Amanda. I could see you weren't yourself for a while after that, and it took me too long to check if you were okay."

I heard a snort, as if Yenay had stifled a laugh.

"What?"

"I guess I can tell you, now that you're no longer my editor."

"Tell me what?"

She cleared her throat. "The 'fat' story? That was my doing." She paused. "I emailed David. Said we should change the angle of the story to Jocelyn's suggestion. The focus on Amanda's body."

I didn't believe her.

"What? No, you didn't."

Another sheepish laugh, laced with guilt.

"Wait, you're serious? Why?"

"Look, if I'd known the backlash was going to be as intense as it was, I would never have done it. Nothing is worth the fact that Annie Klein hates me now and probably always will."

She was quiet for a moment, the memory clearly still painful.

"But that night, when you and Jocelyn were arguing about the story? Honestly, I was on Jocelyn's side. I knew it was harsh, but I was still new at *The Scoop*—you know I didn't start long before you—and I wanted to write some articles that would go viral, get some serious traffic. There's a monthly ranking of how many articles all the reporters write and how many clicks they get, which David looks at—you're shielded from that as an editor. I knew if I had any chance of getting off the night desk, joining the day shift, and finally getting a chance to write some real stories, that's what I had to do. But I was scared to disagree with you, since I was a junior. In the car home, I was kicking myself for not saying what I thought, when you asked for my opinion. So, I emailed David and suggested the change, said I'd thought of it after leaving work and asked if the morning team could do it. I was worried he would tell you, on the phone, when you brought it up to him. I was practically dying of shame inside. But he didn't. And then after he blasted you so hard for disagreeing with him, I thought you'd be angry at me if you knew."

Yenay's confession stunned me; I never would have guessed she was behind the "fat" angle. I might have been angry—after all, I'd felt so bad for her when I got to the office that night, though her tears over the online furor and Annie Klein calling her out were, no doubt, very real—but Amanda was still in the hospital, on life support, and it was unclear if she would survive. Little else seemed worth getting worked up about. Besides, I understood it well, the delicate dance of compromises and trade-offs that must be made to get the things we want, to become who we want to be. I'd done a lot worse than that trying to get ahead at work. A lot, lot worse.

I'd asked Yenay what she would do next. Did she still want to be a celebrity profiler?

"No, fuck the white male celebrity profile writer mafia. They can have it. I'm not going to try to join their club—I'll just start my own. A podcast, or maybe a YouTube channel. Just wait, in ten years those same men will be begging to join *my* club. And I'll tell them, *Keep your chin up!* You just have to work harder, that's all! It's not about you being white, or a man. If you put as much energy into your work as you do whining and complaining, if you find something *important* to say, something *urgent*, impossible to ignore, you'll break through in no time, kid."

"Whoa," I said, laughing despite the gloom, the heaviness of the excruciating wait for news on Amanda. "I've never seen this side of you. I didn't know you could be so...savage."

Yenay laughed. "Why would you? I wore a mask at work. Doesn't everyone?"

"Not everyone," I replied. "Unfortunately, I attended with my real face," I said, referencing Kafka. I don't think Yenay understood what I meant. It didn't matter. Nothing did.

I snapped back to the meeting room with David. Neither of us mentioned Yenay. That she had quit in protest didn't fit his narrative of our inspiring triumph, and so it went unmentioned.

"To that end, given how happy we are with your work, I'm happy to say..."

It couldn't be, could it? Surely David wasn't actually going to come through on his promise to get me a transfer to *Business Day*? I'd forced myself to stop hoping for it. I didn't deserve it, after what I'd done. And yet, I couldn't deny the dream still had its hooks in me. Despite it all, I longed to hear him say it.

"...that you, Jocelyn, and Chris are welcome to treat yourselves to takeout one night this week. Pizza, Chinese, whatever. We've budgeted a hundred and fifty dollars—just expense it by month's end."

My face must have fallen with disappointment, the blow landing hard even though I had told myself I didn't want it anymore, *Business Day*. David leaned forward, concerned.

"What? Is fifty dollars per person not enough to cover dinner these days? You'd think you could get some General Tso's and some of those deep-fried money bags for that. Ridiculous, how expensive New York City is. How anyone but the billionaires survive here is beyond me."

David had landed a heavy blow to my ego. I tried to hide the embarrassment I felt, at briefly allowing myself to believe it might still happen.

"No, it's not that. I..."

"What?"

It felt wrong to bring it up, after everything, but I found myself saying the words anyway.

"*Business Day.*"

"What? Oh, that." David sighed, exasperated. "Why do you want to work there, anyway? I don't understand it. Boring, stuffy, not read by anyone under fifty, going the way of the dinosaurs. Besides, you wouldn't fit in there. Bunch of dull, toffy-nosed twats who summer on Cape Cod. Didn't Peter put you off it? I told him to tell you the truth."

I would have laughed if I wasn't so stung by the betrayal. David sent Peter to cool me on the idea of *Business Day*, not to help me transfer there. He'd probably never had any intention of helping me get a job there, had only said it to lure me in, like Audrey said. I'd been so desperate to see what I wanted to see I'd ignored all the warning signs, all the things that didn't add up.

"You're right," I said, fighting to keep the sarcasm and simmering rage out of my voice. David looked surprised, like he hadn't expected me to loosen my grip on *Business Day* so fast.

"This is where I belong, right? It's the future. *The Scoop* is what readers want now. All the rest is going extinct. *The Scoop* is growing. We make money. I'm one of the lucky ones."

"I'm glad to see you've come around," David said. "You're getting noticed here, Francesca. Give it a couple of years, put your head down, and *you* could be editor in chief. Or you could be upstairs in corporate, in one of those plush jobs with a meaningless title like Director of ESG Initiatives or some utter crap where they pay you half a million a year to lie to Walter Johnson's face and tell him everything is fine so he can claim ignorance down the track. All you have to do is accept that you're never going to be one of them—the stuck-up Yale and Hamptons summer crowd. Once you do, you'll be free. Because instead of trying to become one of them, you can get busy becoming *better* than them. *That* is when you become unstoppable."

I nodded and smiled, acted like I was eating it up. David looked pleased with himself.

"But actually, David, I didn't request this meeting to talk about *Business Day*."

"Oh?"

"No."

"I see. What did you want to talk about?"

David blinked innocently. Did he seriously not think we needed to talk about what happened?

"The night of Amanda's suicide attempt," I began, keeping my eyes on his, not looking away, "when you made me stay back and make those stealth edits, delete that article about the *Fight Club* meme..."

David looked uncomfortable, bristling slightly at the mention of our late-night mission to erase any evidence that we may have gone beyond reason in our reporting on Amanda Myles.

"Mmm."

"How do we make sure nothing like that happens again? I didn't realize until that night how many articles we ran about her in the last month—more than a dozen. I keep wondering what would have happened, if she died, if an article I wrote may have contributed to—"

"You know this is all just business for me, don't you?" David said, interrupting me. "Business, nothing more. The media is a *business*. And when this *business* no longer becomes profitable—in other words, when people stop clicking on stories about gossip and celebrity train wrecks and high-profile people at their worst—I'll be on to the next thing. You can be sure of it."

But I wasn't sure of it. Legacy media was already long past its golden age, budgets and readerships minuscule compared to what they were ten, twenty years ago. Tech moguls had supplanted media titans as the new power brokers and were on track to put all but a few of them out of jobs in the near future. No, David's presence was not purely a business or financial decision. It was tied to something much deeper. I'd seen the way David relished the theatrics of the morning meeting, the way he drank in the attention surrounded by his underlings, the way he loved to drop mentions of his close relationship with Walter Johnson. Outside the Johnson News building, David was no longer someone important, powerful, as he once had been. But inside, he was still somebody, still mattered—as long as he obeyed commands. It couldn't last, not with tech coming to swallow the media whole. Before long, he would be cast out into the real world, his lack of charm, talent, and integrity laid bare. So he would hold on as long as he could.

The sky out the window was dark.

"You haven't let them get to you, have you? *The Guardian* columnist spouting all that self-righteous crap about us being culpable for Amanda's suicide attempt, the people on social media up in arms, when they were the ones who clicked, who drove the frenzied interest in Amanda in the first place? All those people who love to act so holier-than-thou? Who would they be holier than, if not for us? We're the drunk at the pub who falls on his ass and humiliates himself, and all the others get to say, *Oh, wasn't he in an awful state?* And the next day, they all offer to buy him a round. Why? Because they need to keep someone around who looks worse than them. So nobody notices all the hypocritical things *they* do. So they don't have to look in the mirror. Not only do they need us, but they also need the Amanda Myleses of the world, too. You'll see—before long there will be another Amanda, and the media machine, left and right, will chew her up and spit her out to keep themselves alive and relevant, afloat, turning a profit."

That was David's answer? To the question of how we would try to stop something like the events of the last week from happening again? I wanted to make sure I'd heard him correctly.

"You really believe that? There will be another Amanda Myles? Another person who—"

"You think there won't be? Come on, Francesca. These attention-hungry, selfie-posting, emotional wrecks are a dime a dozen, from Hollywood to the West Village to Notting Hill and everywhere in between. There will be another Amanda, with or without *The Scoop*. If we disappeared today, tomorrow someone would replace us. We might as well get our payday."

Despite all the things I'd heard David say in the few short months I'd known him, all the things I'd seen him do, his cold, calculated, completely unfeeling response still shocked me. It was nothing new for a journalist to be detached when reporting on a heavy subject ("'Tragic story, isn't it? But it's a great day for news" was a dark refrain I'd heard more than once during my time at Johnson News), a necessary coping strategy, it could be argued, especially for those with little choice but to face the onslaught of sad, senseless world events day after day, week after week, year after year. But had the incident with Amanda truly not affected him, shaken him, in the slightest? Did he not, like me, spend the weekend sick with worry she might succeed in her attempt to end her life after being pushed to the brink by our relentless invasions into her privacy, and the knock-on effects of tabloid attention? Did he not wonder if the articles we had published about her, about someone who was no longer of genuine public interest (at least not until we forced her back into the spotlight), would become evidence in a courtroom? No, he couldn't possibly be that cold. He couldn't possibly have strayed that far from decency.

"What if the next Amanda doesn't make it?" I pressed. "There'd be blood on our hands."

"Look," David said with a huff, "if I thought there was a chance Amanda would get so upset over a few articles that she'd try to top herself, would I have thought twice about some of them? The ones that were a bit unkind? Perhaps. I will say the *Fight Club* meme story, after her run-in with the paps, was unwise. Too far. The Man Upstairs has been giving me some heat. After the efforts to clean up the image of Johnson News after the spying scandal, it's not ideal."

David was quiet for a moment. Contemplative.

"But will there be another Amanda? Of course there will. And will we publish articles about her? Certainly. And will readers click on those articles? You bet. And will she be driven to near insanity by it all? Quite possibly. Will we stop? No way. Not as long as readers demand it."

A question hung in the air between us, which didn't need to be acknowledged aloud: Would I be there for the next time? Would I be a part of it? Or would I be the next Yenay?

David said he had somewhere to be.

As we stood and made to leave the meeting room, David rested a hand on my shoulder.

"Listen, if *Business Day* is what you want, we can make it happen. But we'll need to give it some time, wait for all this Amanda Myles stuff to blow over. *Business Day* isn't going to hire the journalist whose name was on the articles that made Amanda Myles try to kill herself."

I looked up at David. He was smiling, but in his eyes I saw something menacing. He was, in his own way, putting all the blame on me for what happened to Amanda. Letting me know that I would only go to *Business Day* when he was ready for me to, when he was finished with me.

David turned and strode across the newsroom to his desk, lifted his coat and mailbag from his chair, and headed confidently toward the newsroom doors, not once looking back.

I hurried to the hallway that led to the bathrooms, checked to make sure no one was coming, then reached into my pocket and pulled out my phone. I hit the red round pause button to stop recording. The audio file was twenty-three minutes long. David would be furious if he knew that I'd secretly recorded our conversation, but I hadn't done anything wrong, legally speaking: according to New York state law, only one party needs to consent to a conversation being recorded, and that person was me.

All I'd realistically hoped for, when I'd asked David to meet with me before my shift that day, was to get some proof of the changes David forced me to make to the articles the night Amanda was hospitalized. I wanted evidence, for my own protection, in case David ever acted out of the Johnson News playbook and decided to throw me under the bus, like the juniors in the spying scandal, like Chris said that night: *get rid of the "bad apples" to keep your reputation untarnished and the business operating as normal.* I wasn't about to take the fall on my own. I could also, if necessary, use the evidence as leverage (I preferred "leverage" to blackmail) to negotiate a payout to keep quiet about it all, like that reporter Steve hit with the stapler. But now I had something bigger, much, *much* bigger in my possession: an admission of guilt from the editor in chief of *The Scoop* conceding that the articles had contributed to Amanda's suicide attempt. Not only that, but that *The Scoop* and Johnson News had learned nothing, did not see any reason to review or make changes to its editorial processes, to prevent harm in the future.

I didn't know what I was going to do with the recording, not right then. I only knew it was valuable. And after what David had just said—I was the journalist who had pushed Amanda over the edge—I knew my instinct to gather proof had been right. If anything happened, David would squash me without a second thought. He might even use it to try to control me for years.

I had to name the file. I thought for a second, then had it: *D-Day*. The *D* was for David.

The click of heels on tile. I stuffed my phone in my pocket as Jocelyn rounded the corner.

"Hey," she said, pausing at the entrance to the bathroom and instead coming over to where I was standing. "Did I see you in the meeting room with David just now?"

It hadn't been the same between us since Amanda's suicide attempt. Between Jocelyn, me, and Chris. Yenay's empty chair was a damning reminder, our presence amid her absence saying something none of us wanted to acknowledge: we could have done the same but were still there.

Jocelyn looked confused as she waited for me to explain. I was so angry, felt so foolish, I could have cried if I'd let myself. *The journalist whose articles made Amanda try to kill herself.*

"What happened? Wait, did he fire you?"

"Why would he fire me?" I snapped, her question cutting like an accusation of blame.

"I don't know, that's why I'm asking! I can see you're upset. What did he say to you?"

I'd never told Jocelyn about David's promise to get me a job at *Business Day*. But now that it was obvious it would never happen, that he was going to use his power over me to keep me as his underling, doing his dirty work, possibly forever, there was no point hiding it. I told her everything, about the offer he made in the interview, about my meeting with Peter Lowell.

Jocelyn frowned, said nothing.

"What?"

"Come in here."

Jocelyn signaled for me to follow her into the accessible bathroom, where she rolled the heavy door shut and turned the lock. She sighed, closed her eyes briefly, and then opened them.

"Do you remember when I told you about Steve? The old night editor?"

I remembered her telling me how he threw things across the newsroom, would disappear for hours, come back drunk and sleep it off in a meeting room. The time she discovered him in the kitchen, drinking wine from the bottle, ripping apart a roast chicken with his bare hands.

"Yeah, why?"

"David made Steve the same promise. That if he did a six-month stint, or however long, as night editor at *The Scoop*, that he would get him a job at *Business Day*. But he never made good on the offer. The editor of *Business Day* couldn't give a shit about David Brown."

I blinked at her.

"But I thought Steve went mad," I said, my voice low. "I thought that was why he left."

"Yes, Steve did, very sadly, go mad. And why do you think that is?"

32

As dawn broke over New York City on a bitterly cold November morning, David Brown and half a dozen *Scoop* reporters and editors stood huddled in a circle on the sidewalk outside the building, top heavy and rotund in their winter puffers, like penguins sharing body heat on an Antarctic ice sheet. Police barricades prevented them from getting inside. A group of eight climate activists had staged a protest in the lobby, sitting cross-legged, their arms interlinked in front of the turnstiles, blocking access to the elevators. To *The Scoop*.

I watched the scene from across Seventh Avenue, behind a bus stop, the hood of my coat pulled tight around my face to protect me from the biting chill—and from being recognized. It would have been safer to go home, to not risk being seen. But I couldn't resist staying to watch the results of my mutiny unfold, the plan I still couldn't believe I'd had the courage to carry out.

David, as I'd witnessed from my hiding spot across the street, had tried everything to convince the police to let him upstairs. Shouting, pleading, stomping, even bribing; I'd watched him pull his wallet from his pocket and wave a wad of bills in the face of an unimpressed cop. He was saying "fuck" a lot. But nothing worked. Through the glass of the building, I saw the officers were trying to make the protesters leave, delaying the moment they'd resort to making arrests. I couldn't see the individual faces of the protesters, but I knew Patti was among them.

"There are hundreds of people in our Signal group," she'd said when I'd called her at the start of my shift, crouched in a meeting room whispering into my phone. "It is short notice to plan an action. But the chance to stick it to Johnson News? Incredibly motivating."

When I saw David pull out his phone and study the screen, saw his body stiffen in shock, his face turn an even deeper shade of red, I knew he'd finally seen it, my pièce de résistance. What David saw when he checked *The Scoop* was a rather unexpected story in the splash (surely the worst "dog turd of a home page" he'd ever woken up to, as he'd put it in my interview). A photo of himself, his headshot from the company website, alongside two photos of Amanda Myles: one of her performing onstage during the heyday of the Valentines, the other of her on a stretcher, oxygen mask over her face, being carried out of her home by EMTs after the overdose.

We fucked up! Editor in chief David Brown admits *The Scoop* shares blame for Amanda Myles' suicide attempt: 'If we thought she'd try to kill herself, we would have backed off'

I was there to witness it as David, at the top of his lungs, did what I'd always wondered if he would: called me a cunt. He tilted his head back and howled it to the frozen, gray dawn sky.

I'd pulled the plan together with remarkable speed. After David told me that *Business Day* would never hire "the journalist who made Amanda Myles try to kill herself," after Jocelyn told me that David made the same promise to Steve, to get him a job at *Business Day*, but he never came through, I decided then that after that night, I would never set foot in *The Scoop* newsroom ever again. I understood it, then, why Yenay couldn't bear to stay a second longer, why she'd walked out even though the source of her next paycheck was unknown. If a person does not define the limits of what they will accept, draw a hard line not to be crossed, they won't recognize how far they've strayed from themselves until it is too late; a rip current can carry a person out to sea, quietly, unnoticed, until they lose sight of the shoreline completely.

I didn't know what I would do instead, where I would work, how I would survive, but I was too blind with rage to care. It was as though the rage I felt had set fire to every worry, every fear, every *but*, every *what if*, incinerated everything in me until there was nothing left but the burning desire to make David Brown feel, even just once, what it was like to not be in control. Also, I knew if I was never going to set foot in that newsroom again, that I would have to take action that night. And have to I did. I had to do something with it, with the rage bubbling up within me, on the brink of overflow. Rage at what I had done, not just to Amanda, but to myself.

I said nothing of this to Jocelyn. She was loyal to the job because it allowed her to take care of her mother, and I knew this loyalty could be cause for her to turn on me, snitch on me to David or someone else before I had a chance to carry out my plan. Chris, however, had no such loyalty to David, Johnson News, or *The Scoop*, Robin Hood-ing it as he was. I accosted him in the hall on his way back from the bathroom, confided in him that it would be my last night, told him why.

"So," he said, breaking into a grin, rare for him, "you had enough of being 'demoralized in the shortest possible time, on the largest possible scale, for the lowest possible price'?"

I laughed. "I guess I did."

Once I'd explained exactly what I intended to do—stay back when he and Jocelyn left at two a.m., write an article based on what David said to me in the meeting (the meeting I'd recorded), publish it, put it on the home page, and have Patti and her activist friends block the entrance so no one from *The Scoop* could get inside so it would stay on the website as long as possible—Chris pointed out the hole in my plan.

"But the morning editor, or David, or whoever, will be able to access the website from their home computer or laptop. They'll be able to take it down even with the climate activists blocking the entrance. What you need to do is stop them from being able to log in to the system."

"Shit," I whispered, cursing myself. How had I not thought of that?

"I'm not a hacker," I said, feeling defeated. "I wouldn't have a clue how to do that."

"It's easy," Chris said. "Check the roster to see who is scheduled on for the morning. Try to log in to the content-management system using their credentials until the system bars you for too many wrong password attempts. They'll have to call IT, and since they laid off most of the IT department and moved services to the Philippines, the wait times have been an hour, sometimes longer. Make sure you do the same to David and to all the senior *Scoop* editors."

I stared at Chris, almost rendered speechless at his genius.

"You came up with that just now?"

Chris shrugged, gave a sly smile.

"I fantasize every now and then about taking this place down. I think everyone does."

At two a.m., I made to leave with Chris and Jocelyn as normal but deliberately left behind my coat. I faked realizing this in the elevator, insisted they both go on without me, and pushed the button to go back up, exchanging a private smile with Chris as the doors closed.

Back in the office, alone, I replayed the D-Day recording from the meeting with David and typed out a few key quotes, the ones where he admitted that *The Scoop* had played a role in Amanda Myles's suicide attempt. It also included an "apology" from Johnson News:

> We at Johnson News take seriously our privileged position as one of the world's largest and most influential media companies. For that reason, after reviewing our editorial processes in the wake of the upsetting incident involving Amanda Myles, we have decided to implement a policy that all Johnson News journalists will be trained on and required to follow when reporting on a private citizen, famous or not. This policy requires justification for invasions of privacy in regard to public interest before the publication of sensitive information, or any information that could lead to excessive public scrutiny. We recognize the growing mental health crisis worldwide, the relentless, 24-7 nature of the digital news cycle, and the direct impacts this can have on a person who finds themselves the subject of media attention. We call on other media outlets to implement their own similar policies. Together, we can build a media that's better for us all.

The genius of the fake apology, the made-up policy, was that if my plan succeeded and my inside job went viral, Johnson News would be forced into one of two choices: either clarify there was no such policy, which was not a good look, or, in an attempt to save face, adopt the policy, pretending it had been their idea all along. Either way, Johnson News couldn't win, and I couldn't lose. Sure, I knew David, *The Scoop*, and Johnson News would be incensed at my treason, but what law had I broken? None with the recording. And in terms of the "lie" of the statement, the disinformation...*please*. Johnson News trying to punish one of its journalists for publishing fake news? They *forced* their journalists to publish lies—every day. The idea that by publishing something untrue I had done something outside of company norms was laughable.

By the time I published the article, illustrated with a not totally terrible side-by-side splash image of David and Amanda I'd thrown together in Microsoft Paint, it was nearly five a.m. Patti texted to say she and the other climate protesters she'd wrangled were on their way. It was early enough that they would beat the first *Scoop* reporters and editors coming into the newsroom, but late enough that security had unlocked the building's front doors for the day.

Time to go. I deleted a few personal files off my computer and logged out for the last time. Hands shaking, I gathered up my phone, water bottle, and security pass. Adrenaline kept me moving, stopped me from backing out, from deleting the article, but I was terrified. If by chance somebody—David—had already seen it, they might be on their way. And if it was David, what would he do? I wondered if he'd be able to stop himself from putting his hands around my throat.

For a brief moment, I considered slipping one of Jocelyn's pills to calm me, one last rummage in her magical drawer of treats for the road, but I resisted. Numbing myself was what got me to this place. I was done being numb. I wanted to feel this, *really* feel it. Feel truly alive. After all, what I'd done with my act of rebellion, my defiance, felt more important and powerful than anything I'd done in my entire career as a journalist. Because it wasn't what an editor, or an executive, wanted me to do. It wasn't what colleagues expected of me. It wouldn't earn me a pay raise or a promotion. But it was, for once, the truth—the real, unvarnished truth. Not buried, obscured, or even softened, sharp edges smoothed because we couldn't dare upset the corporate floor, the board, the shareholders—the Man Upstairs—those who enjoyed walking around pretending to be champions of a free press, only to cry like a baby for its mother when that free press stung their own tissue-paper-thin skin. I thought of Patti asking Audrey why *The New York Times* climate change coverage was so inadequate, so weasel-weak, when, as she'd explained to me, class-action lawsuits, mass protests, and a wartime effort to transform the energy industry and prepare communities was the only appropriate response to the dismaying cowardice, greed, and duplicity of the fossil fuel companies. I thought of Chris quoting Kierkegaard—*The media will stir up all those dregs of humanity which no state or government can control*—and wondered how many hate-fueled atrocities were needed, how many centuries-old grievances needed be stoked, for a media company to ensure a quarterly profit, until the inevitable end point of it all scorched the earth. I thought of what Peter Lowell said: *Part of me won't be all that sad to see it go ... Will something better sprout from the ashes?* That last part, at least, gave me hope.

For the first time in my career, I felt my soul on fire. And it felt so much better than being cynical, than telling myself I had no power to change anything. That I had no power at all.

That this was how it was supposed to feel all along.

Standing there, moments from walking out of *The Scoop* forever, I thought of my mom. Had I given her something to be proud of, even if she was not around to see it? Was the time with her I'd sacrificed in what turned out to be her last years, while I was at college, finally worth it? Maybe now I could stop spending my life, as Amanda had said, trying to make a dead person proud. I tried to imagine what my mother would say to me in that moment; probably she would have cracked a joke to break the tension, beneath it blistering anger at those she blamed for "rotting the brains" of people in our town, people everywhere: "If you see Walter Johnson, spit on him for me."

THE SCOOP

The last time I saw my mom, she was leaning on the frame of the open front door as I put my overnight bag in the back seat of my car, preparing to leave after another weekend visit, another two days of cleaning despite her orders not to, of sitting on her couch surrounded by the mess and filth I was supposed to pretend I couldn't see, her hacking cough and ragged breaths I was supposed to not notice, constantly shifting between trying to fix her and sharing in her delusions. Stuck between calling for help and keeping her secret, between defying her wishes and being obedient, wondering which was right. Which would make me a good daughter.

"I was scared," my mother said out of nowhere.

"What?" I walked back up to the porch. I didn't know what she was talking about.

"You asked, yesterday, why we didn't leave. When things got bad with your father."

I'd asked her this, hesitantly, the day before when my golden-tanned, ocean-swimming estranged father had come up in conversation. It had always seemed incongruous to me, the different ways their lives ended up—incongruous, and unfair. I'd asked her why it was him that left and not the other way around. Why did she stay despite his chaos, his rages, his cruelty?

"I was scared," she said again. "Of what people would think, say. Scared because I didn't know what came next. How we'd survive, you and me. But I wish now I had been brave. You deserved better," she said, her voice cracking as she tried not to cry. "You deserved so much better."

I would not make the same mistake, would not let fear of judgment, fear of uncertainty, keep me small. That was the fastest way to the death of the soul. That was no way to live.

The jumbo screen showed no green arrows on my story yet, but I knew they would come, once the readers began to wake up—any minute now. If the Man Upstairs was, indeed, always watching, then I hoped he enjoyed my handiwork. The fear that made my legs shake, made my breath shallow, made my skin break out in goose pimples, was now becoming pure euphoria, energy that surged through my body, soared. Impulsively, I decided I would leave a parting gift for David. I ran over to his desk and with a sweep of my hands pushed some things onto the floor: a newspaper stack, a notebook, a metal cup full of pens. My eyes fell on his wastepaper basket, full of scrunched paper, disposable coffee cups, soda cans, and an apple core, pushed so far under his desk the cleaner missed it. I dragged it out and kicked it over, the trash spilling all over the floor. I was breathing hard. But then it occurred to me that the only person this would hurt would be a member of the building staff, who would be made to deal with it. David, nor any of the other editors—once they regained access to the newsroom—were likely to get down on their hands and knees and clean up the mess. Quickly as I could, I kicked the trash back into the can and set it upright, gathered up the papers and other items, put them back on the desk, and walked out.

In the elevator, I pulled out my phone and sent Chris a text.

Mission complete. Then, **Keep those arrows sharp, Robin Hood.**

Chris would probably tease me for being so corny, but I didn't care. I remembered what he said: *I fantasize every now and then about taking this place down.* Someday, I knew, he, too, would go out in a blaze of glory. And when he did, I would be the first to buy him a drink.

As the traffic picked up on Seventh Avenue, the morning rush beginning in earnest, the rest of my plan unfolded as I'd hoped. David began pointing and yelling at his staff, who began to pull laptops from their bags, either balancing them in their arms or sitting down on the sidewalk. He was urging them to log in, pull the story off the website. After a few moments, their expressions went from serious and scared, to confused and even more scared. The bravest one stood, ambled over to David, and whispered something in his ear. Upon hearing that no one could access the system, David wound his arm back with the skill of a child baseball player and hurled his paper coffee cup onto the sidewalk. Brown liquid splashed on the pants and shoes of several people walking by. Seeing this, a cop came toward him with one hand up to signal *stop*. David cried out something I couldn't hear, but judging by his urgent pointing up at the building, he was still demanding they let him through. Another cop appeared beside the first. David lunged past them, made a run for the entrance. In seconds they had him pinned to the ground, one of the cops speaking into the radio pinned to their chest, presumably calling for backup. David, thrashing under the weight of the cops holding him down, twisted until he was facing the editors, who stood frozen in shock, screaming instructions at them. His face purpling, his mouth open, he reminded me of a newborn baby—enraged at his helplessness. I couldn't hear him, wasn't certain, but watching his lips move, I was pretty sure David shouted that they, too, were all cunts.

Carefully, not wanting to be seen, I slipped my phone from my pocket, leaned around the edge of the bus shelter, and took a photo of my former boss prone on the ground. I knew I would want to savor it forever, the sight of David Brown weakened, overpowered, if only for a moment.

I stayed just long enough to see David being led to a police car in handcuffs. I figured someone would post his bail and he'd be out in no time, probably back at his desk and barking orders by lunch, somehow turning the humiliating display of him lying on the cement, powerless, into a story of his heroism by day's end—at least this would be the version of events he'd relay to the Man Upstairs. But maybe, just maybe, I'd planted a seed in his mind that would someday sprout. A whisper, a niggling voice inside he'd find harder to ignore as time went on: that he was building nothing of his life but a toxic legacy—and not even his own legacy, but that of the Man Upstairs. That he could feel his soul on fire, too, if he wanted. That it wasn't too late. But probably not. Probably I'd only fueled him to grasp tighter to the safety of his favorite illusion: that he was simply holding a mirror up to an ugly world. That he himself was not the ugly world.

I was cold and tired, and my work was done. Time to go. I would have liked to call a car, collapse into the back seat, but the subway stairs behind me were an escape chute, too tempting to resist. I disappeared down into the underground. As I waited for the train, I decided there were some people I wanted to see my last ever story for *The Scoop*. I went to the home page, clicked on the article, and took screenshots, which I texted to three people, each with a personal note.

First, Yenay. **Any advice for someone who just quit their job at a tabloid in protest? Asking for a friend.**

Next, Audrey. **Got a hot tip for the Times media desk. Also, truce?**

And finally, Amanda.

> **Is it revenge? Or just telling the truth?**

EPILOGUE

THREE MONTHS LATER, I WOKE to a text from Audrey, asking me to call her. We hadn't spoken since the day I staged my revolt at *The Scoop*, and even then, it had only been brief, and stilted. I'd given her details for a story about it, our instincts as journalists strong enough to overcome the fact that we were not, technically, speaking. The hurt was still too raw to try to heal our broken friendship. The sight of her name on my screen jolted me awake.

I got up, used the bathroom, and went into the kitchen to find Patti there, dressed for work and making herself breakfast.

"Coffee?" she asked, lifting the pot she'd made. I nodded and let her pour me a cup.

"Audrey texted," I said, rubbing my face, still half asleep. "She wants me to call her."

Patti's eyes widened. She knew what it meant, to finally hear from Audrey, could probably sense my guts churning as I anticipated finally talking to my ex–best friend.

"On Valentine's Day? Maybe she's calling to confess her love for you. I always knew there had to be an explanation for your unlikely friendship with an Upper East Side WASP."

Patti was clearly trying to ease the tension I felt, and I was grateful. I laughed.

"Thanks for the coffee."

I took my mug over to the living room window and perched on the sill. I should have felt satisfied, smug, that Audrey was breaking the silence first. But all I felt was sad—at what had happened to us and at my own inability to try to fix it sooner. I decided I would take whatever happened, whether she yelled, angrily blamed me for everything, told me she hated me, if she cried. I could handle her emotions. She wasn't my father, and I was no longer a child. I was safe. In the distance I could see the Manhattan skyline, as always, in the center, the Empire State Building. Every time I looked lately, I could have sworn it was getting smaller, farther away.

I dialed Audrey. She picked up after a few rings.

"Frankie, hi."

"Hey," I said. We were both silent for an awkward moment. "I was surprised to get your text," I said finally. "It's been a long time."

"Yeah, I know. We should have talked before now. But I—"

"I wanted to reach out," I said, my nerves causing me to interrupt, "but I didn't know what to say. But I want you to know I understand, why you wrote the article . . . you were only doing your job and—"

"I think we should get together soon, to talk," she said, cutting me off. "About all of that. But . . . I was actually wondering what you're up to these days. Do you have a new job yet?"

I did not, at least not in the sense I knew Audrey meant. I'd been making coffees and bussing tables at a café in my neighborhood, which paid barely enough to cover my rent but would allow me to get by as long as I paid for what I could with credit until the start of summer, when I'd be leaving New York City. I still had credit card debt, and almost no savings, but I had it all worked out. On Patti's advice, I'd consolidated my credit cards into one monthly payment with a lower interest rate. I'd begun the process of selling most of my belongings; my clothes, furniture. I intended to sell almost everything in the storage unit in North Carolina, get rid of it next time I could get down there. None of Mom's belongings made me feel connected to her, and she wasn't around to guilt me into keeping them. It had been long enough. I was ready to let go.

I'd lined up a job starting Memorial Day weekend in a small town in the Catskills, at a bookstore, where I would work for the summer for a not terribly great hourly rate. But I was invited to live there rent-free, in a small studio above the store. Not needing to pay rent, not doing anything with my time but working in the store and hiking, I'd put everything I earned toward my debt. If I stuck to the plan, I'd be debt-free and have at least a few thousand in savings by Labor Day. In addition to working at the bookstore, I'd signed up to do an online marketing course, with the aim of getting a full-time job after the summer. If everything worked out, I would come back to New York City, or start a new life in San Francisco, Seattle, Austin, or even somewhere overseas, maybe London, in the fall. I was terrified; that something would go wrong, that my plan would fall apart. And I was still bitter, sad, about my media career coming to an end the way it did. But I knew it was right to leave the industry, after everything I'd done.

I told all this to Audrey. Patti unlocked the apartment door. I waved as she walked out.

"Frank, I was talking to my boss, Margaret Lester-Jones; she oversees the Media desk. She wants you to come into the *Times* and meet with her. About a possible job opportunity."

I listened as Audrey explained. Hillary Clinton was expected to announce as soon as April that she would be running in the 2016 presidential election. There was speculation, and worry, that as the country faced its first serious shot at a woman president, the longtime misogynistic lens that America Now and the other Johnson News outlets applied to women in the public eye would be kicked up a notch, with troubling ramifications for the race, for the country.

The media will stir up all those dregs of humanity which no state or government can control.

Audrey said the *Times* intended to dedicate significant resources to Johnson News' anticipated sexist coverage.

"We want to know what their decision-making processes are, both in the newsroom and the C-suite. We want to know who's really pulling the levers of power. We want to be able to take the sting out of any sexist coverage by being quick to call it out. I know I don't have to say this, but given what happened with Amanda Myles, we know how serious the consequences of such coverage can be."

The mention of Amanda's name, as always, made me feel sick, though not as much as it used to, since I'd heard she'd signed a deal to make a documentary about her life—the rise and fall of the Valentines, the music industry sexism, her marriage and swift divorce from Alexander, her sobriety struggle, the blackface photo scandal, the way her mental health unraveled under the glare of tabloid attention. Her suicide attempt. I was, admittedly, nervous about what she might say about *The Scoop*, about the articles, even about me. But, despite the ethical gray area of a controversial figure earning money from said controversy, especially when she had caused real pain by wearing blackface, I understood why she would, given the chance, grab the opportunity to tell her own story in her own words. It would be up to the public to decide if she deserved redemption, and it was far from guaranteed. But at least the public would hear it all straight from Amanda, without her words being twisted. People could decide for themselves.

"Let me make sure I understand," I said to Audrey now. "Your boss

THE SCOOP

wants Johnson News to become its own Media desk beat, and she wants to talk about that with...me?"

"You're a Johnson News insider. You would be perfect, given your understanding of the inner workings there, your contacts. In fact, there might not be anyone else who can do it."

I kept my gaze on the Empire State Building, the way you should keep your eyes on the horizon when seasick.

"I'm flattered, but..." It pained me to say what I said next, but I saw no alternative.

"What?"

"Surely your boss, Margaret—she knows everything that happened with Amanda, right? How I was involved? What I did? And what I did when I left *The Scoop*? Why would she—"

"You have something she needs, Frankie. It's as simple as that. Don't overthink it."

"How could I *not* overthink this?"

"Nothing is guaranteed. It's a meeting. That's all."

"I know."

I was closer than I'd ever been to getting what I'd always wanted, and I hadn't seen it coming. And yet, there was that word, on the tip of my tongue: *no*. Since Amanda's suicide attempt, as the guilt, shame, and regret rose up in me daily like bile I had to swallow down, I'd convinced myself, at least on my better days, that there was a path to redemption for me, despite what I'd done, the harm I'd caused. I'd made my plan to leave the industry and start anew. If I couldn't do work as a journalist that made the world better in some way, then the least I could do was leave the industry altogether. Find a better way to be useful. Stop taking up space.

But now, despite everything I'd done—documented in the very pages of the *Times* itself—here was the paper of record, the Gray Lady, reaching out a hand to bring me in. I thought of all I'd had to go through to get them to notice me: compromised my values, splashed around in the mud, hounded a woman until she tried to kill herself. Ironic, that the very actions that had seen me chastised in its pages, what I'd become, was now the thing that made them want me. I almost began to weep, thinking of all I'd done, all I'd given, all I'd lost, to get to this point.

I didn't want to be a part of it, if this was what it was. Because if the *Times* wanted me after what I'd done, then there really was nowhere to go in the industry anymore that was clean. Or maybe there never had been, and I'd been too idealistic and naïve to see it. Audrey selling me out to impress her boss at the *Times*, me exploiting Amanda to impress mine. At *Marie Claire*, the articles we wrote that were really for the rich white lady at her Hamptons house, not the brown woman working inside. For the Washington insider, not the local mechanic, nurse, or teacher. It was becoming apparent that all this time, since I was a kid reading *Seventeen* magazine, I'd been clinging to a version of the media, of myself, that existed only in my mind. I hadn't seen it for what it really was. All this time I'd believed an illusion and had been calling it a dream. But at what point do the dreams that fuel the fire within us threaten to burn up everything, even ourselves? Do we simply give ourselves over to the flames because it's become so familiar we can't imagine another way?

Our lives mostly march along incrementally, small daily choices shaping our existence; the decision to turn down this block or that one, rather than standing at a crossroads. But every now and then, we do face a juncture that will shape our fates, and this was one of them. Two wildly different futures stood before me, all hinging on the next words to come out of my mouth.

"Frankie? What should I tell her?"

In my mind I imagined myself in a few weeks' time, walking into the foyer of *The New York Times* building, balancing a coffee cup as I swiped my security pass and was let through the turnstiles. Sitting at a desk in that most hallowed of newsrooms. On the inside again. Powerful, important. Would I ever be able to forget what I had done to get there? The price of admission?

"Frankie?"

"Tell Margaret thanks for thinking of me, but I'm not the person for the job. I do know someone who would be perfect, though. A talented, hungry young reporter who is passionate, has integrity, and is just as much of a Johnson News insider as me. You know her: Yenay Tan."

Yenay didn't need any favors from me, of that I was well aware. I wasn't sure she would even want it; burned by legacy media, she might have already set her sights on starting that podcast or YouTube channel she mentioned, or ditching the media completely and becoming a Pilates teacher in her hometown. Yenay had big ambitions, but at the same time, she didn't seem as desperately attached to the journalist identity as I had been, as dependent on it for self-worth. I smiled, imagining Yenay walking into *The New York Times* building, a media reporter now, and then what? Maybe the white male celebrity profile writer mafia would be broken up after all.

Audrey was quiet for a moment, shocked, I think, that I'd turn down the meeting. After my desperate, agonized, rejection-filled summer trying to get a job, after the heated discussion at her birthday party. Back then, I would've given anything for the opportunity she was presenting to me now. I knew that, once again, Audrey wouldn't understand. She was still in the inner circle, embraced, celebrated, was still empowered to do valuable work. But the game of musical chairs, the ever-shrinking circle, was becoming more ruthless by the year, and though it would take a while—Audrey sure to be one of the last ones to feel the squeeze—one day, when she inevitably lost her seat, maybe then she would understand. But until then, she wouldn't. Not yet.

"Frankie, this is the opportunity of a lifetime. Anyone in our industry would kill for this. You're guaranteed near limitless *Times* resources to cover this beat for the next year, and beyond. You're seriously going to turn it down? You won't even meet Margaret, just to see?"

I was still perched on the windowsill. I'd been staring at a spot on the rug, but I looked out the window again, toward the Manhattan skyline. It was a freezing February morning, people on the sidewalk below bundled in thick coats, shoulders hunched against the gusts of icy air slicing against strips of exposed skin on necks, wrists, ankles. But before long the first signs of spring would appear, the morning frosts would thaw, buds would swell, burst open, fill the parks and gardens with color. Everyone would shed their heavy layers and welcome the warming sun.

"Like I said, I'll send you Yenay's details."

"I'm sure Yenay's great. But she's young, right? Isn't she too green? And what's she like? I've noticed the younger ones coming through lately, they're not like you and me. They're impatient. They don't want to wait their turn. They have no respect for hierarchy, for norms. No respect for the way things have always been done, or that they're done that way for a reason."

I couldn't help but smile.

"That's why she'll be great, Audrey. That's why she'll be great."

ACKNOWLEDGMENTS

To my literary agent, Hayley Steed. You took this story seriously when I was just a woman with a Word document and a dream, and in doing so you changed my life. You saw what was not yet on the page, but could be, and had the wisdom (and patience) to coax it out of me. I am so grateful for your guidance, support, and all your tireless work. My deepest thanks also to the entire Janklow & Nesbit UK team for your support, especially Mina Yakinya.

To my editor, Nicole Luongo. Your vision was essential for *The Scoop* to become the novel I'd hoped and dreamed it would be. Thank you for seeing my work so clearly, and for making this process a joy. I'm so lucky my novel found a home with Grand Central Publishing; thank you to the entire team, especially production editor Anjuli Johnson, copyeditor Carrie Andrews, proofreaders Alayna Johnson and Pam Rehm, production coordinator Emily Baker, manufacturing coordinator Sara Schaller, interior designer Taylor Navis, cover designer YY Liak, Albert Tang, Rachel Rodriguez, Cordelia Calvert, and Allison Schuster. There is so much work that goes into publishing a book, much of which the author and the public never see, and I'm

ACKNOWLEDGMENTS

very grateful to every single person who has helped *The Scoop* become a real book in readers' hands.

It is because of my brilliant editor across the pond, Rachel Hart, that *The Scoop* made it to readers in the UK, and also in my home country of Australia. My deepest gratitude to the entire Wildfire/Headline team for championing me and this book.

Leigh Stein! You understood this book at a time when I was beginning to wonder if anyone else ever would, and your feedback and encouragement kept me going when I was entertaining the idea of giving up. The amount of energy you give to other writers and their books, as an author yourself, is surely unmatched. Please never stop explaining satire to people on the internet.

In the fall of 2024, while preparing to go out on submission with *The Scoop*, I got the news I'd been selected as a Spruceton Inn Artist Resident. Thank you to Casey Sciezska and Steven Weinberg for recognizing me as a novelist at a vulnerable time—it meant a great deal—and for everything you do for artists at all stages of their careers.

To Rebecca Rodriguez at Subtext Literary, for seeing a vision for *The Scoop* on the screen.

For thirteen years I worked as a journalist in Australia and the United States, and throughout that time I got to know many wonderful colleagues, with whom I shared all kinds of experiences, from the funny, to the stressful, to the weird, to the wild, and many of you became good friends beyond the newsroom or office. I appreciate you all. A special shout-out to my Aussie journos in New York: Tiffany Bakker, Lena Bell, Jules Corderoy, James Law, Megan Palin, and Katie Robertson. Thank you for feeling like home when home is so far away.

To Belinda, dear cousin, for the childhood hours we spent watching outrageously bad comedies (how many times did we rewind the *Weekend At Bernie's II* parasailing shark bite scene?), writing fake horoscopes, and recording songs inspired by Wesley Willis, which formed

ACKNOWLEDGMENTS

a core part of my personality, for better or worse. Thank you also to Mitchell, Judy, Beverley, Kerrie, and the entire Milner side; coming from a family of voracious readers with a dark sense of humor is an inheritance for which I'm grateful. To Bell, Matt, Aurora, Johnny, Dean, and Sarah, for always feeling like home no matter how long it's been.

To Leonie. Your love and support have been a steady foundation from which I've been able to reach for my dreams. You've been an enormously positive influence on me, showing me that with hard work and commitment one can build a life they love. You have made so much possible. Thank you to the Connallys for making me one of your own.

To the friends who became family: Kimberly Gillan, Jessica Martin, Leda Ross, Josephine Rozenberg-Clarke, Emilie Shane, and Gabrielle Tozer. Each of you have made my life more fun, funny, interesting, and full of love than I could ever properly find the words to say. Thank you for loving and understanding me as my full, messy self. Little Erin couldn't have known that out there in the world, her people were waiting to meet her.

To my mother, Janis. You would have been more excited than anyone to read *The Scoop*, if only you had stuck around on this earthly plane a little longer. But you had other, surely better places to be, and I know that wherever you are, you know.

And now, because I had to save the best for last: Sam. I'm endlessly grateful to you for your patience and good humor as our lives were overtaken by a Word document for so many years. You made sacrifices so I could do this, supported me in every way a writer could hope to be supported, from the practical to the existential. Your unwavering belief that I could pull this off carried me all the way to the end. I don't know who I'd be without your generosity, selflessness, jokes, wisdom, and love, but I do know that there would be no *The Scoop*.

RAISING READERS
Books Build Bright Futures

Dear Reader,

We'd love your attention for one more page to tell you about the crisis in children's reading, and what we can all do.

Studies have shown that reading for fun is the **single biggest predictor of a child's future life chances** – more than family circumstance, parents' educational background or income. It improves academic results, mental health, wealth, communication skills, ambition and happiness.[1]

The number of children reading for fun is in rapid decline. Young people have a lot of competition for their time. In 2024, 1 in 10 children and young people in the UK aged 5 to 18 did not own a single book at home.[2]

Hachette works extensively with schools, libraries and literacy charities, but here are some ways we can all raise more readers:

- Reading to children for just 10 minutes a day makes a difference
- Don't give up if children aren't regular readers – there will be books for them!
- Visit bookshops and libraries to get recommendations
- Encourage them to listen to audiobooks
- Support school libraries
- Give books as gifts

There's a lot more information about how to encourage children to read on our website: **www.RaisingReaders.co.uk**

Thank you for reading.

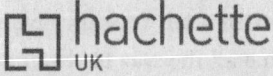

---

[1] OECD, '21st-Century Readers: Developing Literacy Skills in a Digital World', 2021, https://www.oecd.org/en/publications/21st-century-readers_a83d84cb-en.html

[2] National Literacy Trust, 'Book Ownership in 2024', November 2024, https://literacytrust.org.uk/research-services/research-reports/book-ownership-in-2024